Song of the Court

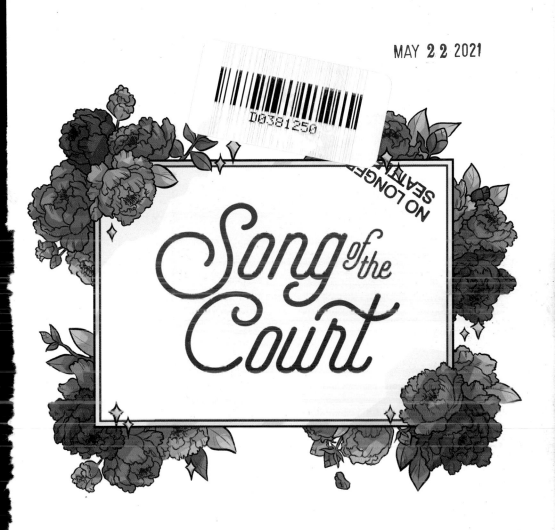

STERLING CHILDREN'S BOOKS
New York

An Imprint of Sterling Publishing Co., Inc.
1166 Avenue of the Americas
New York, NY 10036

ISBN 978-1-4549-3301-4

Library of Congress Cataloging-in-Publication Data

Names: Farina, Katy, author, artist. I Fortson, Ashanti, colourist.
Title: Song of the court / story and art by Katy Farina ; colors by Ashanti
Fortson.
Description: New York : Sterling Children's Books [2020] I Audience: Ages
6-8 I Summary: "To buy seeds for her beautiful garden, Arietta plans to
sell her treasured family violin--until Princess Cassia spots the
instrument and begs Arietta to perform at her birthday party. Although
she has never played, Arietta decides to learn a special song for the
occasion."-- Provided by publisher.
Identifiers: LCCN 2020007706 I ISBN 9781454933014 I ISBN 9781454939993
(epub)
Subjects: LCSH: Graphic novels. I CYAC: Graphic novels. I Violin--Fiction.
I Music--Fiction.
Classification: LCC PZ7.7.F364 So 2020 I DDC 741.5/973--dc23
LC record available at https://lccn.loc.gov/2020007706

Distributed in Canada by Sterling Publishing Co., Inc.
c/o Canadian Manda Group, 664 Annette Street
Toronto, Ontario M6S 2C8, Canada

For information about custom editions, special sales, and premium and corporate purchases, please
contact Sterling Special Sales at 800-805-5489 or
specialsales@sterlingpublishing.com.

Manufactured in Malaysia

Lot #:
2 4 6 8 10 9 7 5 3 1
06/20

sterlingpublishing.com

Design by Heather Kelly and Julie Robine

Colors by Ashanti Fortson

Song of the Court

Story and art by
KATY FARINA

Colors by
ASHANTI FORTSON

STERLING CHILDREN'S BOOKS
New York

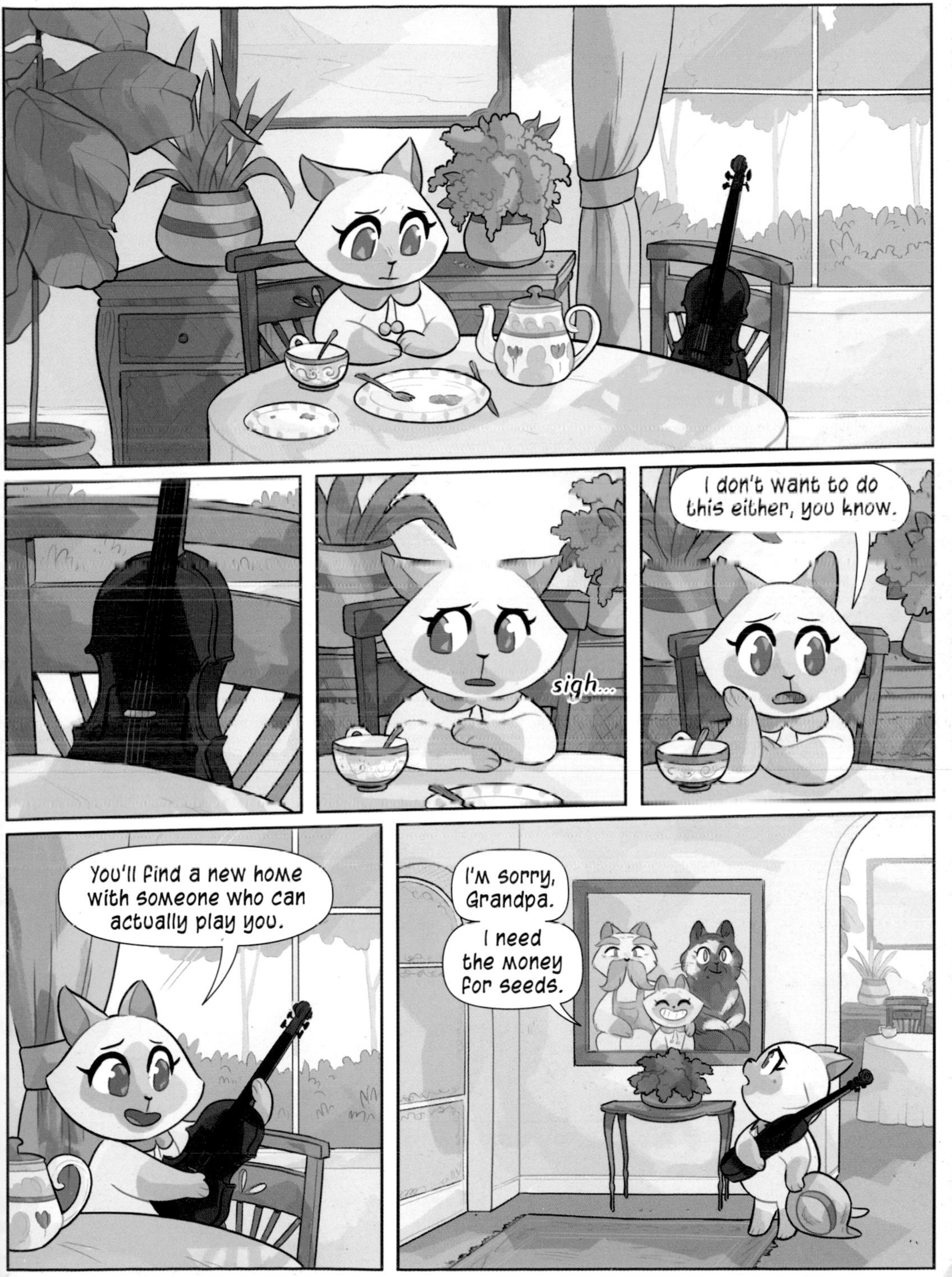
sigh...
I don't want to do this either, you know.
You'll find a new home with someone who can actually play you.
I'm sorry, Grandpa.
I need the money for seeds.

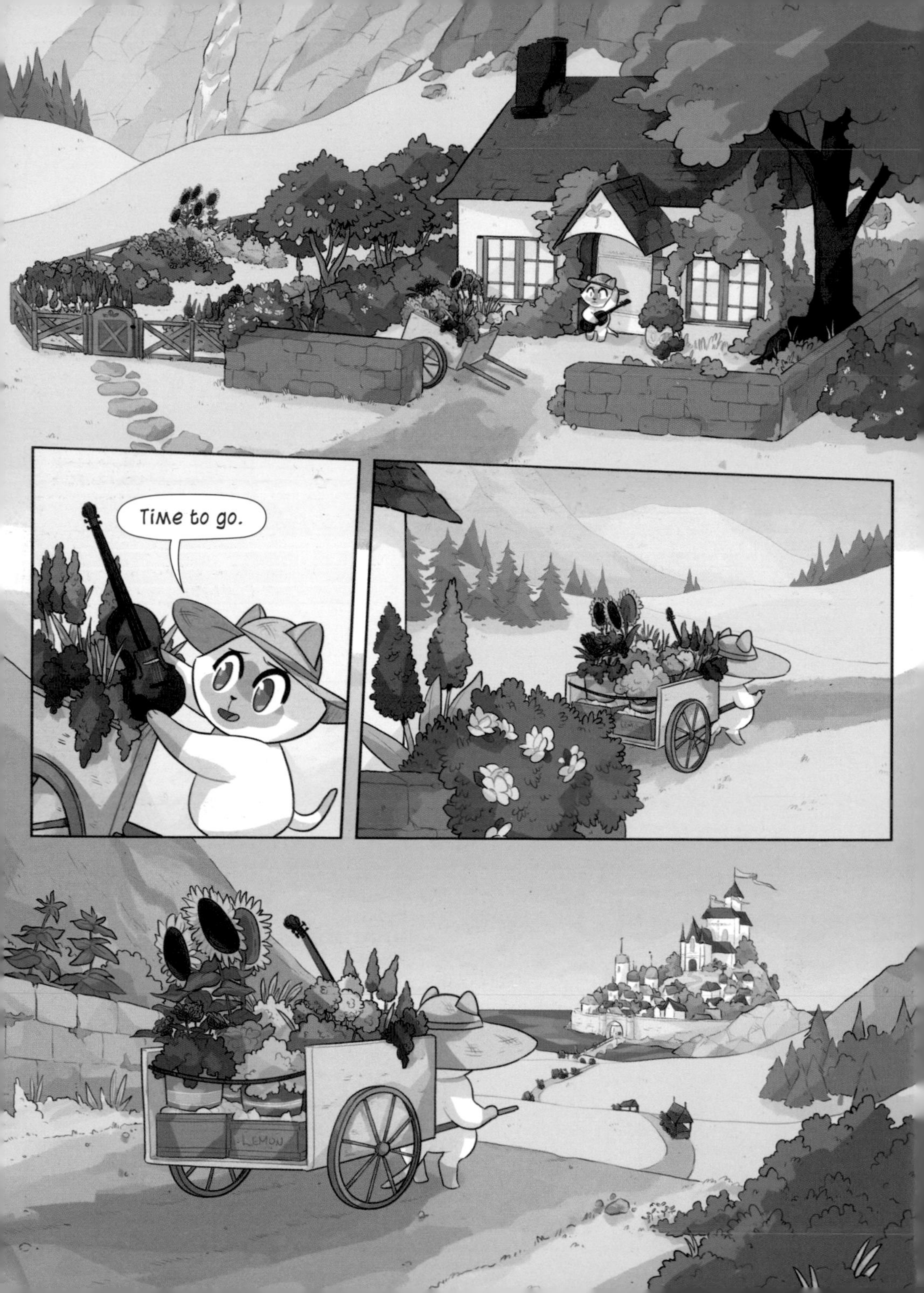
Time to go.
LEMON

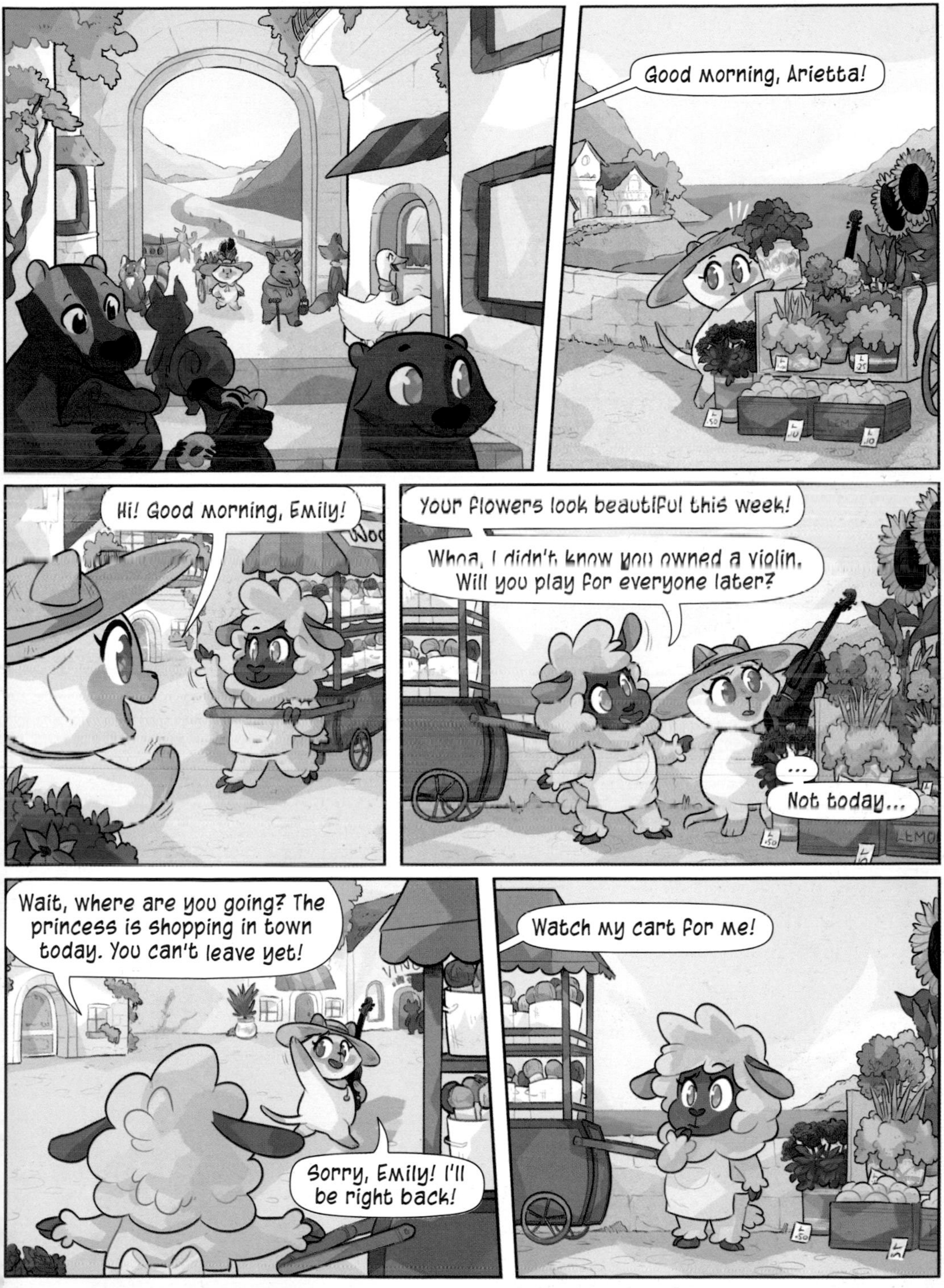
Good Morning, Arietta!
Hi! Good morning, Emily!
Your flowers look beautiful this week!
Whoa, I didn't know you owned a violin. Will you play for everyone later?
...
Not today...
Wait, where are you going? The princess is shopping in town today. You can't leave yet!
Sorry, Emily! I'll be right back!
Watch my cart for me!

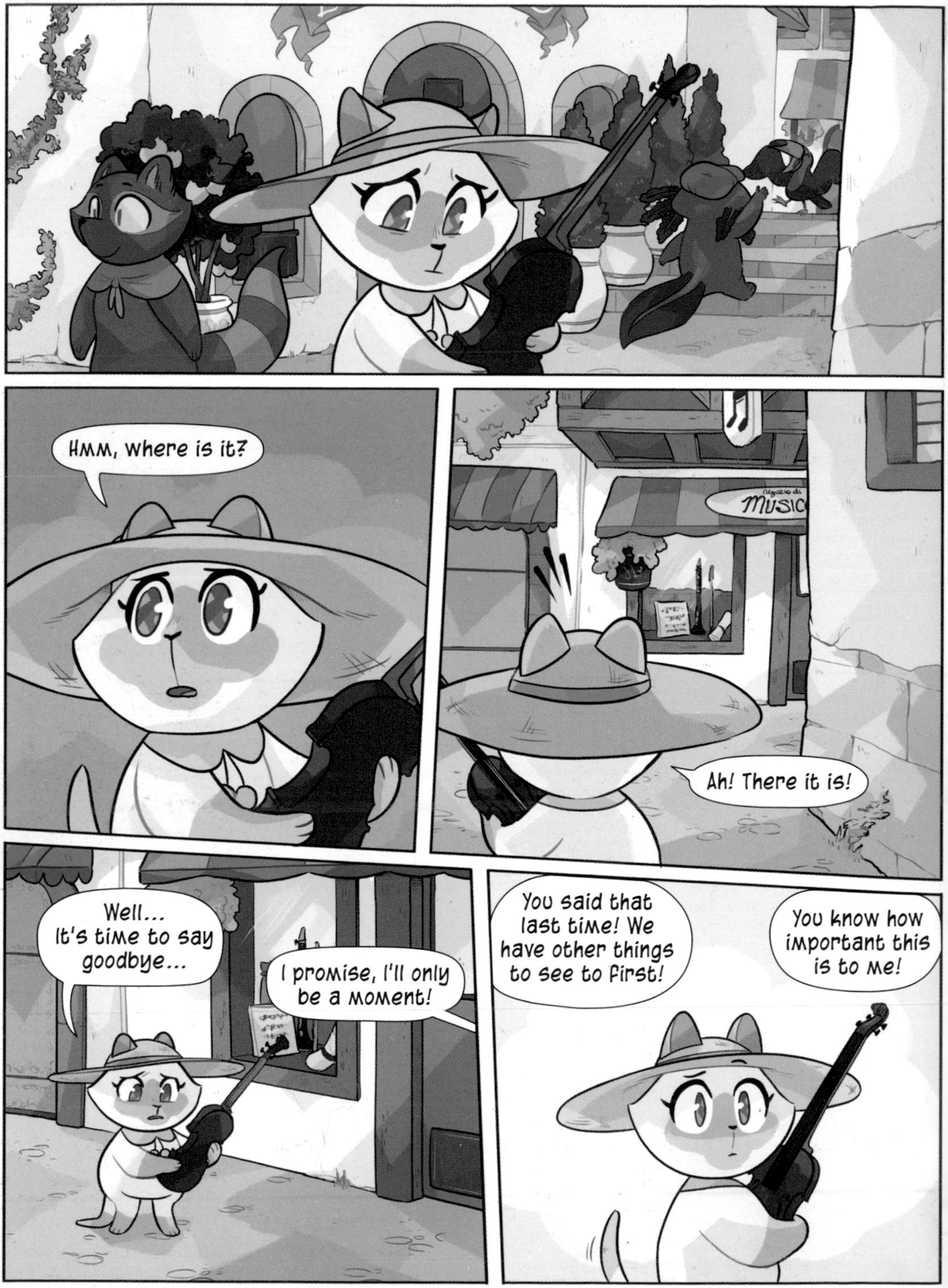
Hmm, where is it?
negozio di MUSIC
Ah! There it is!
Well... It's time to say goodbye...
I promise, I'll only be a moment!
You said that last time! We have other things to see to first!
You know how important this is to me!

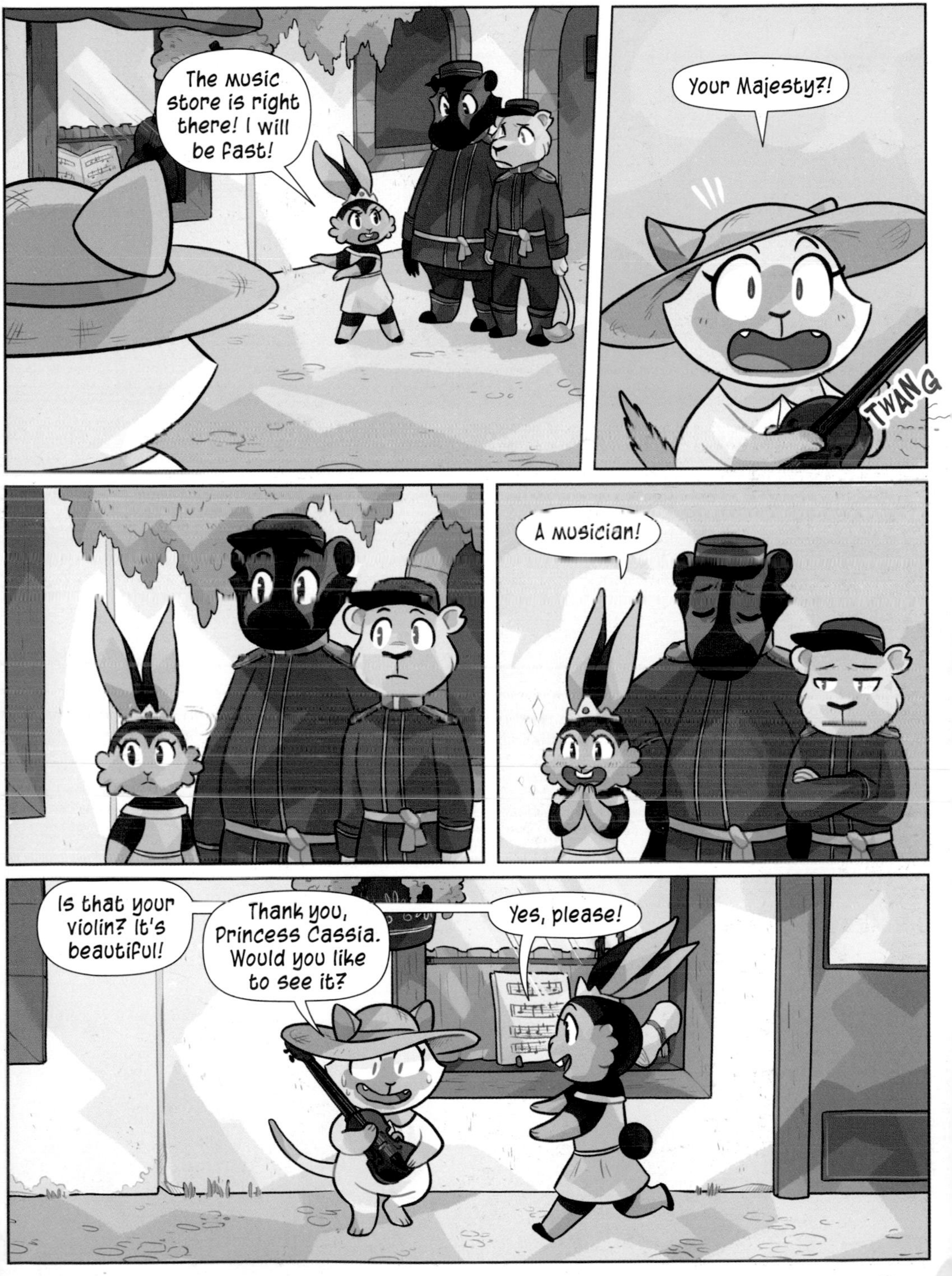
The music store is right there! I will be fast!
Your Majesty?!
TWANG
A musician!
Is that your violin? It's beautiful!
Thank you, Princess Cassia. Would you like to see it?
Yes, please!

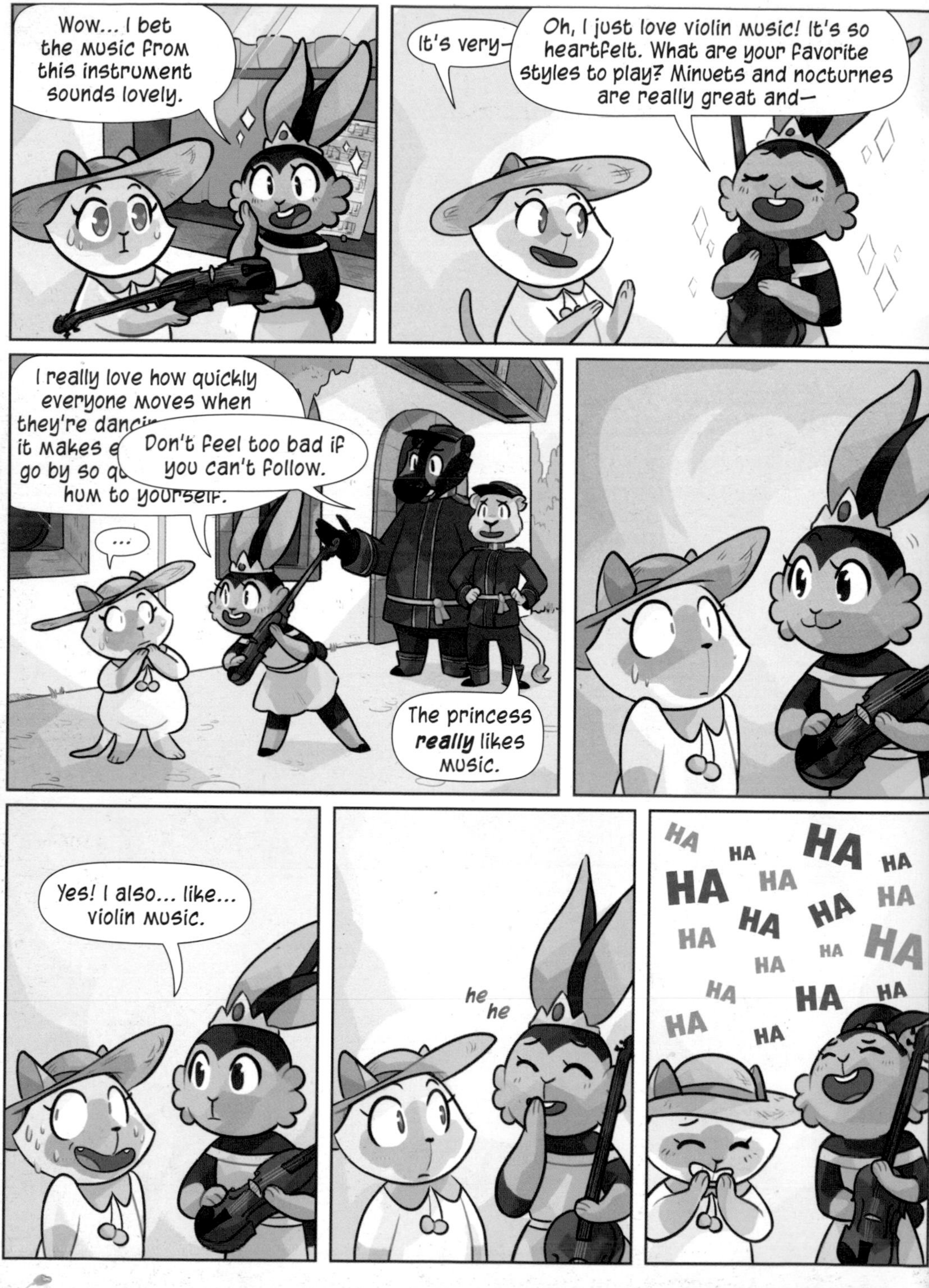
Wow... I bet the music from this instrument sounds lovely.
It's very—
Oh, I just love violin music! It's so heartfelt. What are your favorite styles to play? Minuets and nocturnes are really great and—
I really love how quickly everyone moves when they're dancin
it makes e
go by so q
hum to yourself.
Don't feel too bad if you can't follow.
...
The princess **really** likes music.
Yes! I also... like... violin music.
he he
HA HA HA HA HA HA HA HA HA HA HA HA HA HA HA HA HA HA HA HA

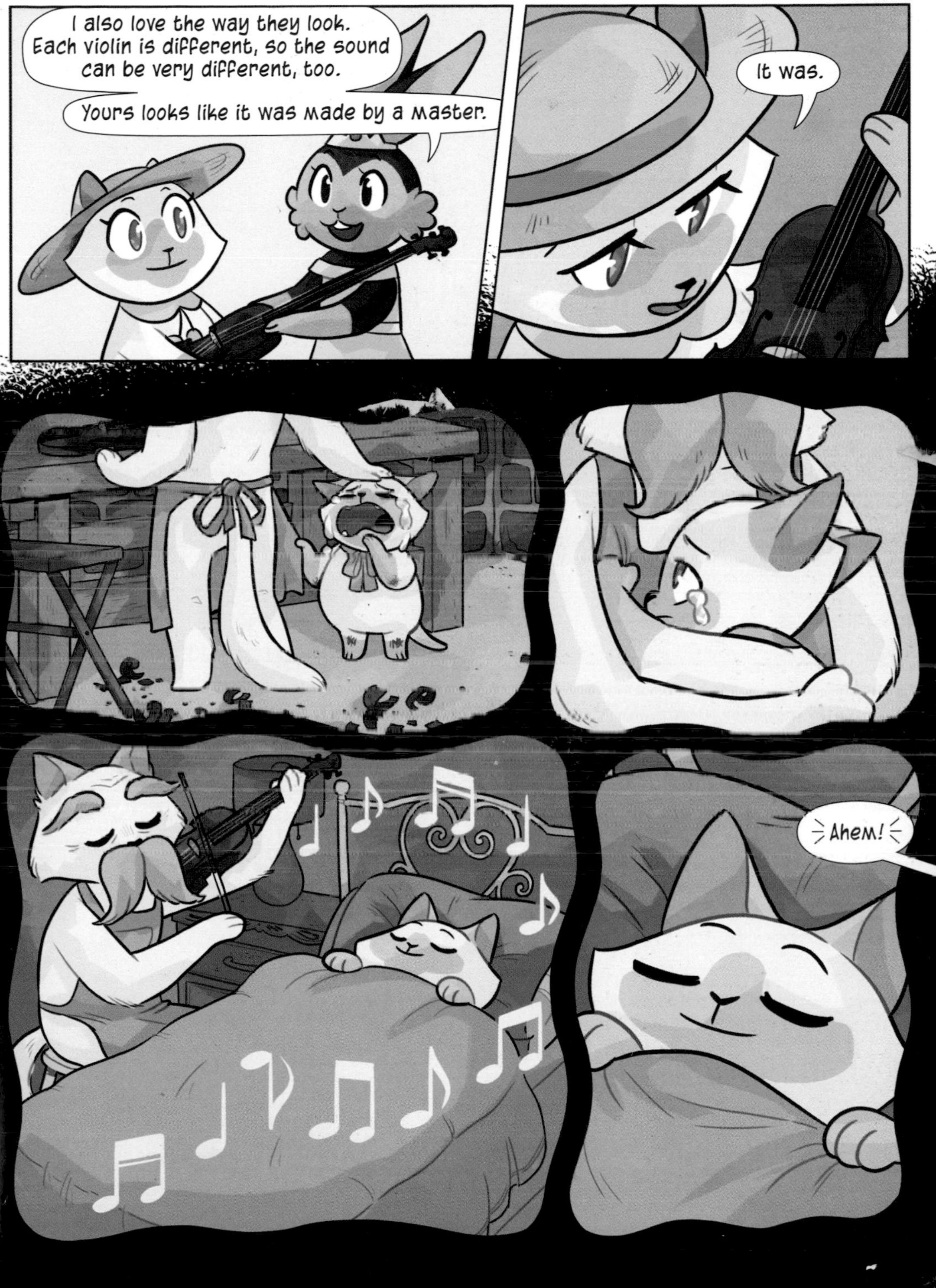
I also love the way they look. Each violin is different, so the sound can be very different, too.
Yours looks like it was made by a master.
It was.
Ahem!

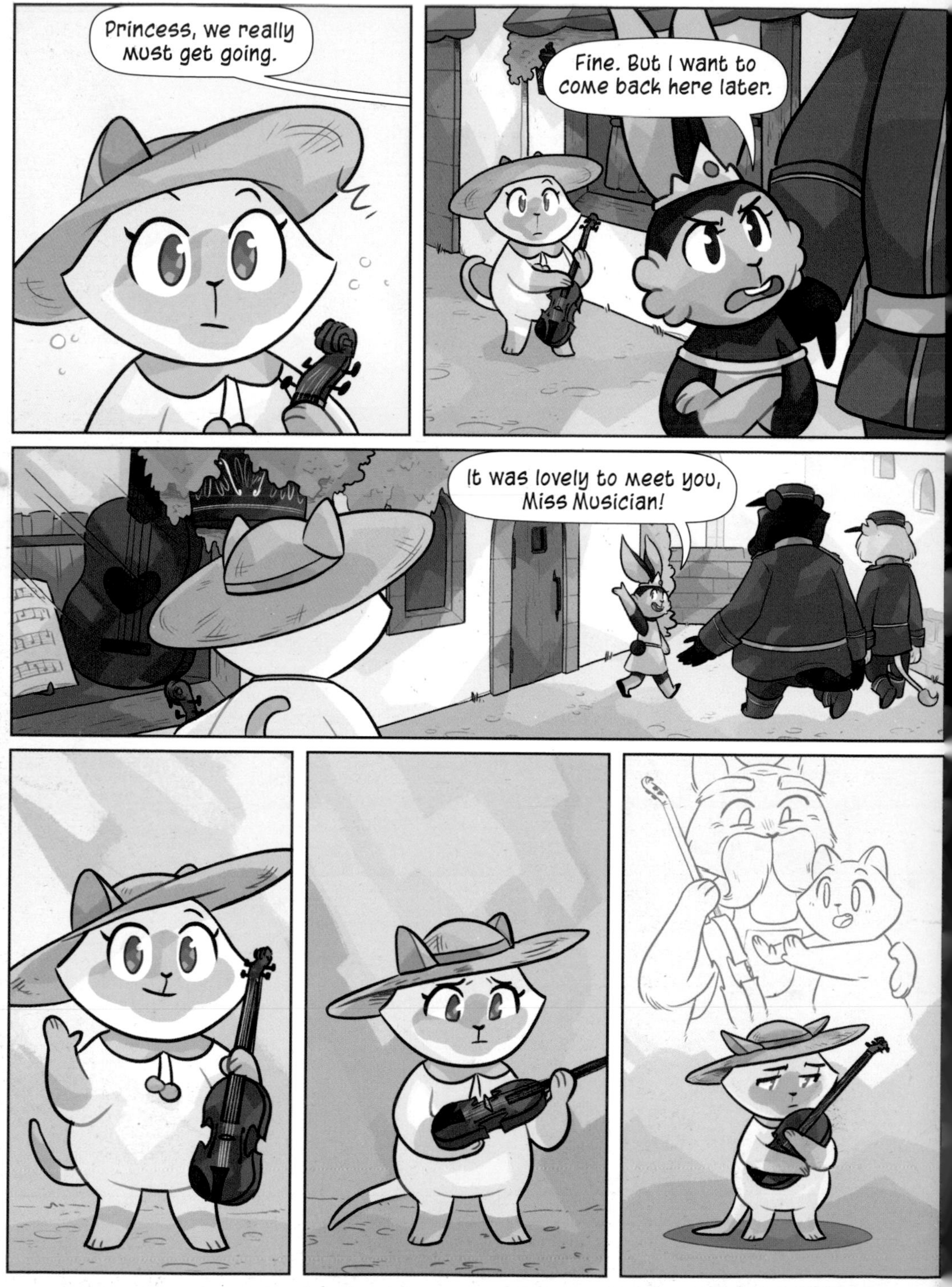
Princess, we really must get going.
Fine. But I want to come back here later.
It was lovely to meet you, Miss Musician!

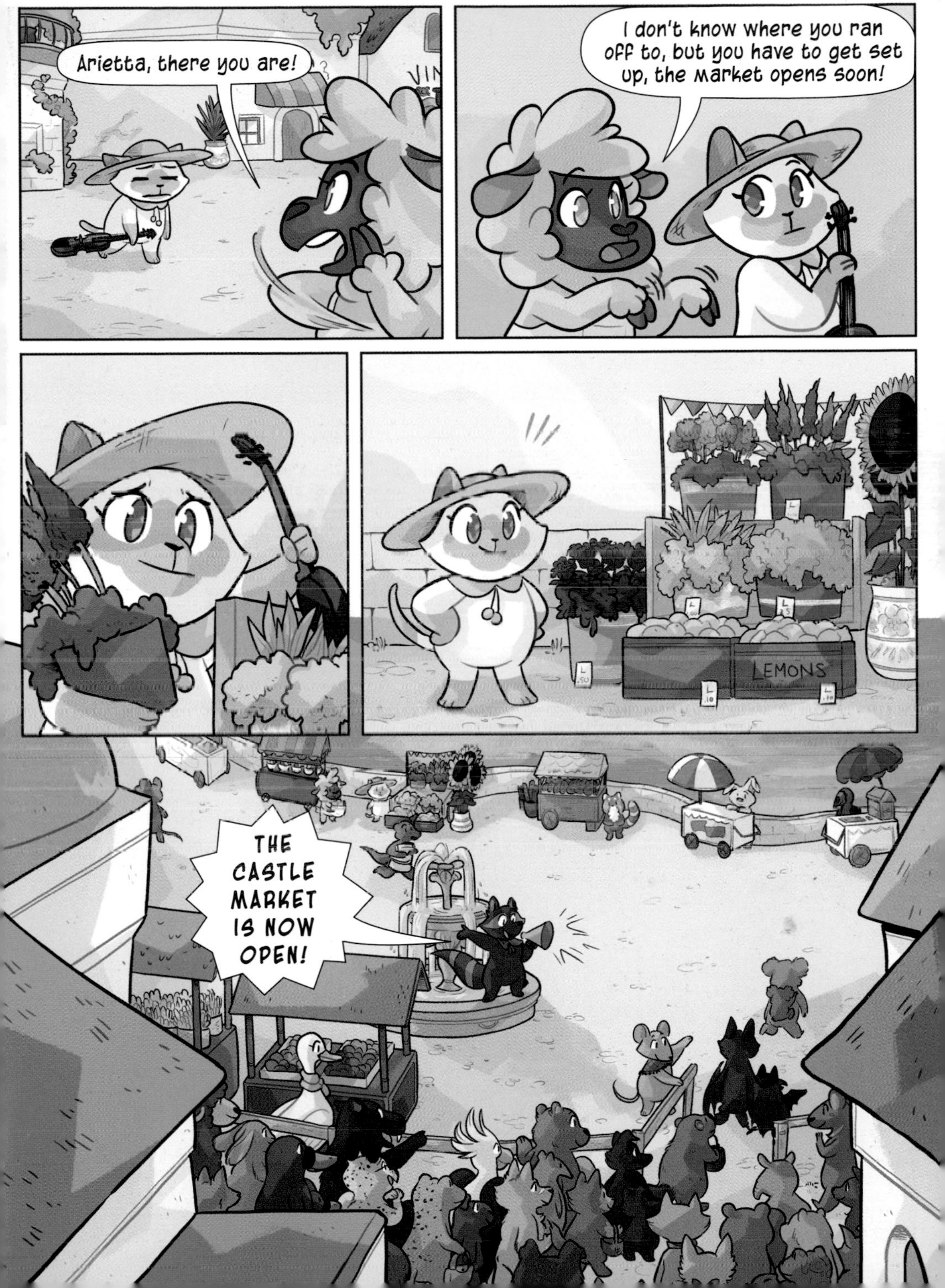
Arietta, there you are!
I don't know where you ran off to, but you have to get set up, the market opens soon!
LEMONS
THE CASTLE MARKET IS NOW OPEN!

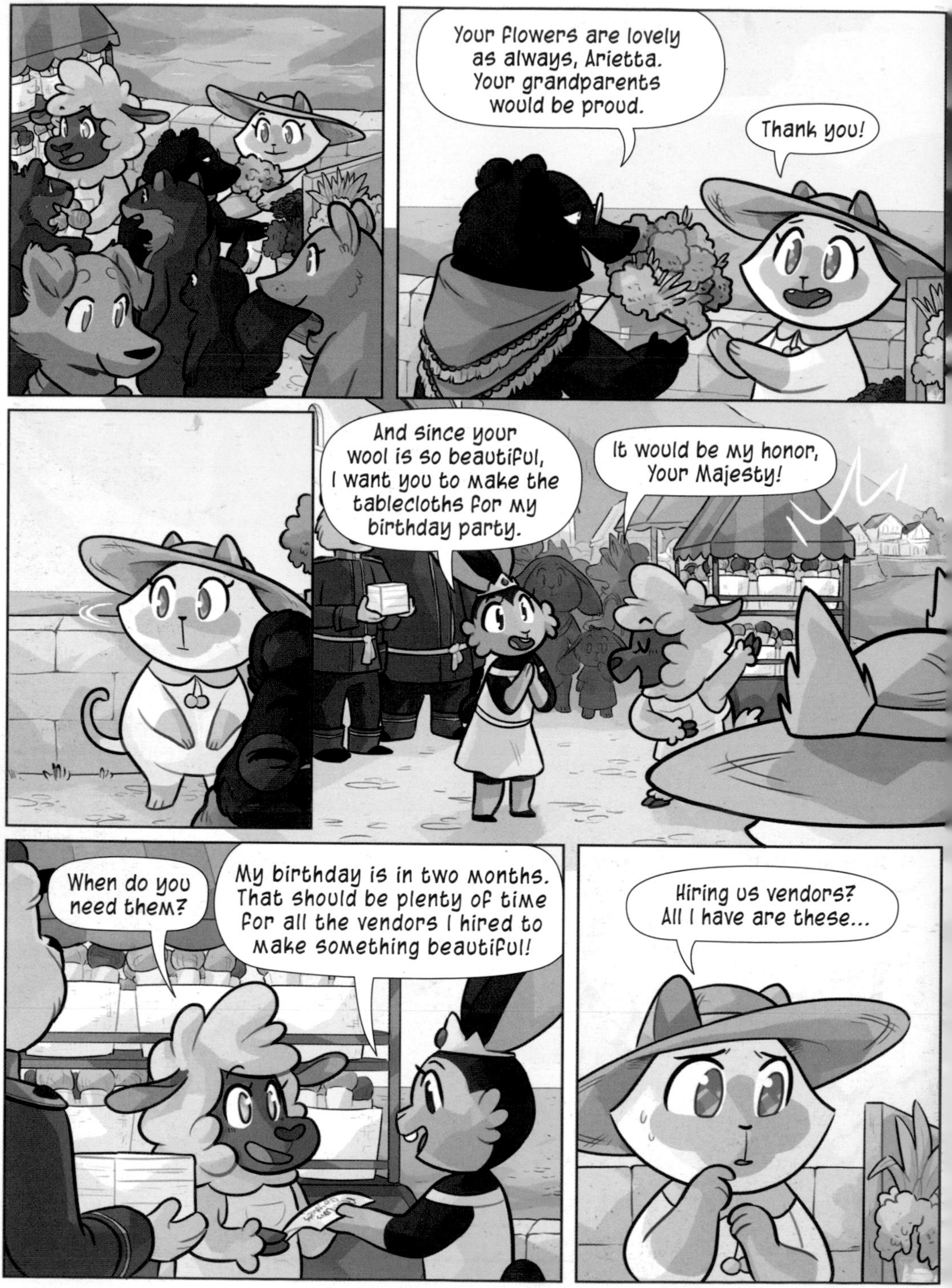
Your flowers are lovely as always, Arietta. Your grandparents would be proud.
Thank you!
And since your wool is so beautiful, I want you to make the tablecloths for my birthday party.
It would be my honor, Your Majesty!
When do you need them?
My birthday is in two months. That should be plenty of time for all the vendors I hired to make something beautiful!
Hiring us vendors? All I have are these...

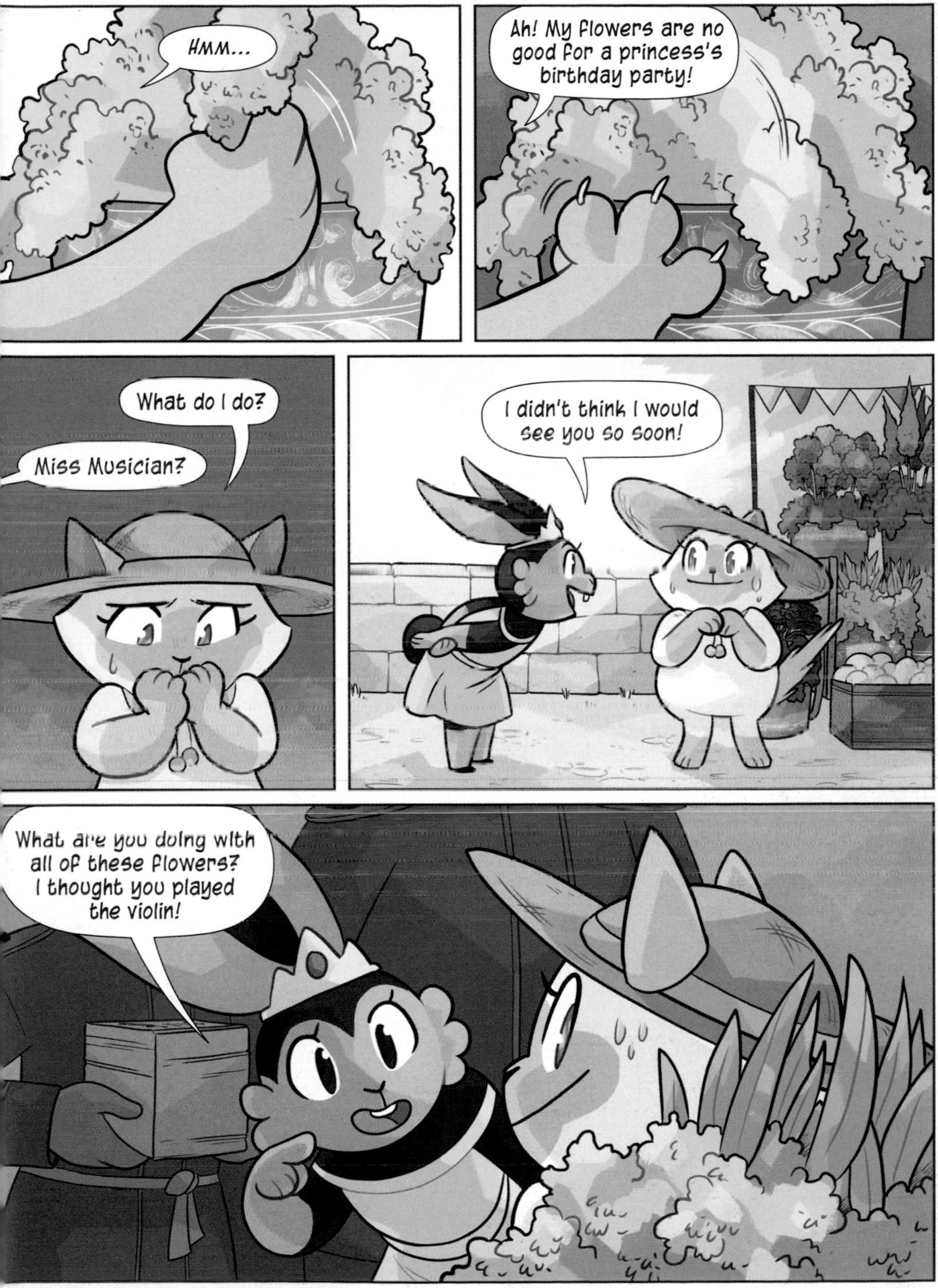
HMM...
Ah! My flowers are no good for a princess's birthday party!
What do I do?
Miss Musician?
I didn't think I would see you so soon!
What are you doing with all of these flowers? I thought you played the violin!

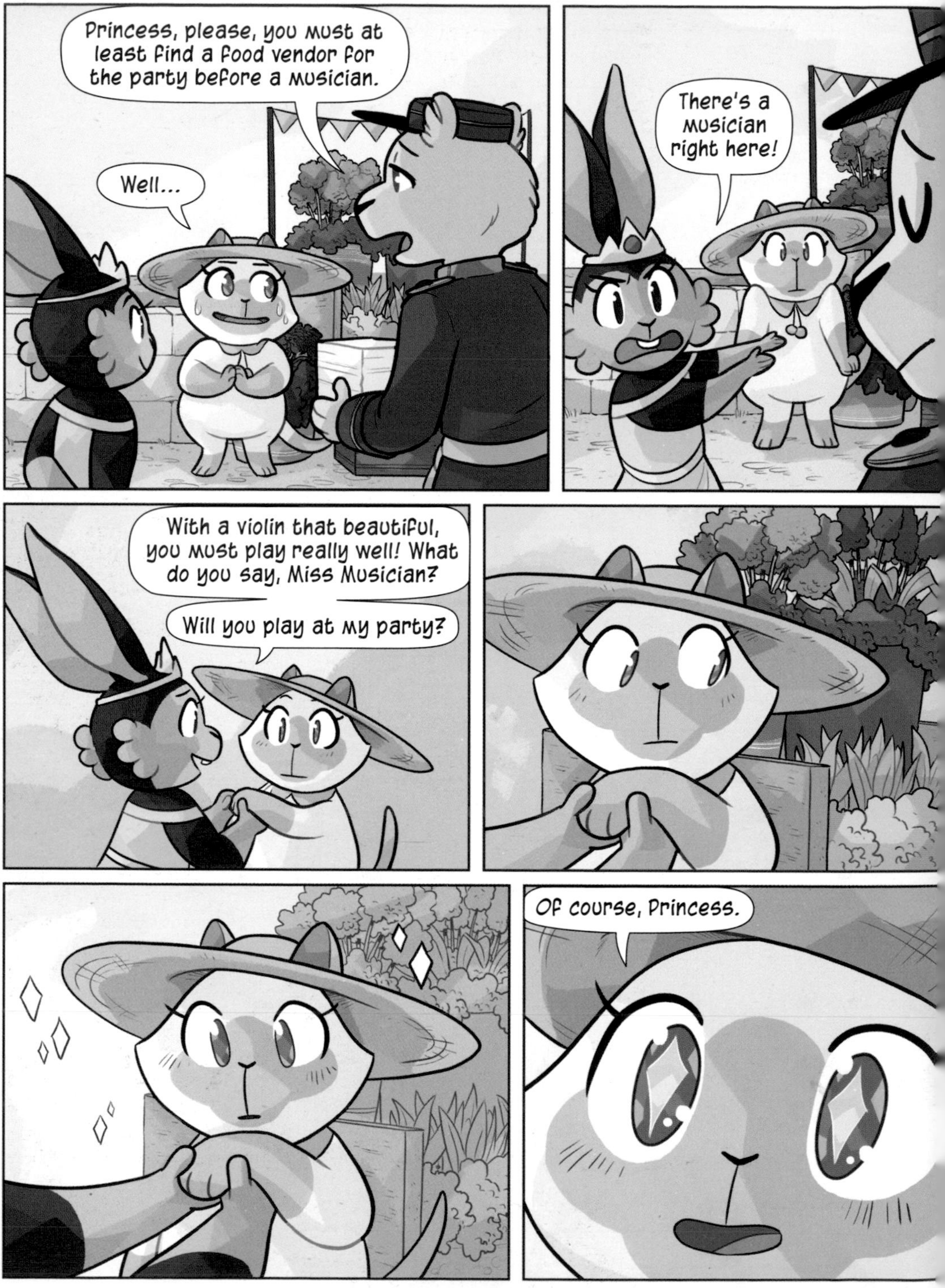
Princess, please, you must at least find a food vendor for the party before a musician.
Well...
There's a musician right here!
With a violin that beautiful, you must play really well! What do you say, Miss Musician?
Will you play at my party?
Of course, Princess.

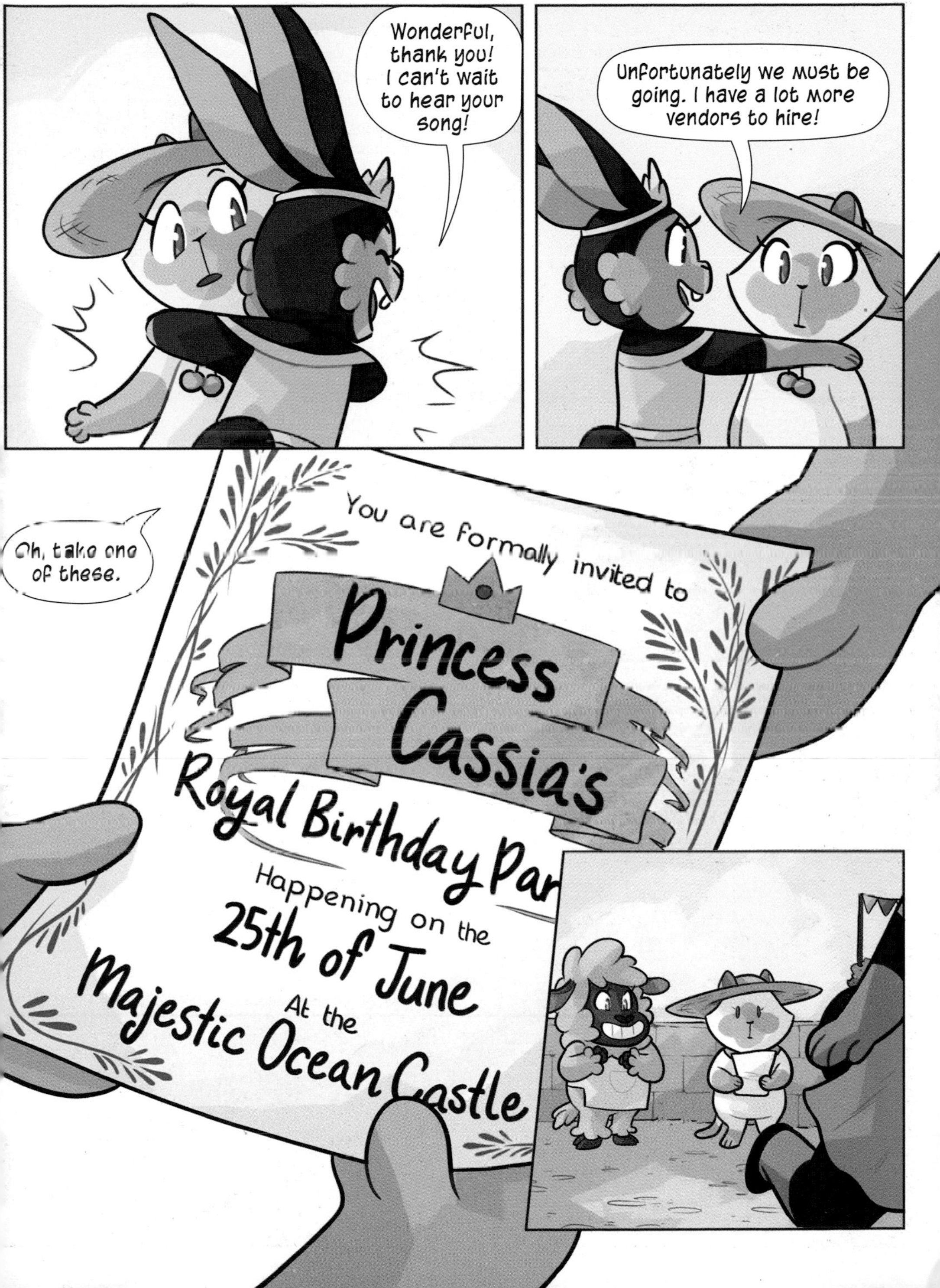

Wonderful, thank you! I can't wait to hear your song!
Unfortunately we must be going. I have a lot more vendors to hire!
Oh, take one of these.
You are formally invited to
Princess Cassia's
Royal Birthday Par
Happening on the
25th of June
At the
Majestic Ocean Castle

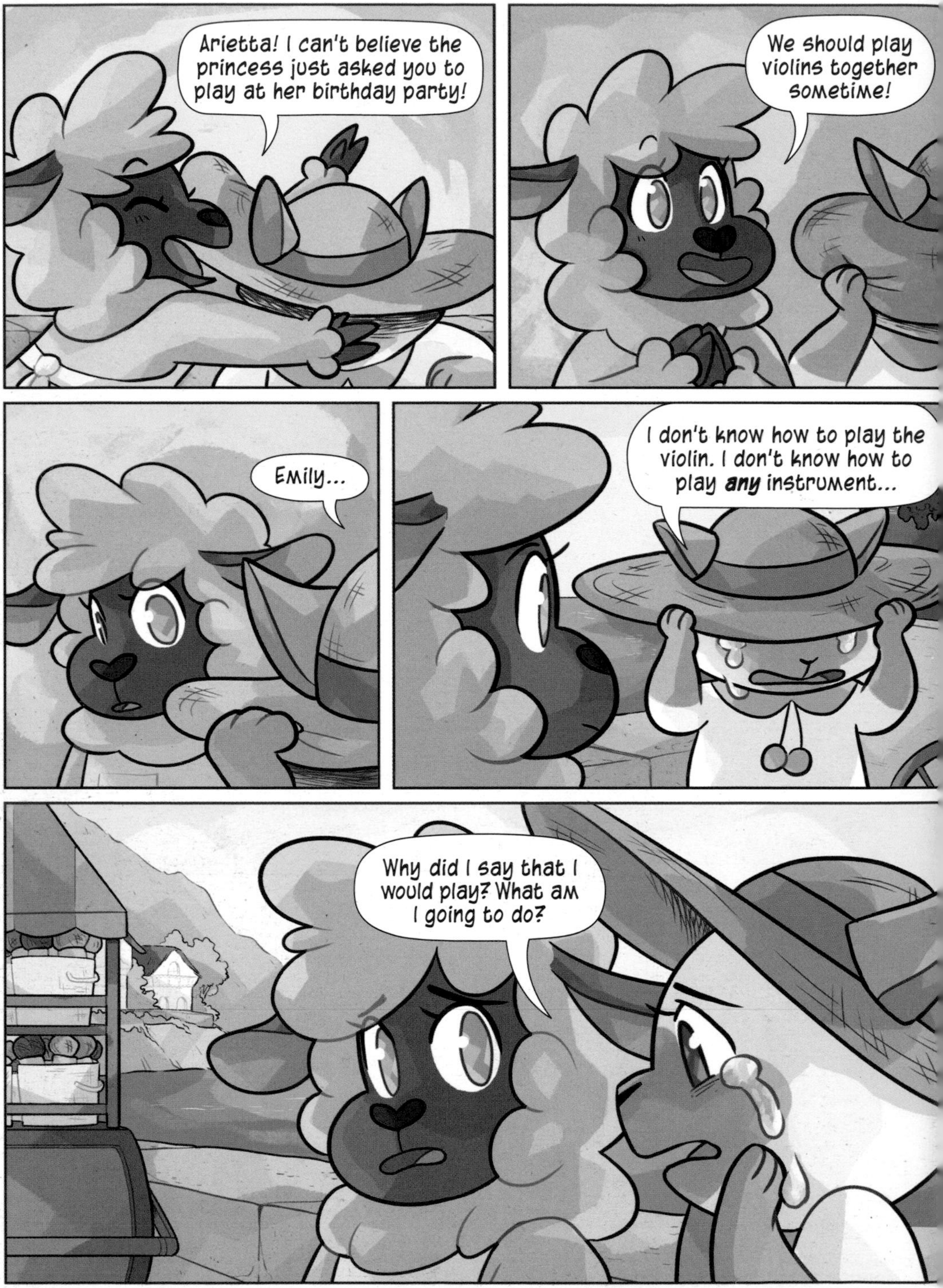
Arietta! I can't believe the princess just asked you to play at her birthday party!
We should play violins together sometime!
Emily...
I don't know how to play the violin. I don't know how to play **any** instrument...
Why did I say that I would play? What am I going to do?

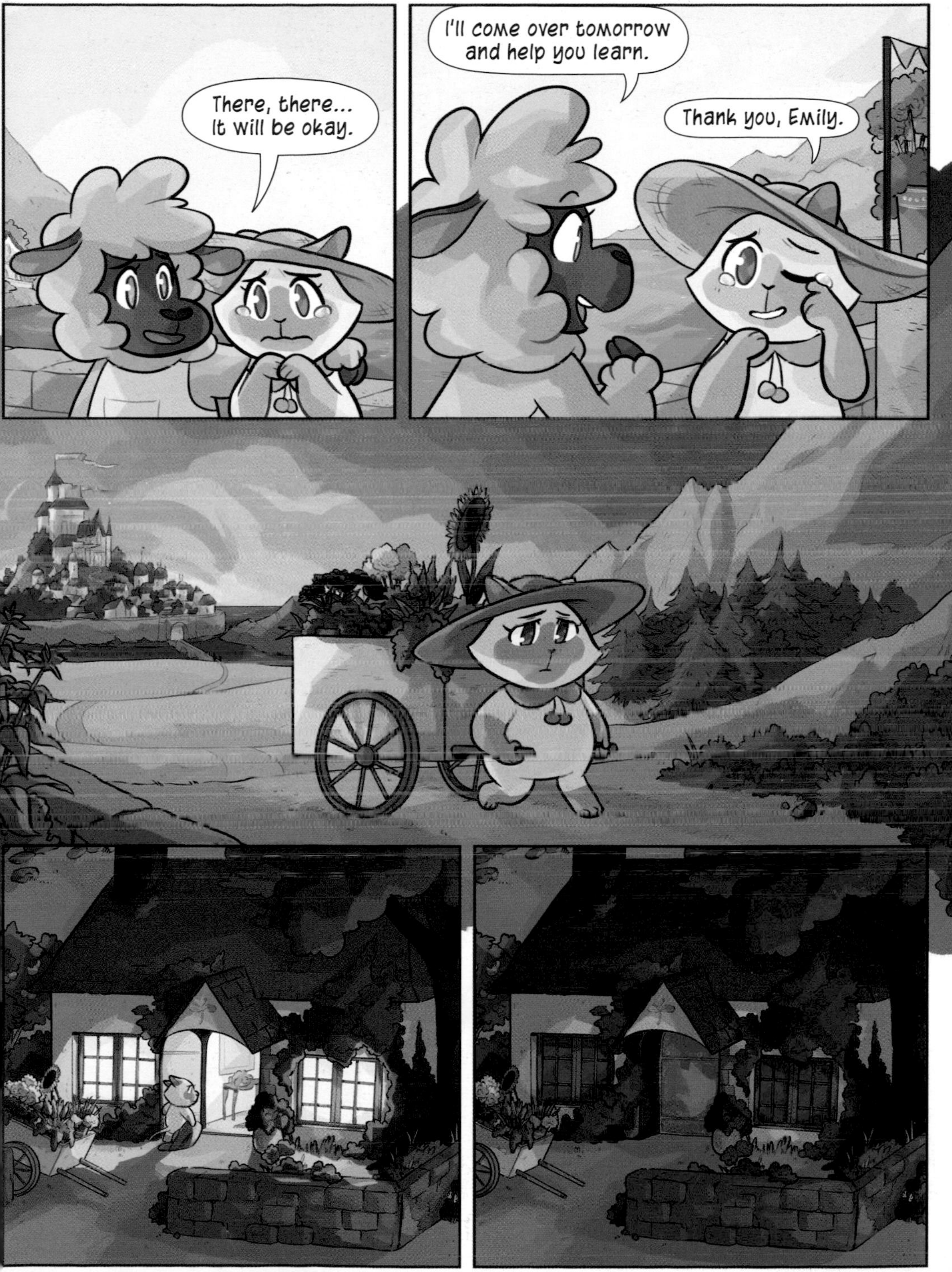
There, there...
It will be okay.
I'll come over tomorrow and help you learn.
Thank you, Emily.

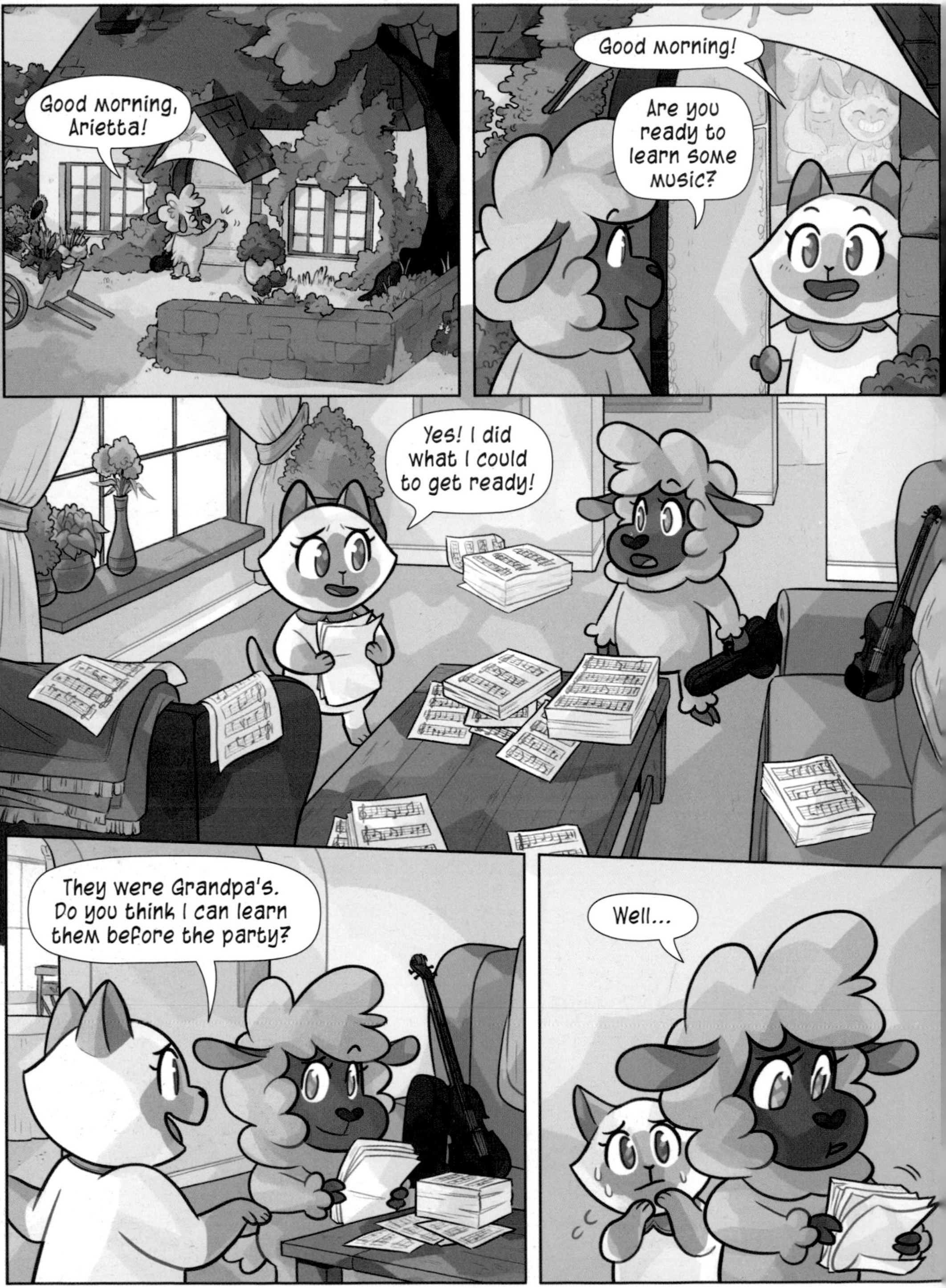
Good morning, Arietta!
Good morning!
Are you ready to learn some music?
Yes! I did what I could to get ready!
They were Grandpa's. Do you think I can learn them before the party?
Well...

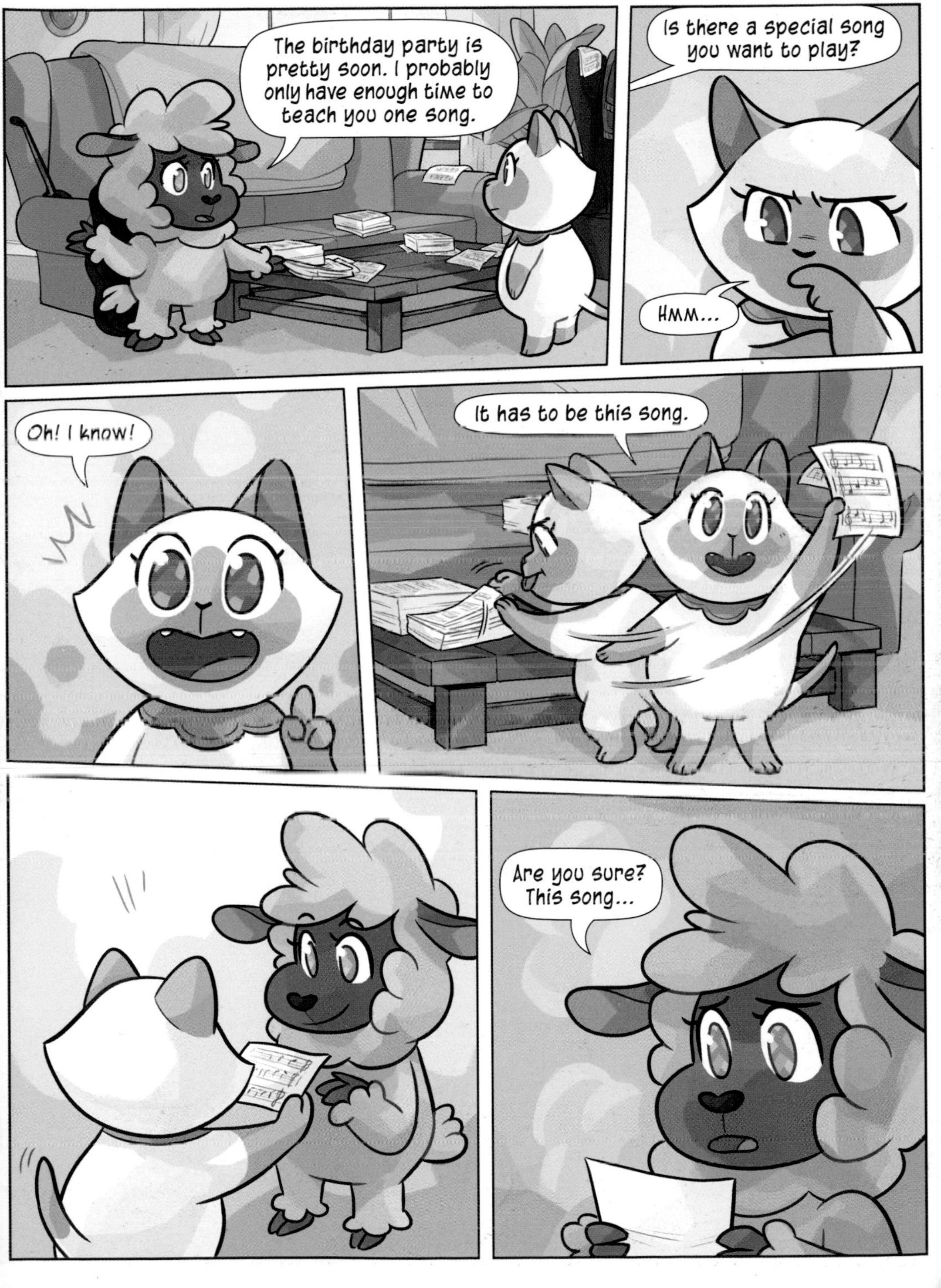
The birthday party is pretty soon. I probably only have enough time to teach you one song.
Is there a special song you want to play?
HMM...
Oh! I know!
It has to be this song.
Are you sure? This song...

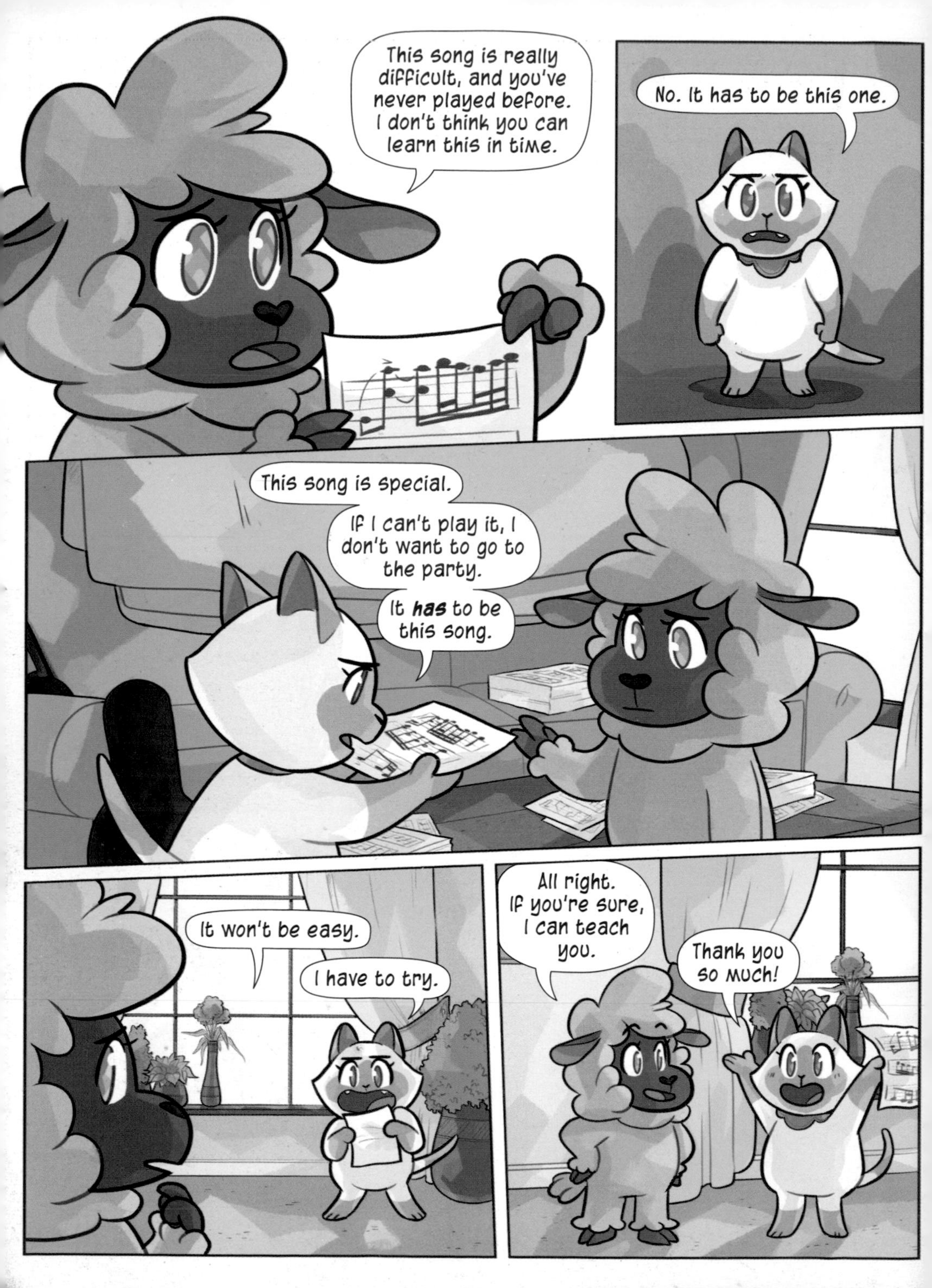
This song is really difficult, and you've never played before. I don't think you can learn this in time.
No. It has to be this one.
This song is special.
If I can't play it, I don't want to go to the party.
It **has** to be this song.
It won't be easy.
I have to try.
All right. If you're sure, I can teach you.
Thank you so much!

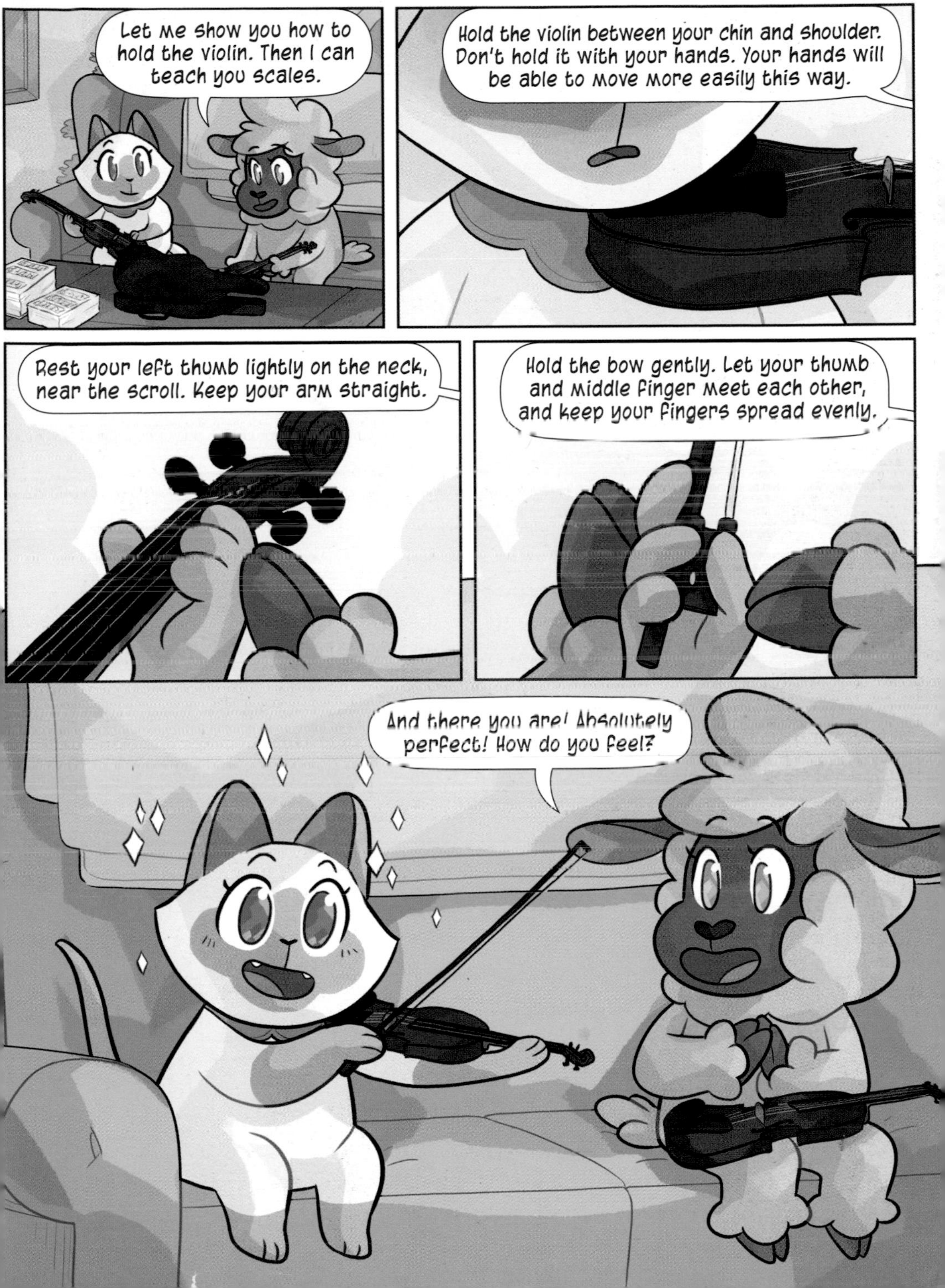
Let me show you how to hold the violin. Then I can teach you scales.
Hold the violin between your chin and shoulder. Don't hold it with your hands. Your hands will be able to move more easily this way.
Rest your left thumb lightly on the neck, near the scroll. Keep your arm straight.
Hold the bow gently. Let your thumb and middle finger meet each other, and keep your fingers spread evenly.
And there you are! Absolutely perfect! How do you feel?

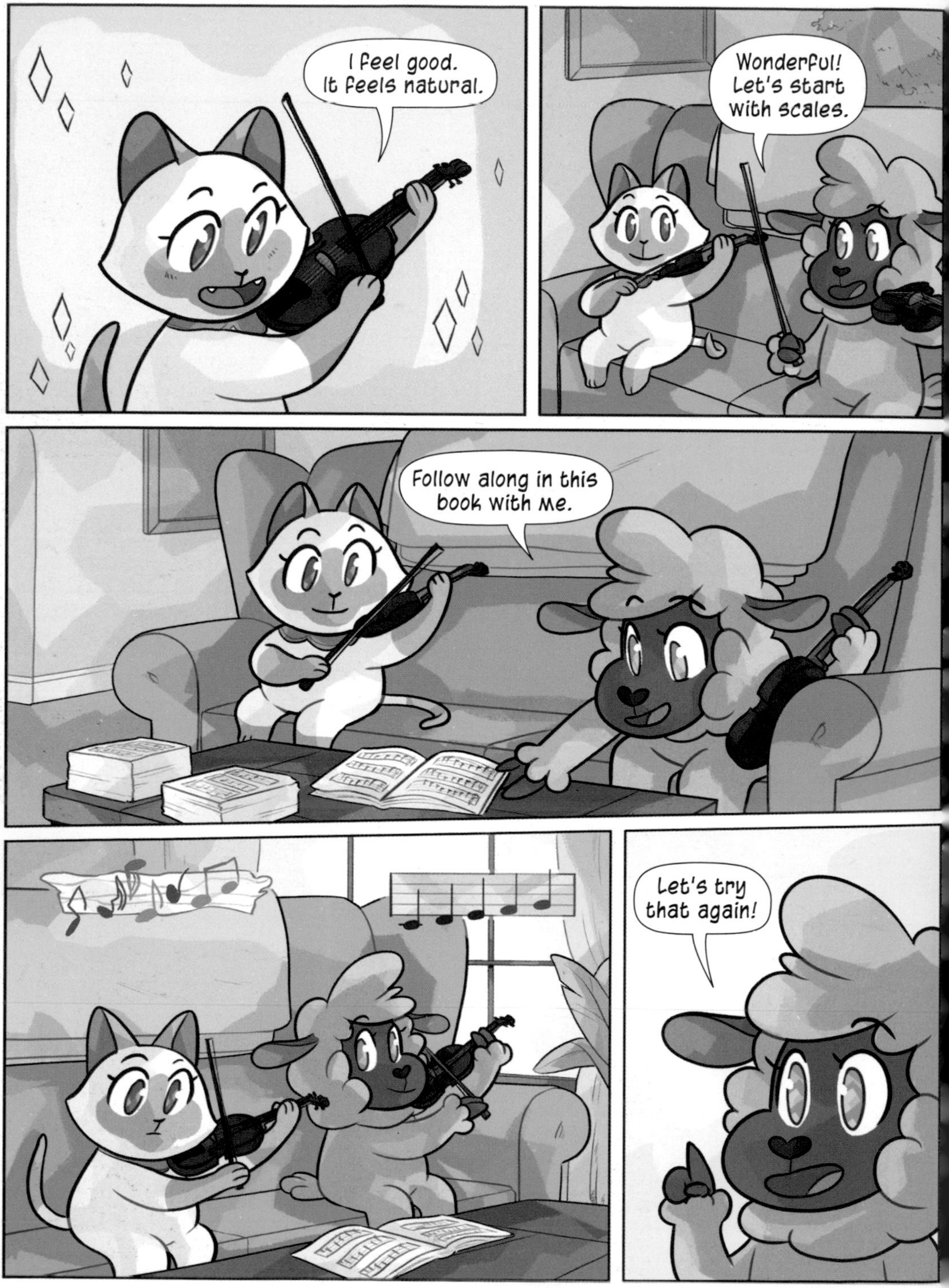
I feel good.
It feels natural.
Wonderful!
Let's start
with scales.
Follow along in this
book with me.
Let's try
that again!

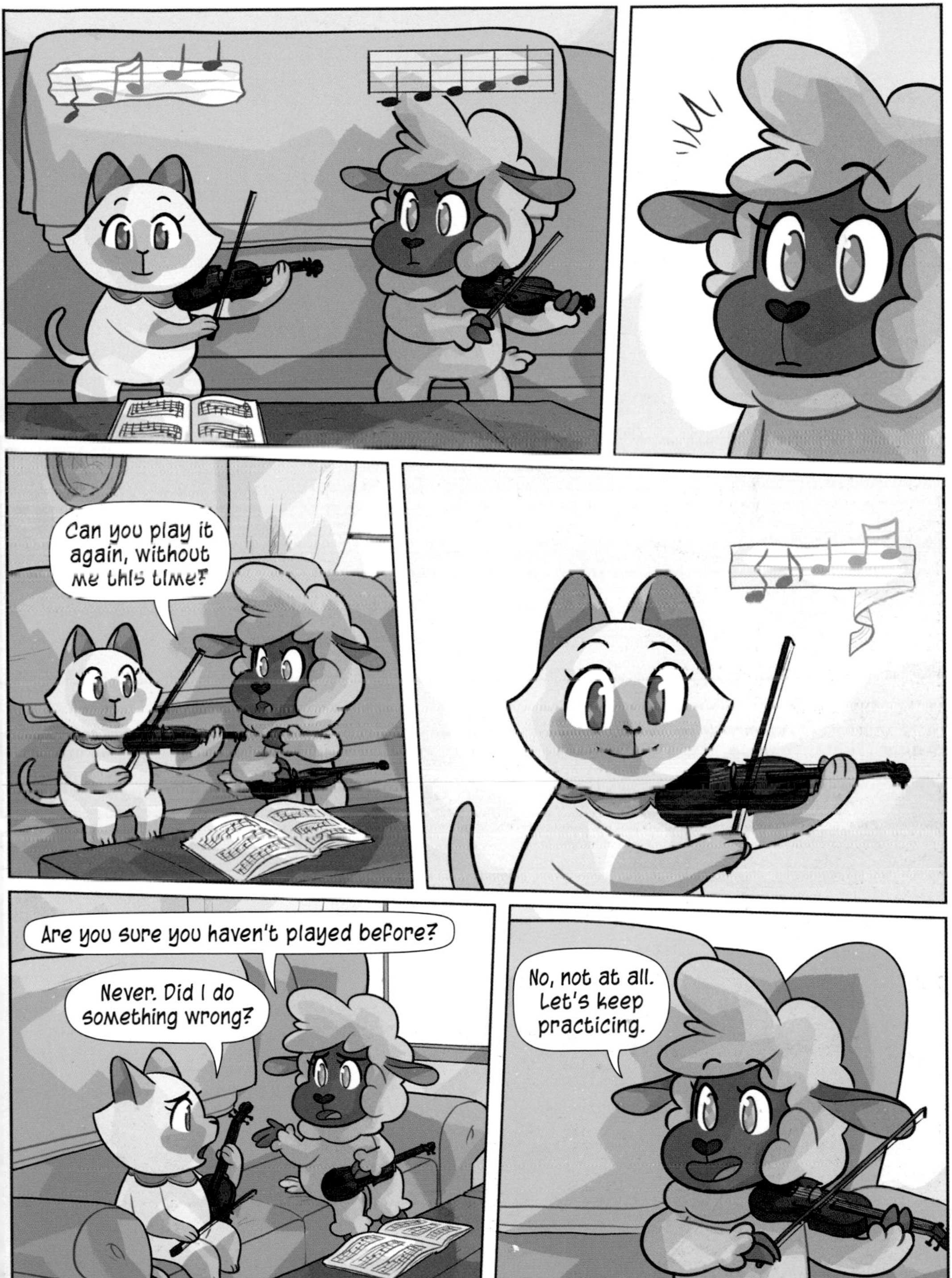
Can you play it again, without me this time?
Are you sure you haven't played before?
Never. Did I do something wrong?
No, not at all. Let's keep practicing.

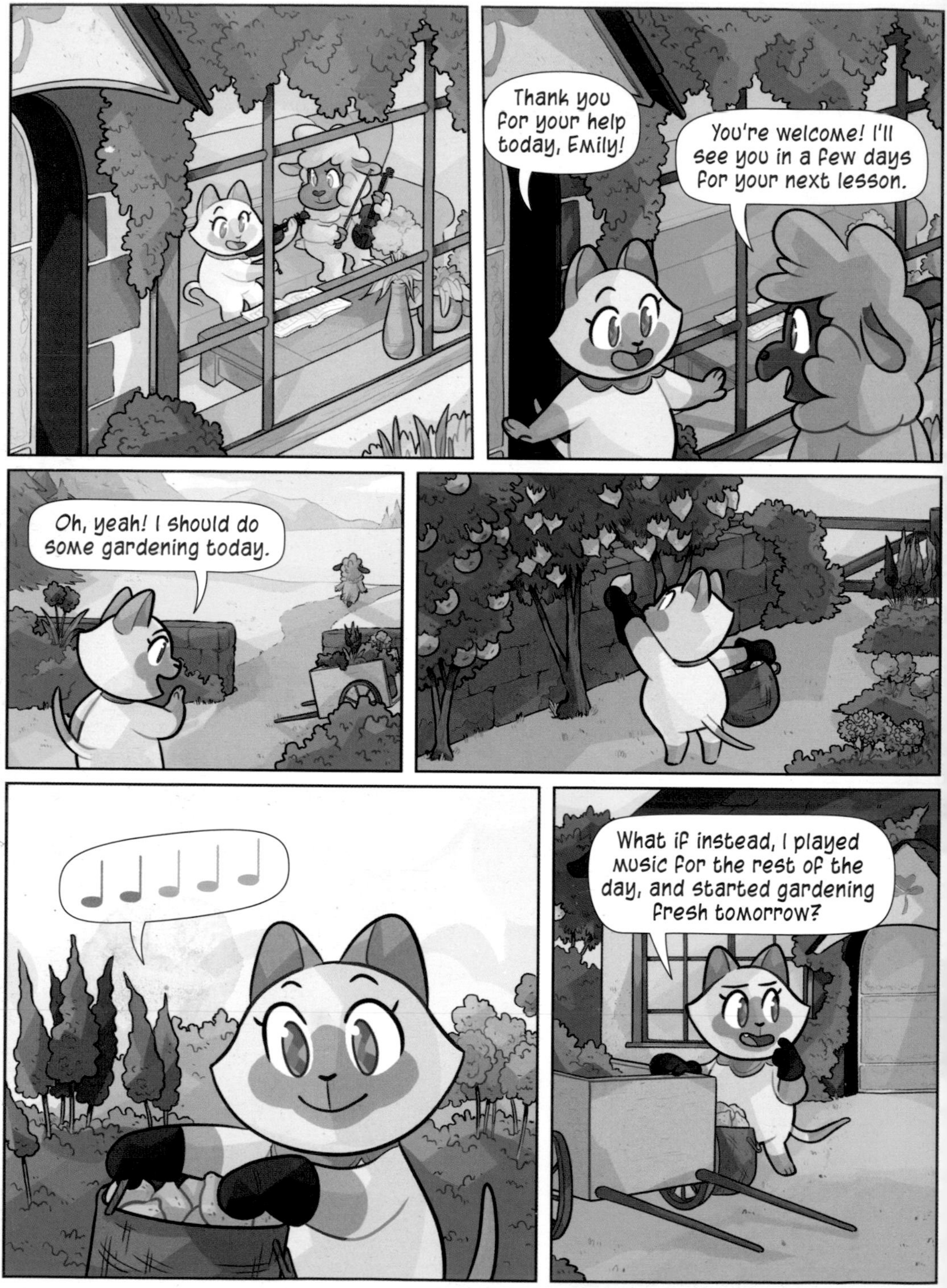
Thank you for your help today, Emily!
You're welcome! I'll see you in a few days for your next lesson.
Oh, yeah! I should do some gardening today.
What if instead, I played music for the rest of the day, and started gardening fresh tomorrow?

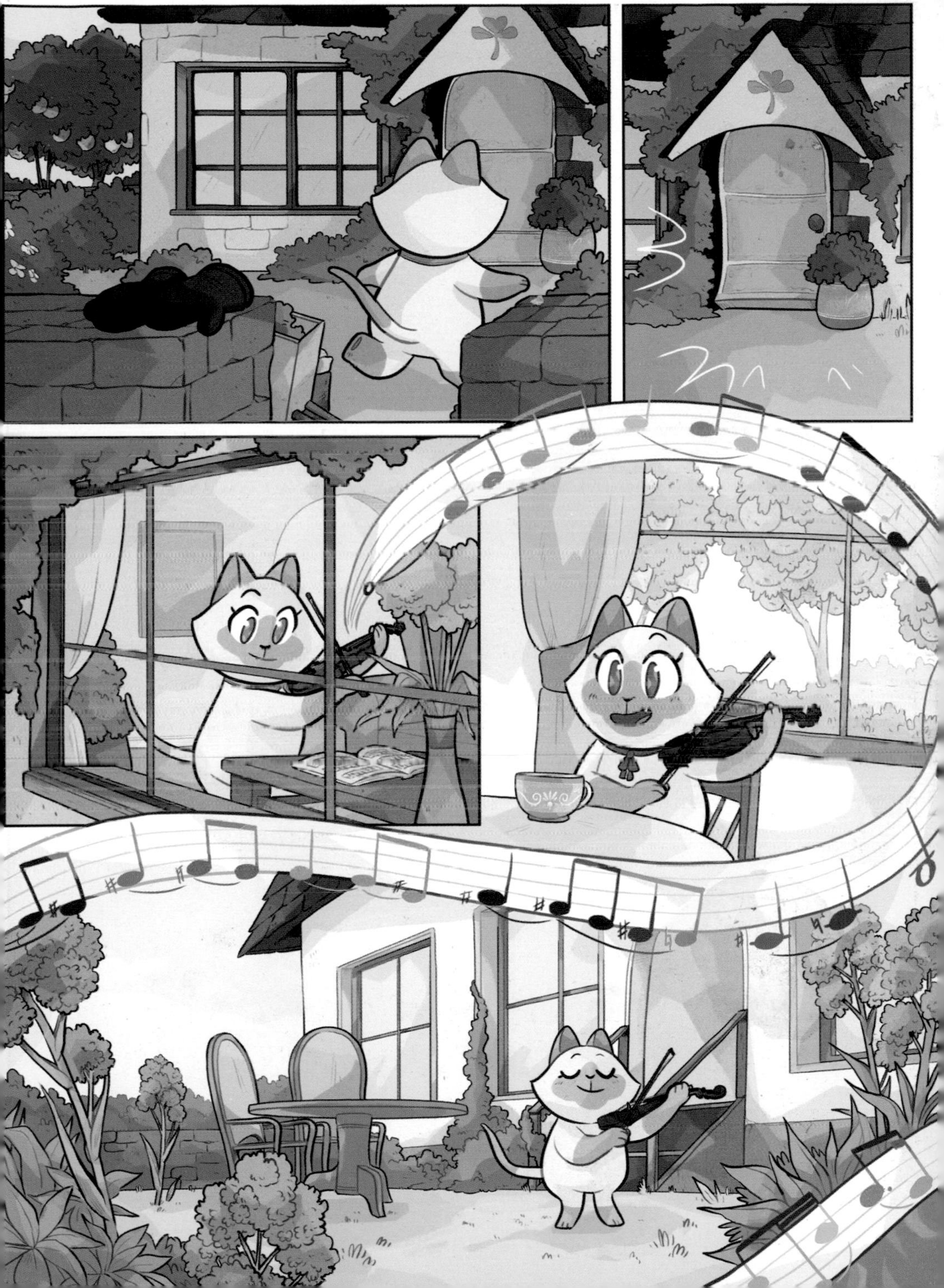

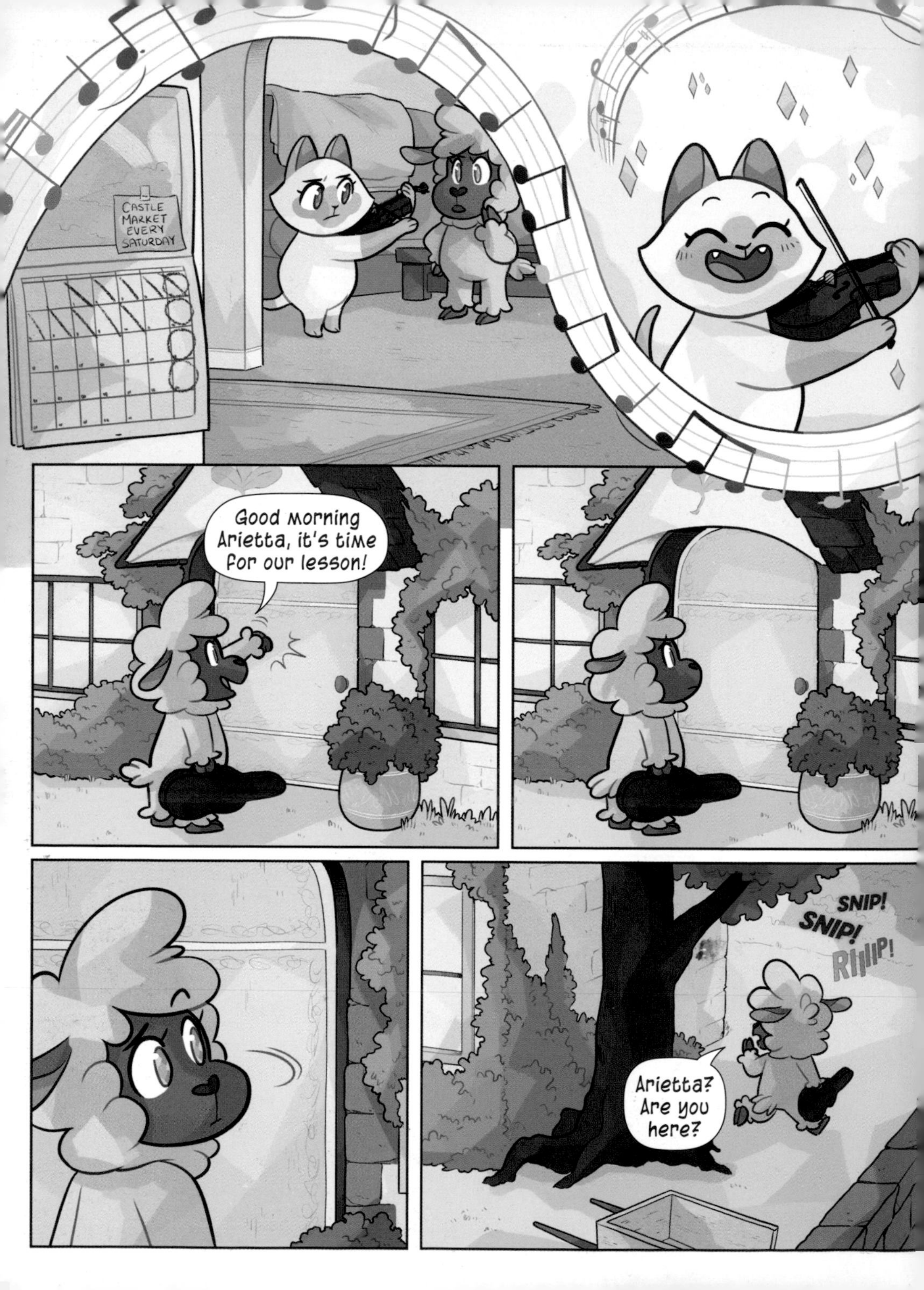
CASTLE MARKET EVERY SATURDAY
Good morning Arietta, it's time for our lesson!
SNIP!
SNIP!
RIIIIP!
Arietta? Are you here?

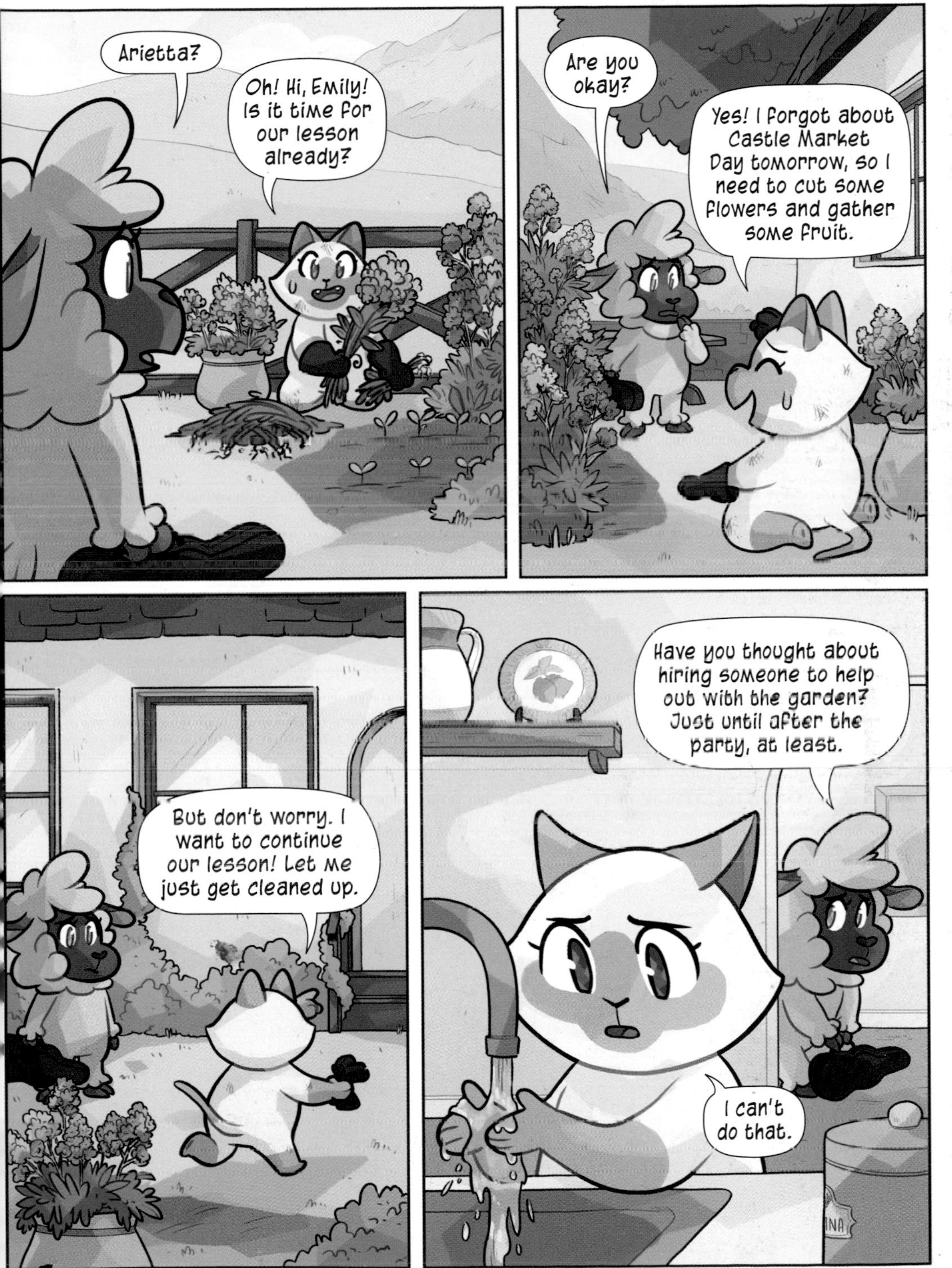
Arietta?
Oh! Hi, Emily! Is it time for our lesson already?
Are you okay?
Yes! I forgot about Castle Market Day tomorrow, so I need to cut some flowers and gather some fruit.
But don't worry. I want to continue our lesson! Let me just get cleaned up.
Have you thought about hiring someone to help out with the garden? Just until after the party, at least.
I can't do that.

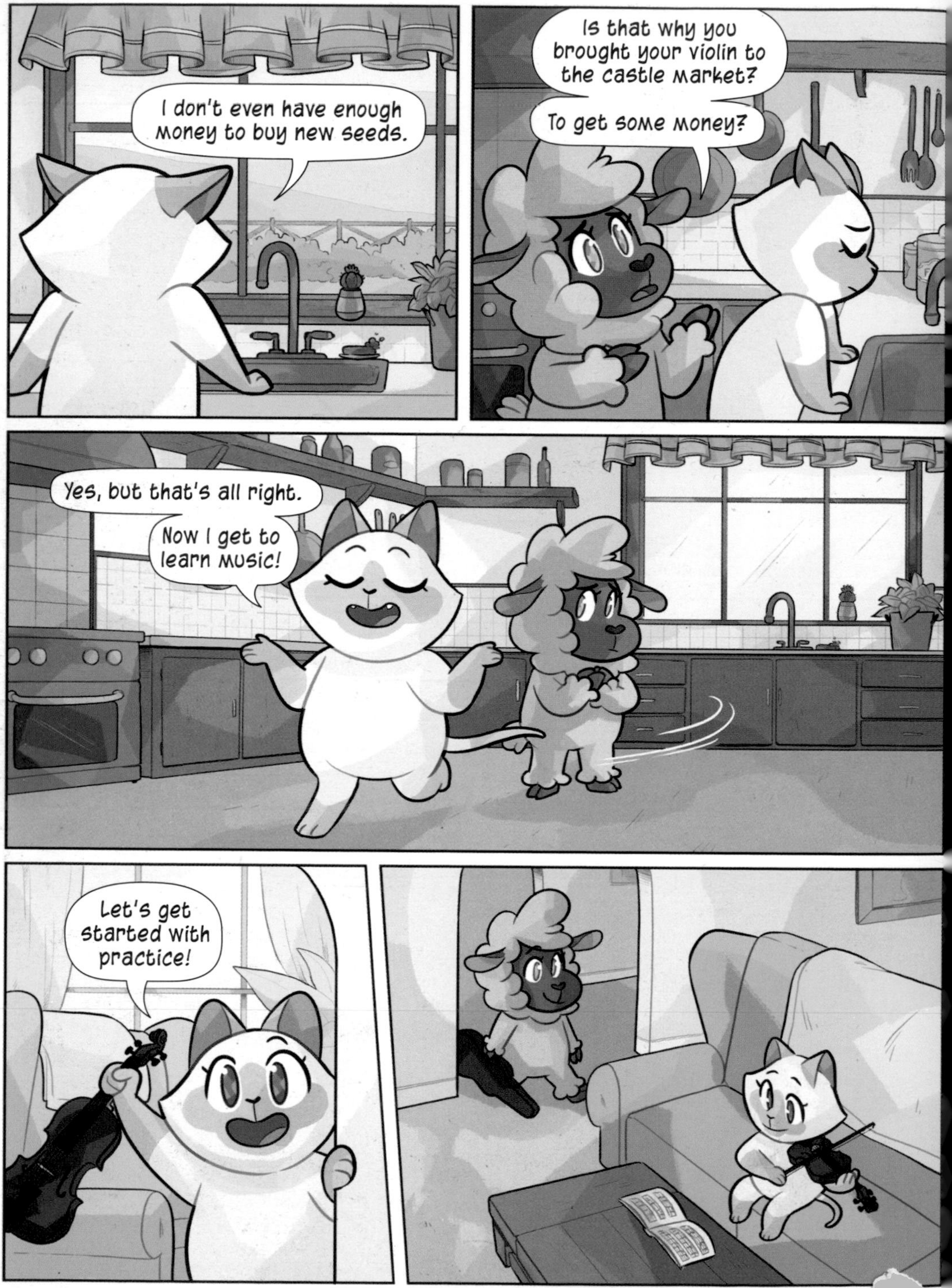
I don't even have enough money to buy new seeds.
Is that why you brought your violin to the castle market?
To get some money?
Yes, but that's all right.
Now I get to learn music!
Let's get started with practice!

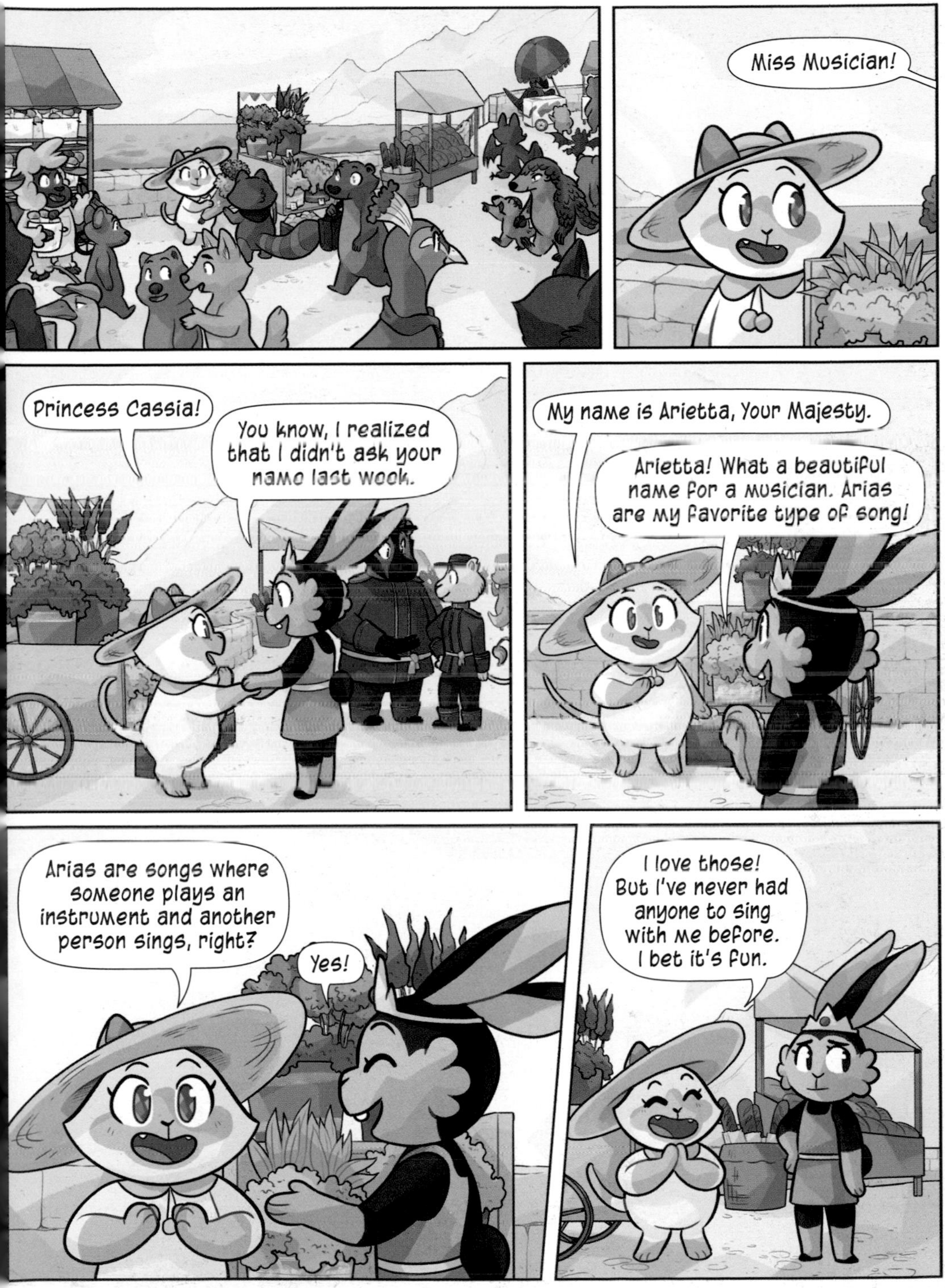
Miss Musician!
Princess Cassia!
You know, I realized that I didn't ask your name last week.
My name is Arietta, Your Majesty.
Arietta! What a beautiful name for a musician. Arias are my favorite type of song!
Arias are songs where someone plays an instrument and another person sings, right?
Yes!
I love those! But I've never had anyone to sing with me before. I bet it's fun.

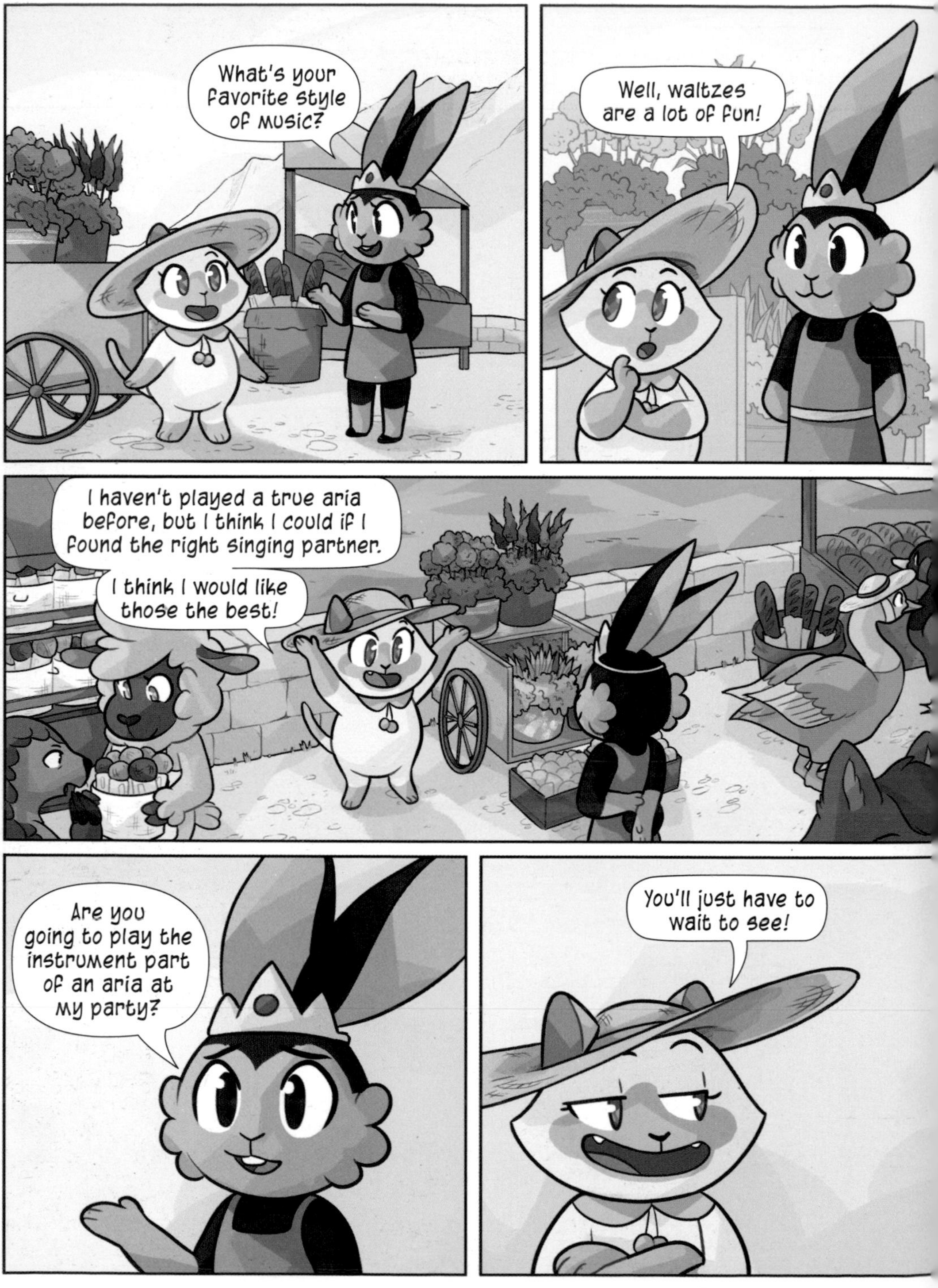
What's your favorite style of music?
Well, waltzes are a lot of fun!
I haven't played a true aria before, but I think I could if I found the right singing partner.
I think I would like those the best!
Are you going to play the instrument part of an aria at my party?
You'll just have to wait to see!

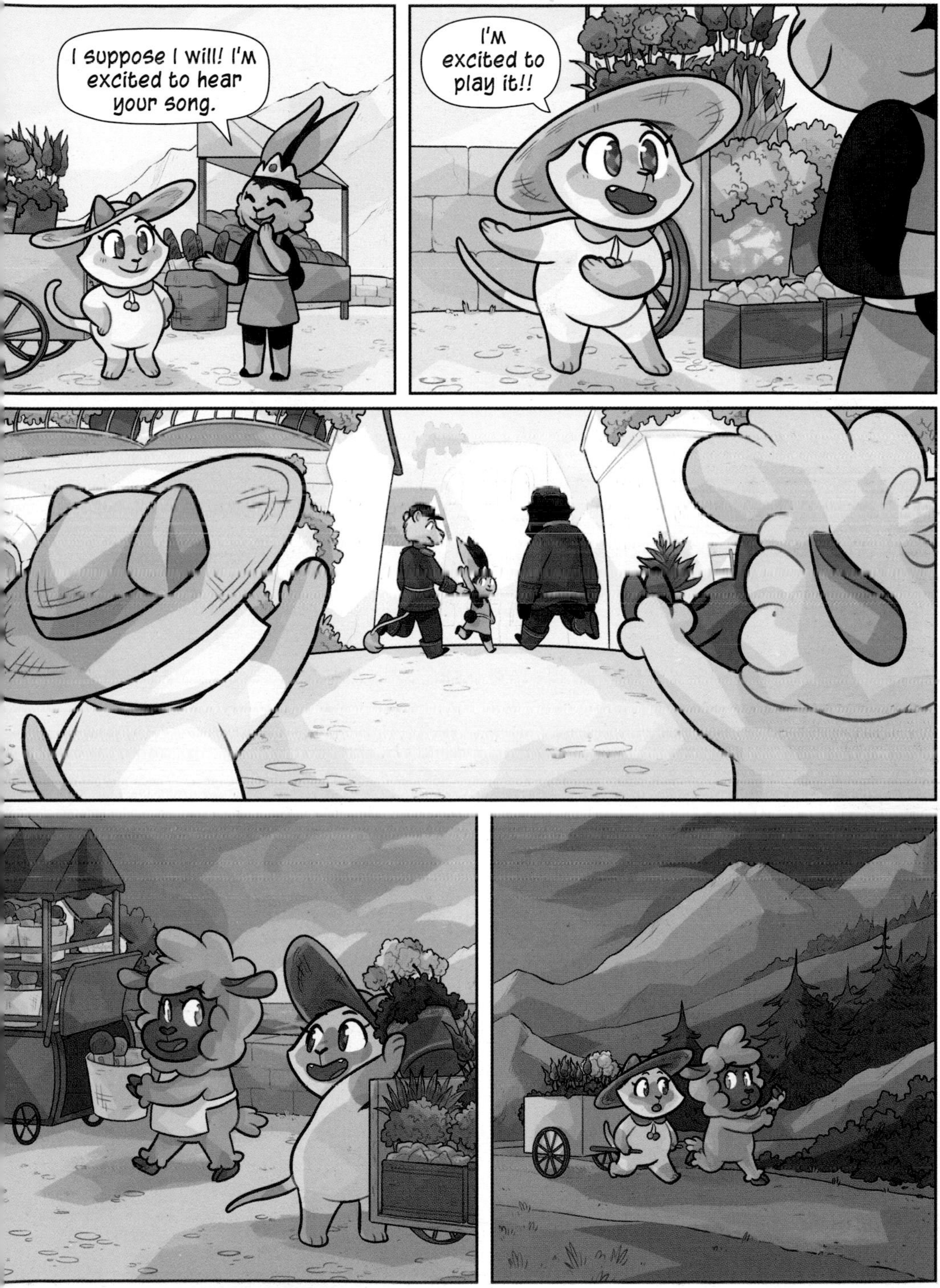
I suppose I will! I'M excited to hear your song.
I'M excited to play it!!

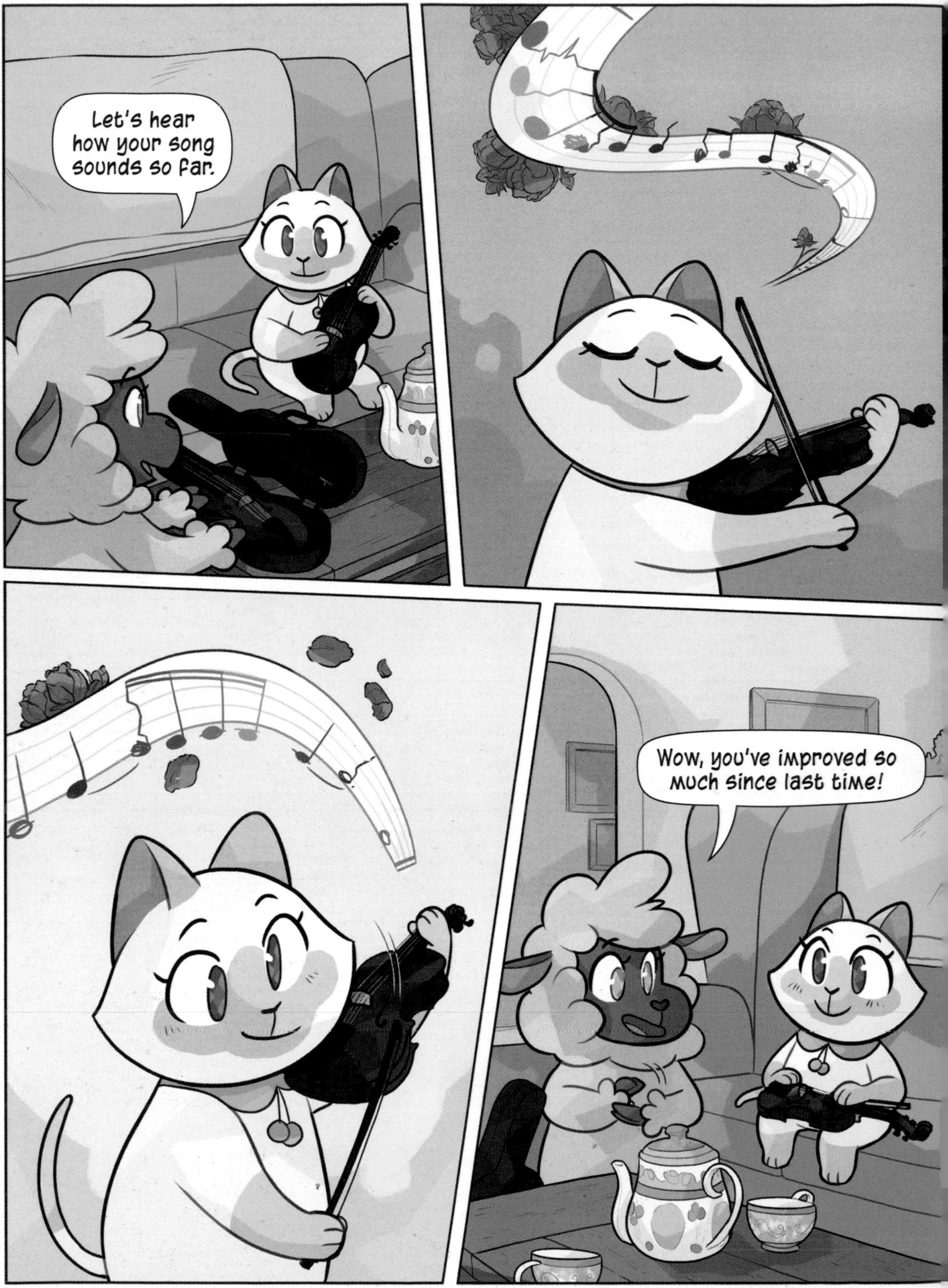
Let's hear how your song sounds so far.
Wow, you've improved so much since last time!

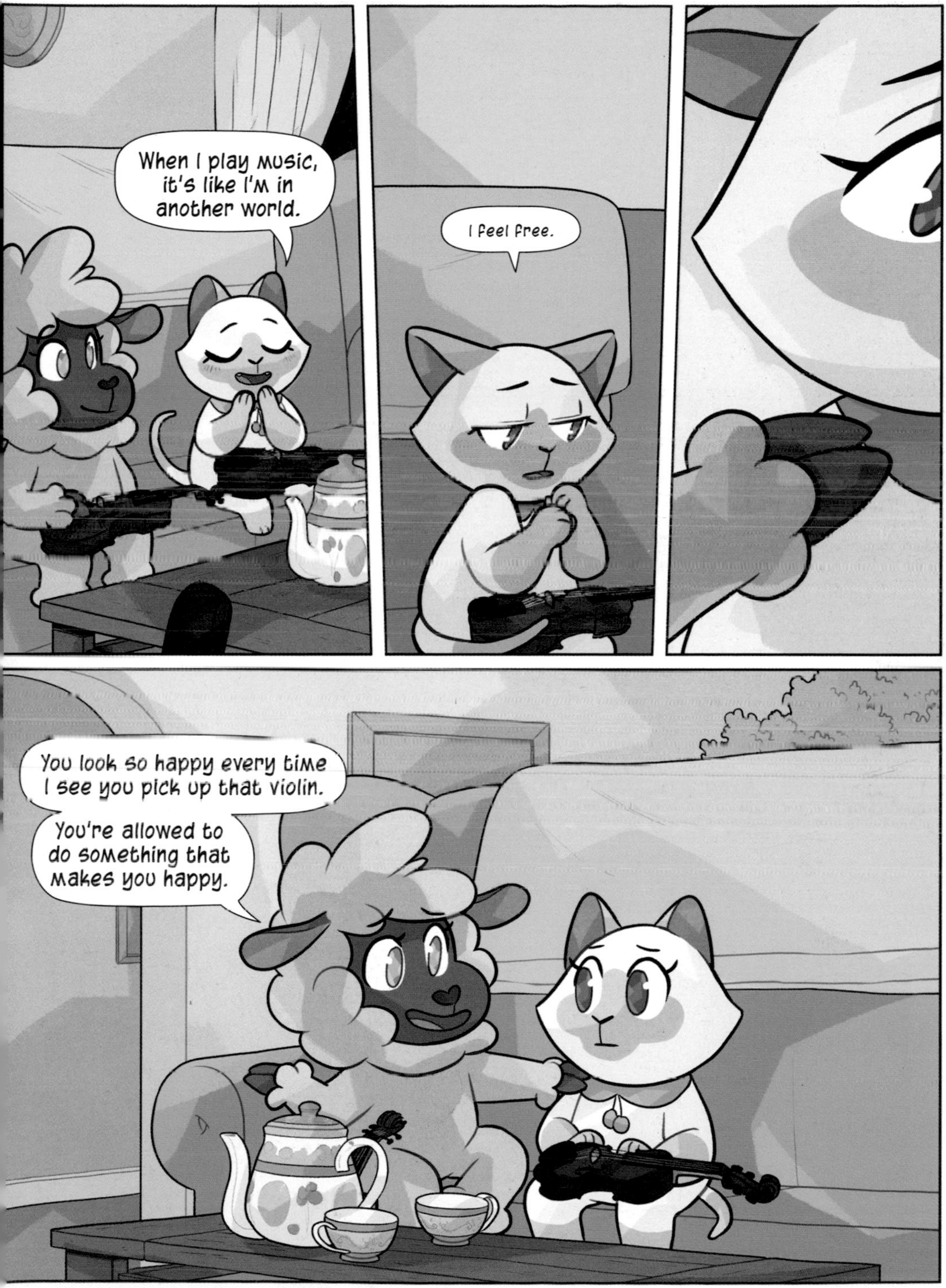
When I play music, it's like I'm in another world.
I feel free.
You look so happy every time I see you pick up that violin.
You're allowed to do something that makes you happy.

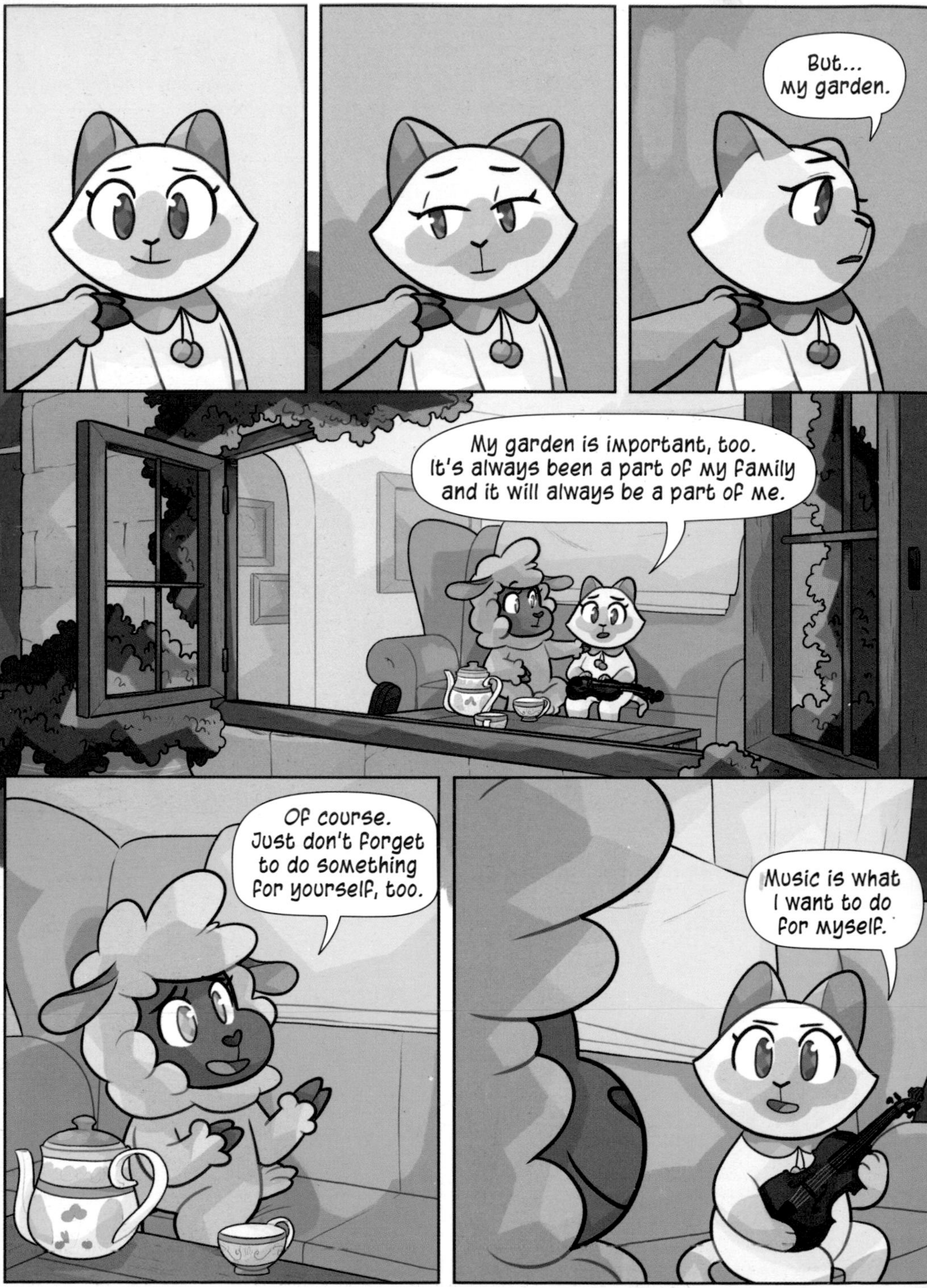

But...
my garden.
My garden is important, too.
It's always been a part of my family
and it will always be a part of me.
Of course.
Just don't forget
to do something
for yourself, too.
Music is what
I want to do
for myself.

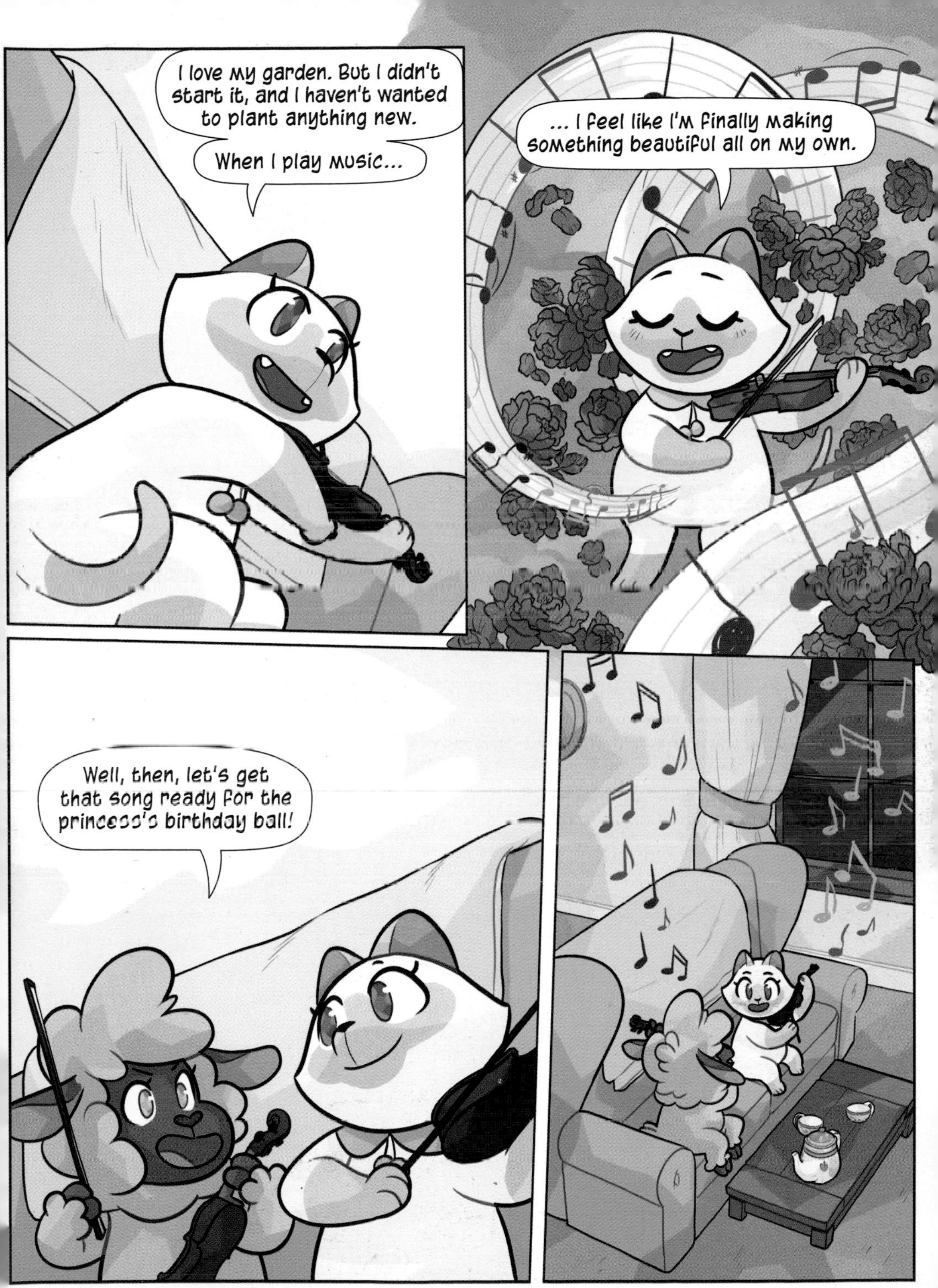
I love my garden. But I didn't start it, and I haven't wanted to plant anything new.
When I play music...
... I feel like I'm finally making something beautiful all on my own.
Well, then, let's get that song ready for the princess's birthday ball!

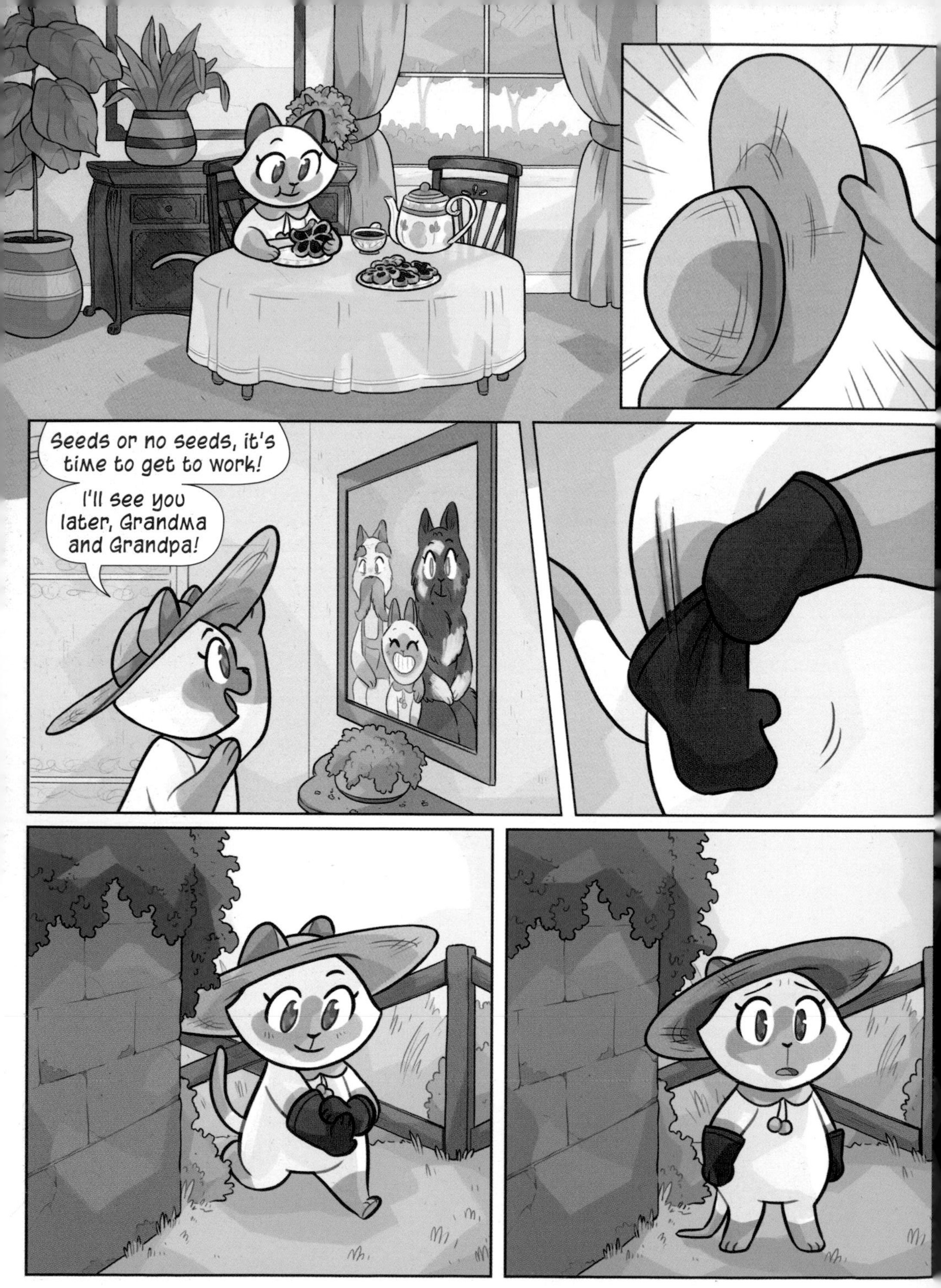
Seeds or no seeds, it's time to get to work!
I'll see you later, Grandma and Grandpa!

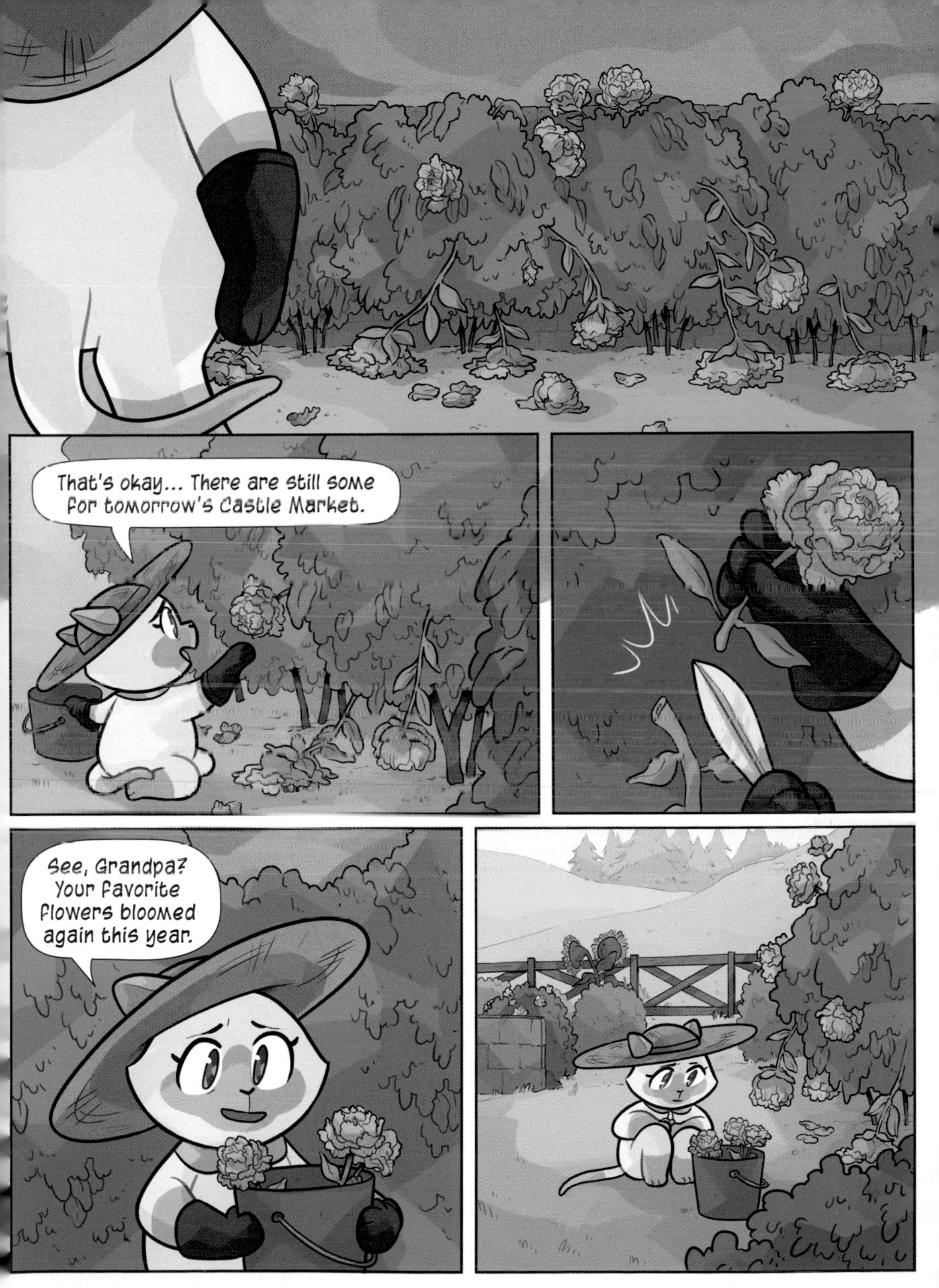
That's okay... There are still some for tomorrow's Castle Market.
See, Grandpa? Your favorite flowers bloomed again this year.

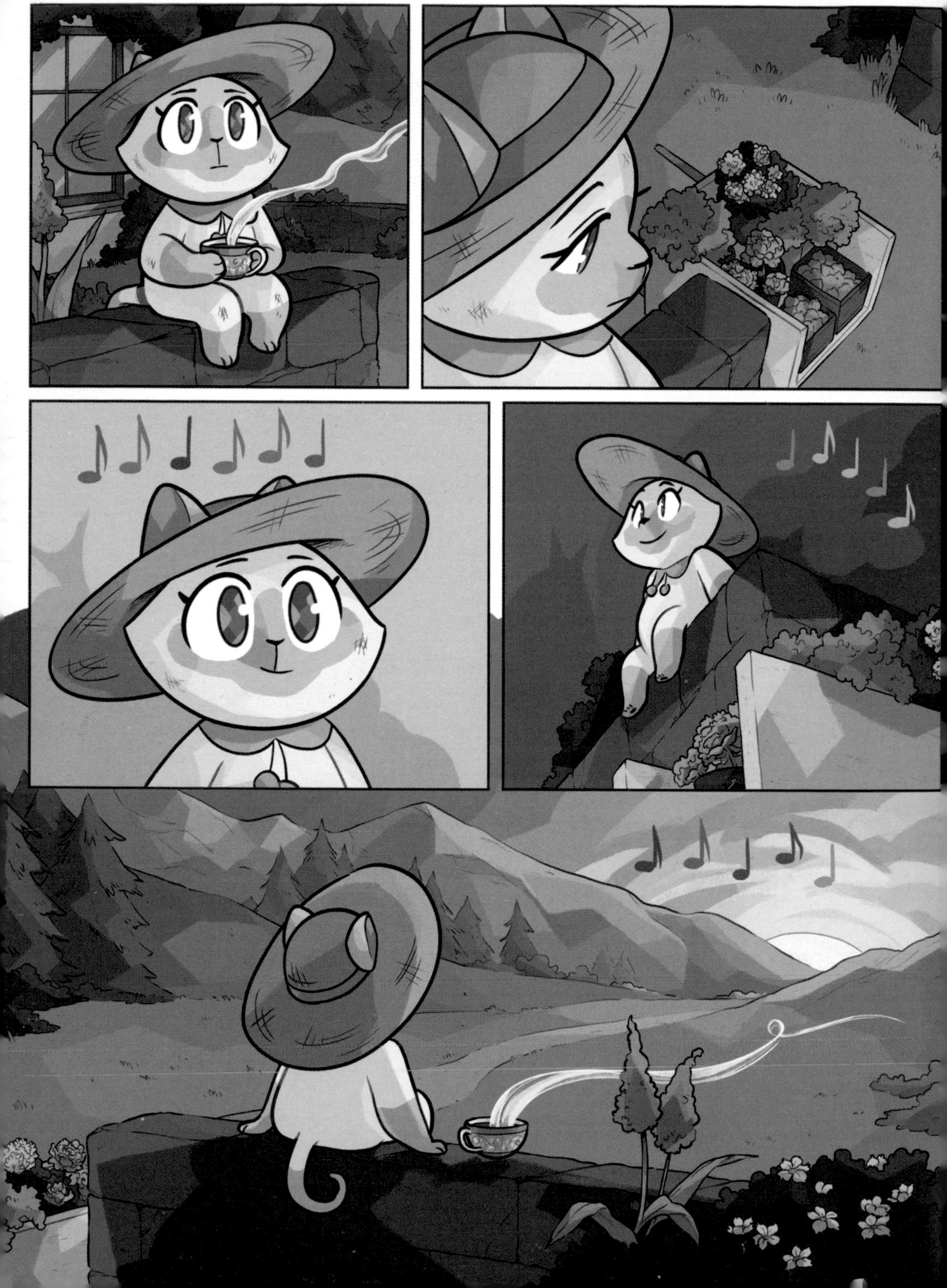

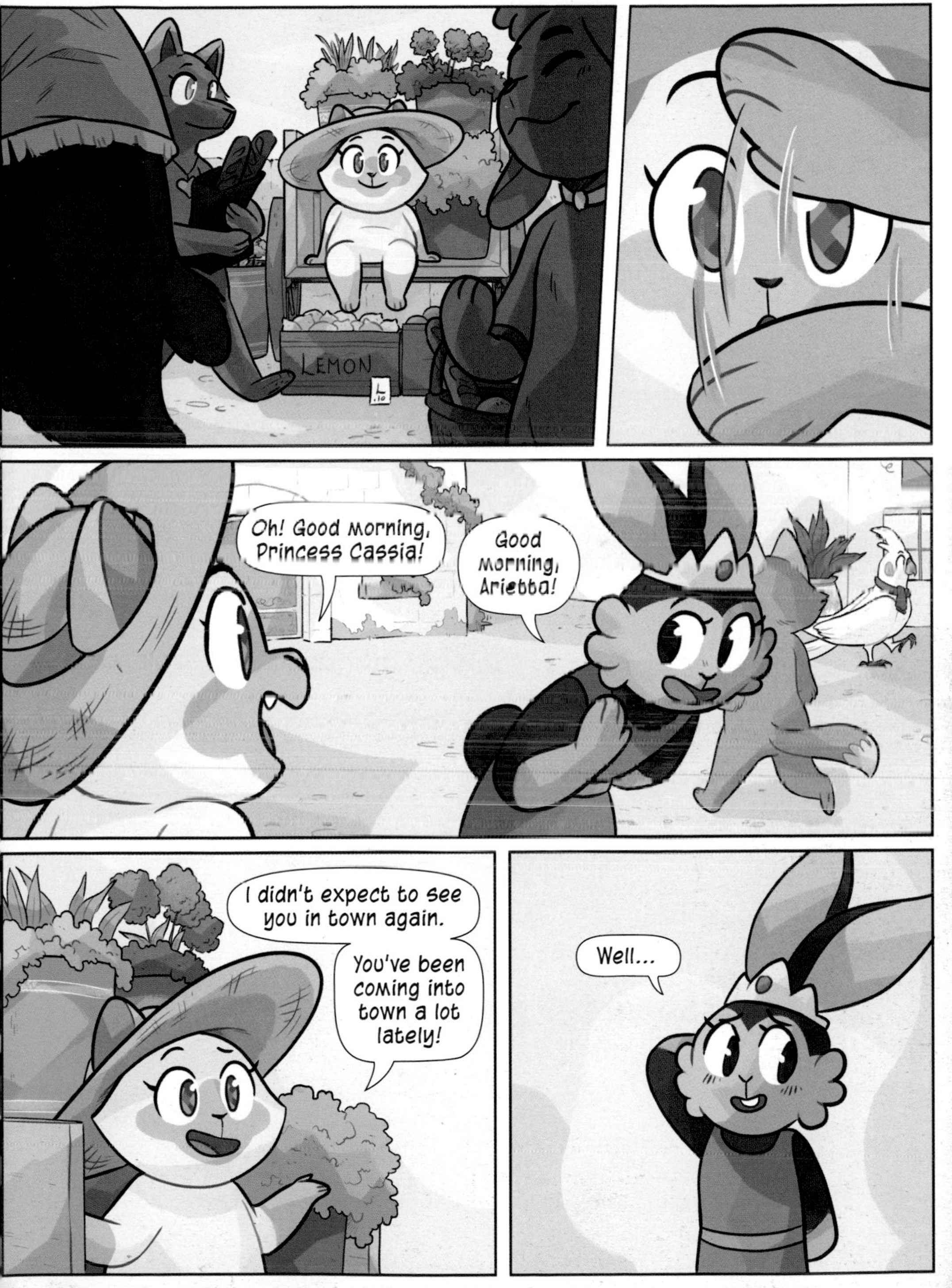
LEMON
Oh! Good morning, Princess Cassia!
Good morning, Arietta!
I didn't expect to see you in town again.
You've been coming into town a lot lately!
Well...

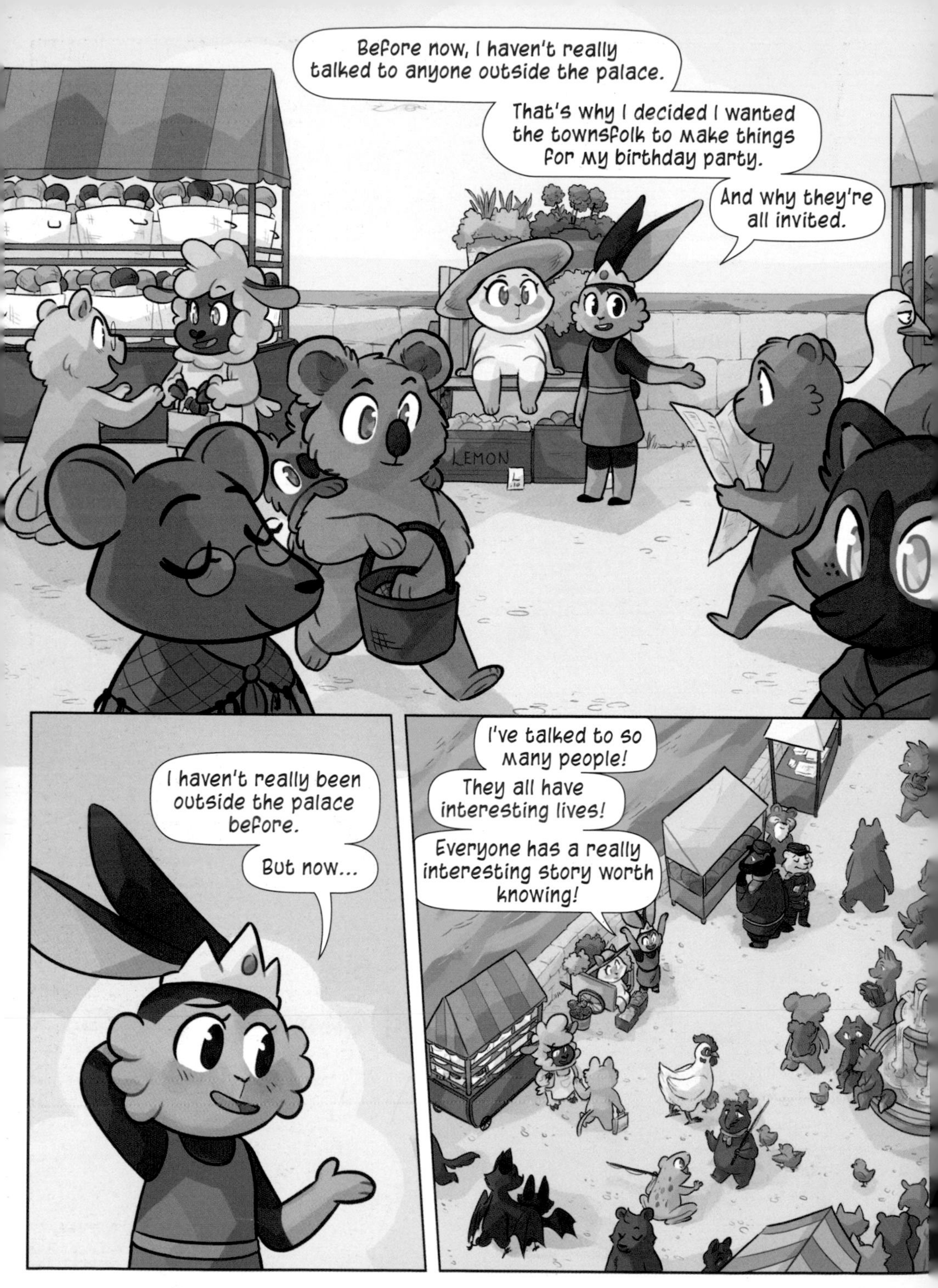
Before now, I haven't really talked to anyone outside the palace.
That's why I decided I wanted the townsfolk to make things for my birthday party.
And why they're all invited.
LEMON
I haven't really been outside the palace before.
But now...
I've talked to so many people!
They all have interesting lives!
Everyone has a really interesting story worth knowing!

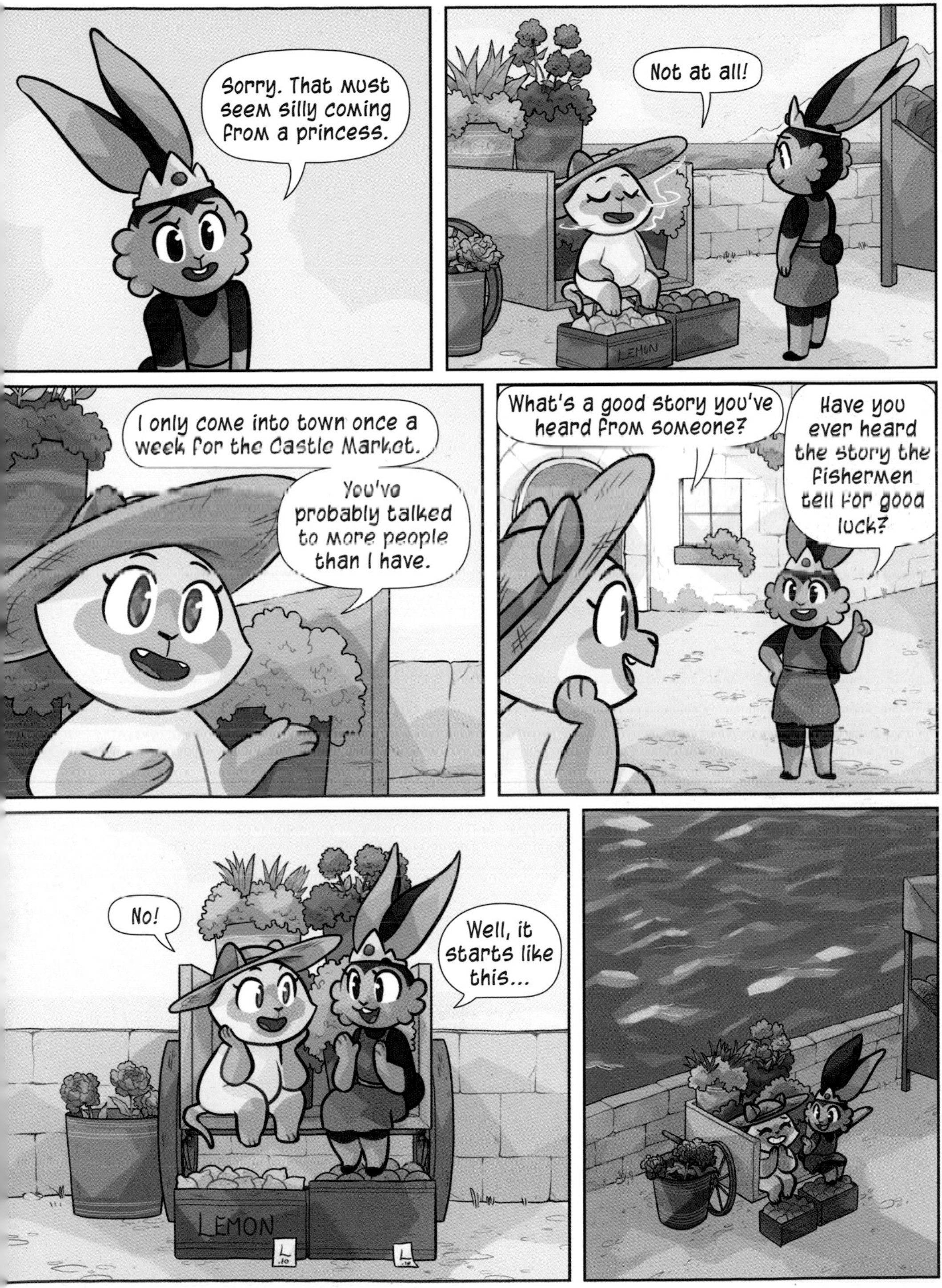
Sorry. That must seem silly coming from a princess.
Not at all!
I only come into town once a week for the Castle Market.
You've probably talked to more people than I have.
What's a good story you've heard from someone?
Have you ever heard the story the fishermen tell for good luck?
No!
Well, it starts like this...
LEMON

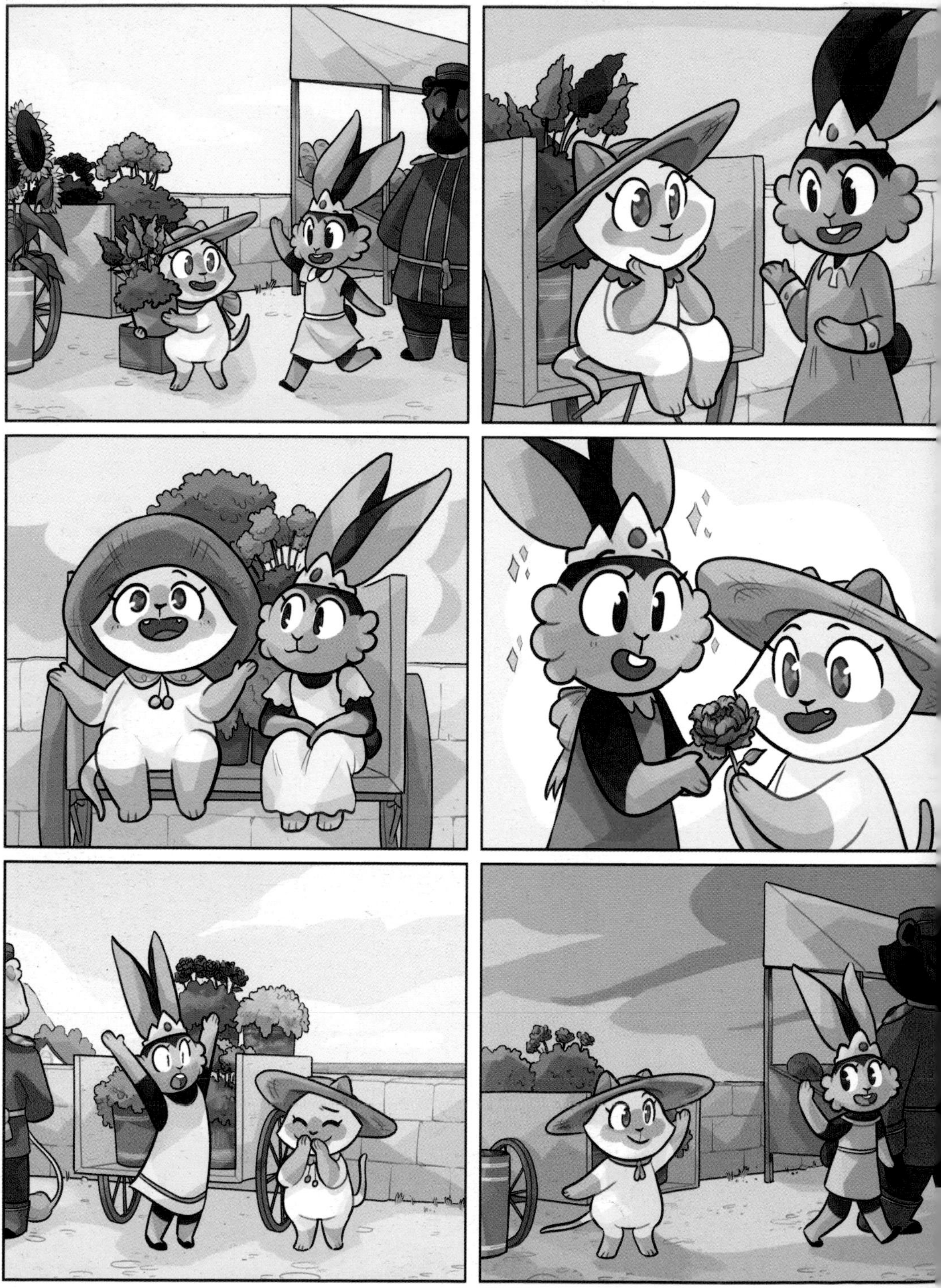

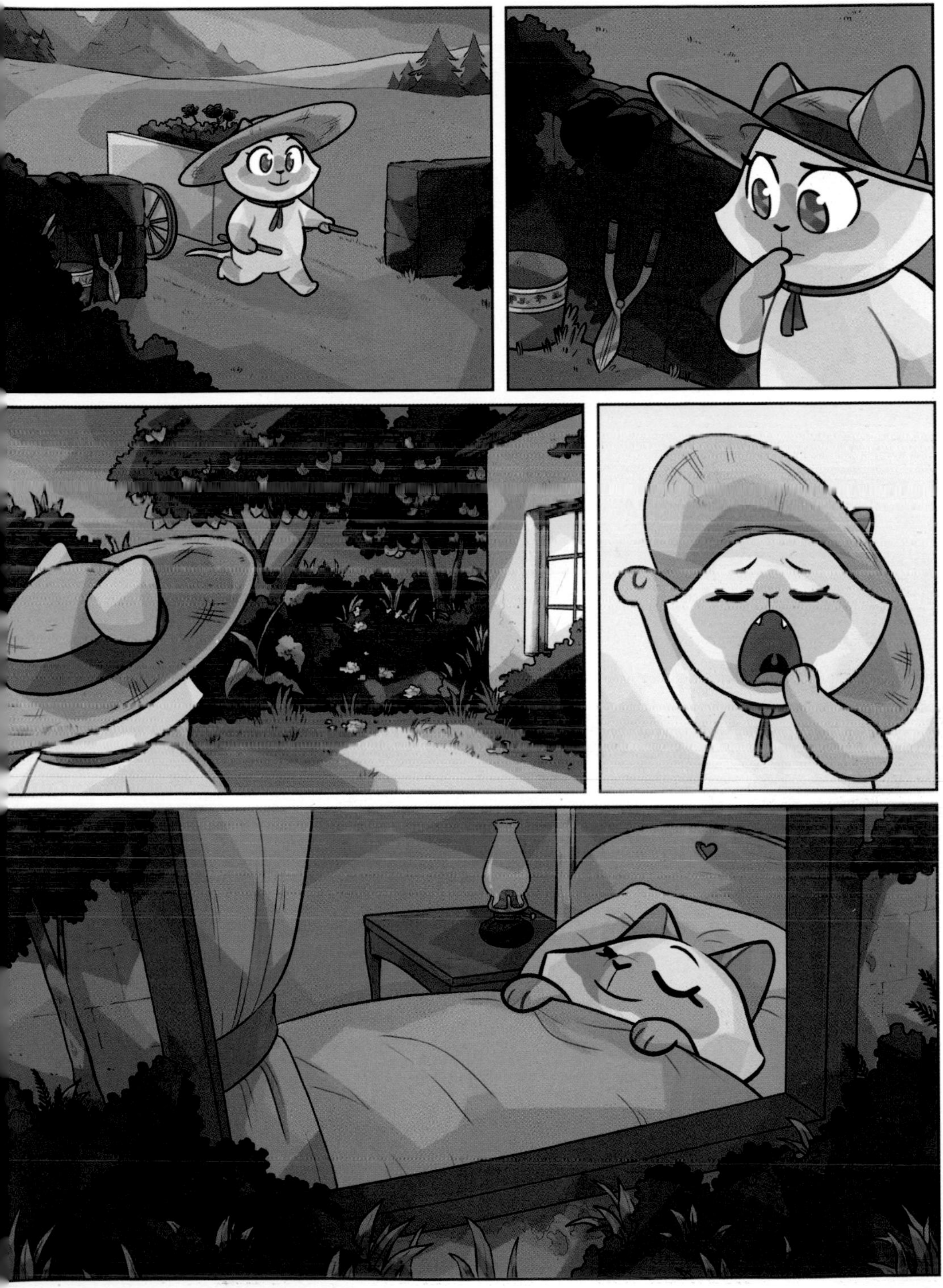

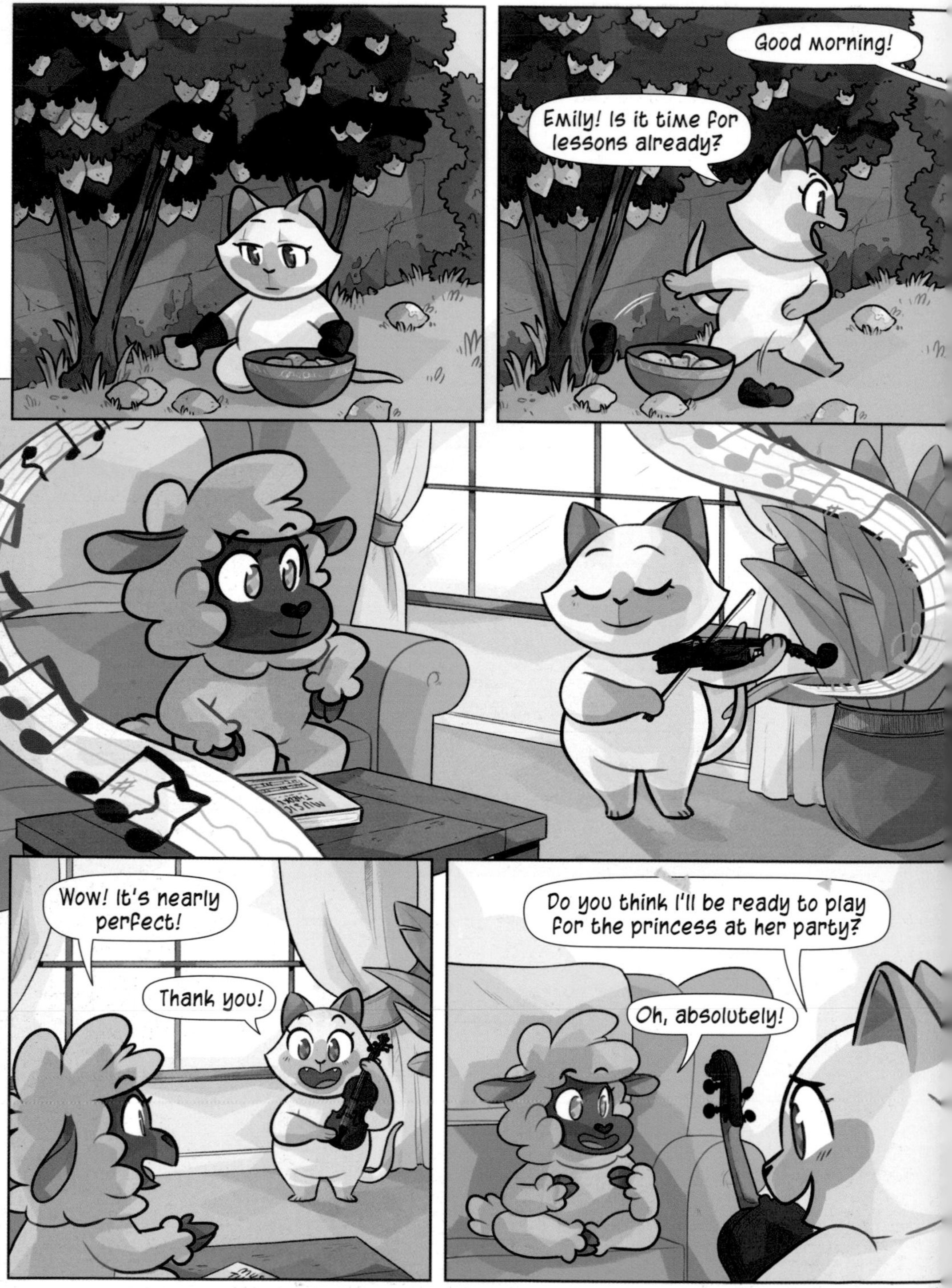
Good morning!
Emily! Is it time for lessons already?
Wow! It's nearly perfect!
Thank you!
Do you think I'll be ready to play for the princess at her party?
Oh, absolutely!

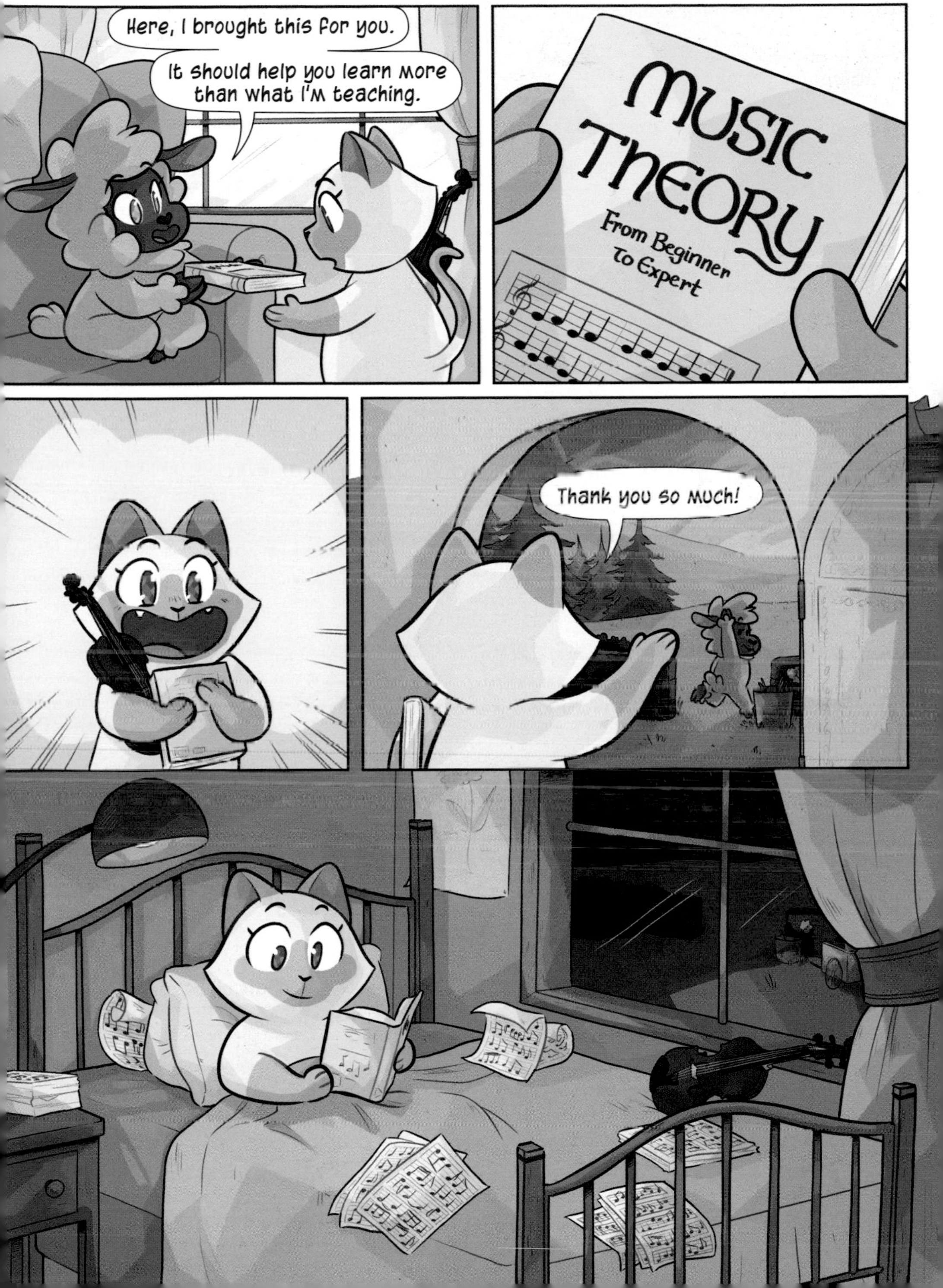
Here, I brought this for you.
It should help you learn more than what I'm teaching.
MUSIC THEORY
From Beginner to Expert
Thank you so much!

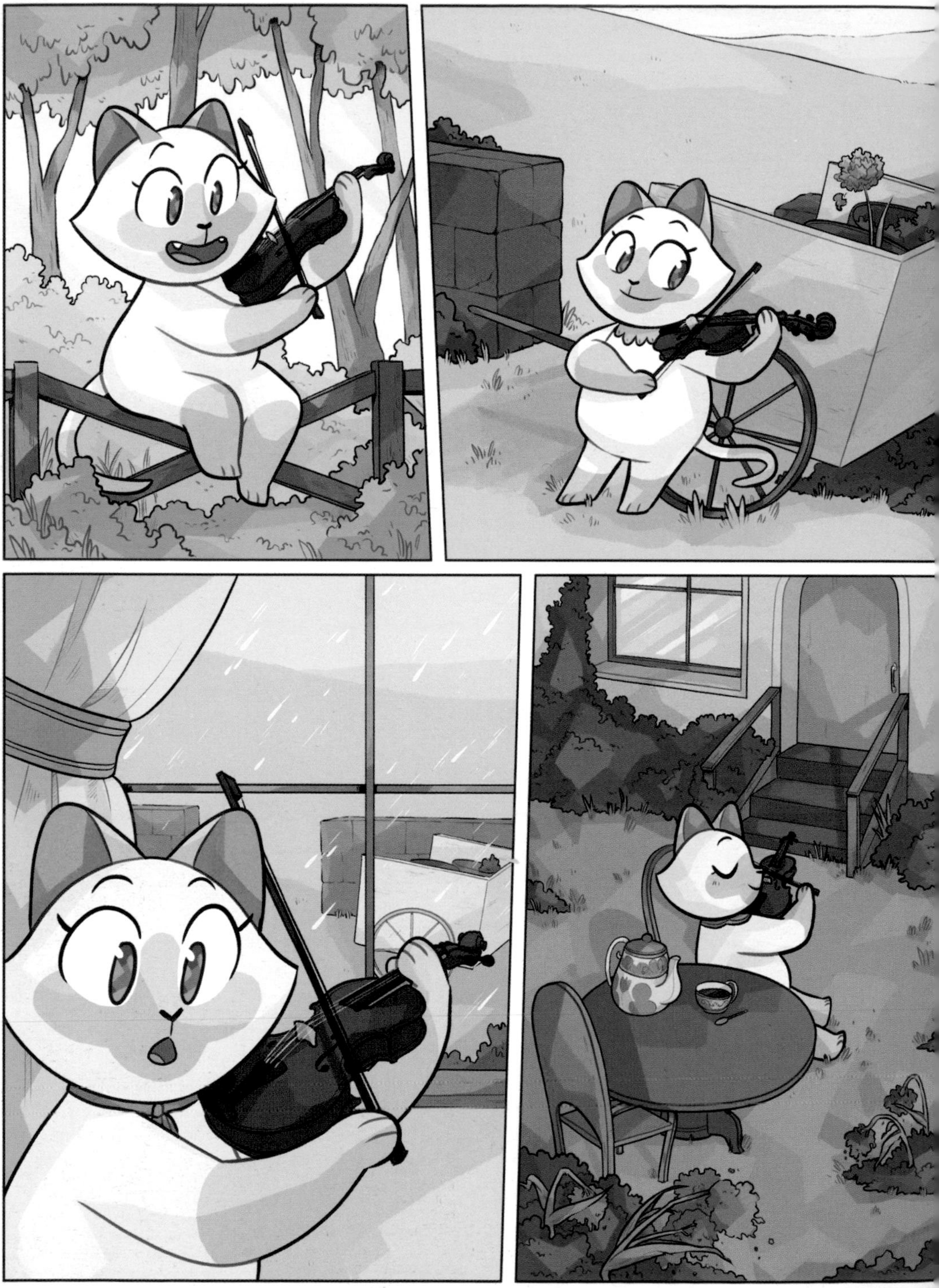

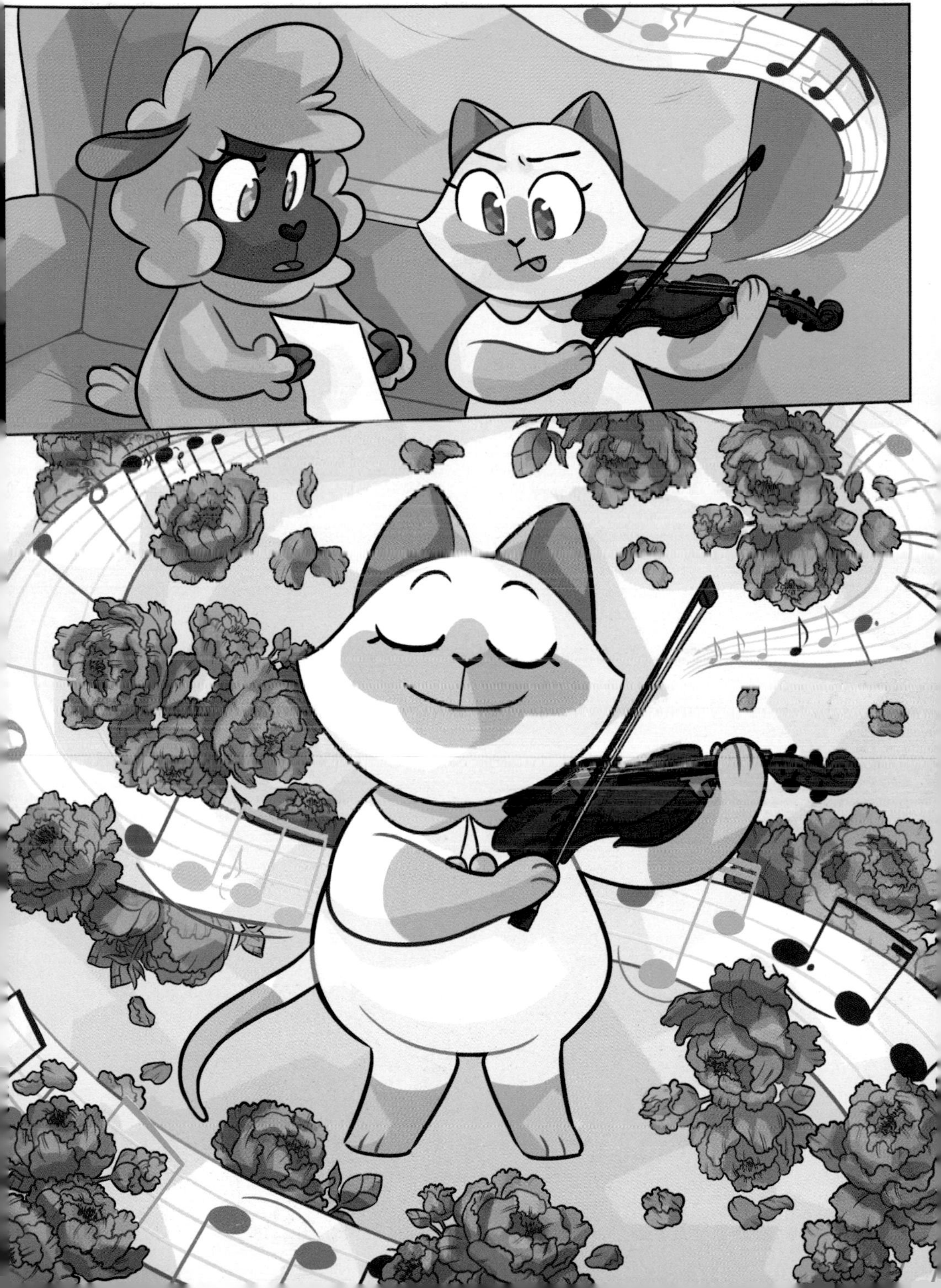

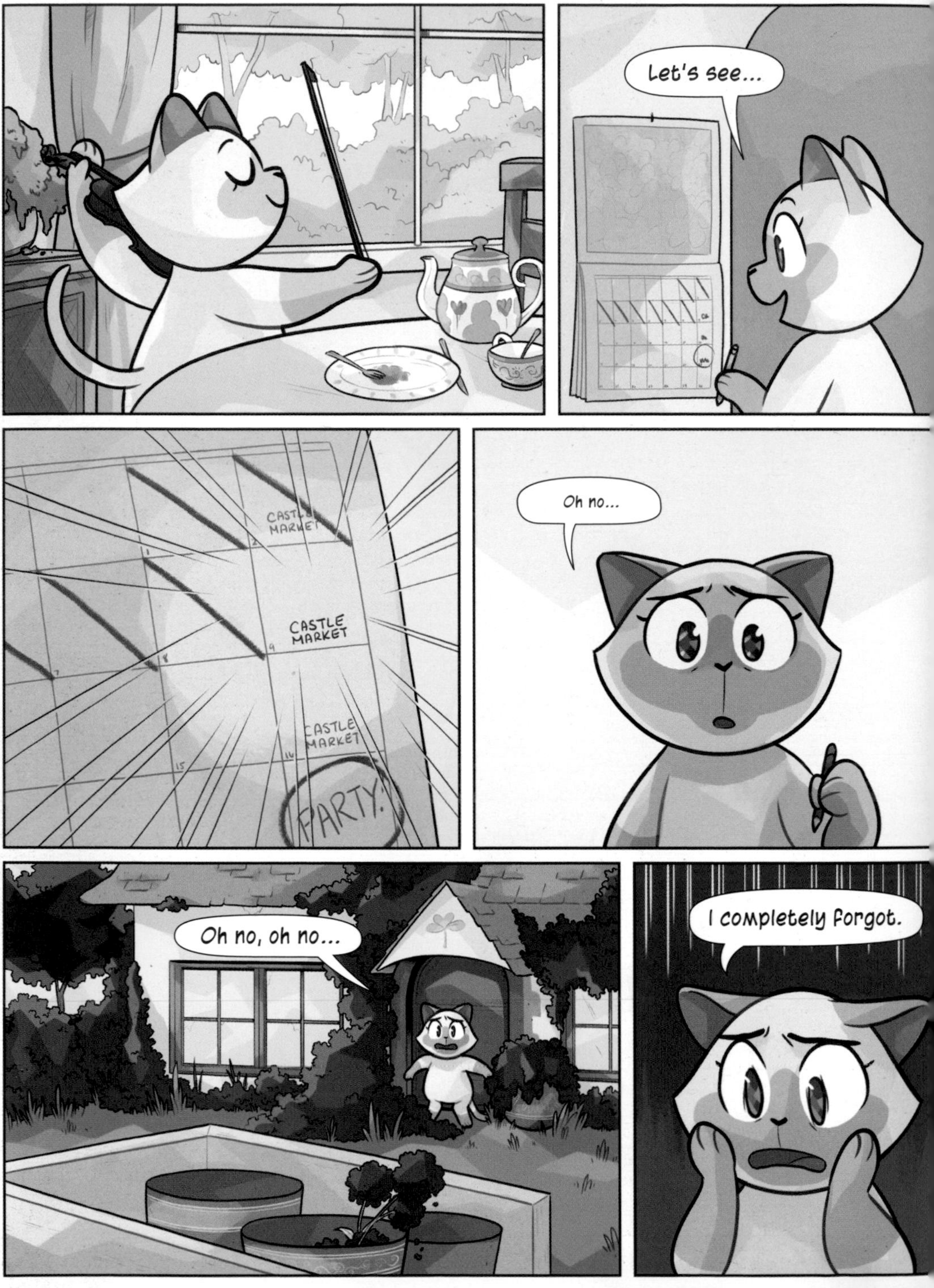
Let's see...
CASTLE MARKET
CASTLE MARKET
CASTLE MARKET
PARTY!
Oh no...
Oh no, oh no...
I completely forgot.

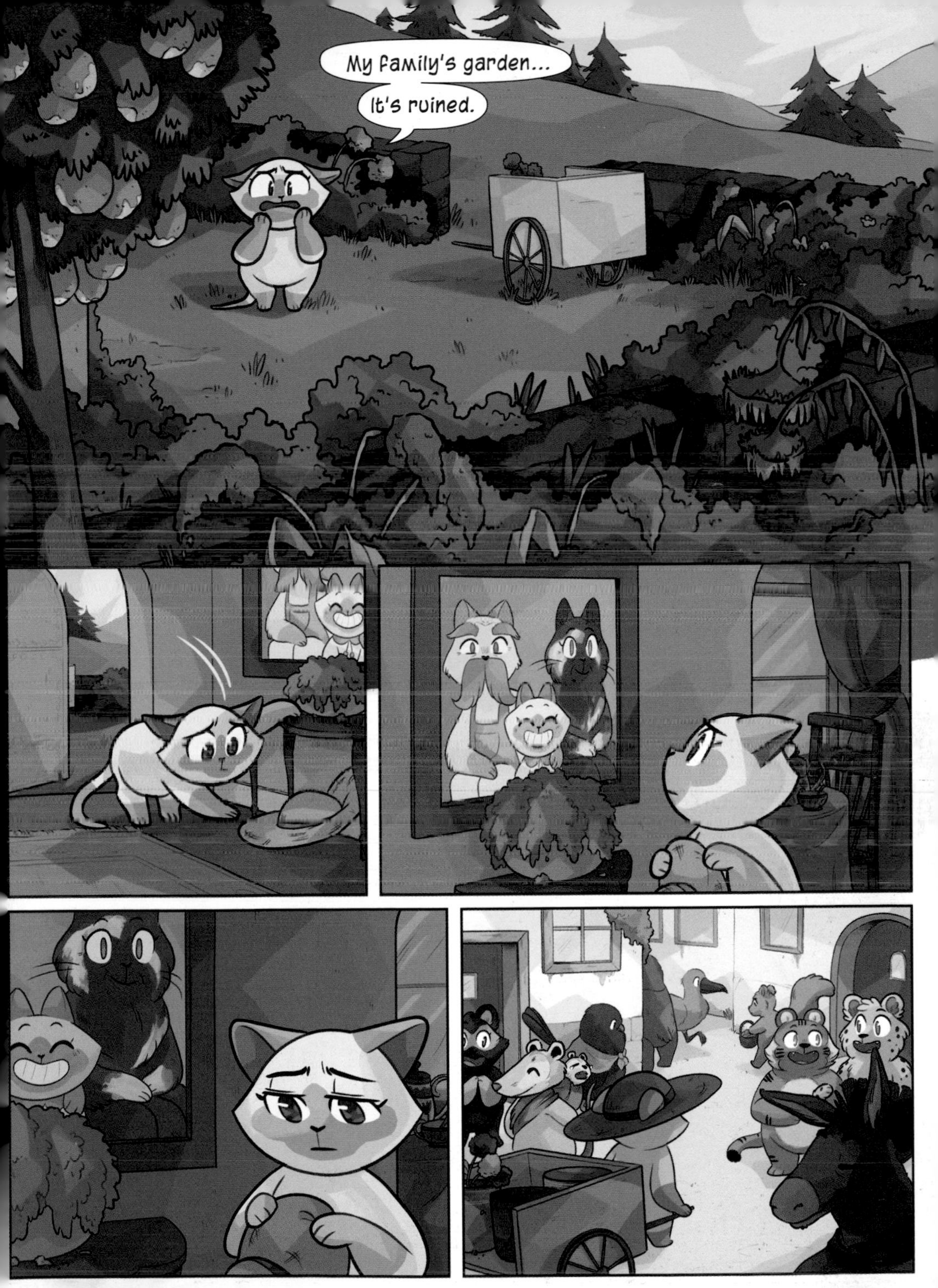
My family's garden...
It's ruined.

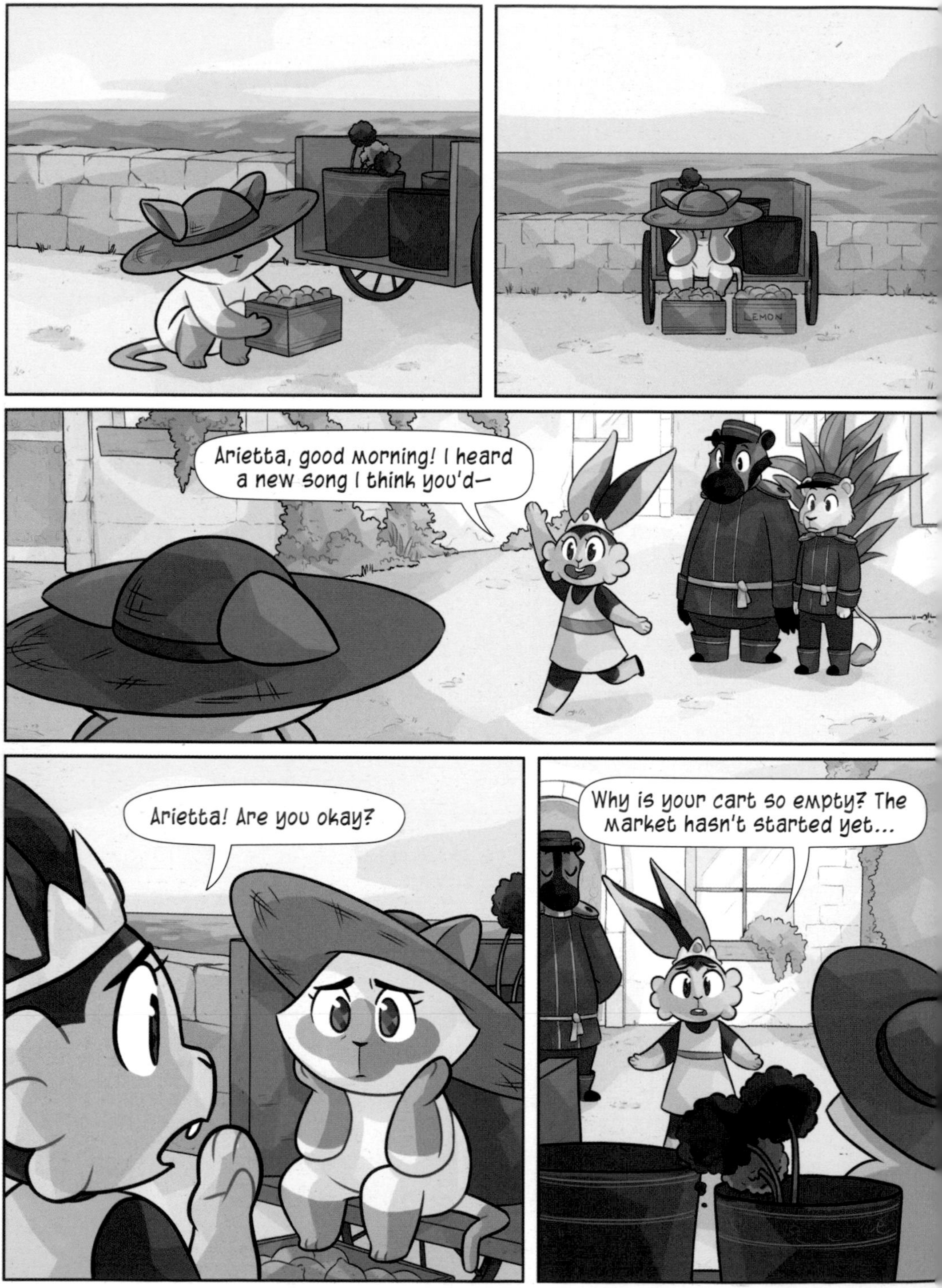
LEMON
Arietta, good morning! I heard a new song I think you'd—
Arietta! Are you okay?
Why is your cart so empty? The market hasn't started yet...

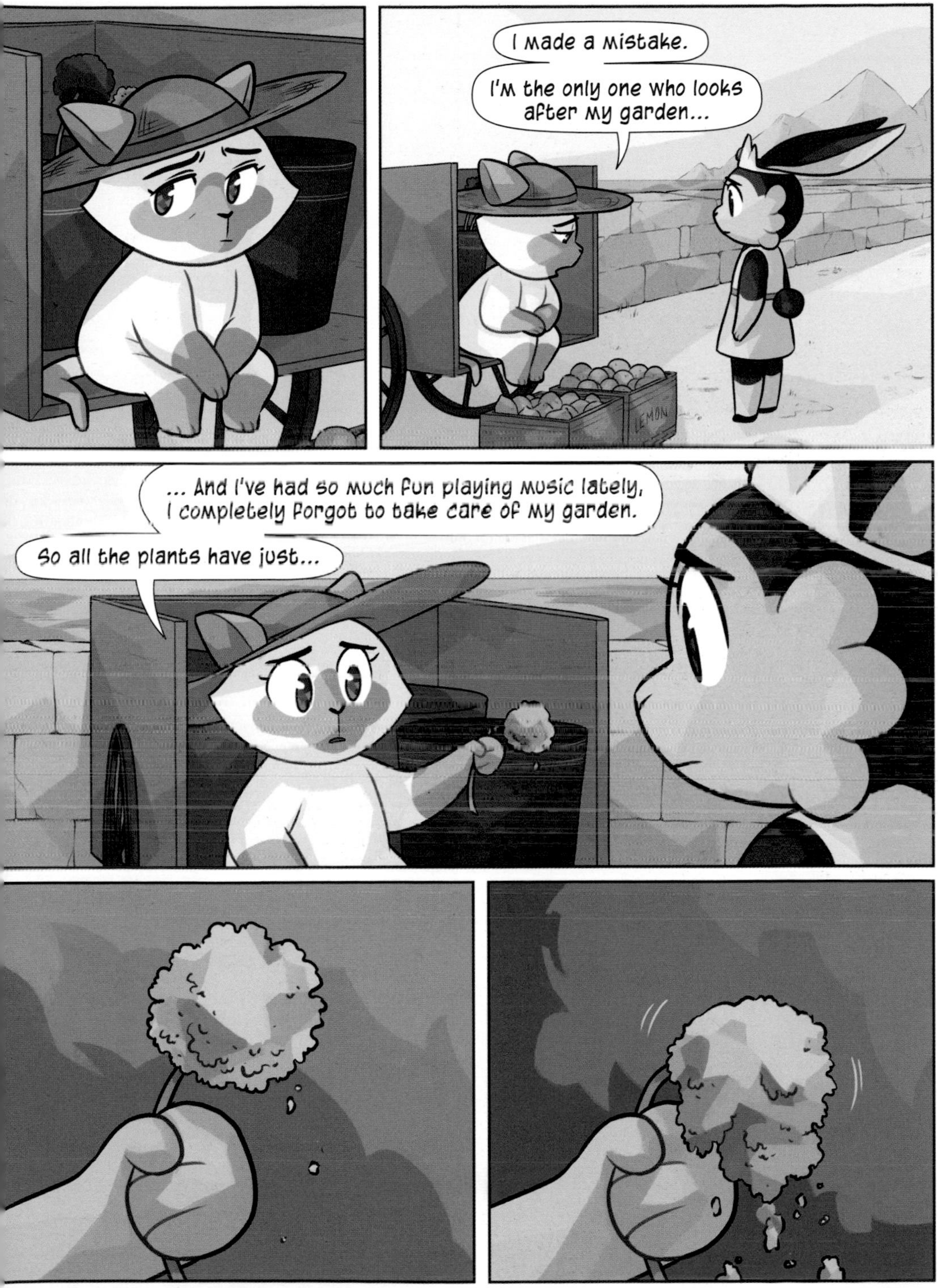
I made a mistake.
I'm the only one who looks after my garden...
LEMON
... And I've had so much fun playing music lately, I completely forgot to take care of my garden.
So all the plants have just...

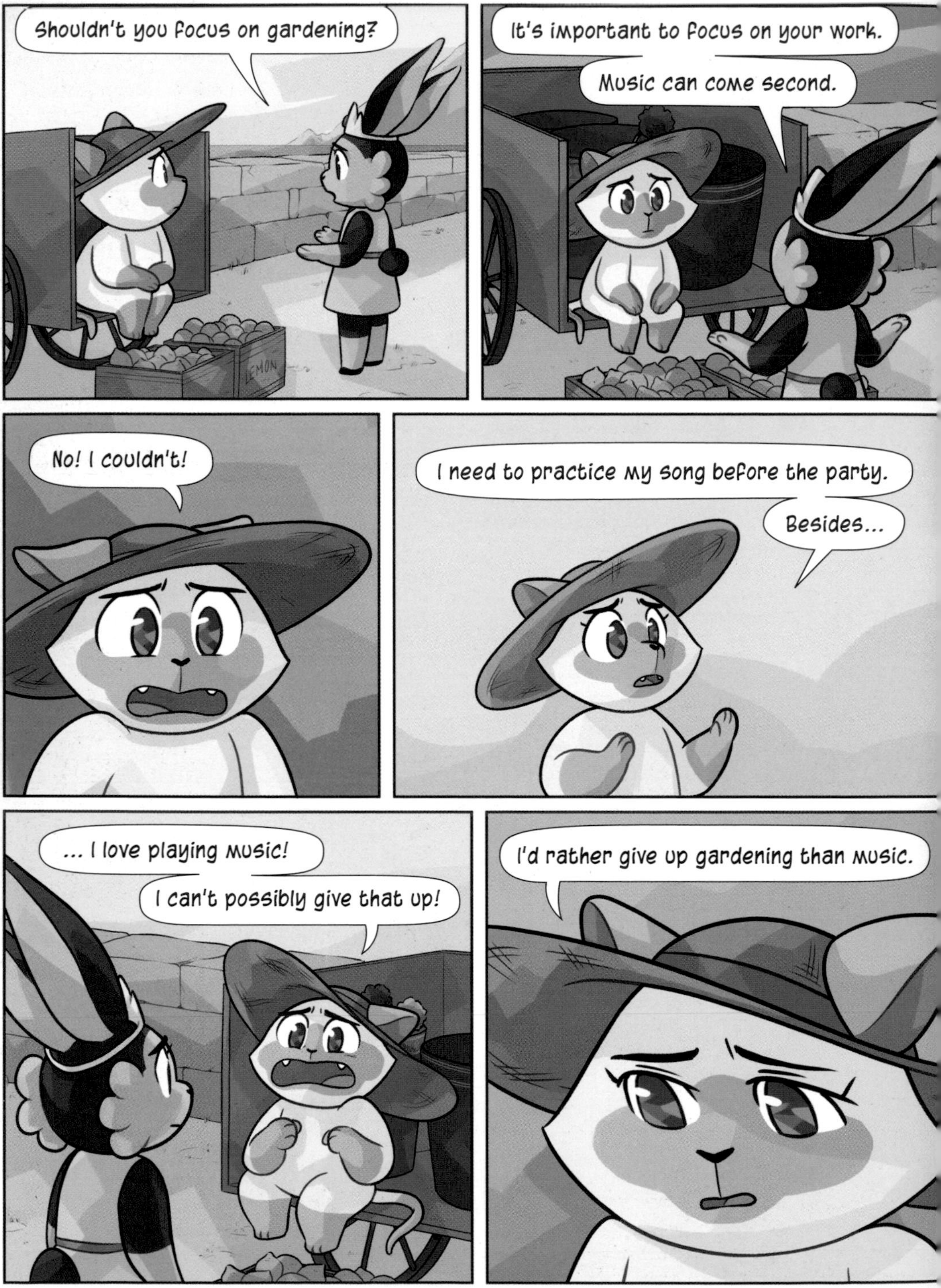
Shouldn't you focus on gardening?
It's important to focus on your work.
Music can come second.
No! I couldn't!
I need to practice my song before the party.
Besides...
... I love playing music!
I can't possibly give that up!
I'd rather give up gardening than music.

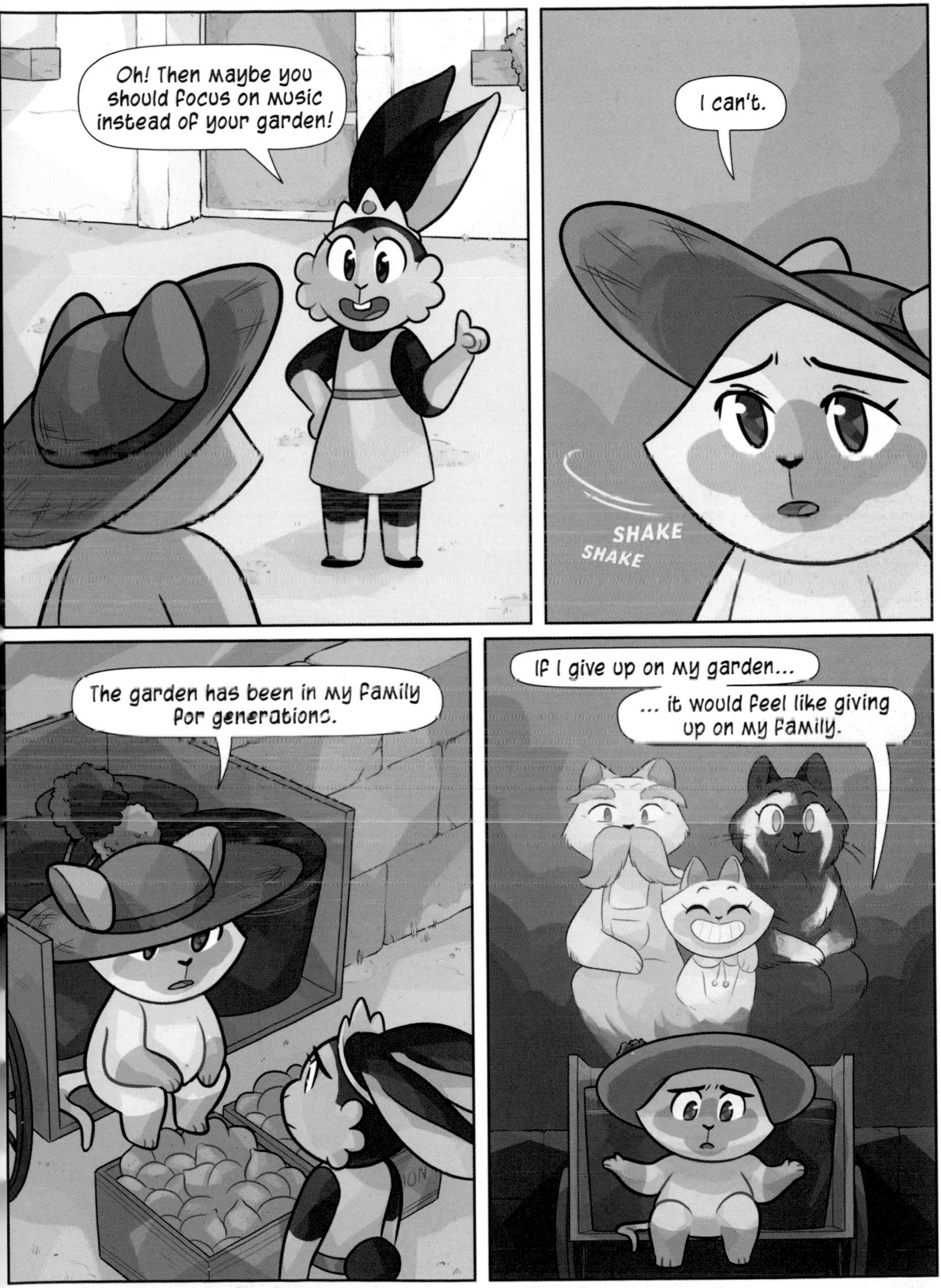
Oh! Then maybe you should focus on music instead of your garden!
I can't.
SHAKE SHAKE
The garden has been in my family for generations.
If I give up on my garden...
... it would feel like giving up on my family.

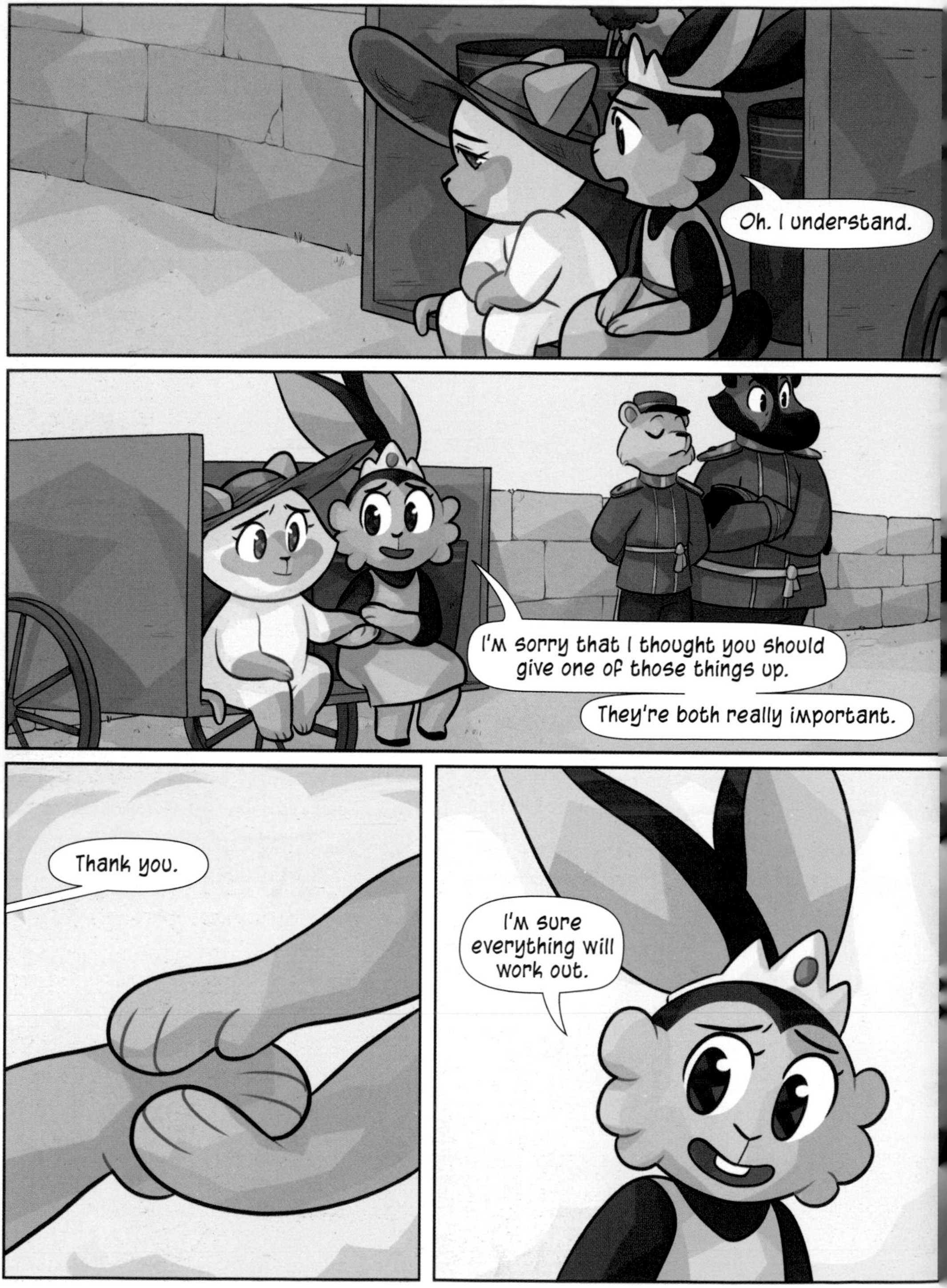
Oh. I understand.
I'm sorry that I thought you should give one of those things up.
They're both really important.
Thank you.
I'm sure everything will work out.

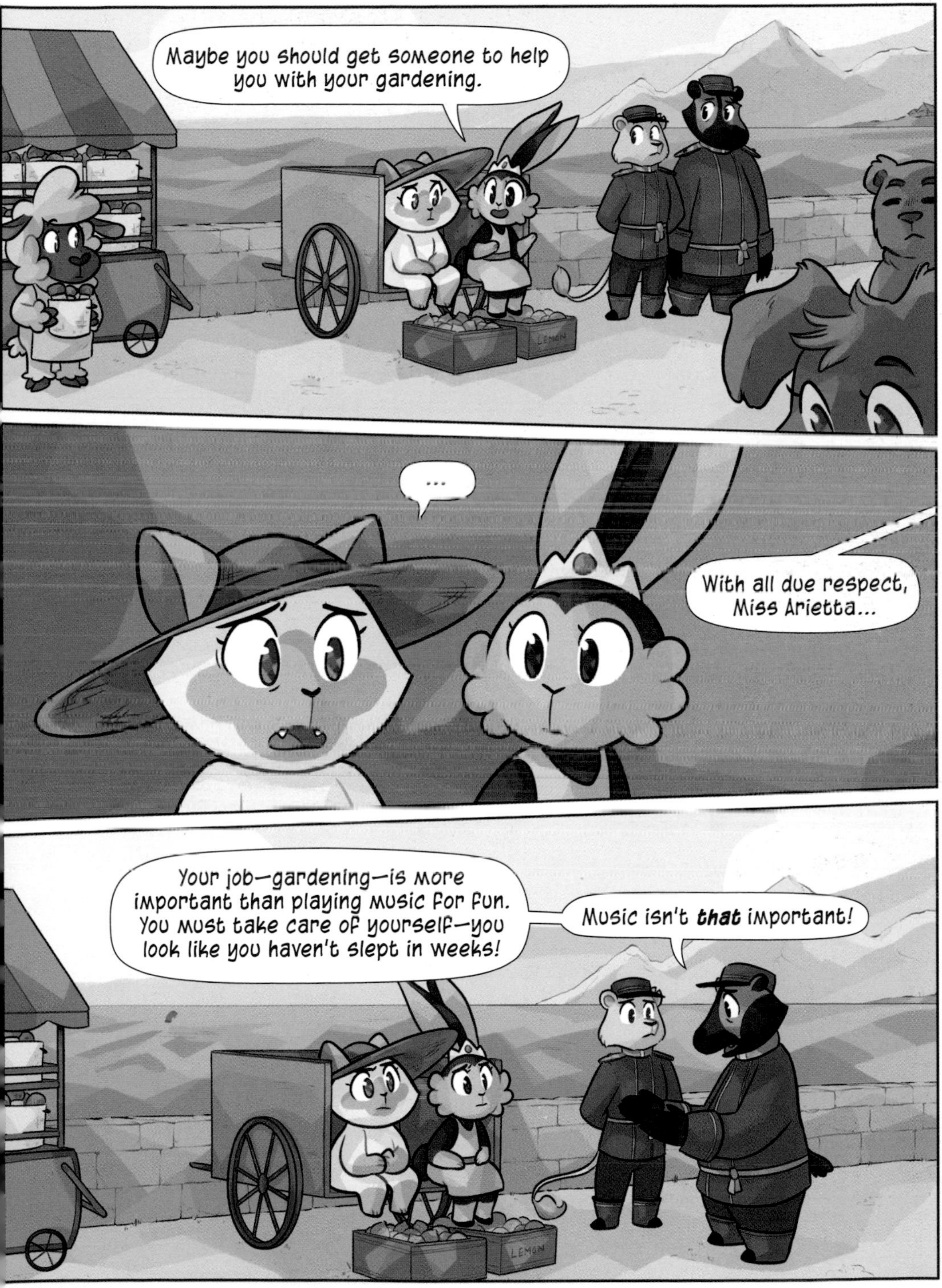
Maybe you should get someone to help you with your gardening.
...
With all due respect, Miss Arietta...
Your job—gardening—is more important than playing music for fun. You must take care of yourself—you look like you haven't slept in weeks!
Music isn't ***that*** important!
LEMON

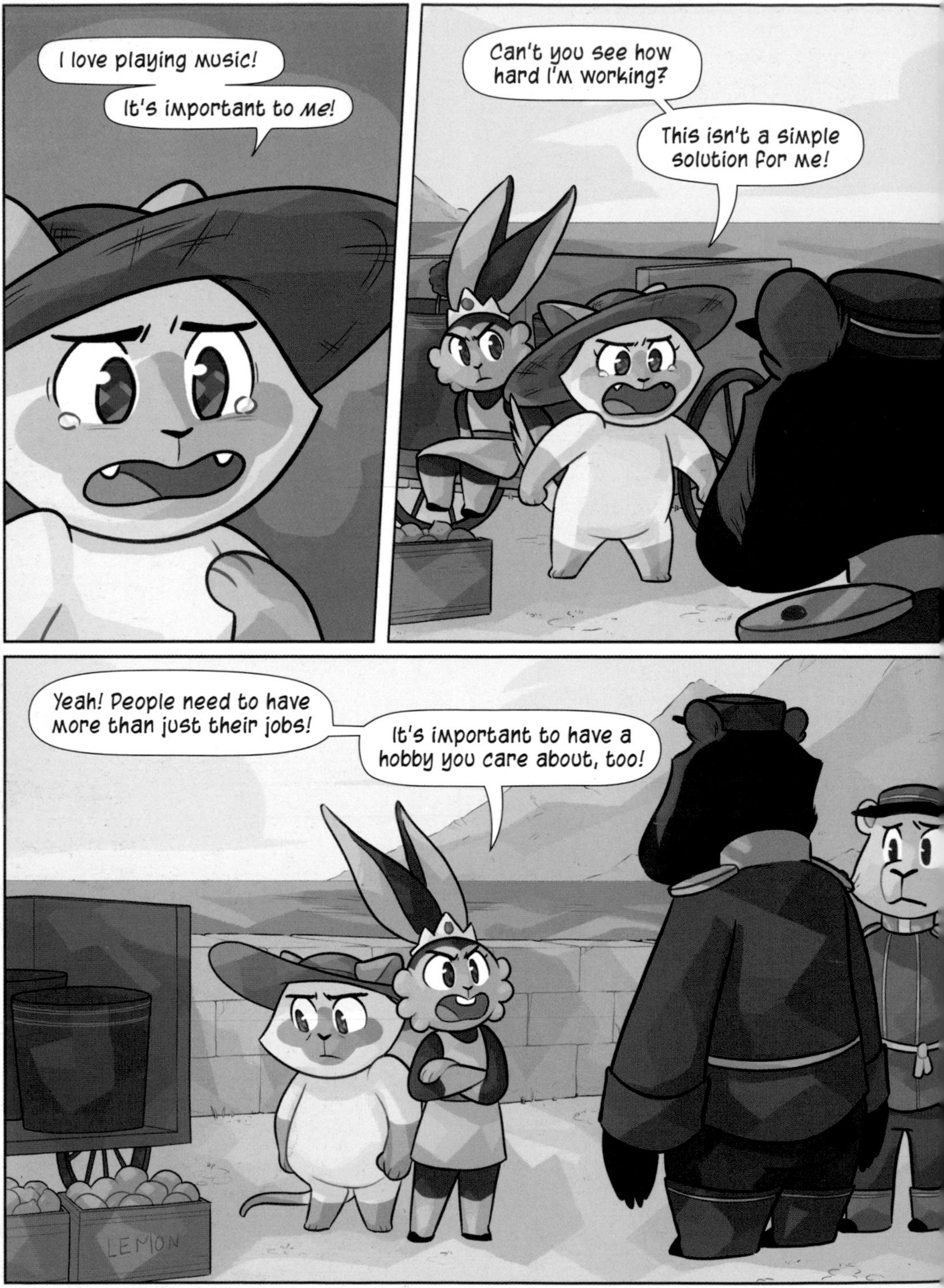
I love playing music!
It's important to me!
Can't you see how hard I'm working?
This isn't a simple solution for me!
Yeah! People need to have more than just their jobs!
It's important to have a hobby you care about, too!
LEMON

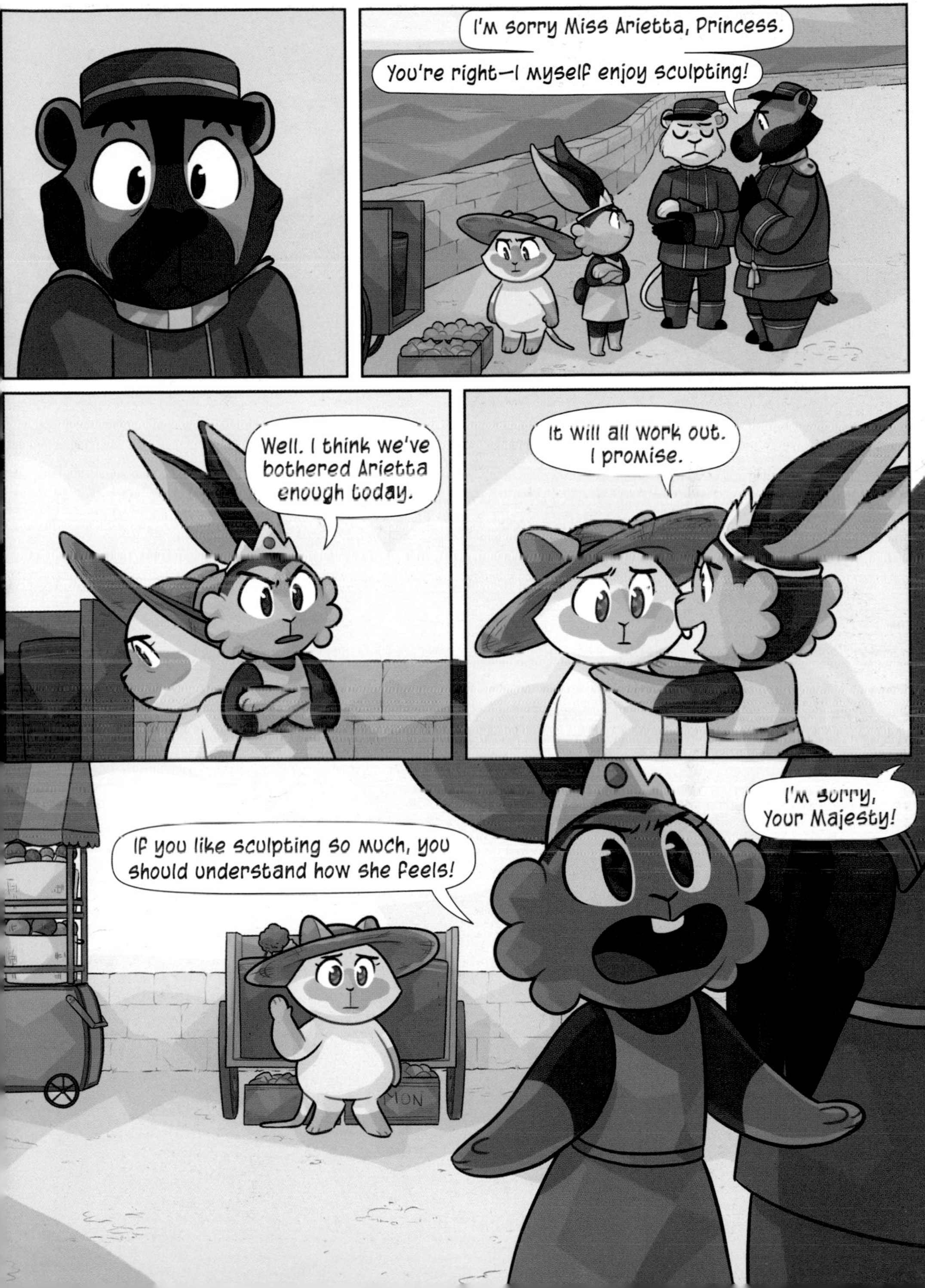
I'm sorry Miss Arietta, Princess.
You're right—I myself enjoy sculpting!
Well. I think we've bothered Arietta enough today.
It will all work out. I promise.
If you like sculpting so much, you should understand how she feels!
I'm sorry, Your Majesty!
MON

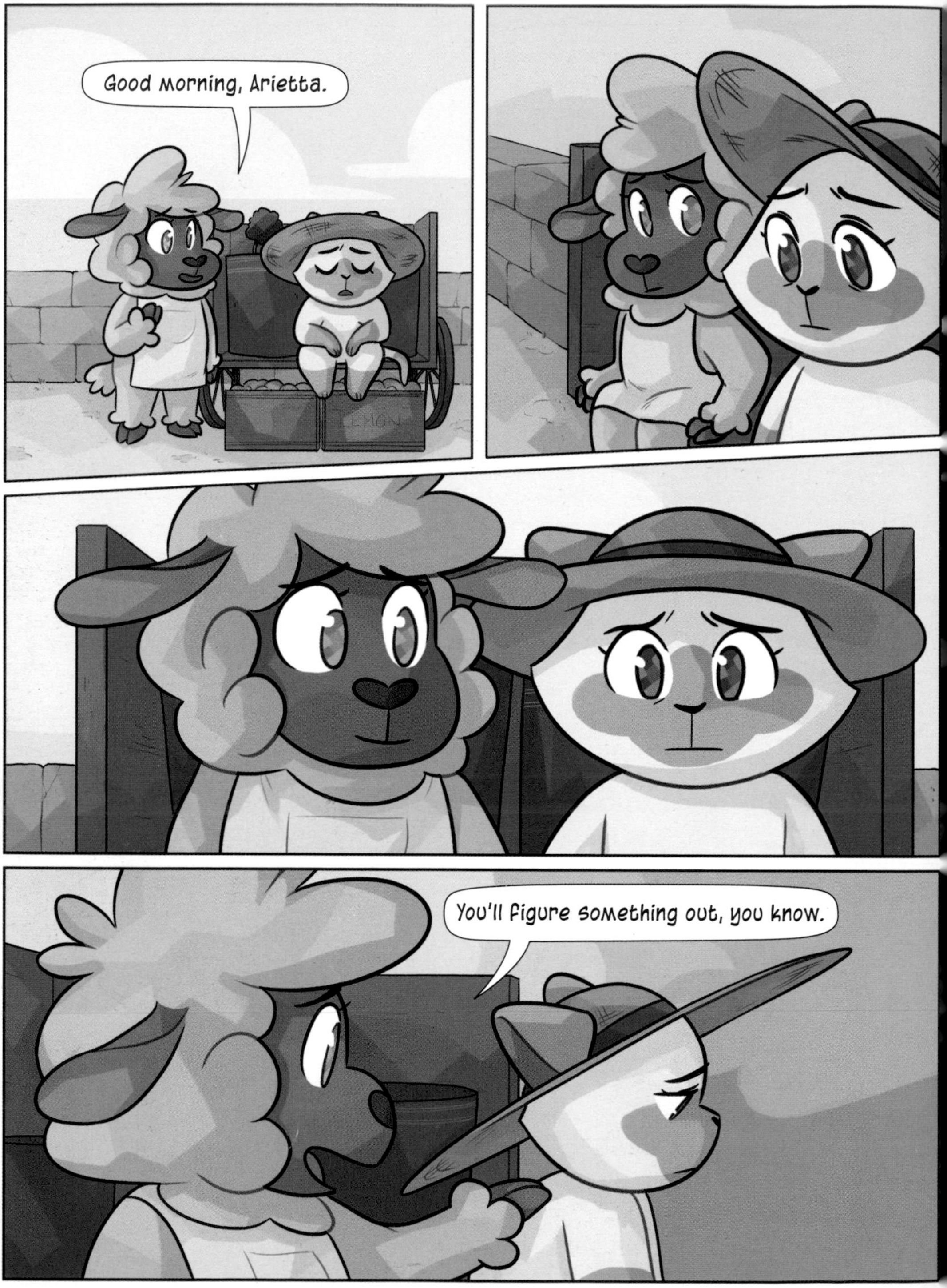

Good Morning, Arietta.
LEMON
You'll figure something out, you know.

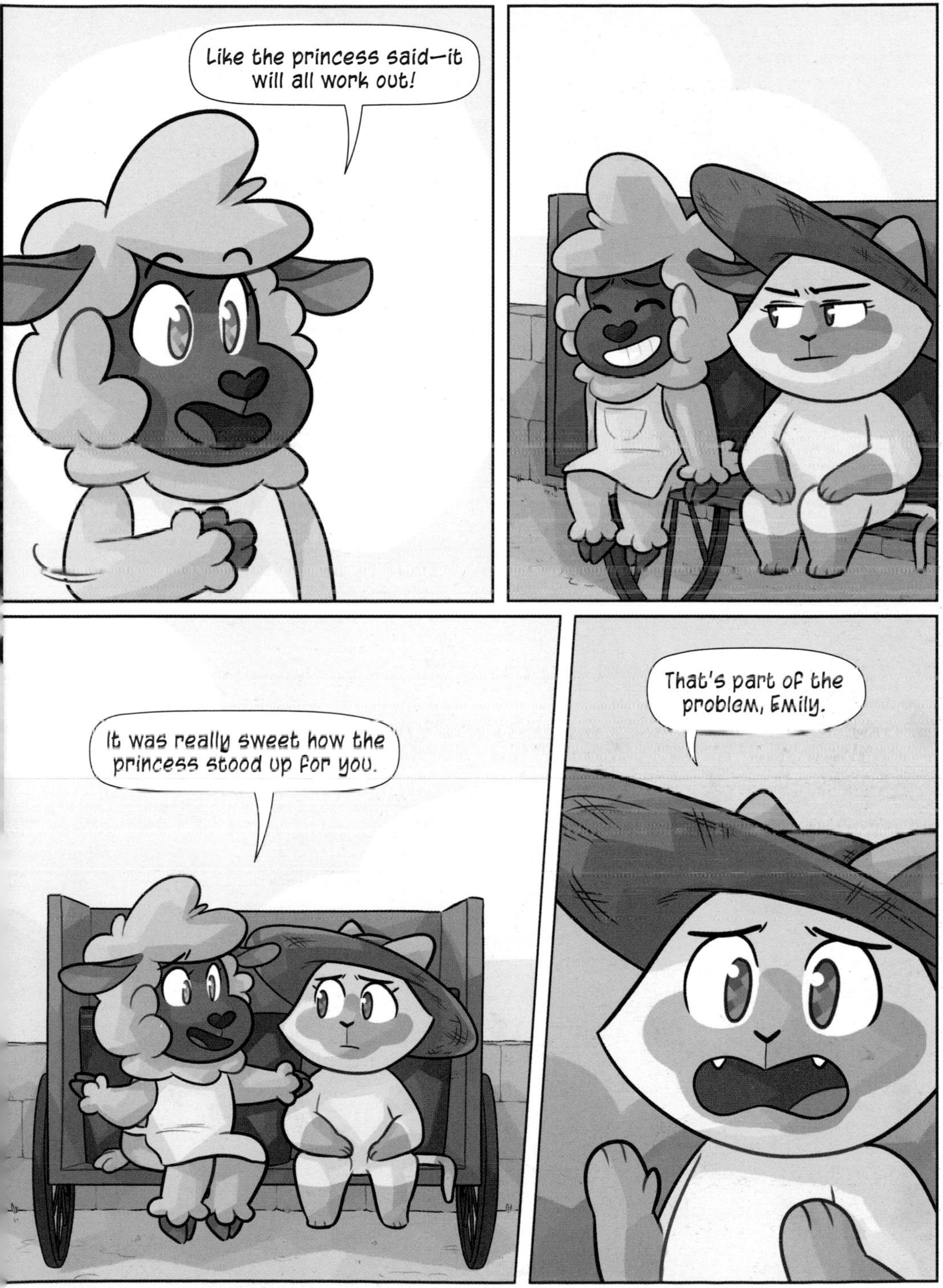
Like the princess said—it will all work out!
It was really sweet how the princess stood up for you.
That's part of the problem, Emily.

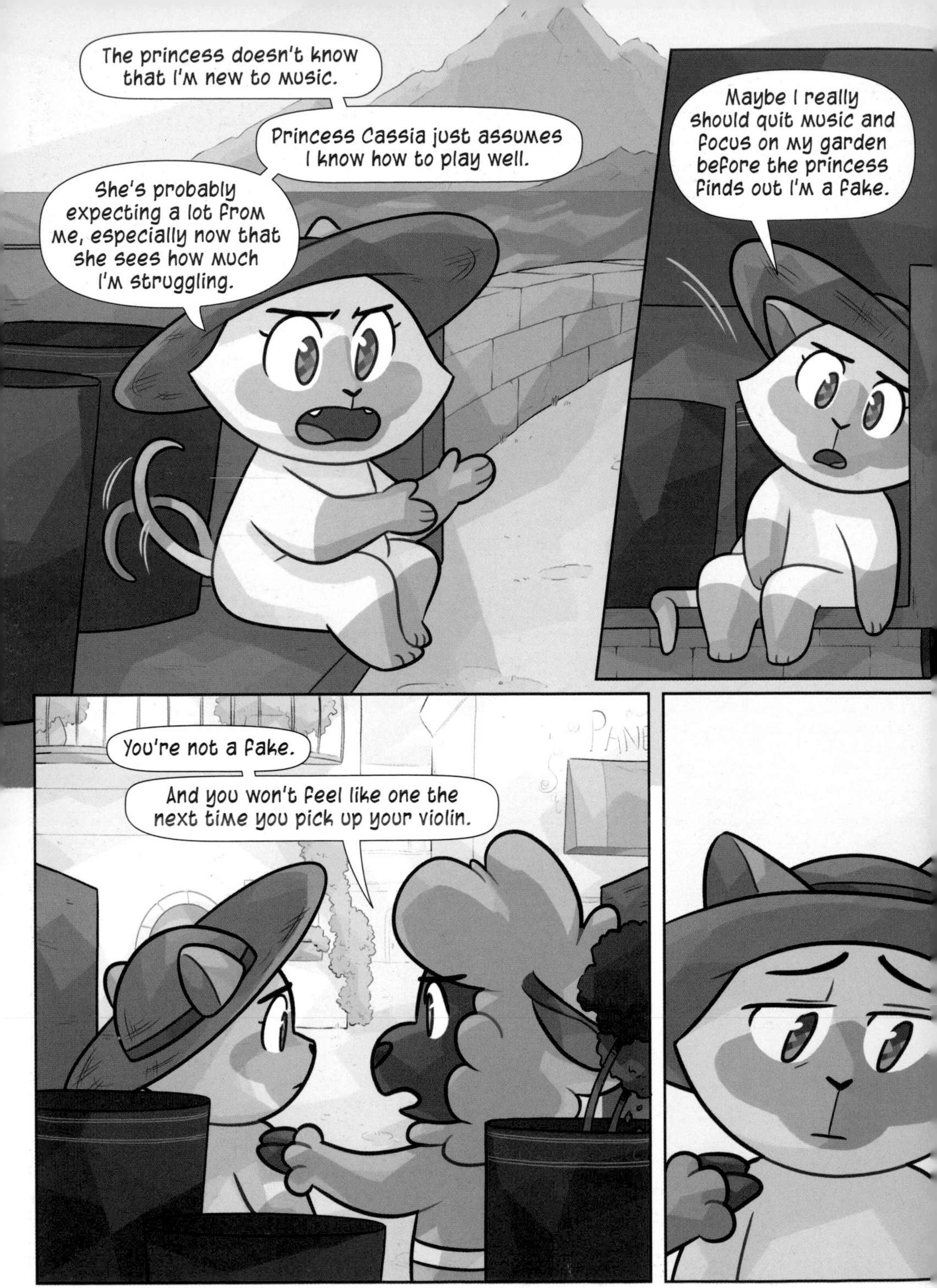
The princess doesn't know that I'm new to music.
Princess Cassia just assumes I know how to play well.
She's probably expecting a lot from me, especially now that she sees how much I'm struggling.
Maybe I really should quit music and focus on my garden before the princess finds out I'm a fake.
You're not a fake.
And you won't feel like one the next time you pick up your violin.

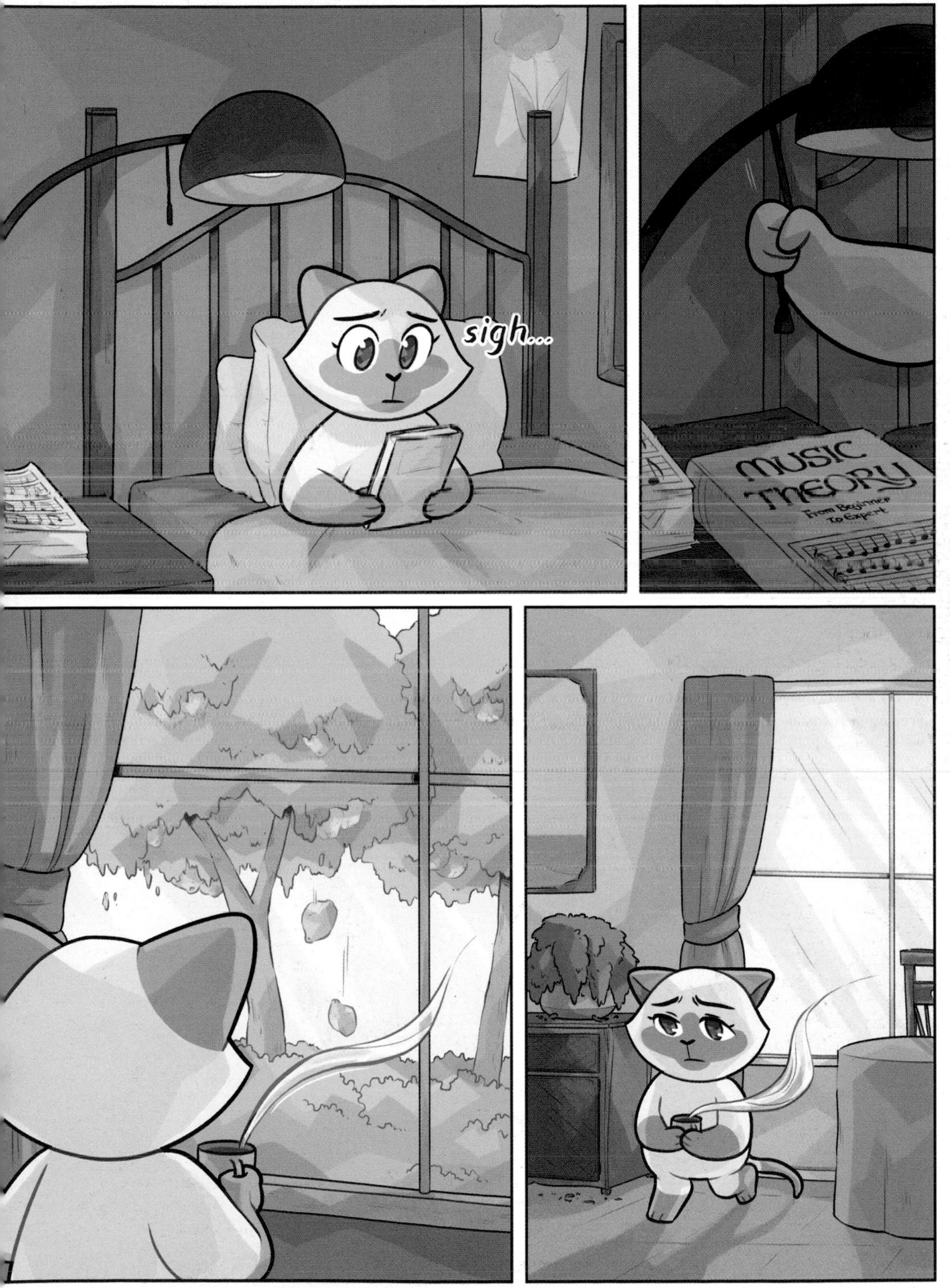
sigh...
MUSIC THEORY
From Beginner To Expert

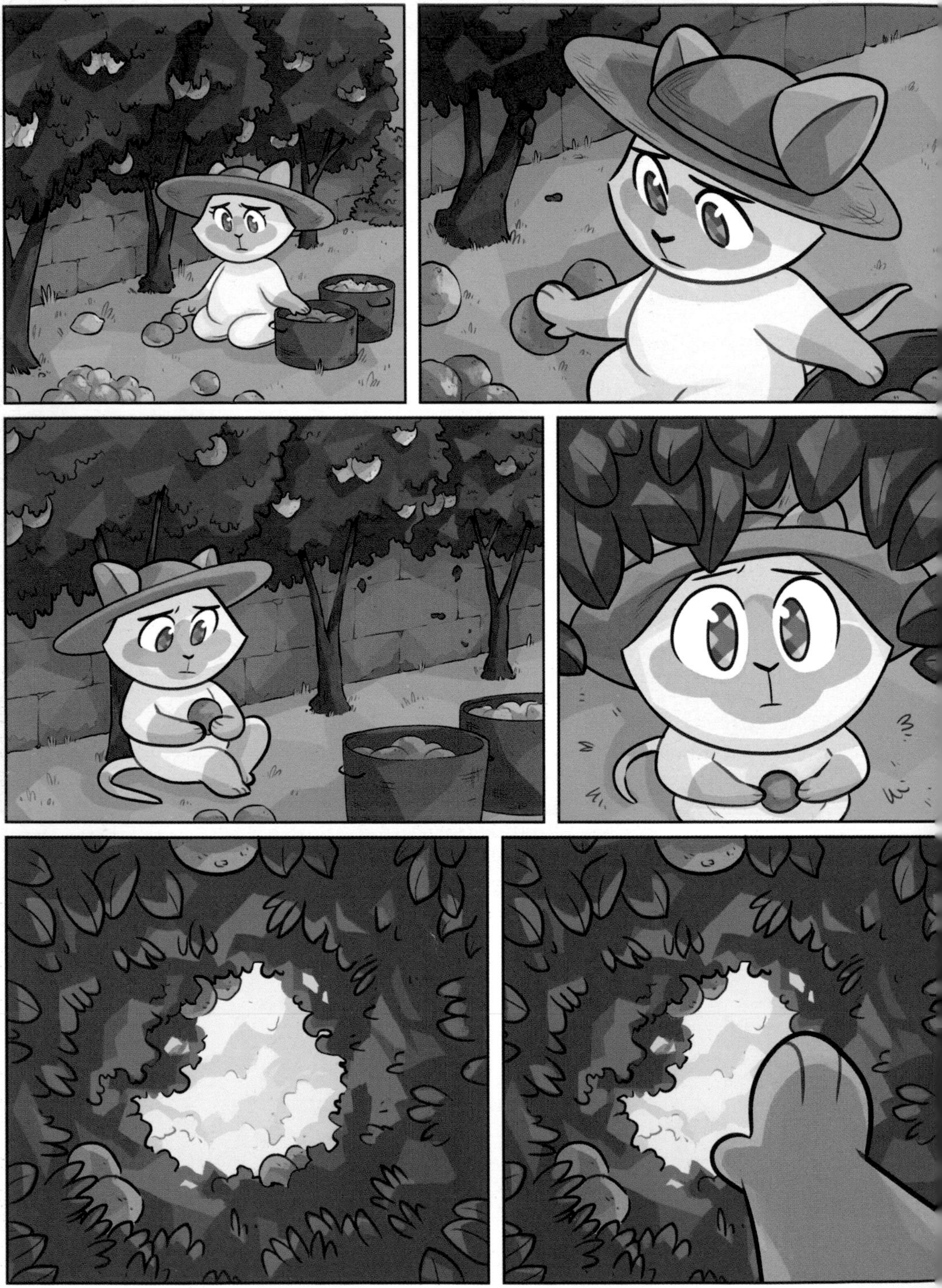

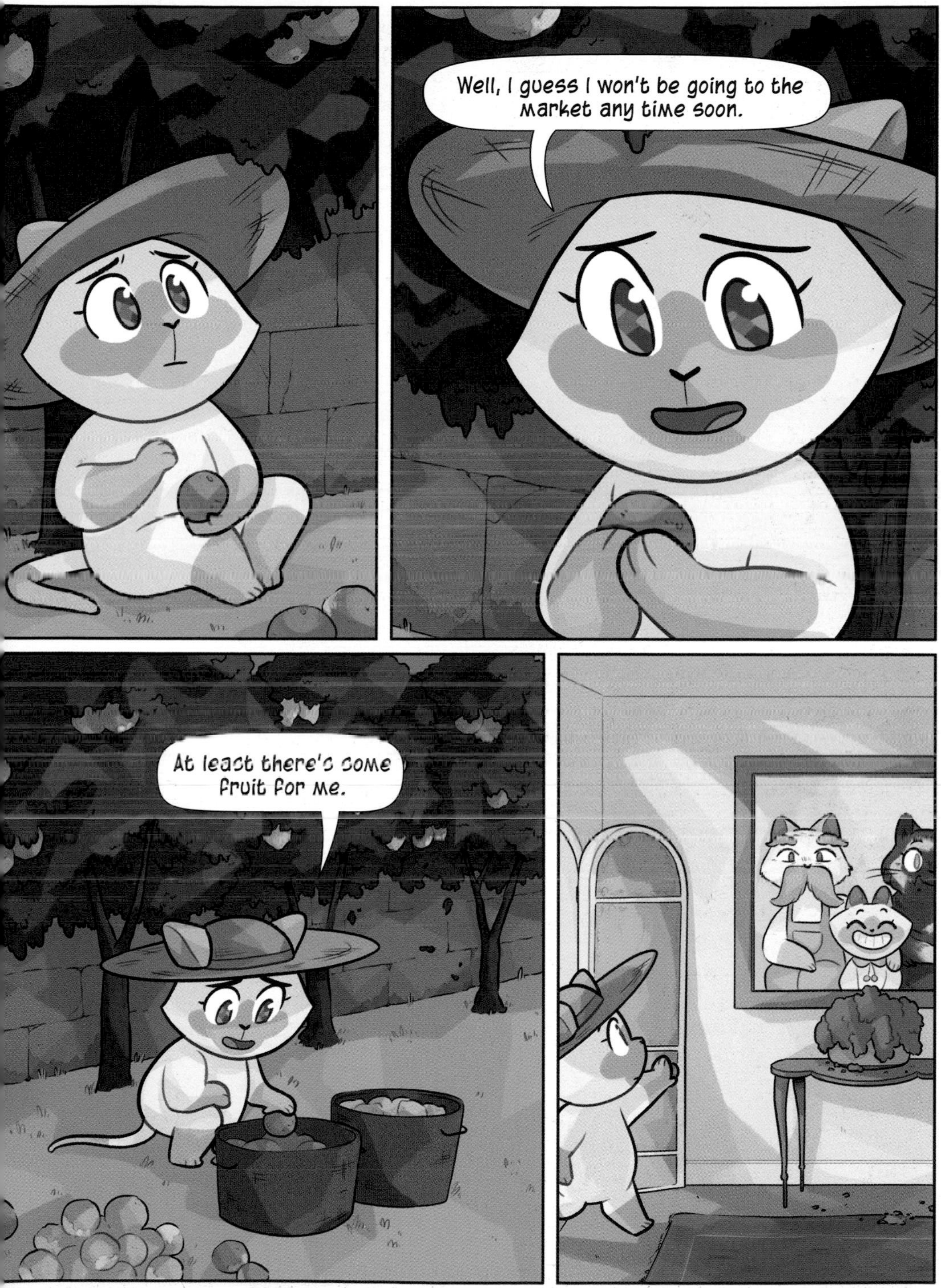
Well, I guess I won't be going to the market any time soon.
At least there's some fruit for me.

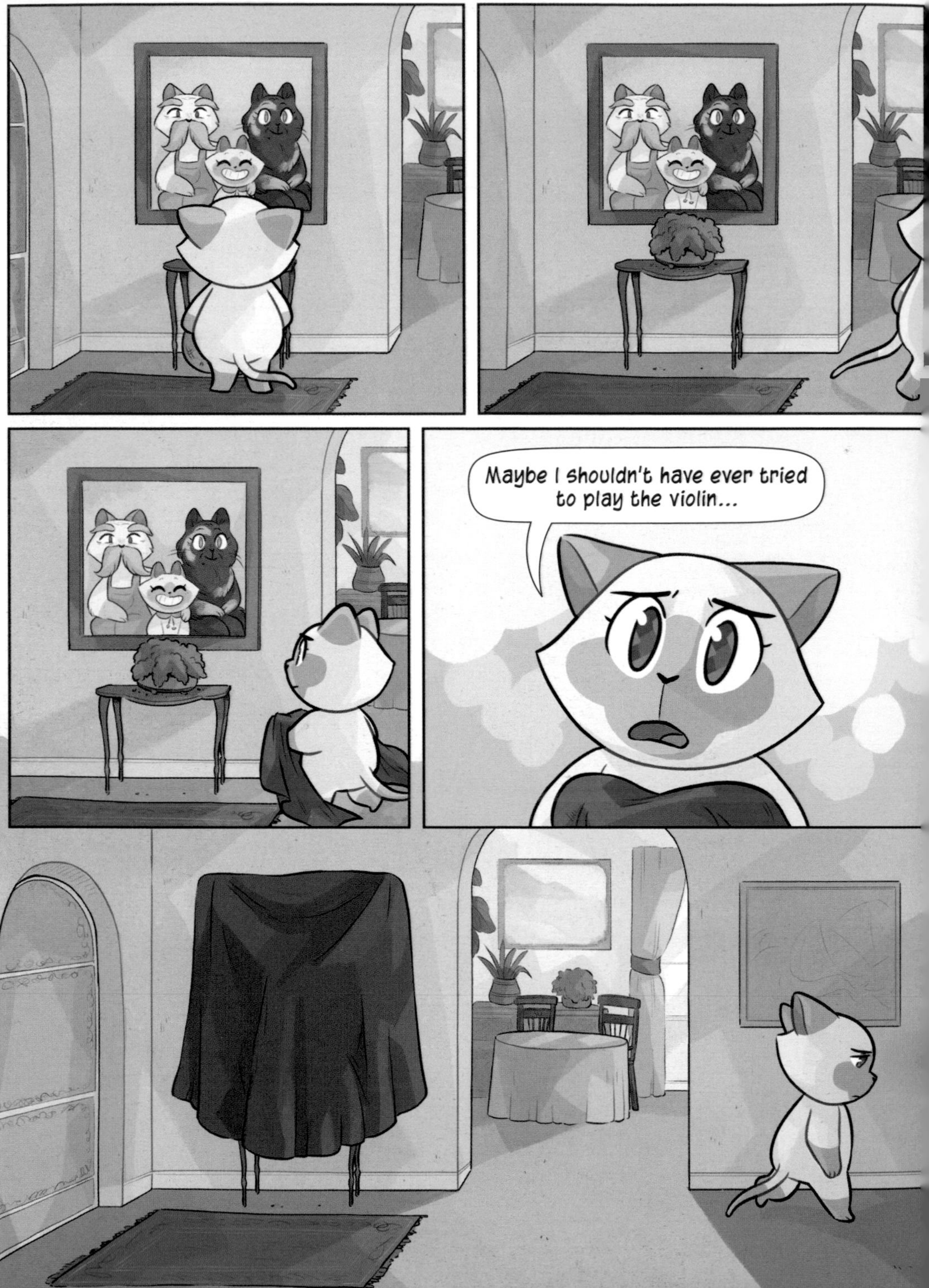
Maybe I shouldn't have ever tried to play the violin...

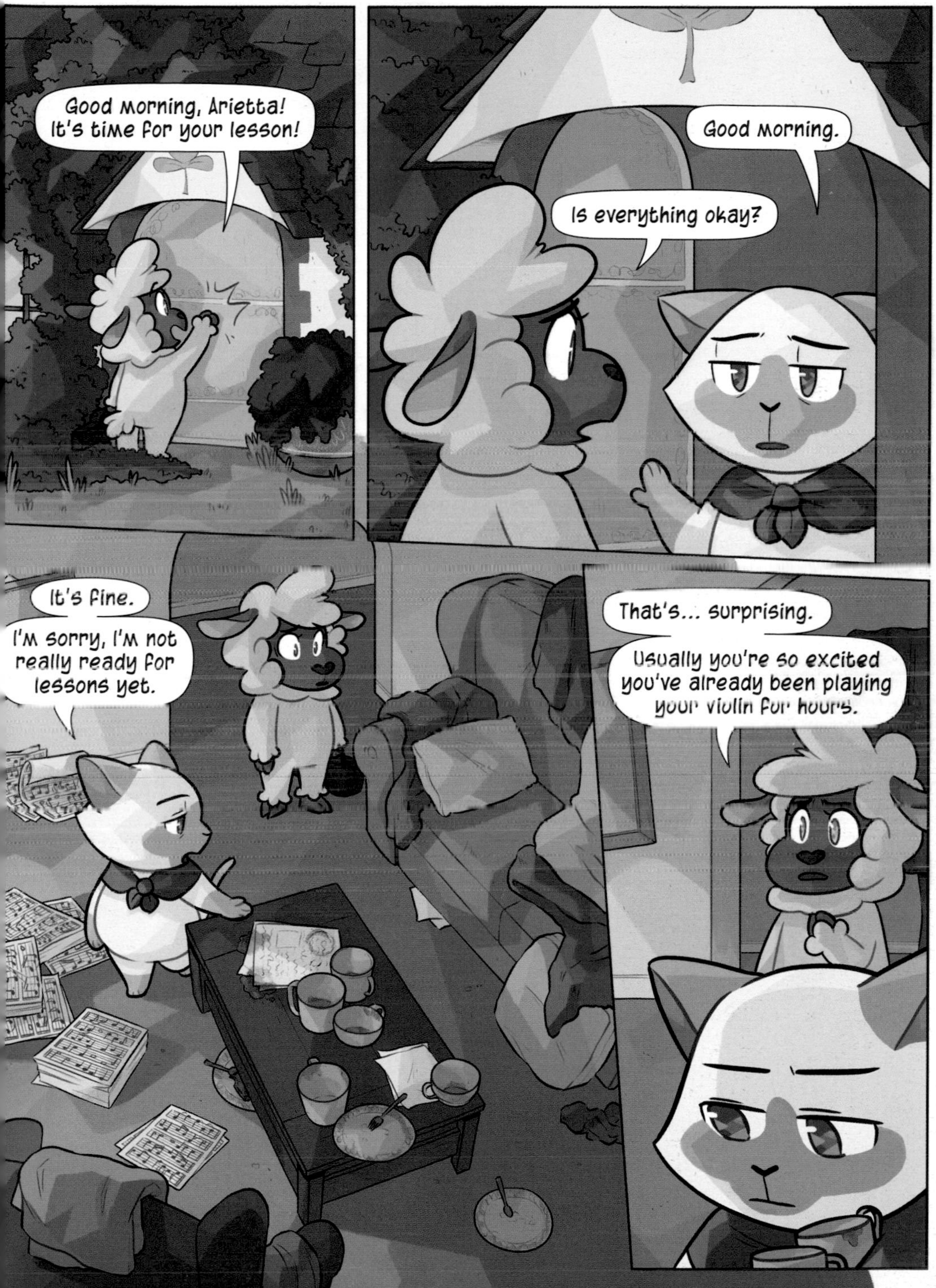
Good morning, Arietta! It's time for your lesson!
Good morning.
Is everything okay?
It's fine.
I'm sorry, I'm not really ready for lessons yet.
That's... surprising.
Usually you're so excited you've already been playing your violin for hours.

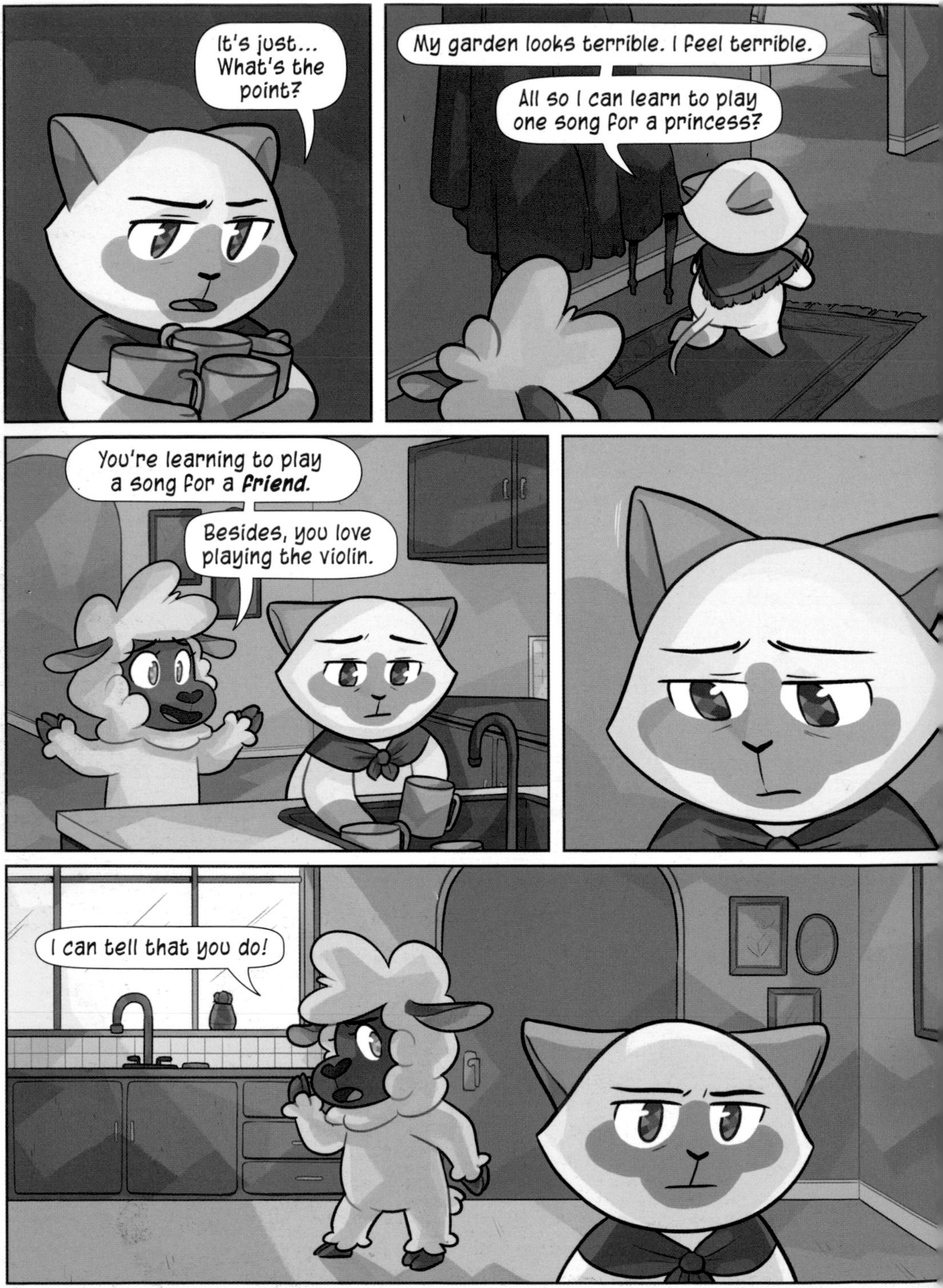

It's just... What's the point?
My garden looks terrible. I feel terrible.
All so I can learn to play one song for a princess?
You're learning to play a song for a **friend**.
Besides, you love playing the violin.
I can tell that you do!

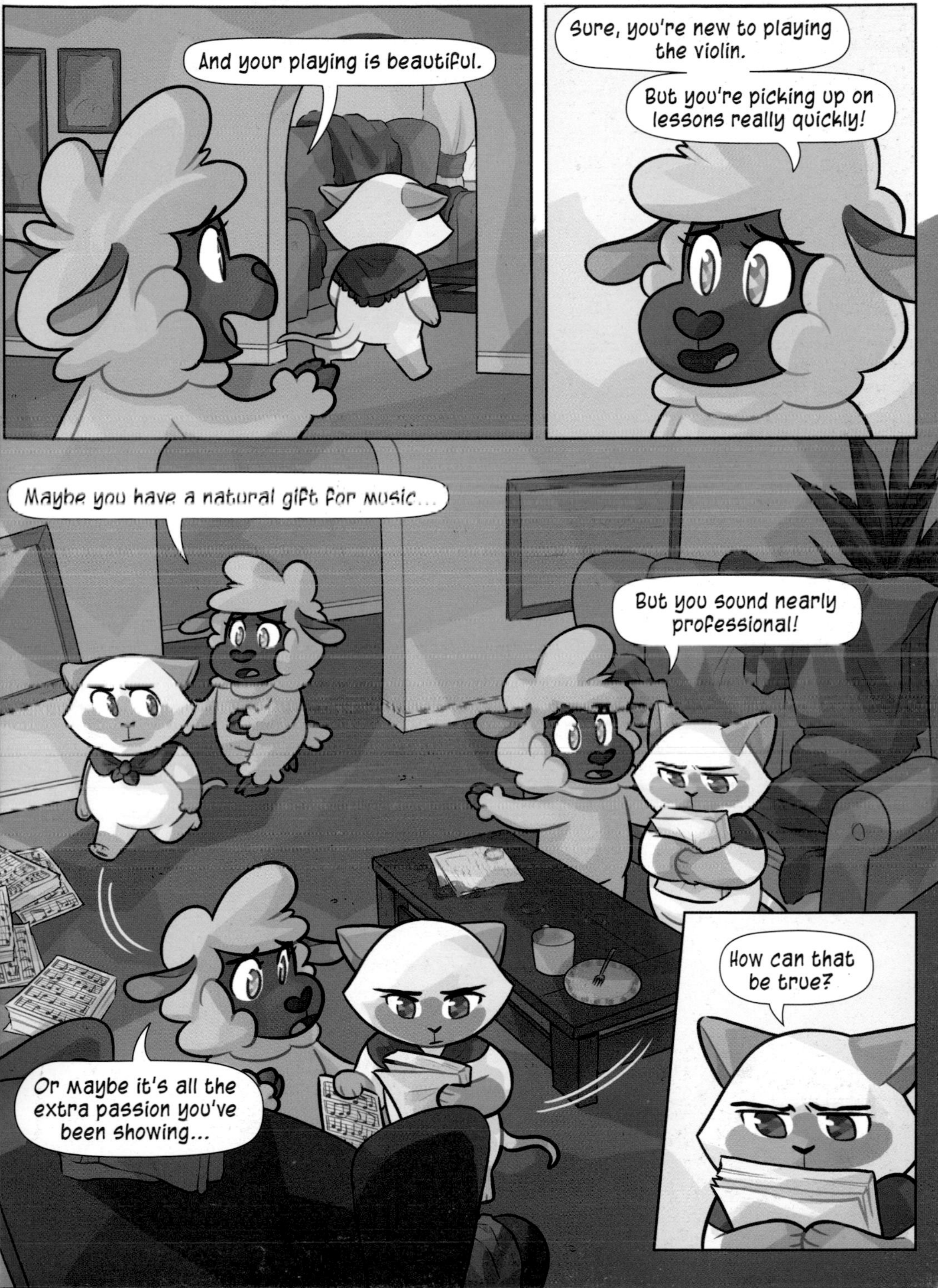
And your playing is beautiful.
Sure, you're new to playing the violin.
But you're picking up on lessons really quickly!
Maybe you have a natural gift for music...
But you sound nearly professional!
Or maybe it's all the extra passion you've been showing...
How can that be true?

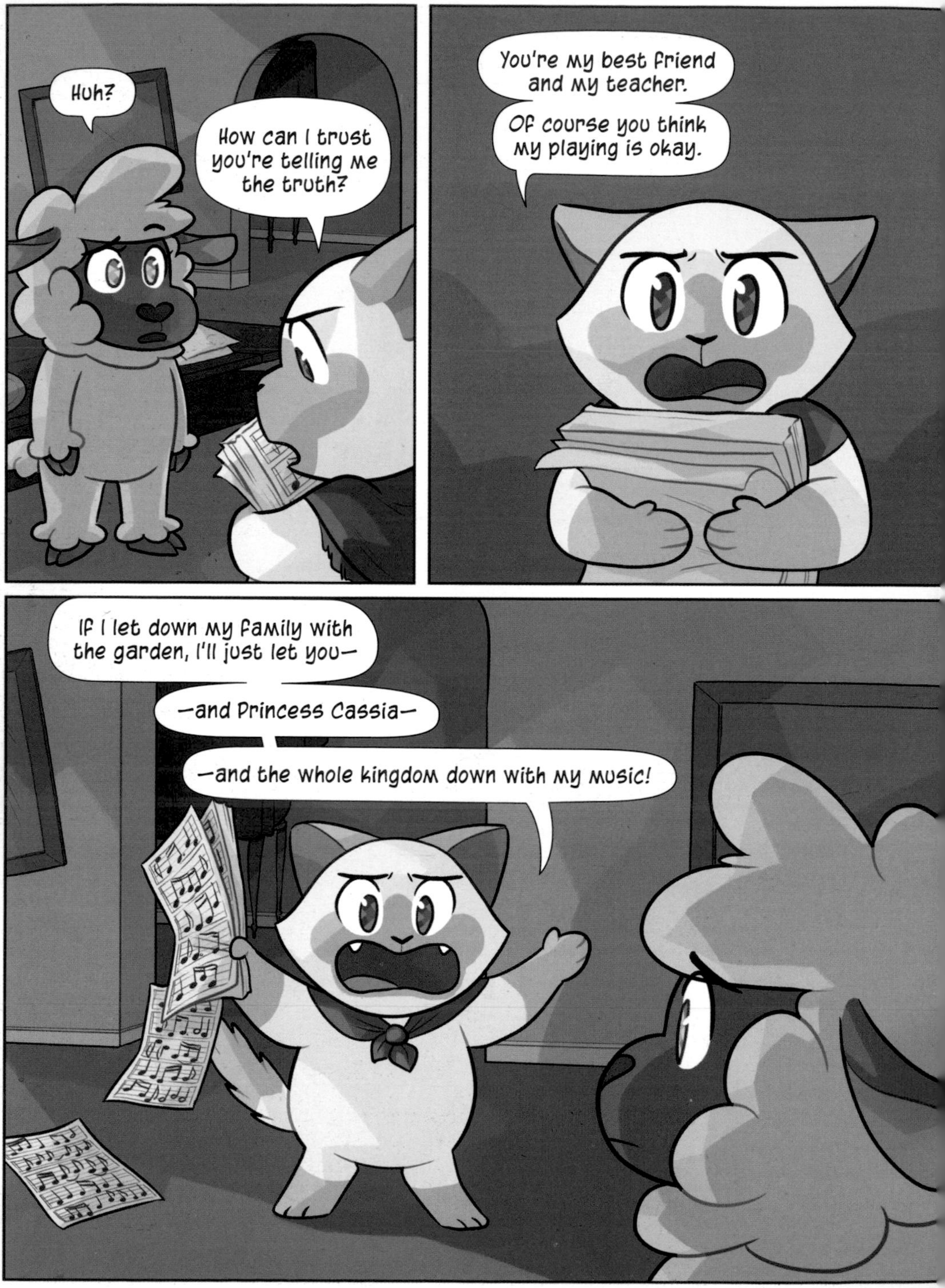
Huh?
How can I trust you're telling me the truth?
You're my best friend and my teacher.
Of course you think my playing is okay.
If I let down my family with the garden, I'll just let you—
—and Princess Cassia—
—and the whole kingdom down with my music!

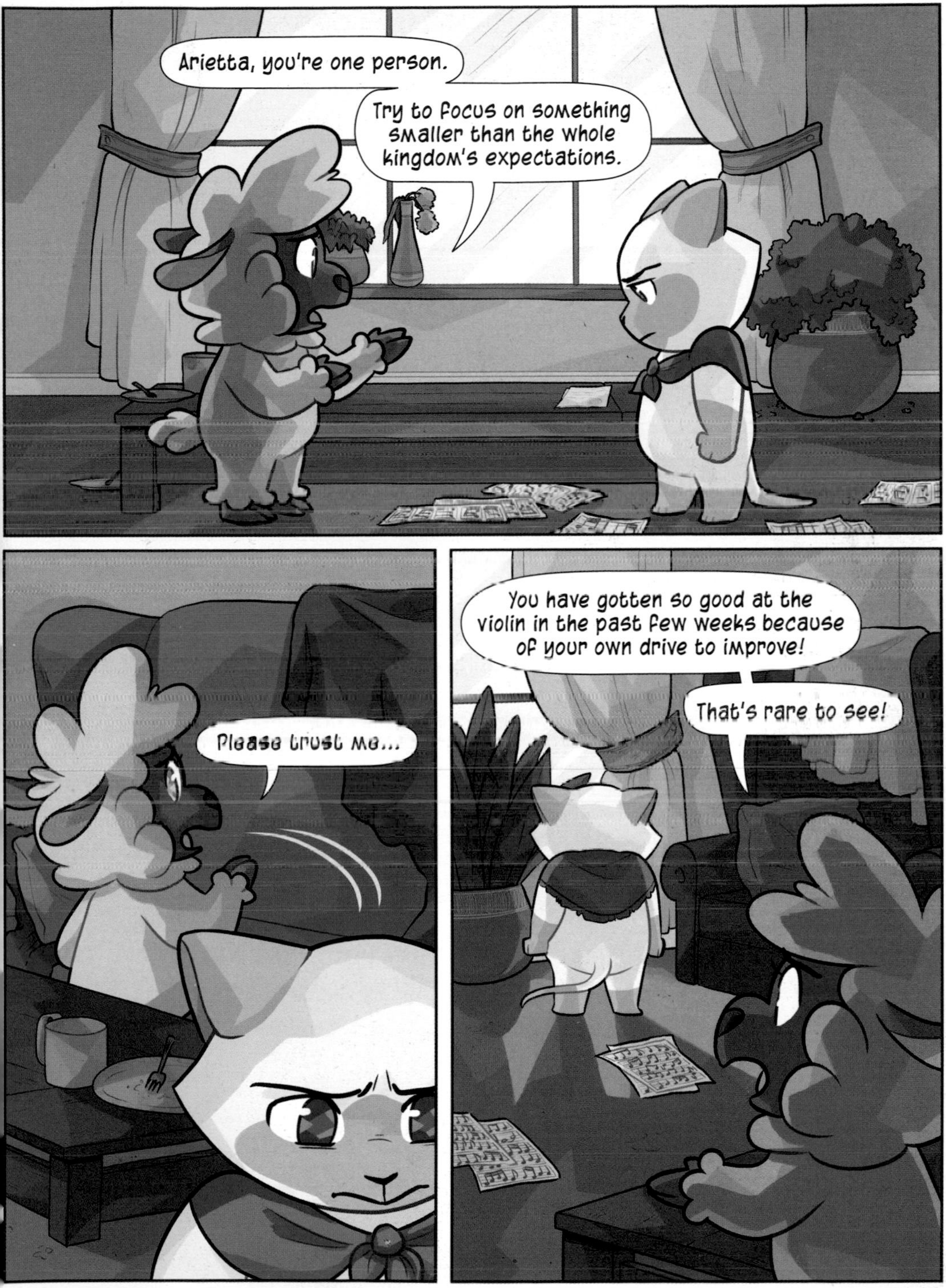
Arietta, you're one person.
Try to focus on something smaller than the whole kingdom's expectations.
Please trust me...
You have gotten so good at the violin in the past few weeks because of your own drive to improve!
That's rare to see!

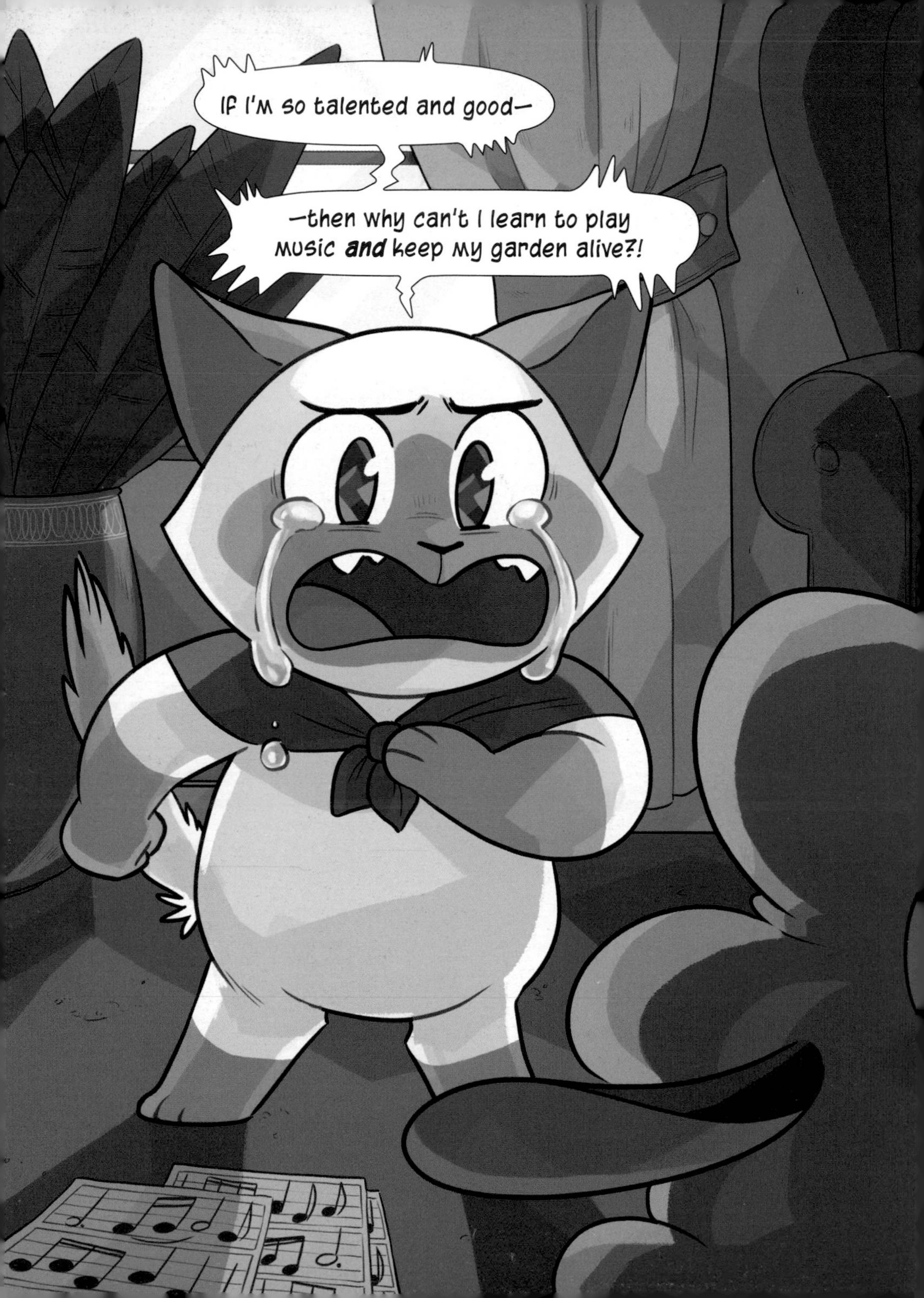
If I'm so talented and good—
—then why can't I learn to play music **and** keep my garden alive?!

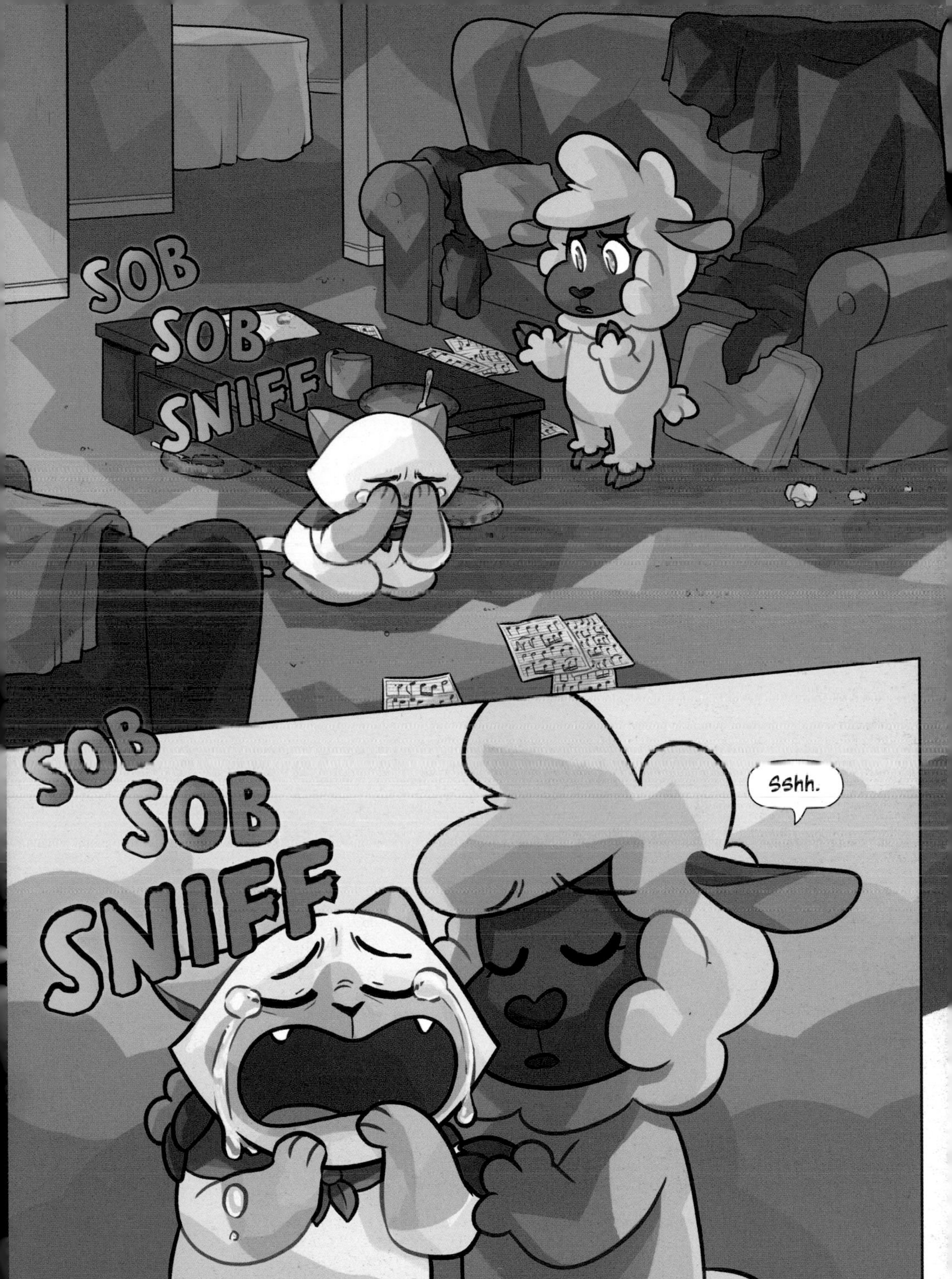
SOB
SOB
SNIFF
SOB
SOB
SNIFF
Sshh.

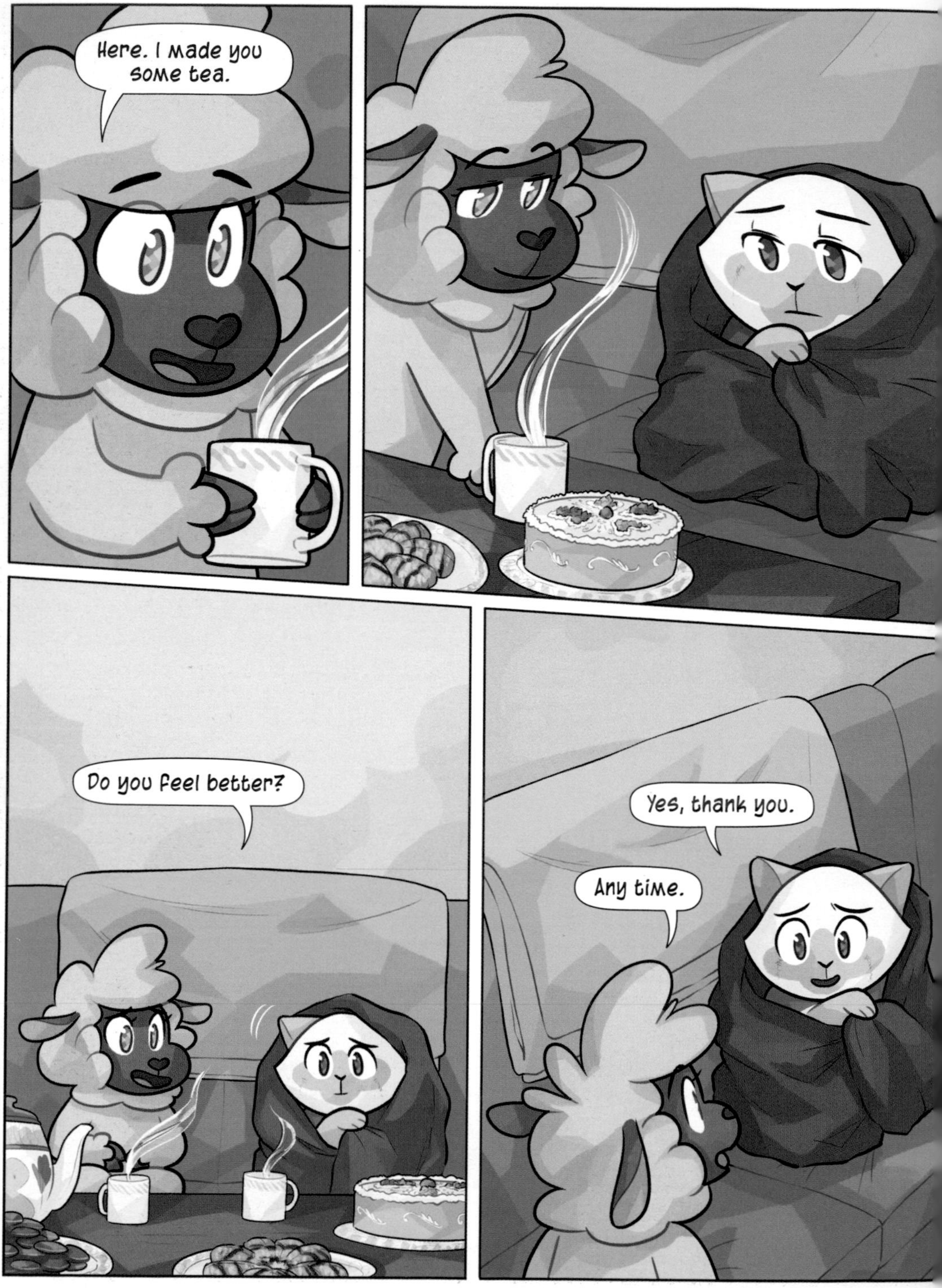
Here. I made you some tea.
Do you feel better?
Yes, thank you.
Any time.

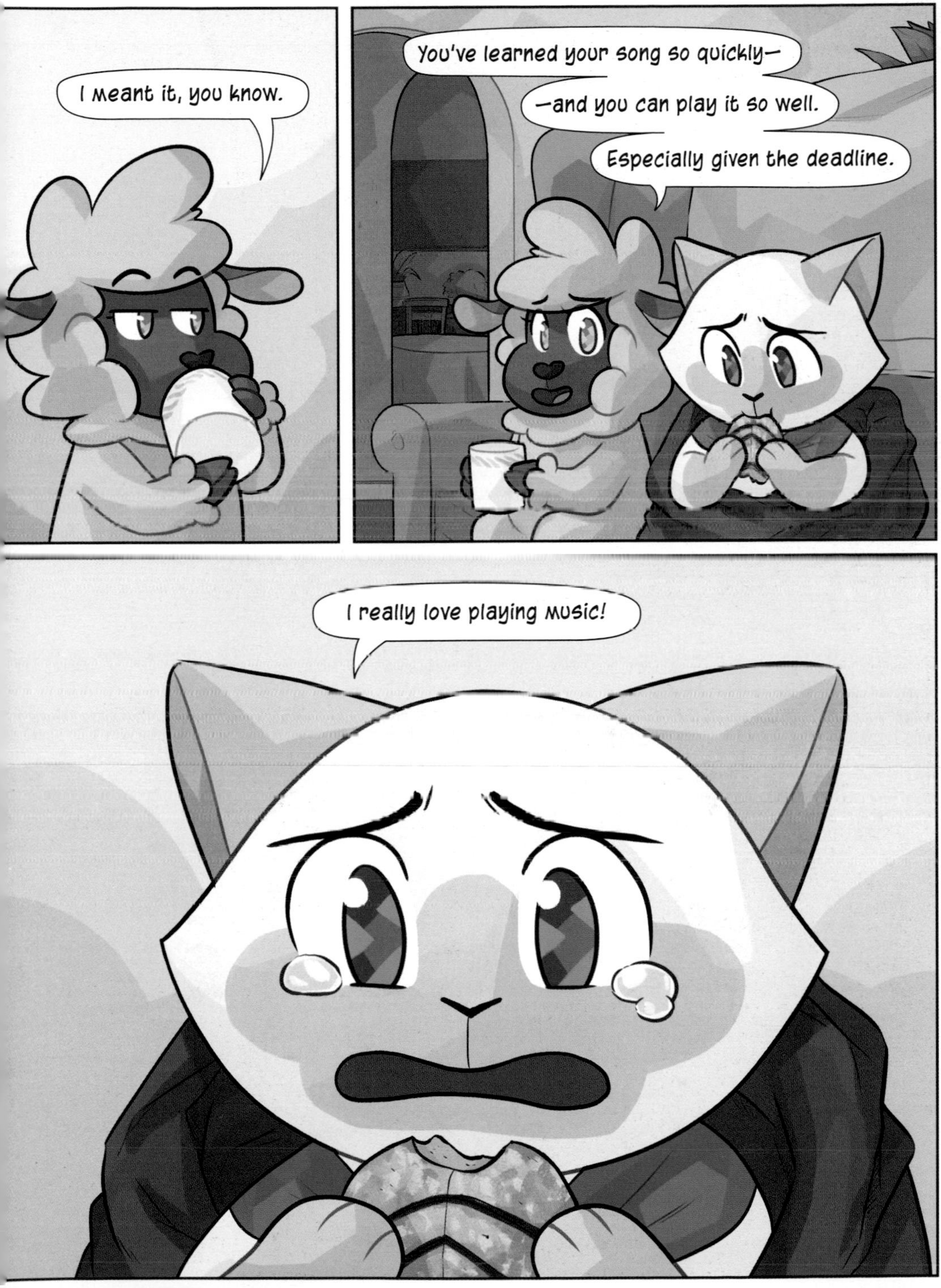
I meant it, you know.
You've learned your song so quickly—
—and you can play it so well.
Especially given the deadline.
I really love playing music!

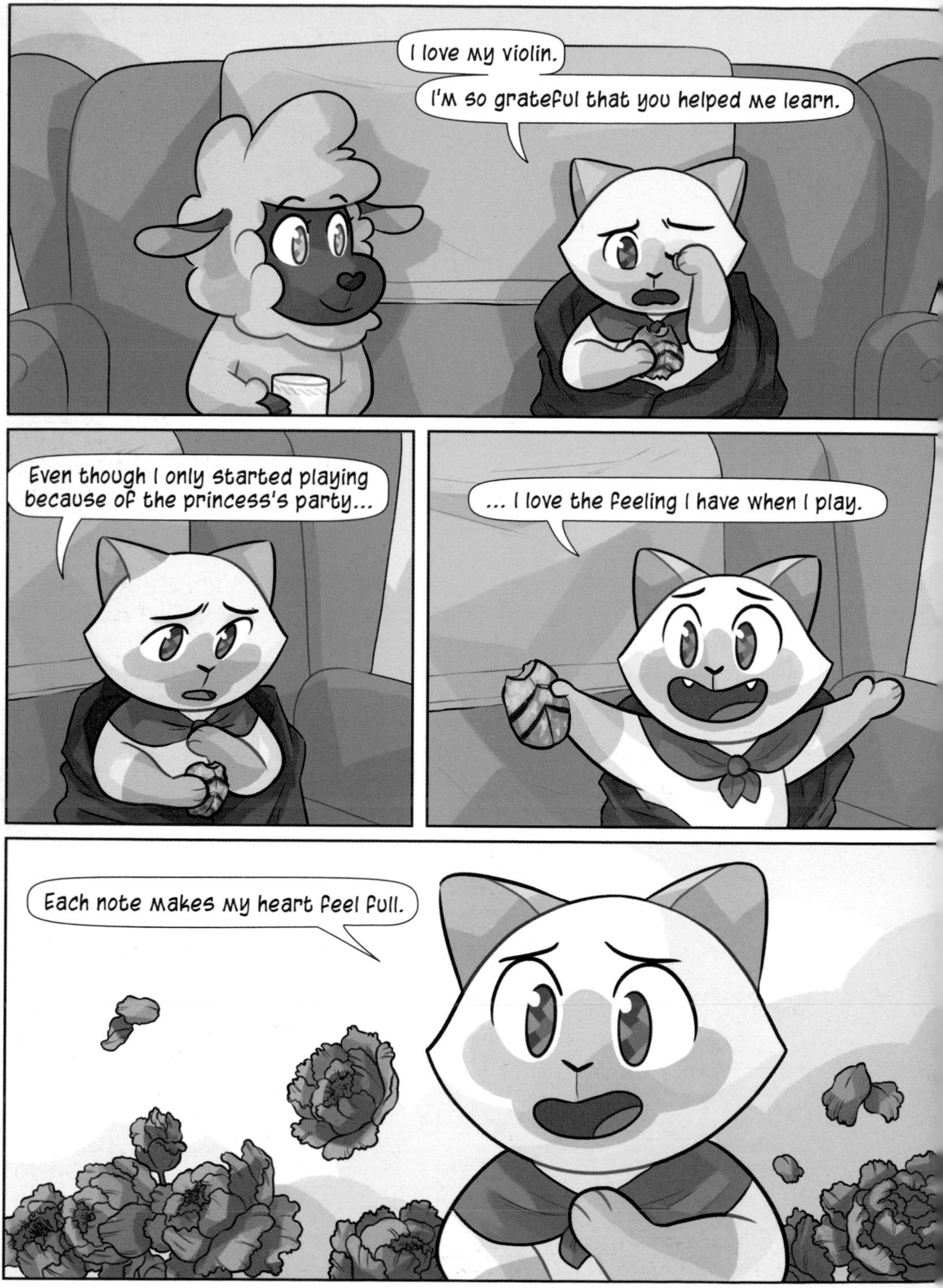
I love my violin.
I'm so grateful that you helped me learn.
Even though I only started playing because of the princess's party...
... I love the feeling I have when I play.
Each note makes my heart feel full.

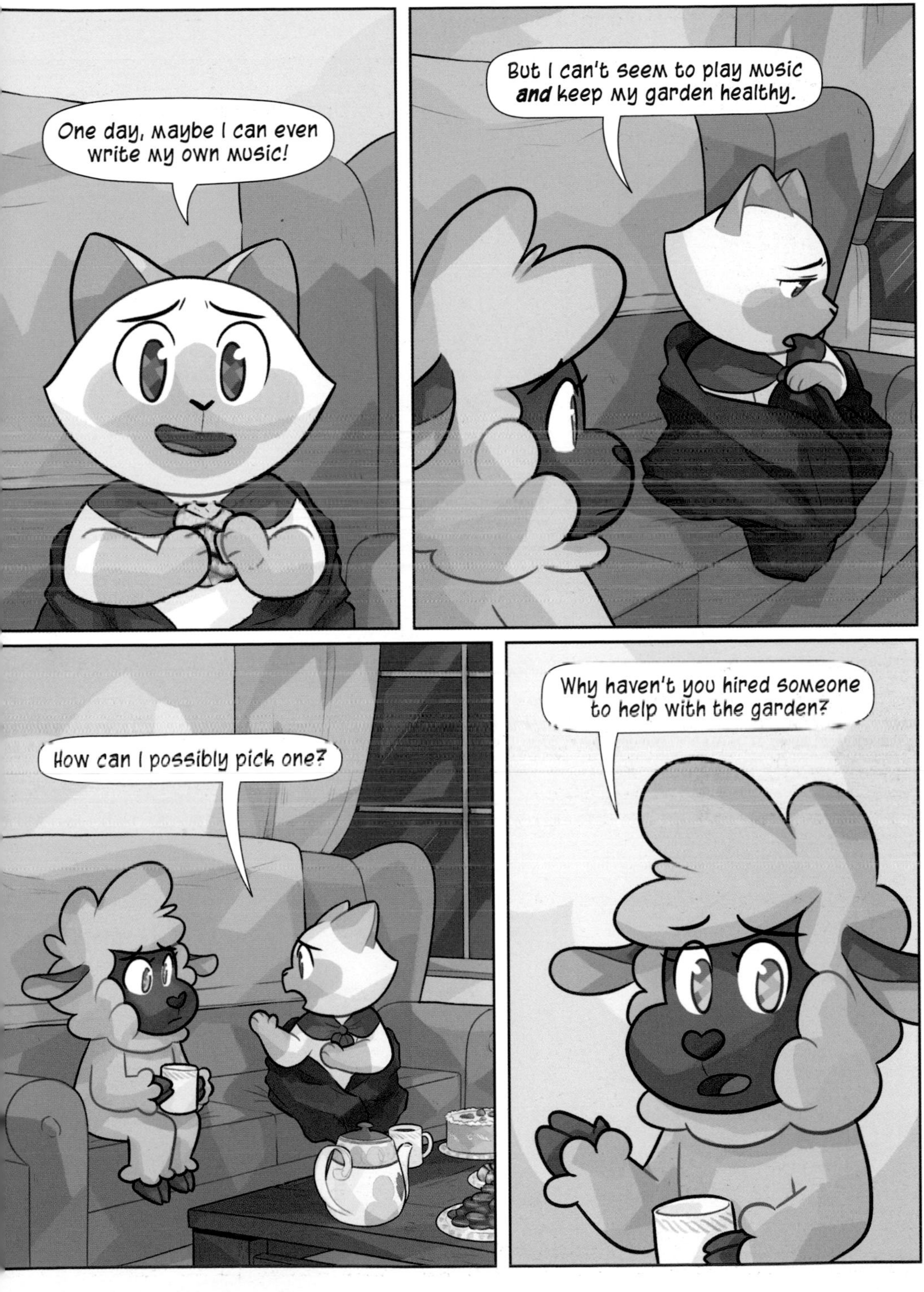
One day, maybe I can even write my own music!
But I can't seem to play music **and** keep my garden healthy.
How can I possibly pick one?
Why haven't you hired someone to help with the garden?

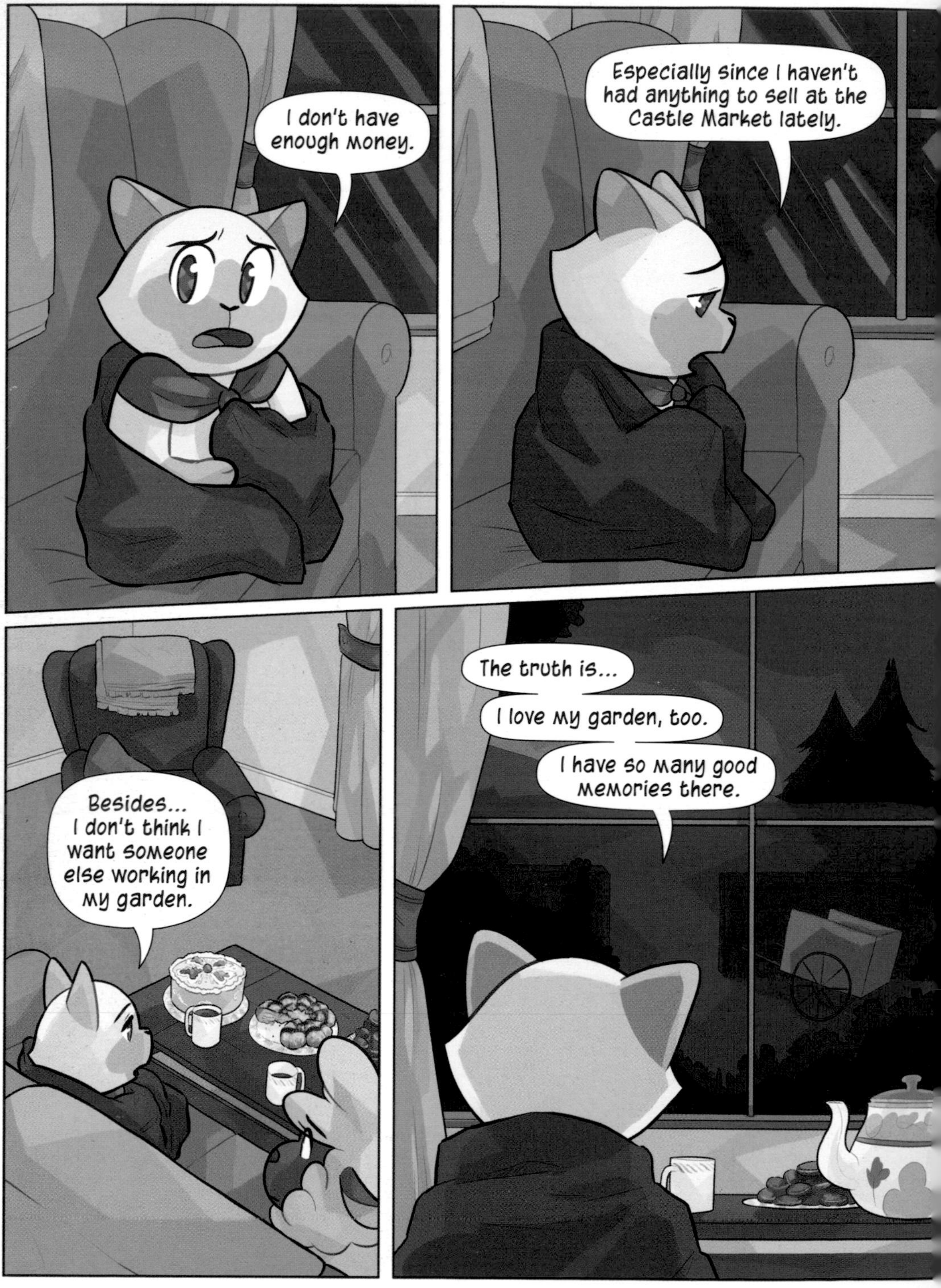
I don't have enough money.
Especially since I haven't had anything to sell at the Castle Market lately.
Besides... I don't think I want someone else working in my garden.
The truth is...
I love my garden, too.
I have so many good memories there.

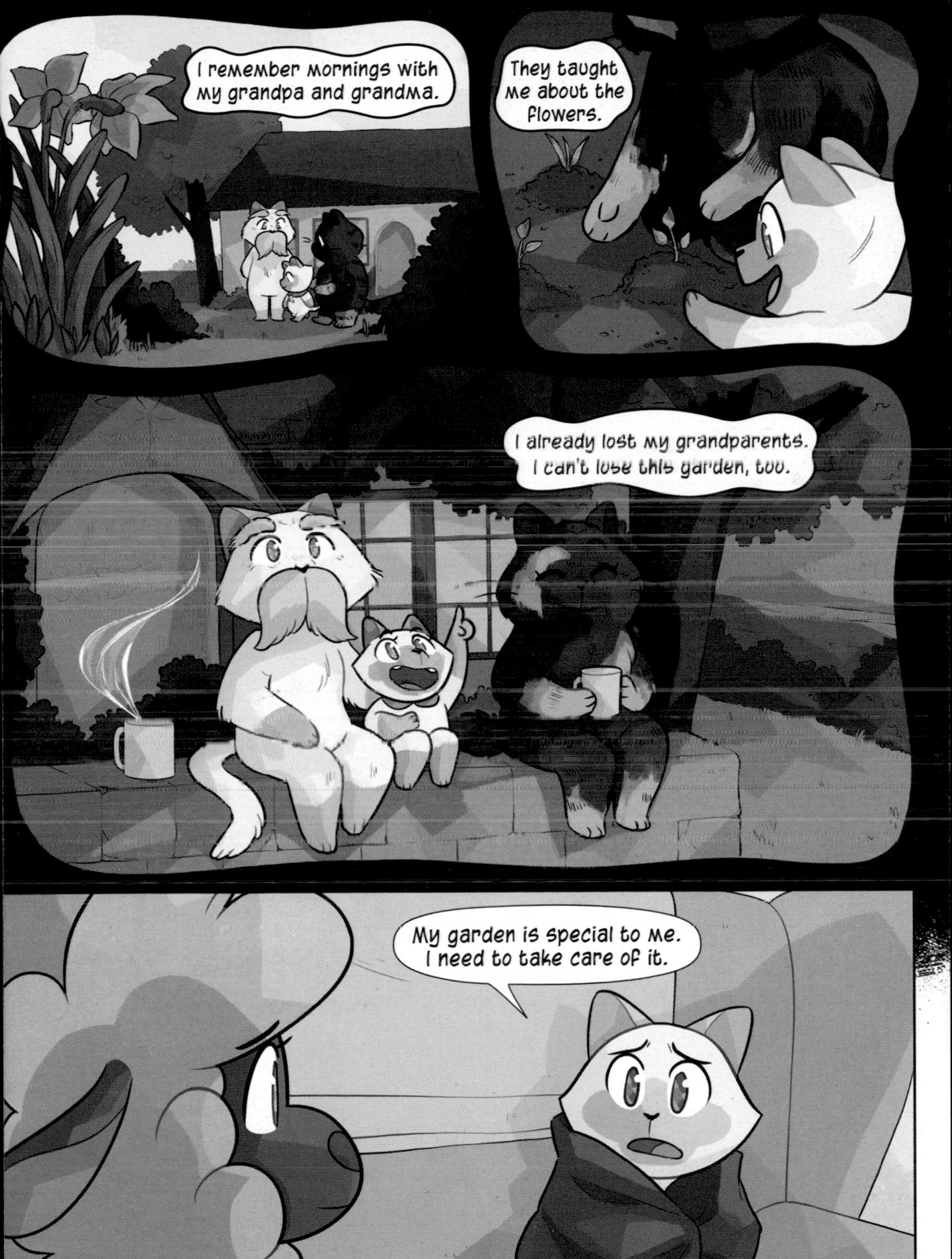
I remember mornings with my grandpa and grandma.
They taught me about the flowers.
I already lost my grandparents. I can't lose this garden, too.
My garden is special to me. I need to take care of it.

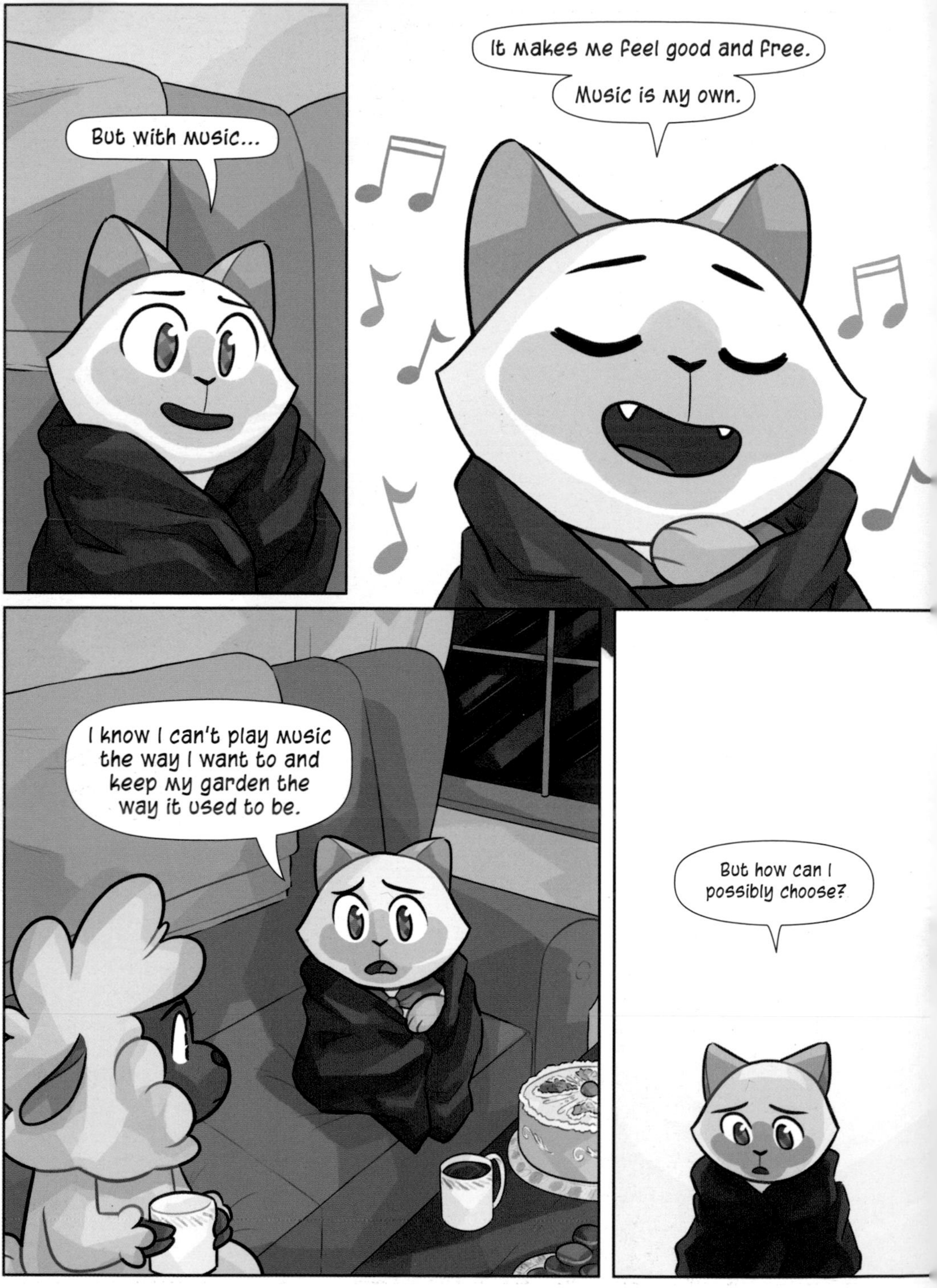

But with music...
It makes me feel good and free.
Music is my own.
I know I can't play music the way I want to and keep my garden the way it used to be.
But how can I possibly choose?

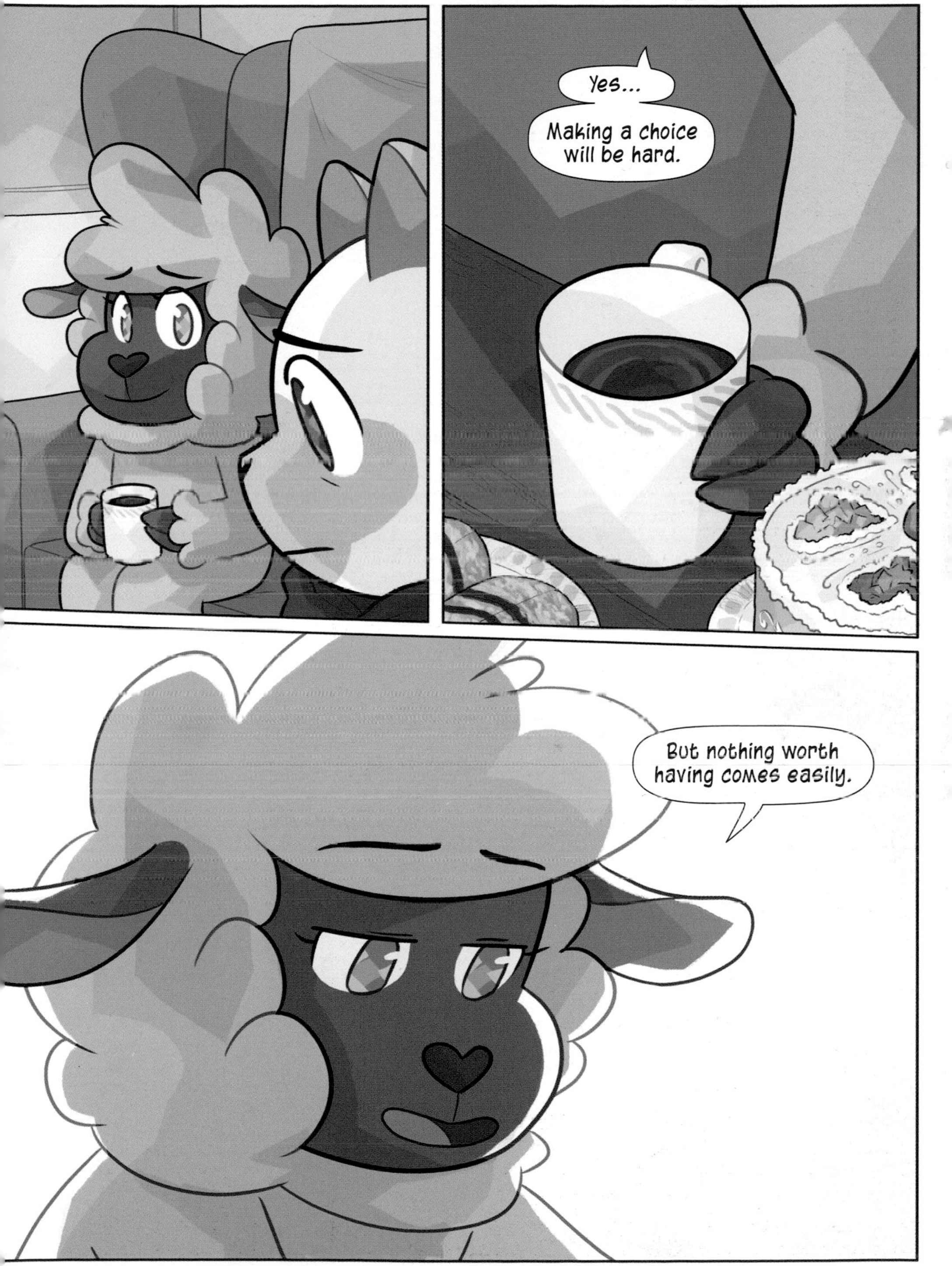
Yes...
Making a choice will be hard.
But nothing worth having comes easily.

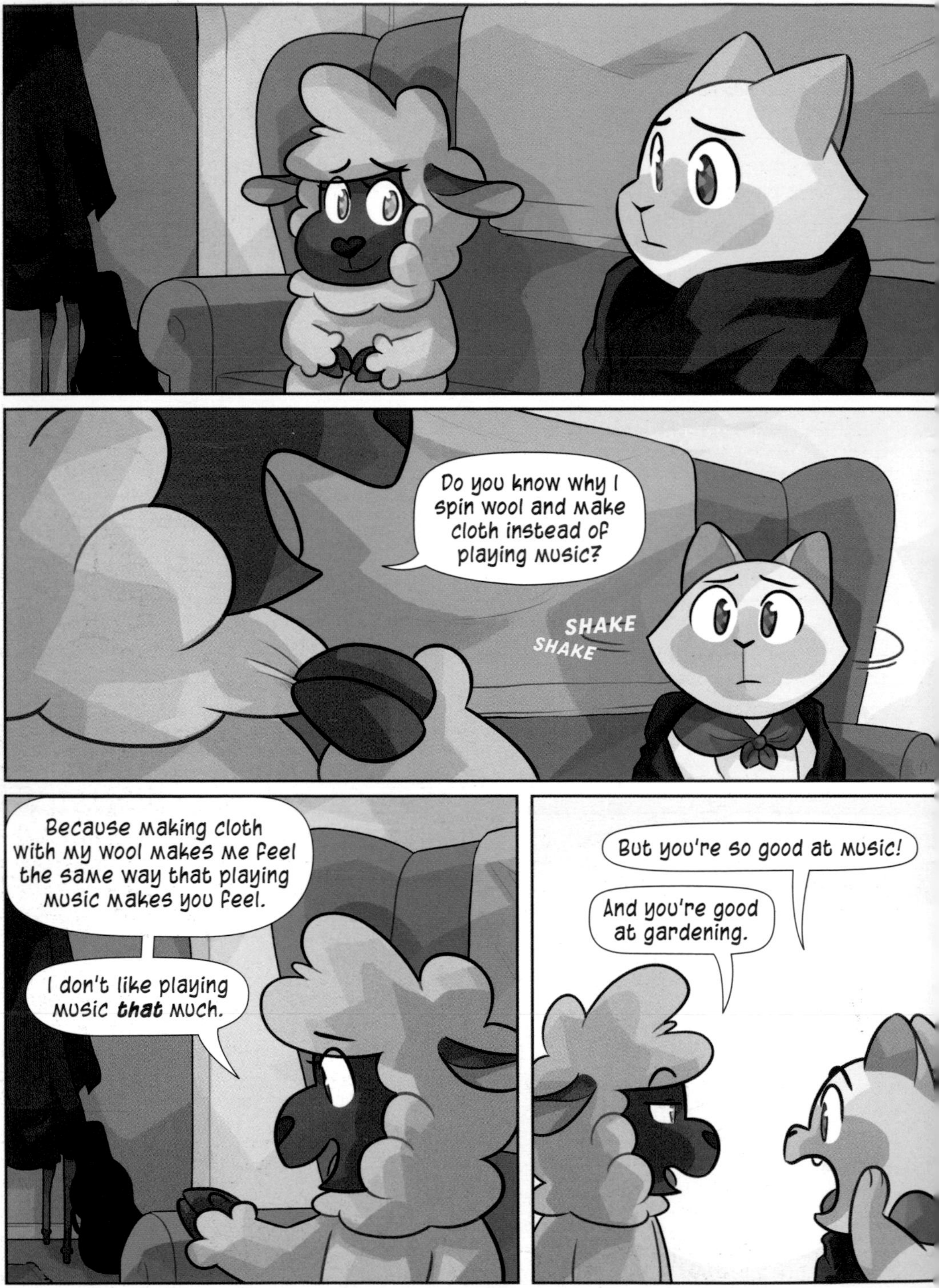
Do you know why I spin wool and make cloth instead of playing music?
SHAKE
SHAKE
Because making cloth with my wool makes me feel the same way that playing music makes you feel.
I don't like playing music ***that*** much.
But you're so good at music!
And you're good at gardening.

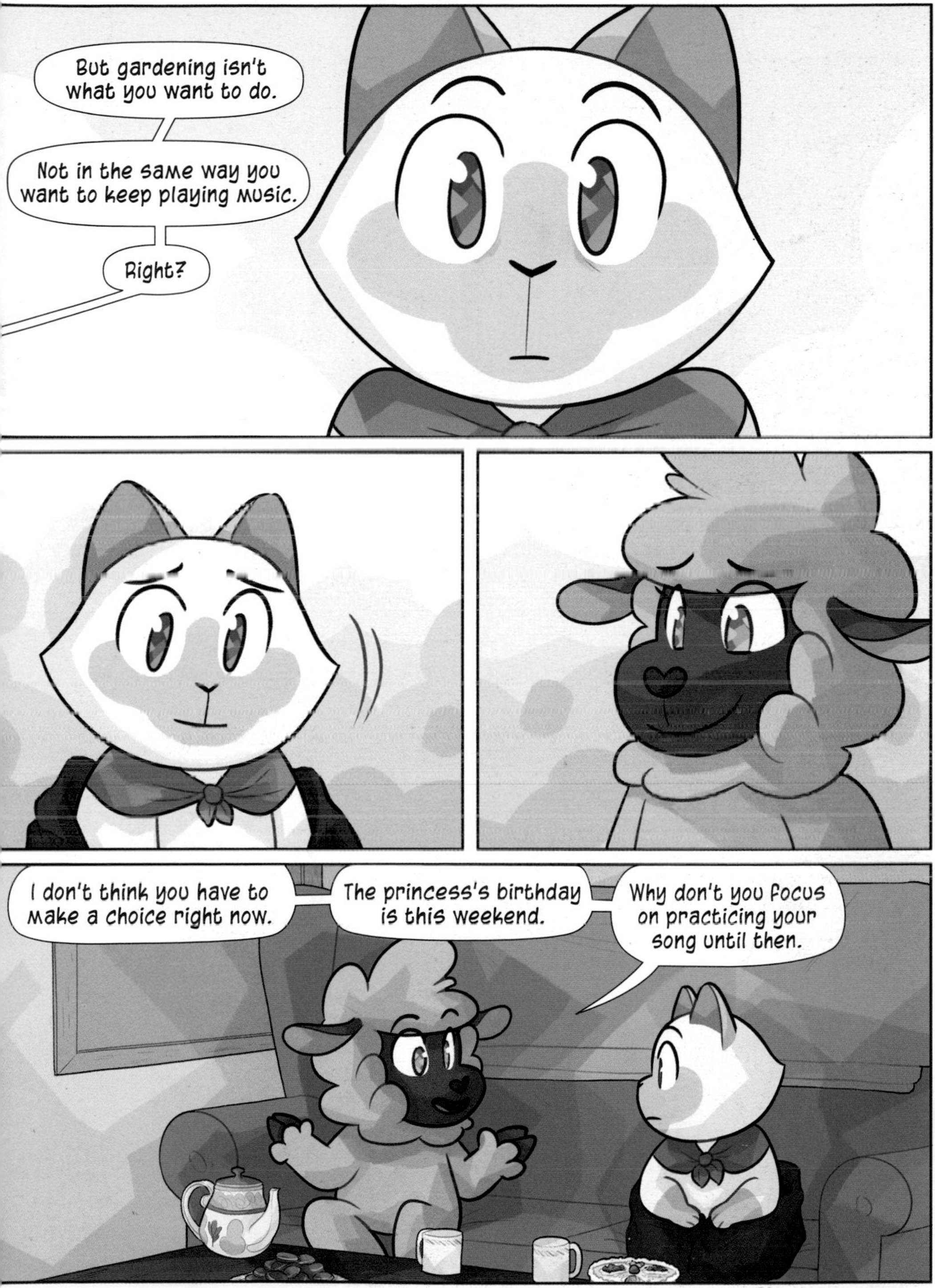

But gardening isn't what you want to do.
Not in the same way you want to keep playing music.
Right?
I don't think you have to make a choice right now.
The princess's birthday is this weekend.
Why don't you focus on practicing your song until then.

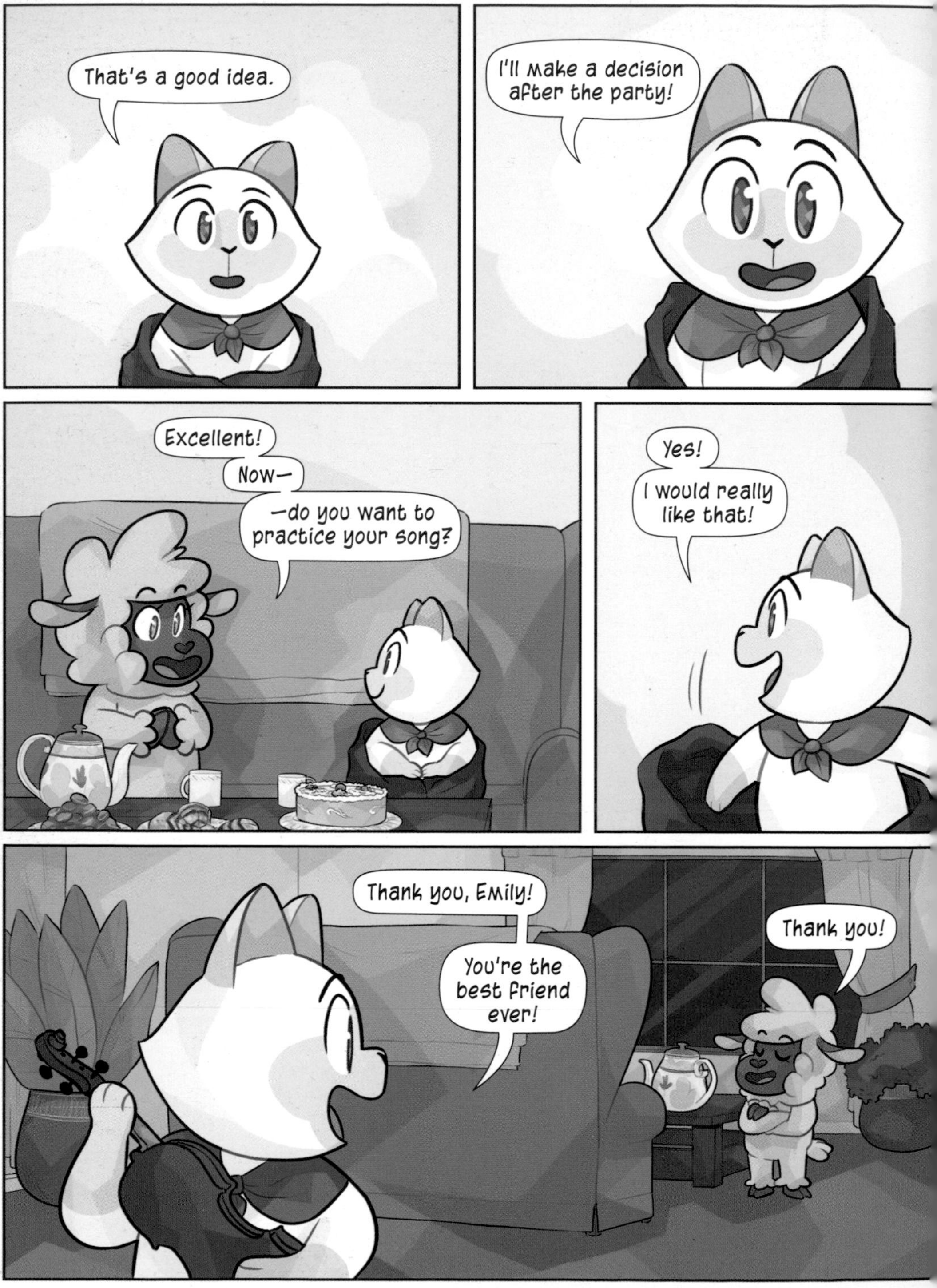
That's a good idea.
I'll make a decision after the party!
Excellent!
Now—
—do you want to practice your song?
Yes!
I would really like that!
Thank you, Emily!
You're the best friend ever!
Thank you!

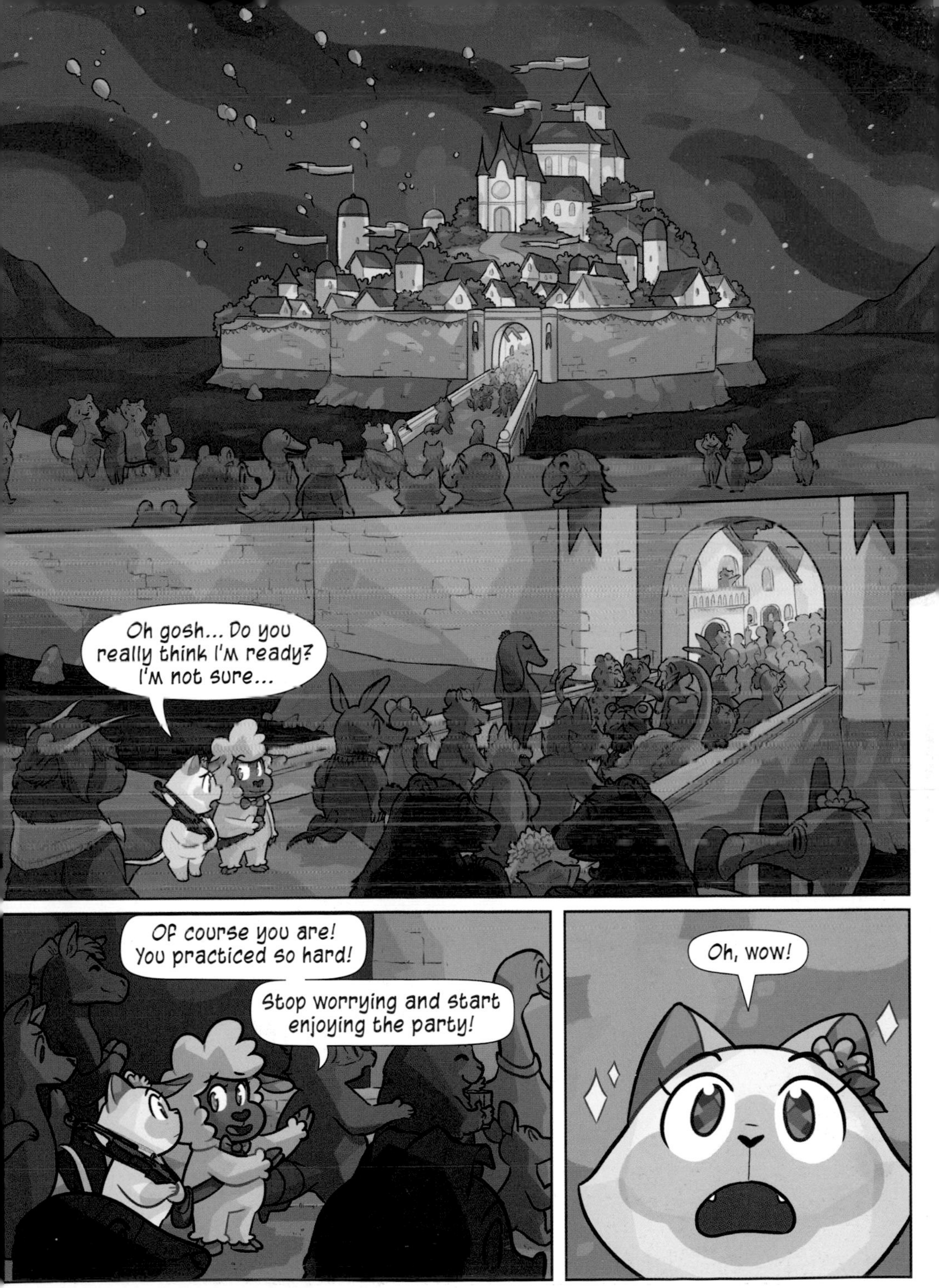
Oh gosh... Do you really think I'm ready? I'm not sure...
Of course you are! You practiced so hard!
Stop worrying and start enjoying the party!
Oh, wow!

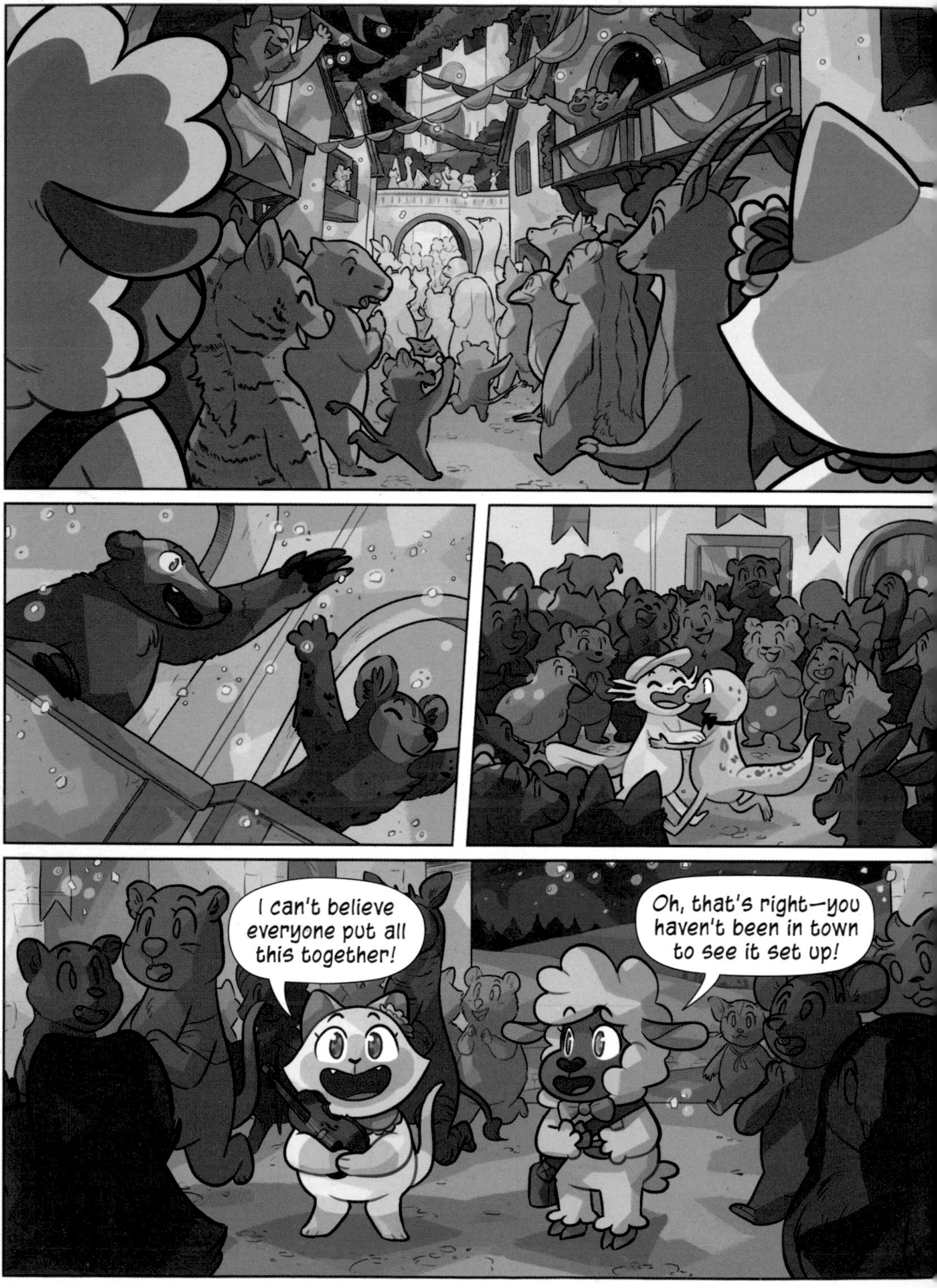
I can't believe everyone put all this together!
Oh, that's right—you haven't been in town to see it set up!

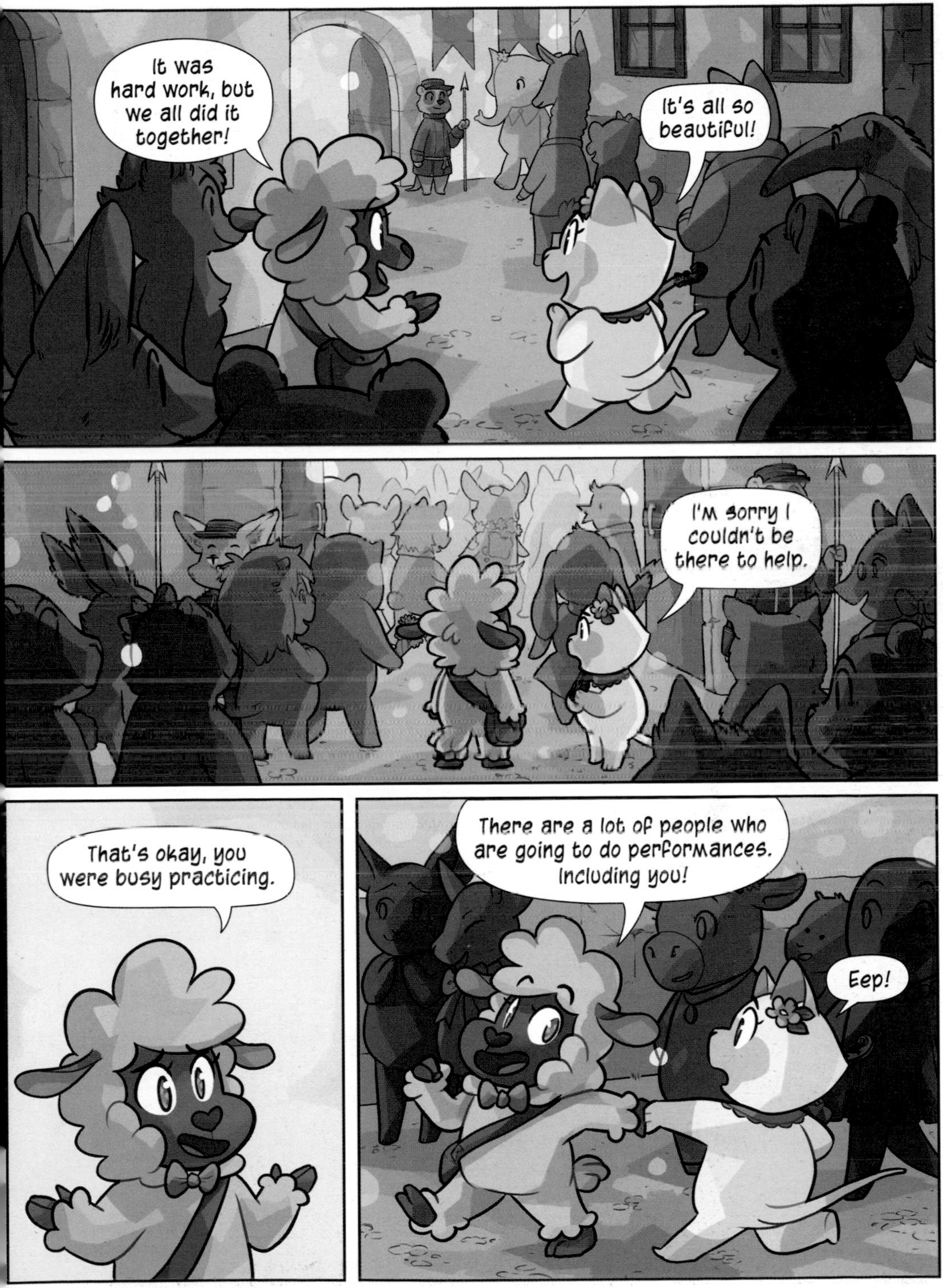
It was hard work, but we all did it together!
It's all so beautiful!
I'm sorry I couldn't be there to help.
That's okay, you were busy practicing.
There are a lot of people who are going to do performances. Including you!
Eep!

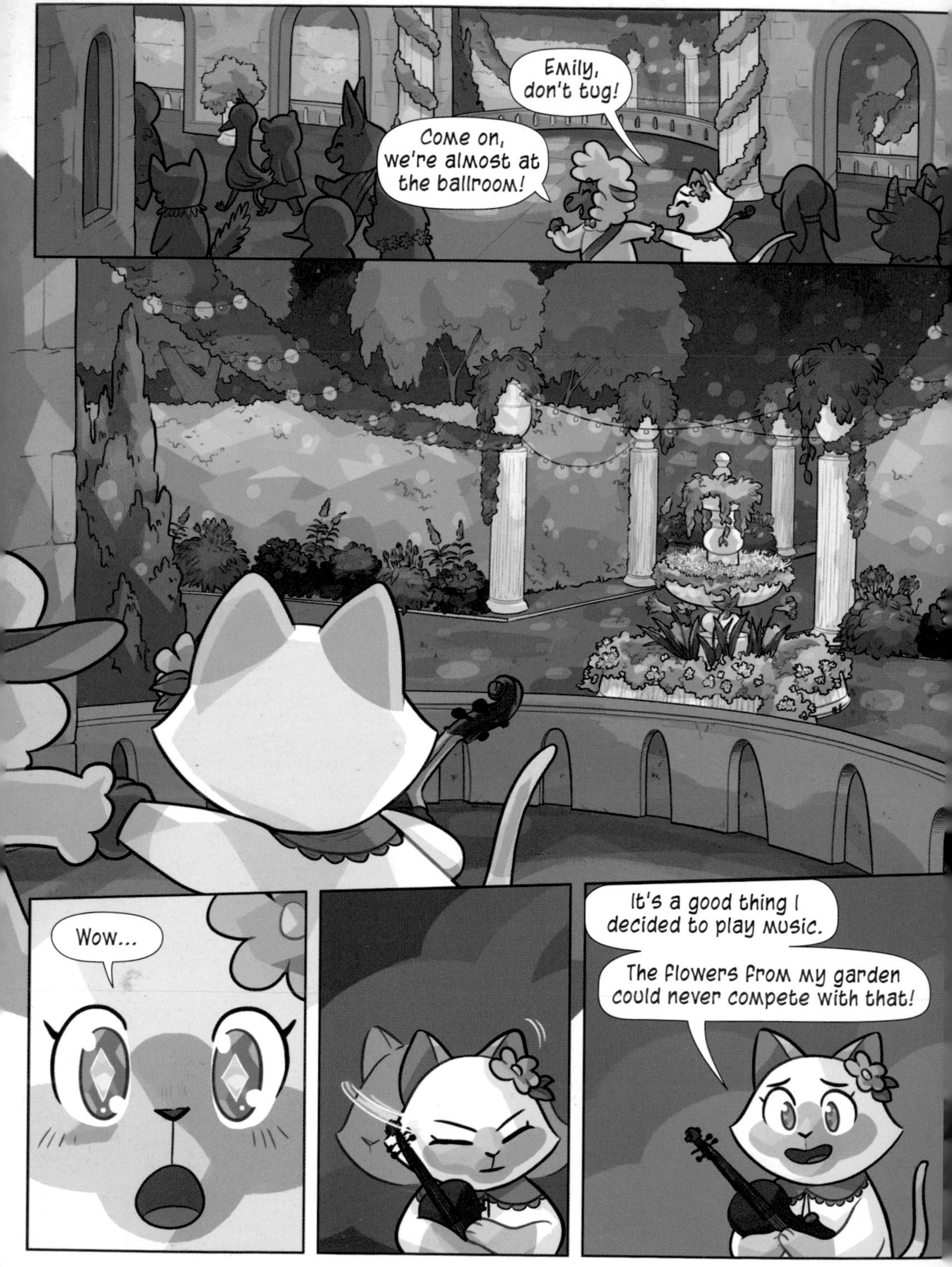
Emily, don't tug!
Come on, we're almost at the ballroom!
Wow...
It's a good thing I decided to play music.
The flowers from my garden could never compete with that!

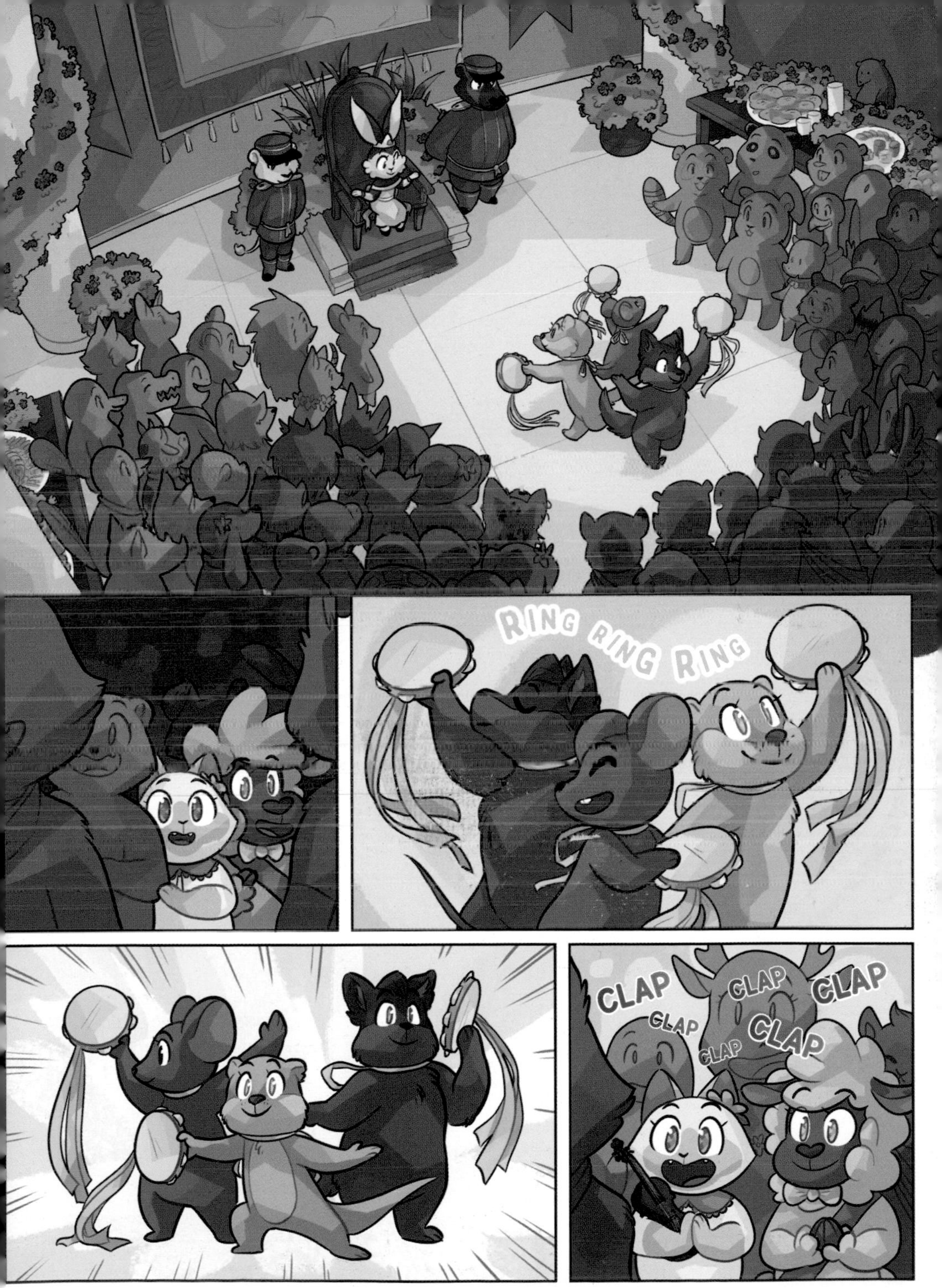
RING RING RING
CLAP
CLAP
CLAP
CLAP
CLAP
CLAP
CLAP

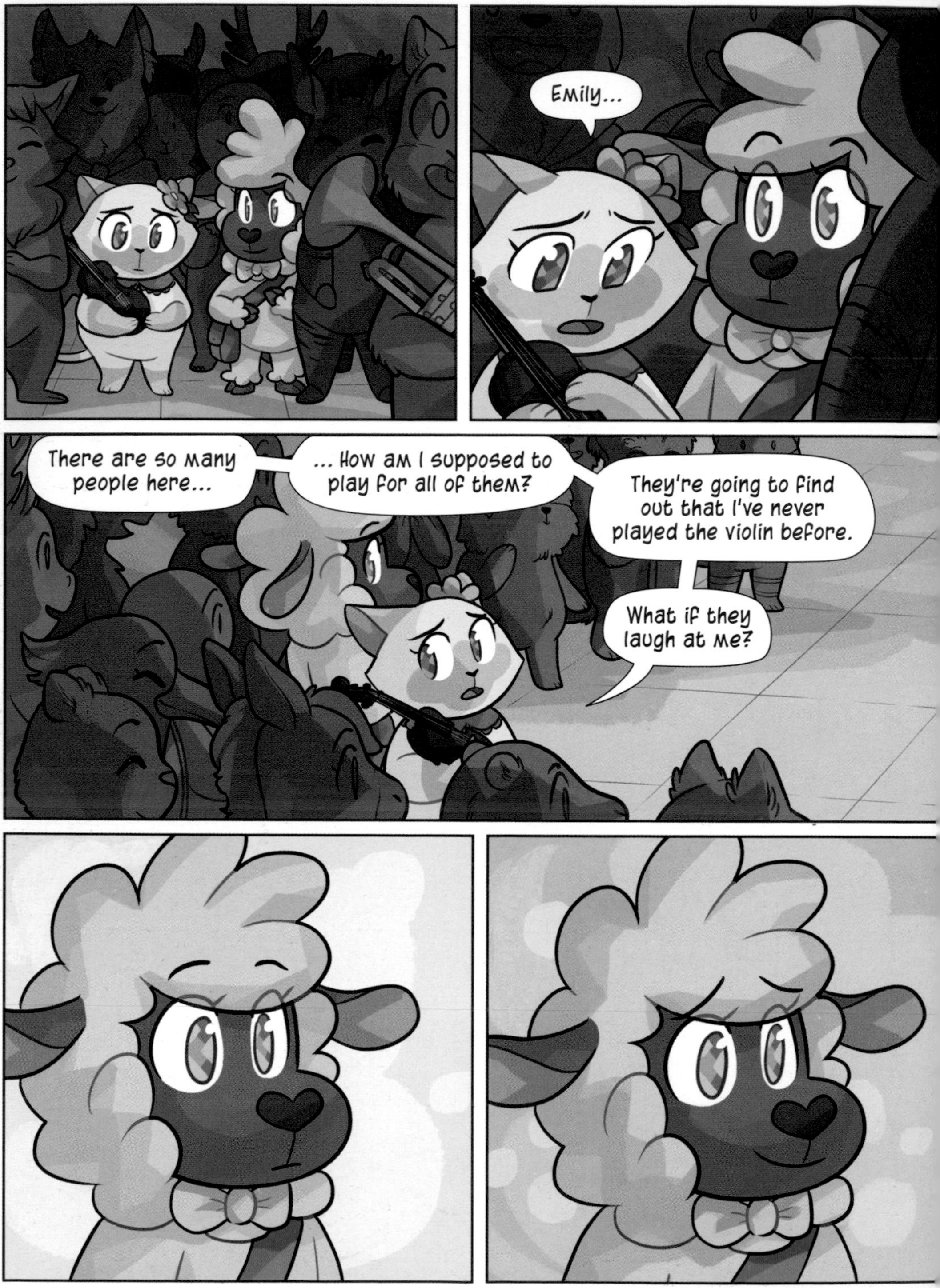
Emily...
There are so many people here...
... How am I supposed to play for all of them?
They're going to find out that I've never played the violin before.
What if they laugh at me?

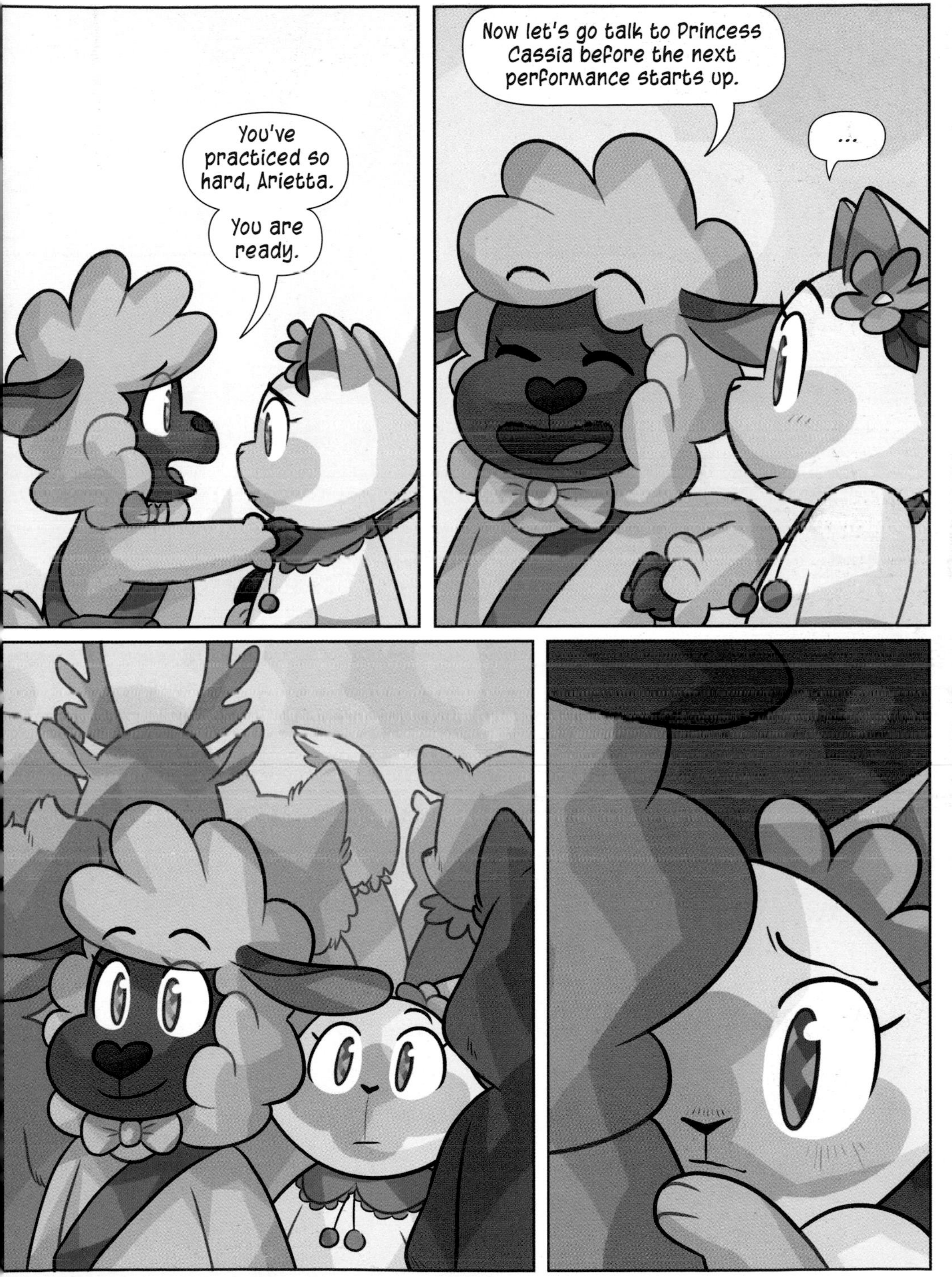
You've practiced so hard, Arietta.
You are ready.
Now let's go talk to Princess Cassia before the next performance starts up.
...

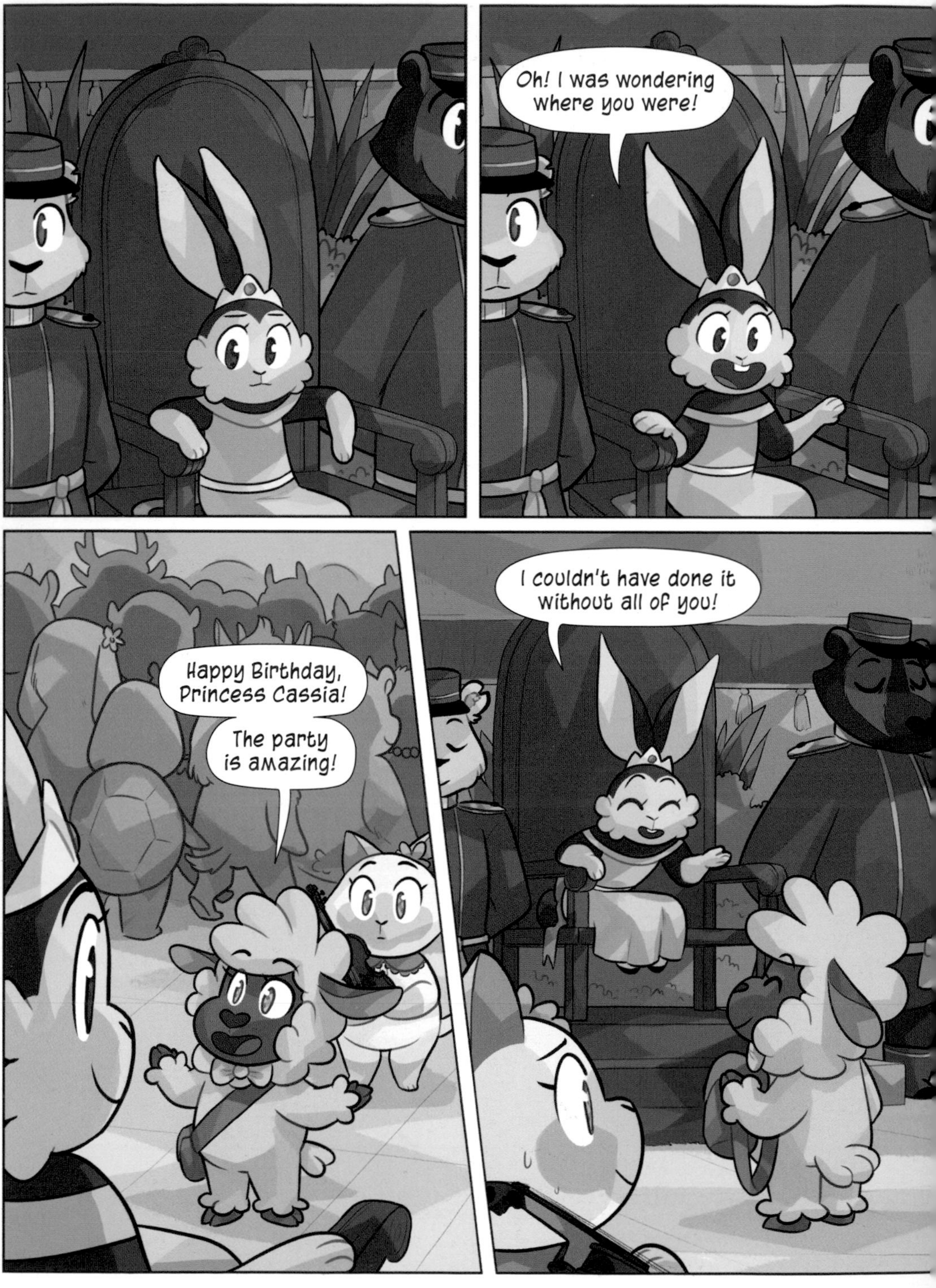
Oh! I was wondering where you were!
Happy Birthday, Princess Cassia!
The party is amazing!
I couldn't have done it without all of you!

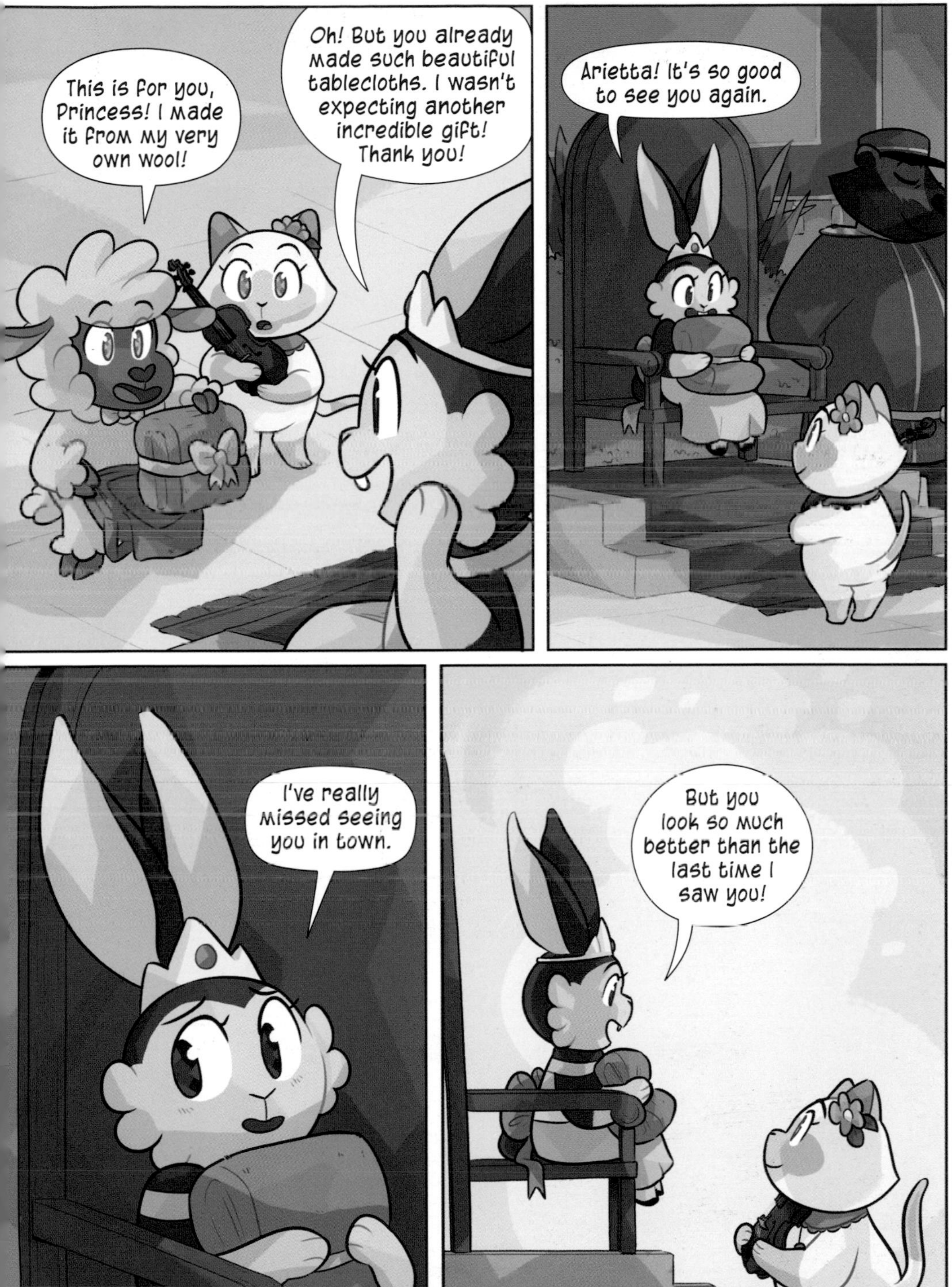
This is for you, Princess! I made it from my very own wool!
Oh! But you already made such beautiful tablecloths. I wasn't expecting another incredible gift! Thank you!
Arietta! It's so good to see you again.
I've really missed seeing you in town.
But you look so much better than the last time I saw you!

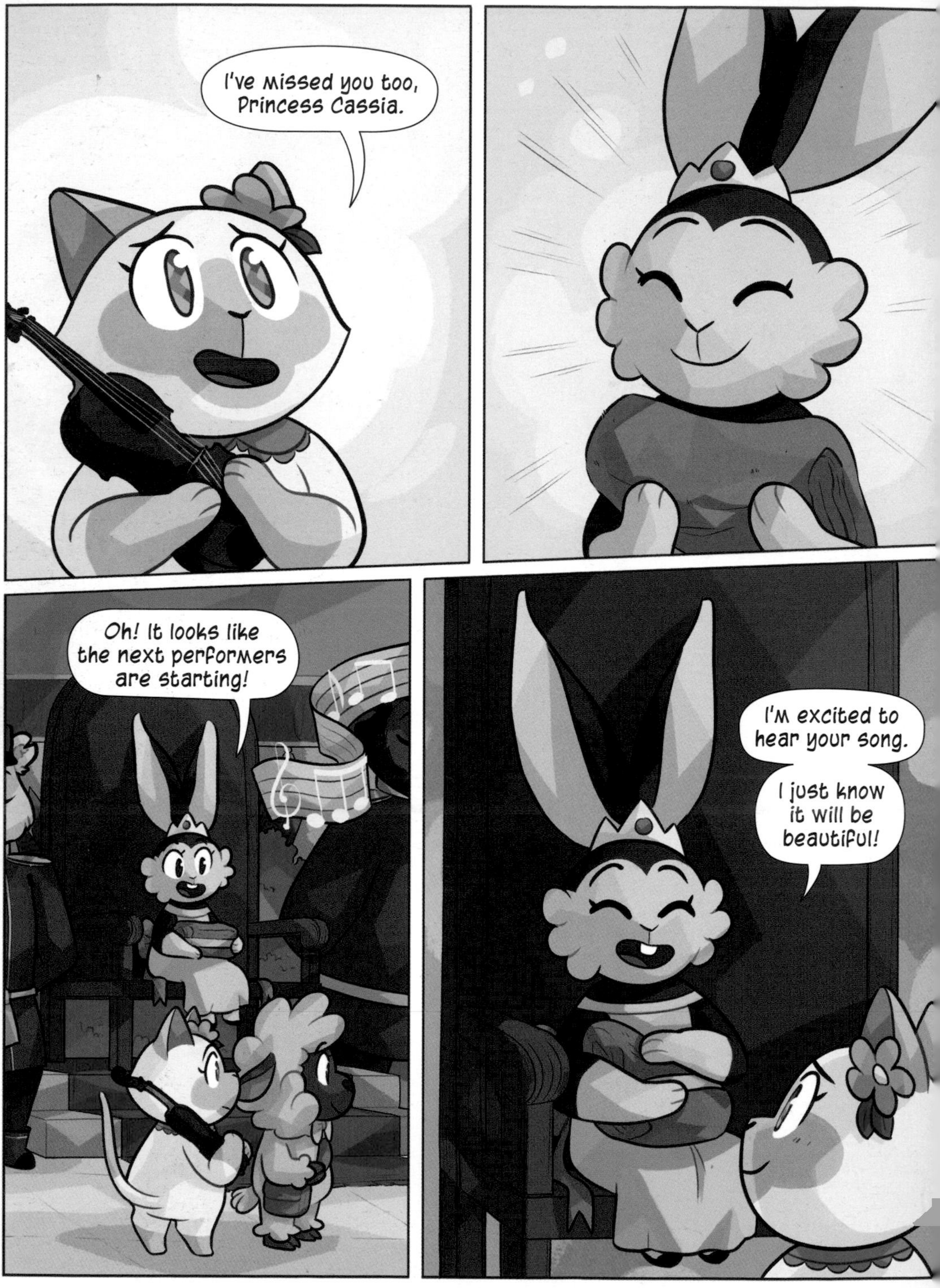
I've missed you too, Princess Cassia.
Oh! It looks like the next performers are starting!
I'm excited to hear your song.
I just know it will be beautiful!

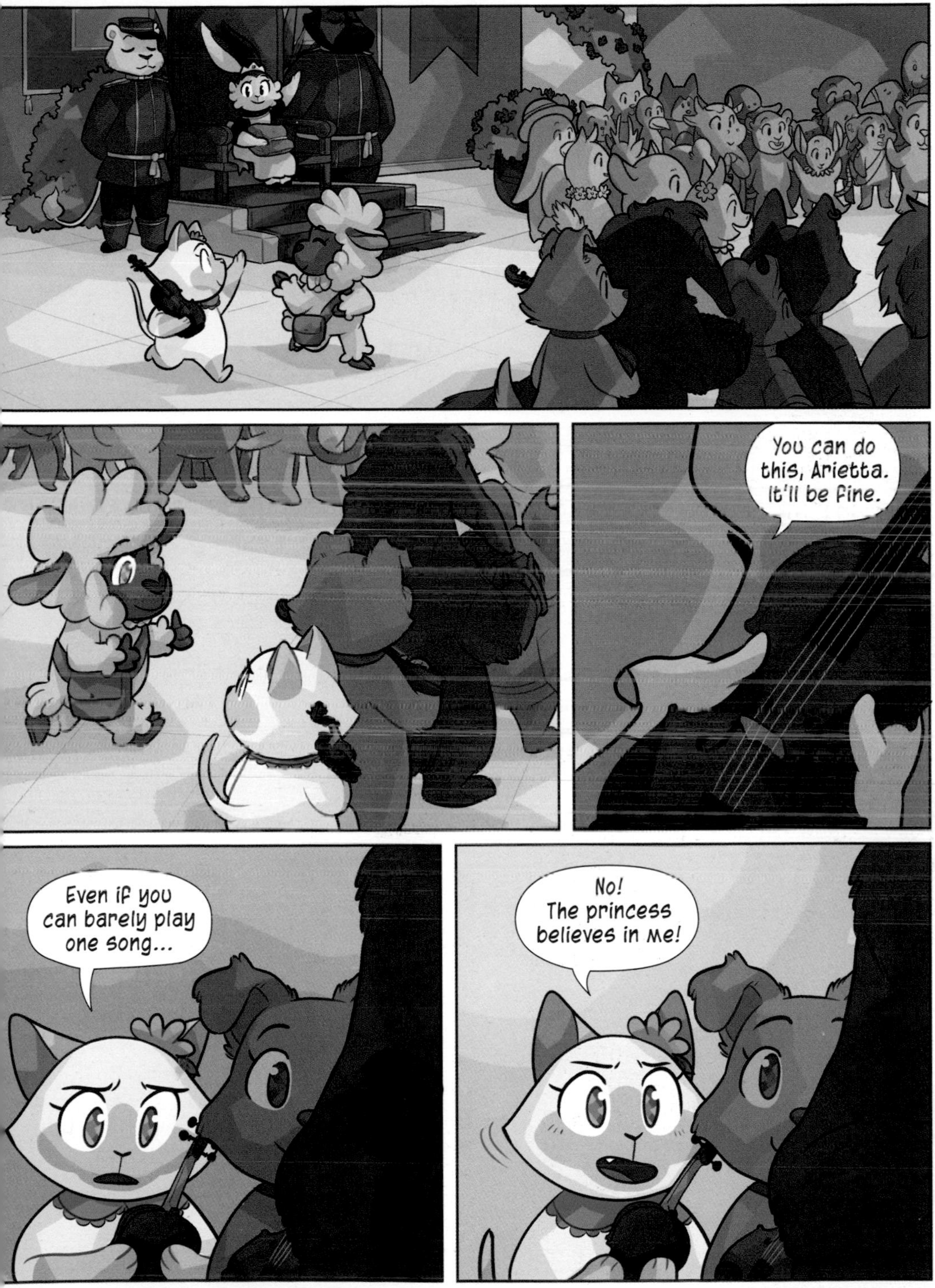
You can do this, Arietta. It'll be fine.
Even if you can barely play one song...
No! The princess believes in me!

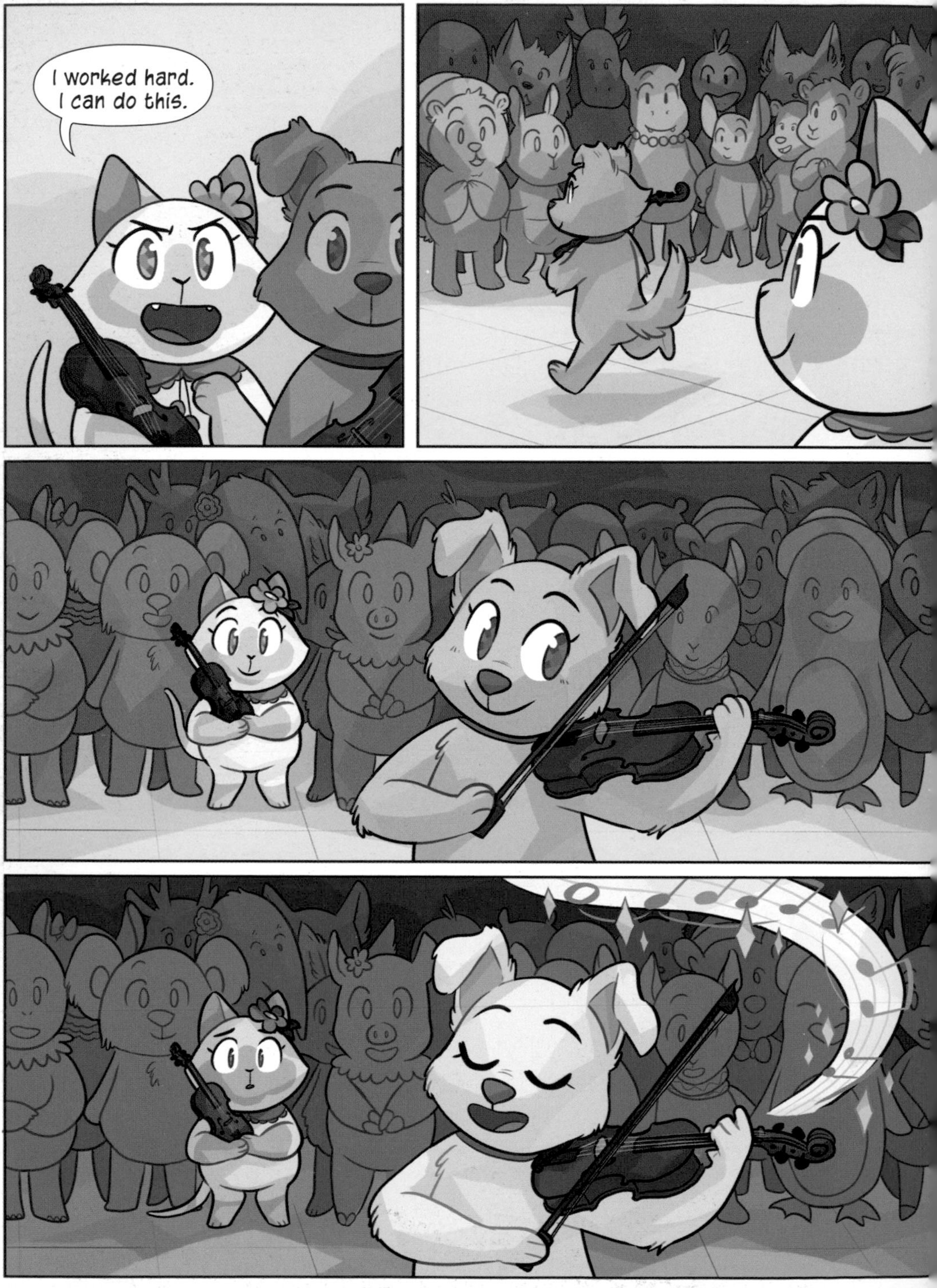
I worked hard.
I can do this.

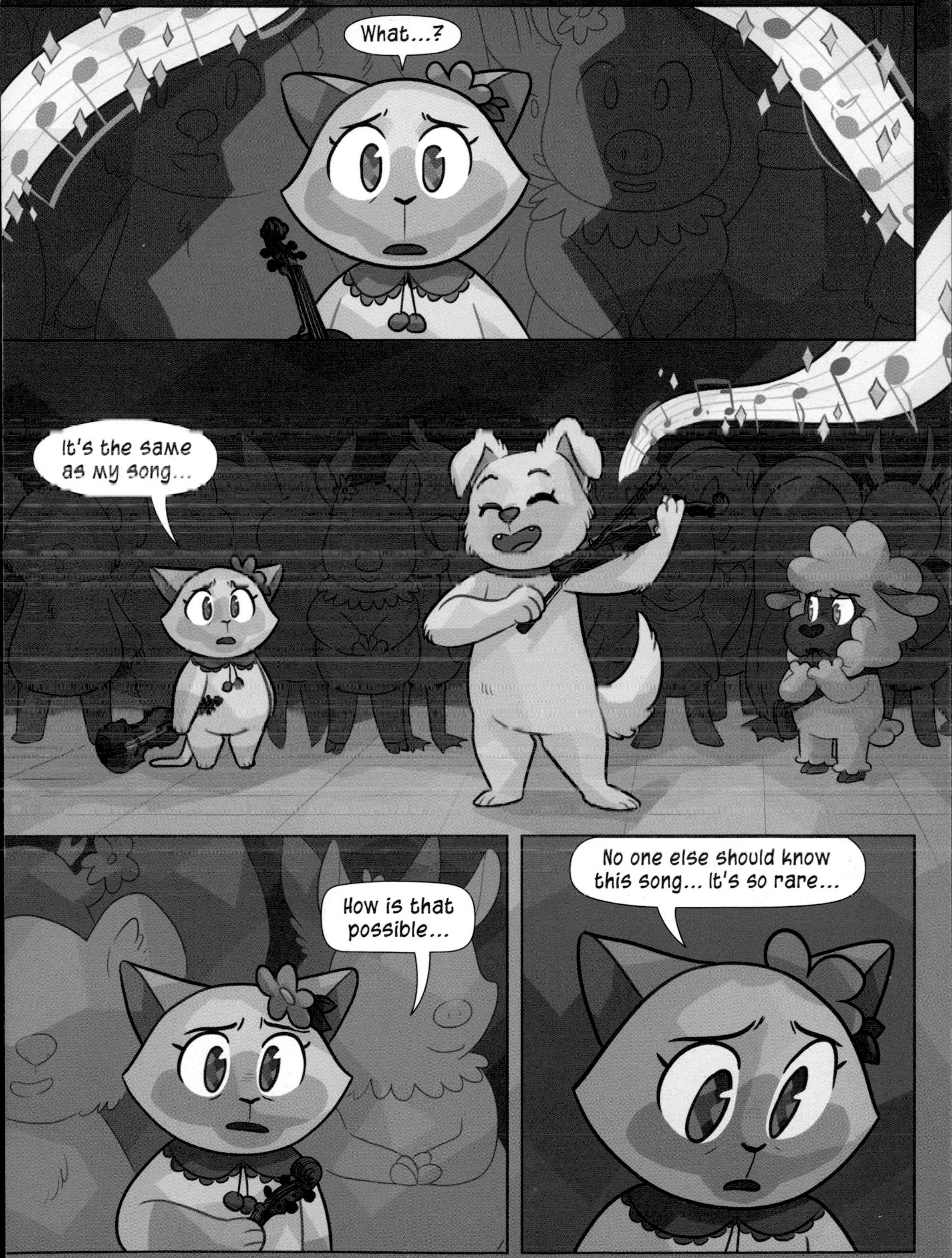
What...?
It's the same as my song...
How is that possible...
No one else should know this song... It's so rare...

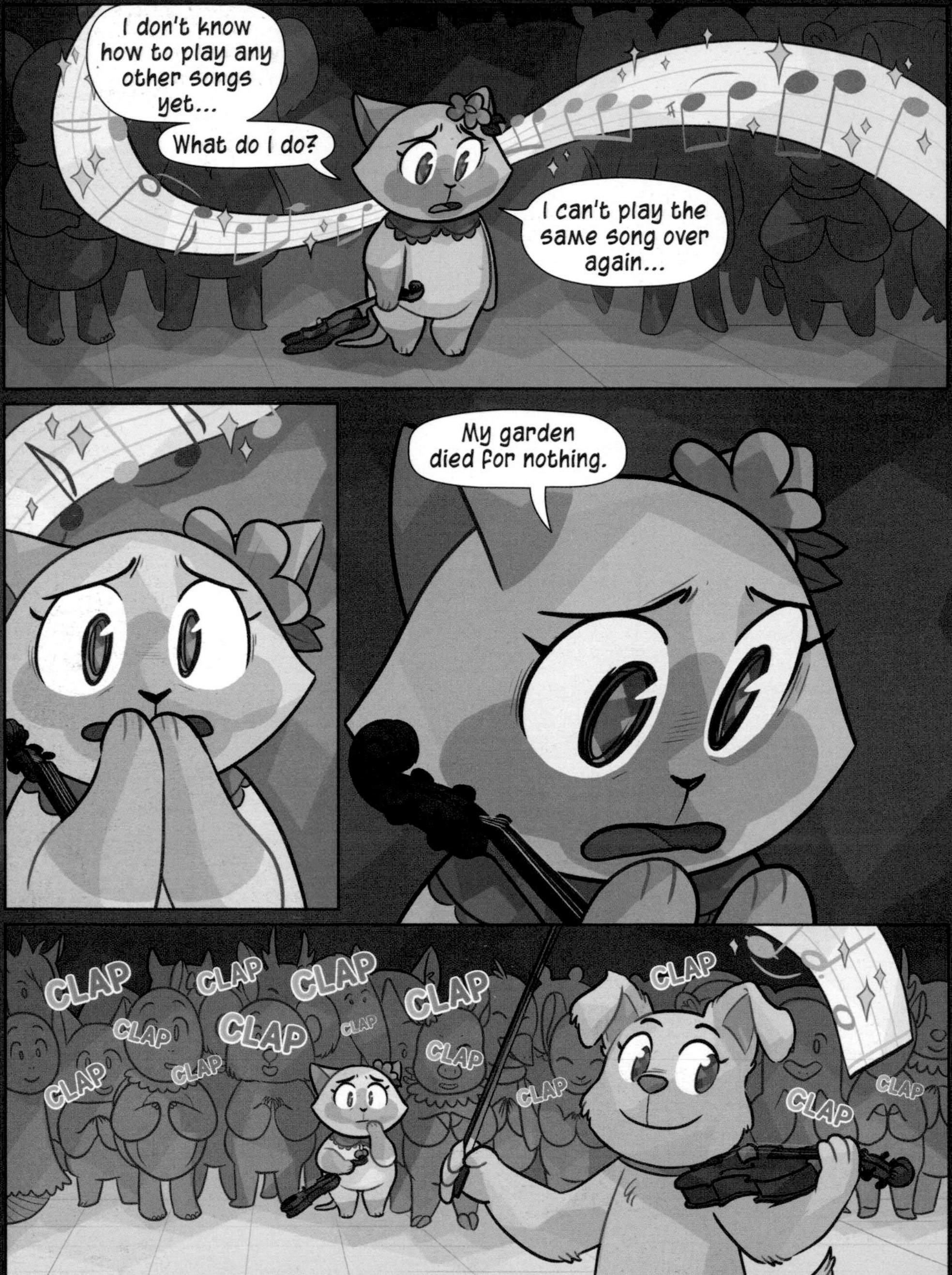
I don't know how to play any other songs yet...
What do I do?
I can't play the same song over again...
My garden died for nothing.
CLAP
CLAP
CLAP
CLAP
CLAP
CLAP
CLAP
CLAP
CLAP
CLAP
CLAP
CLAP
CLAP
CLAP

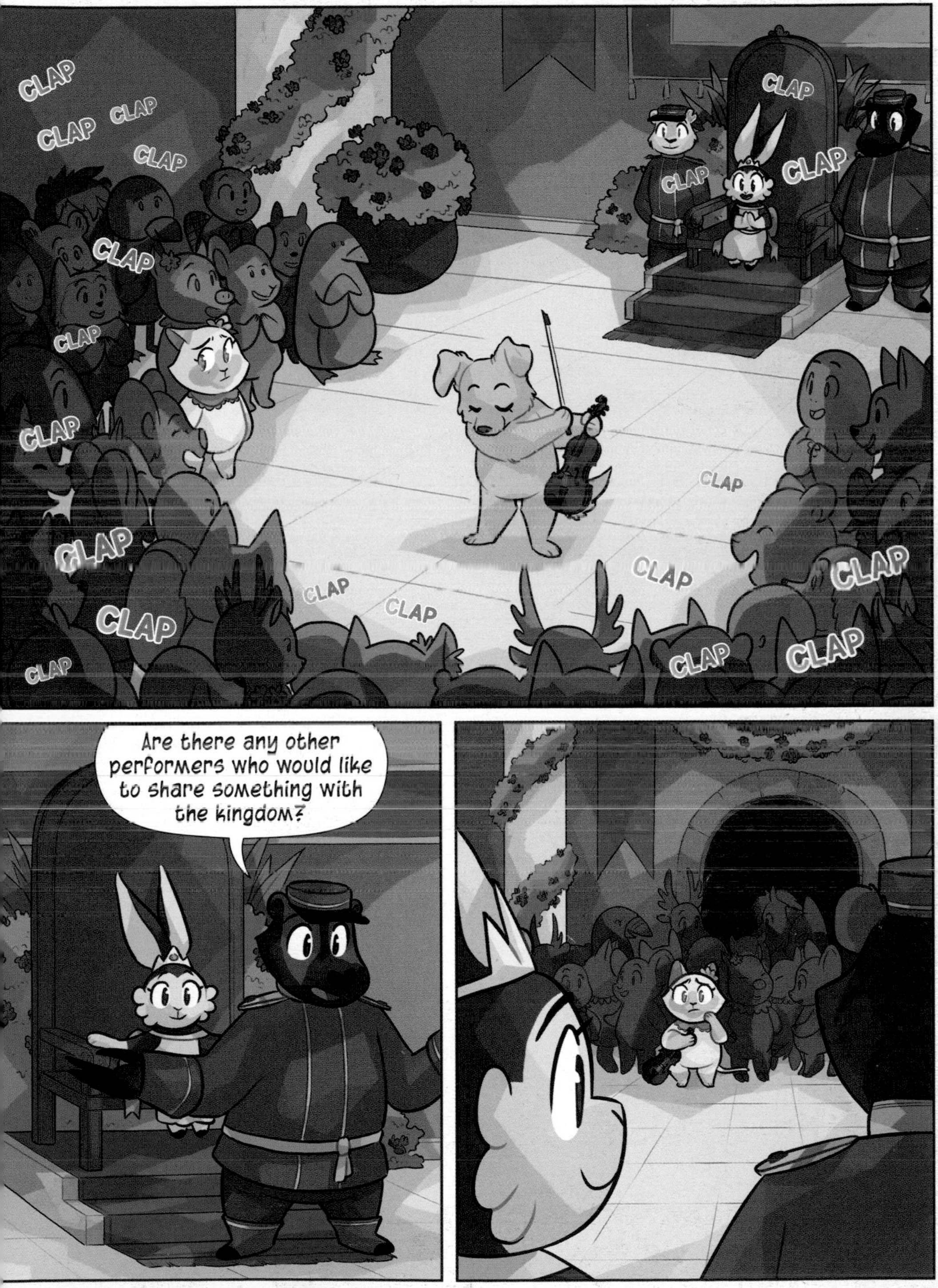
CLAP
CLAP CLAP
CLAP
CLAP
CLAP
CLAP
CLAP
CLAP
CLAP
CLAP
CLAP
CLAP
CLAP
CLAP
CLAP
CLAP
CLAP
CLAP
Are there any other performers who would like to share something with the kingdom?

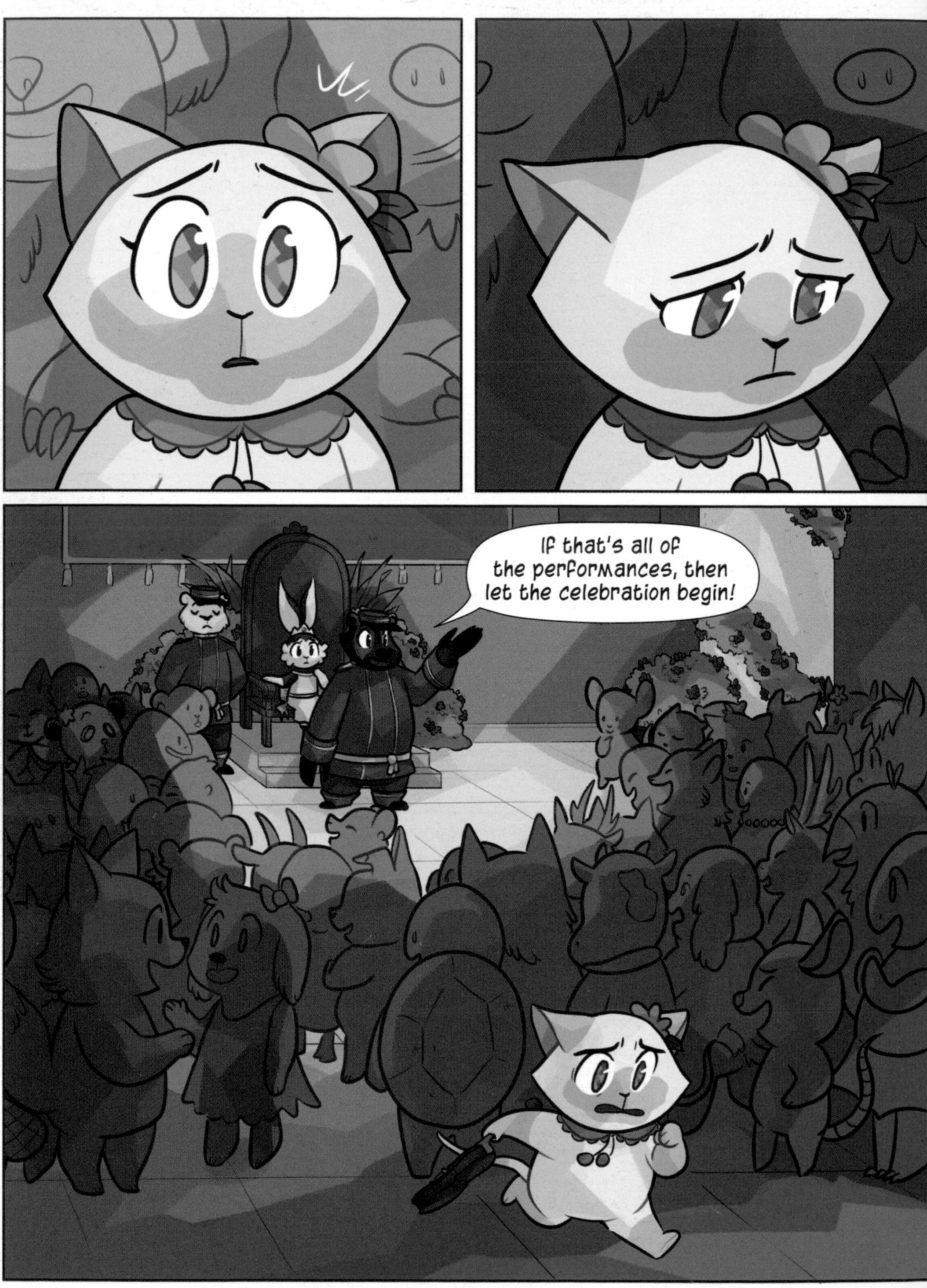
If that's all of the performances, then let the celebration begin!

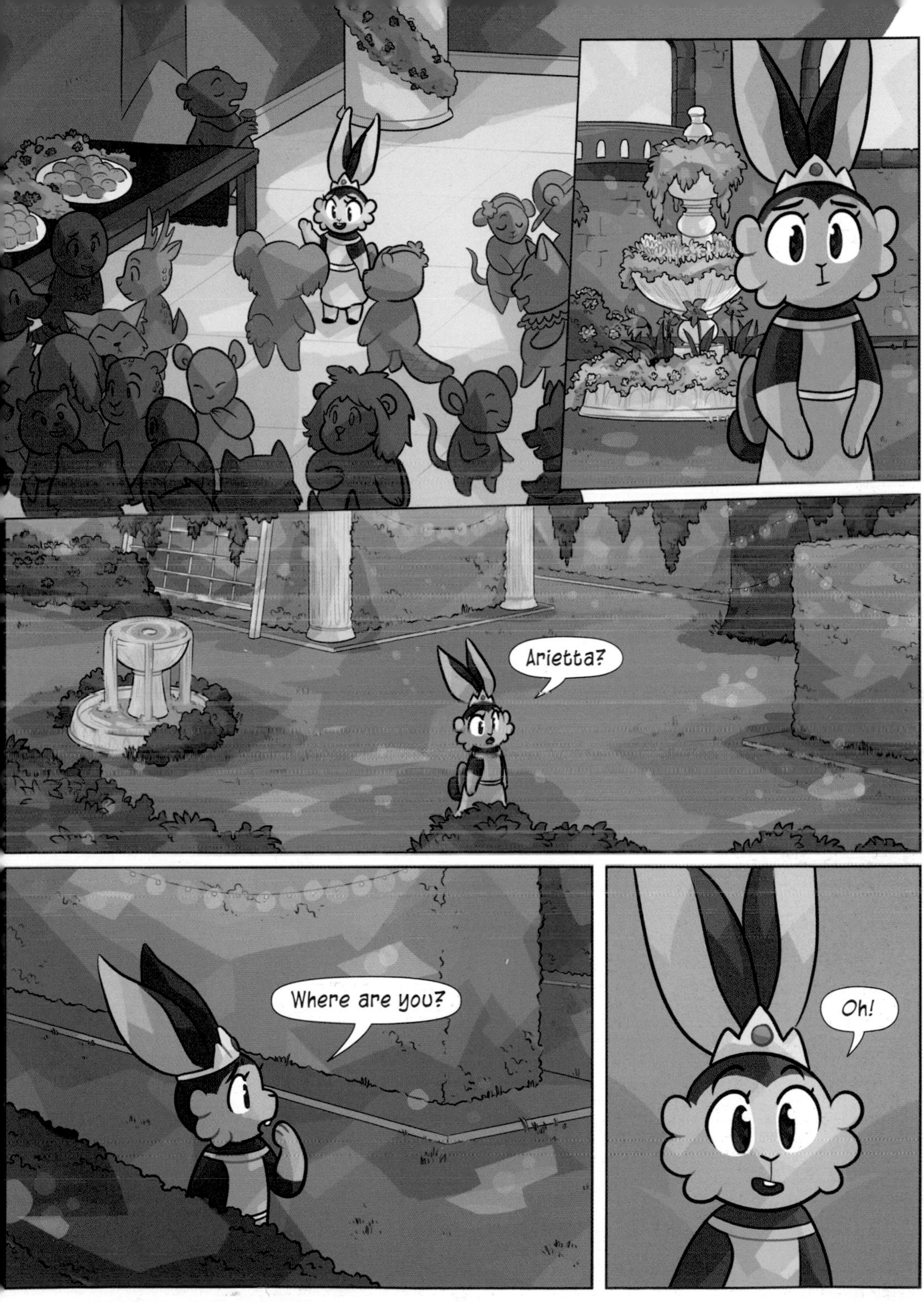
Arietta?
Where are you?
Oh!

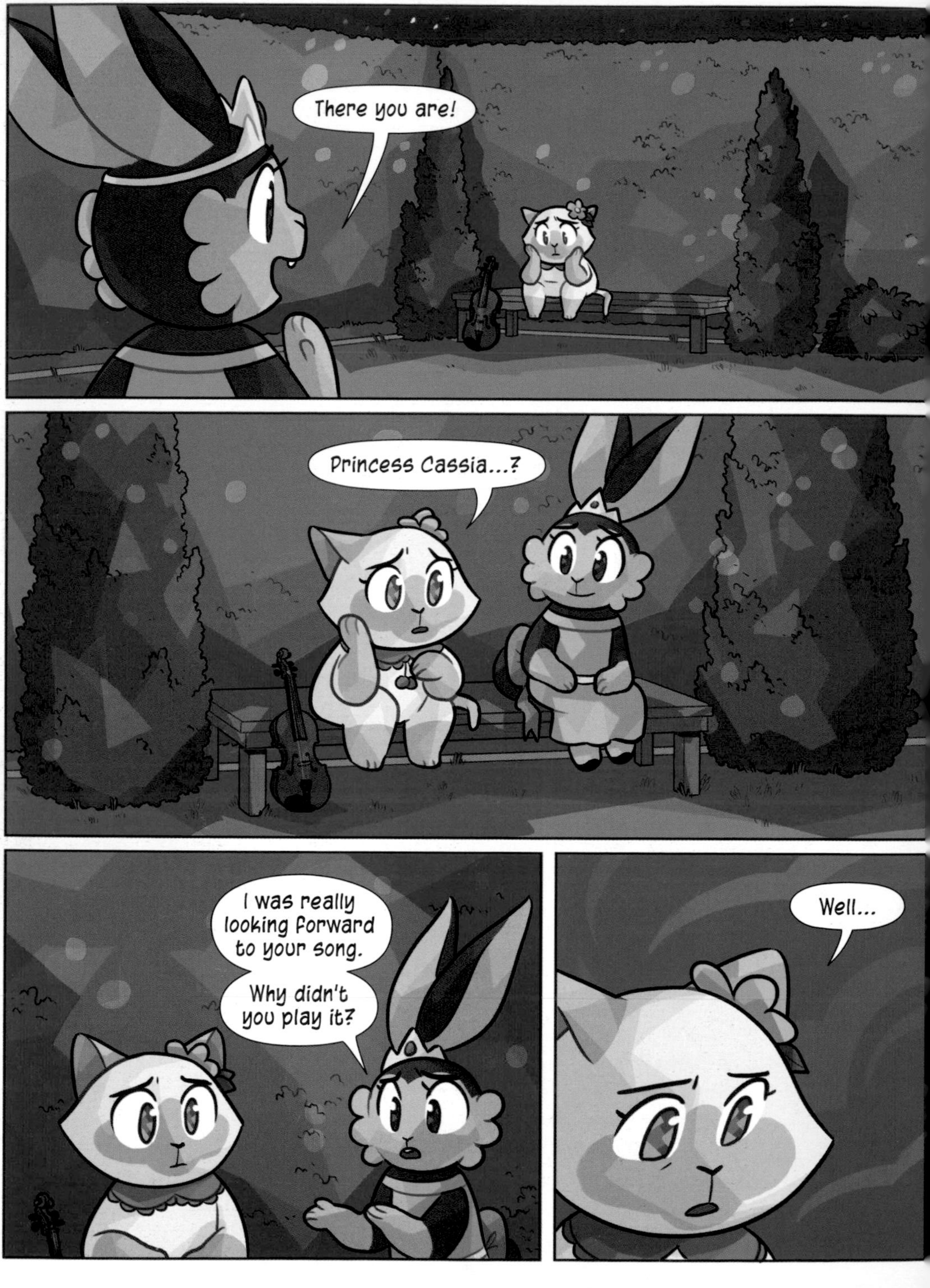
There you are!
Princess Cassia...?
I was really looking forward to your song.
Why didn't you play it?
Well...

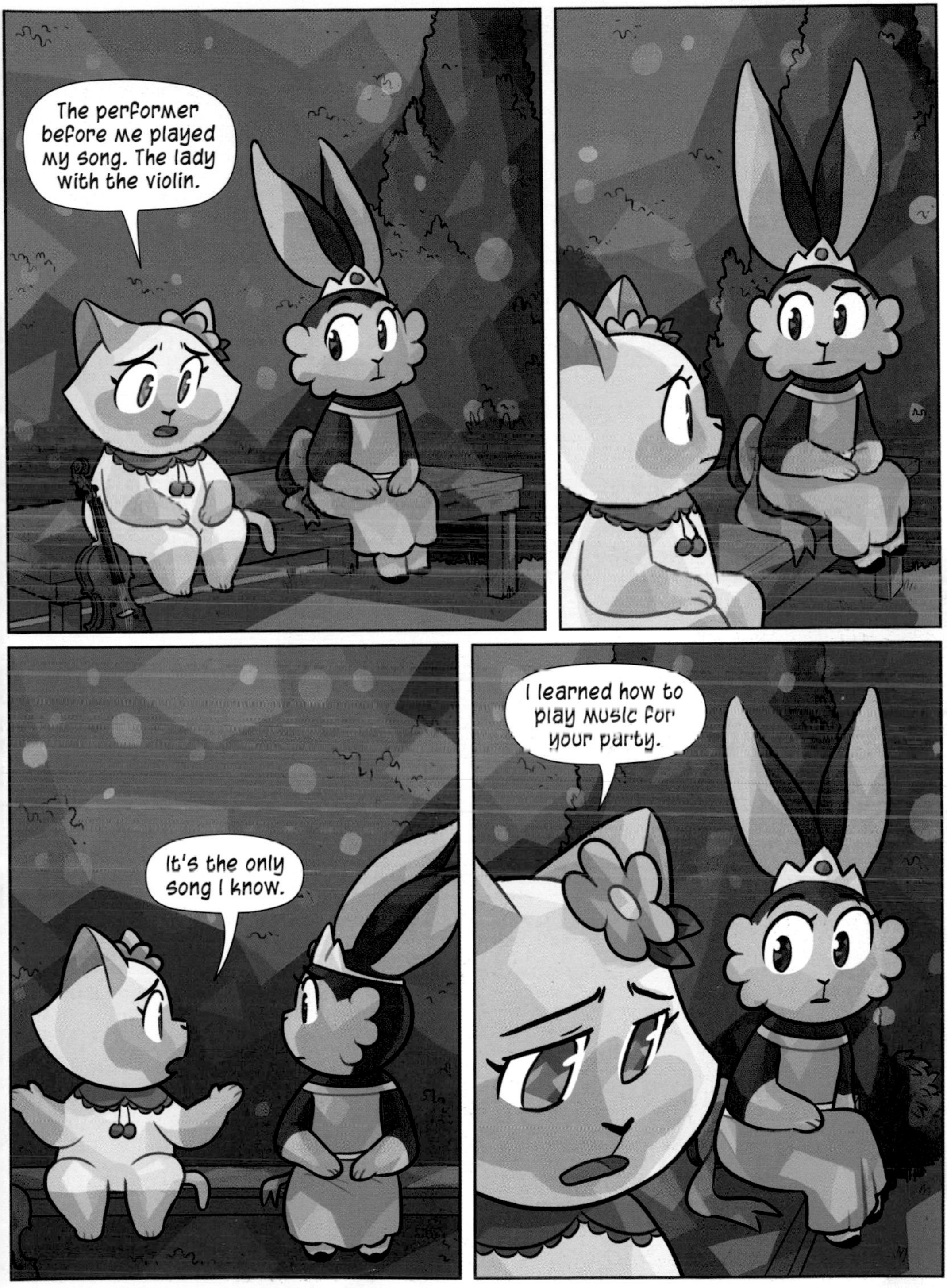
The performer before me played my song. The lady with the violin.
It's the only song I know.
I learned how to play music for your party.

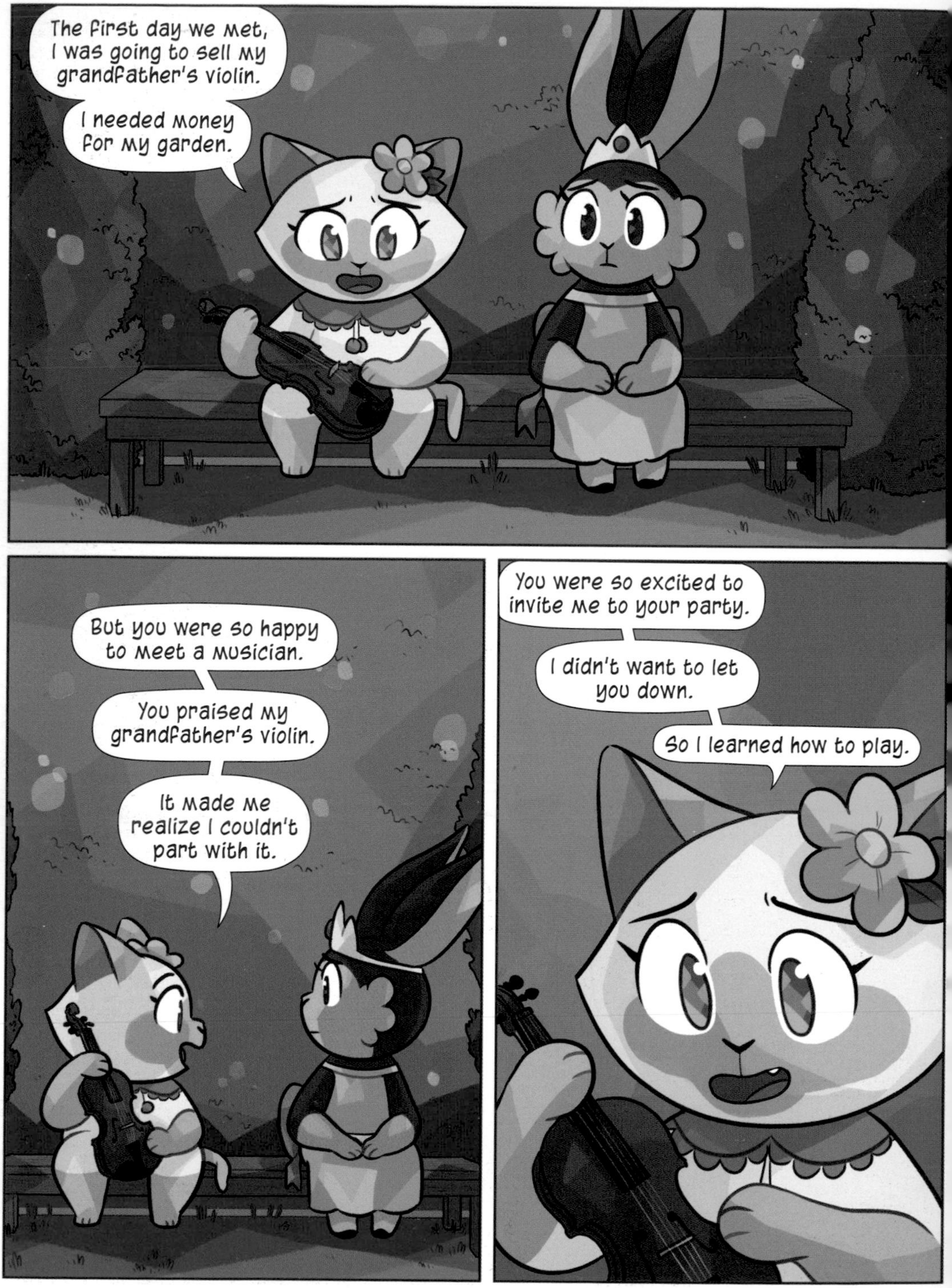

The first day we met, I was going to sell my grandfather's violin.
I needed money for my garden.
But you were so happy to meet a musician.
You praised my grandfather's violin.
It made me realize I couldn't part with it.
You were so excited to invite me to your party.
I didn't want to let you down.
So I learned how to play.

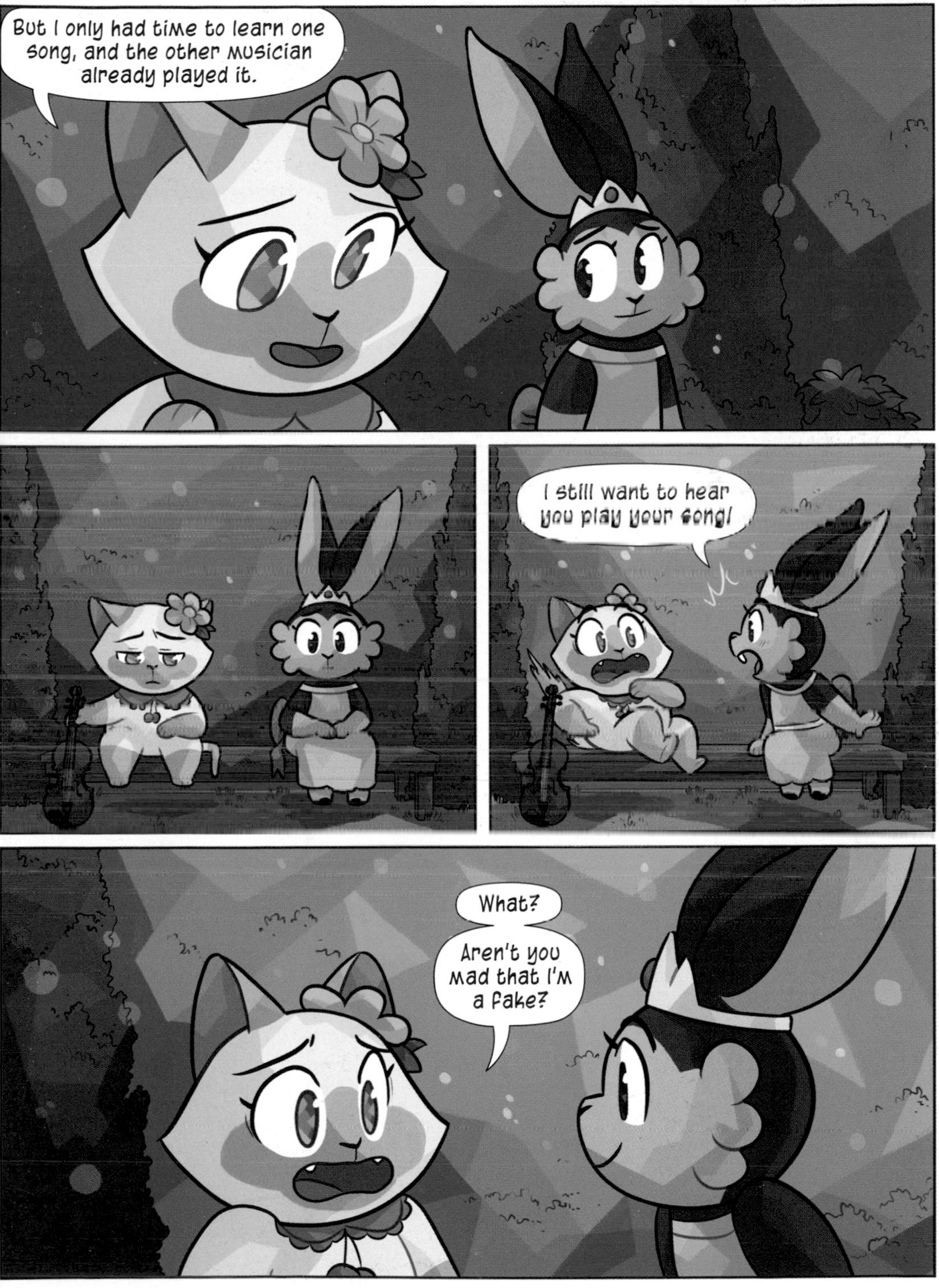
But I only had time to learn one song, and the other musician already played it.
I still want to hear you play your song!
What?
Aren't you mad that I'm a fake?

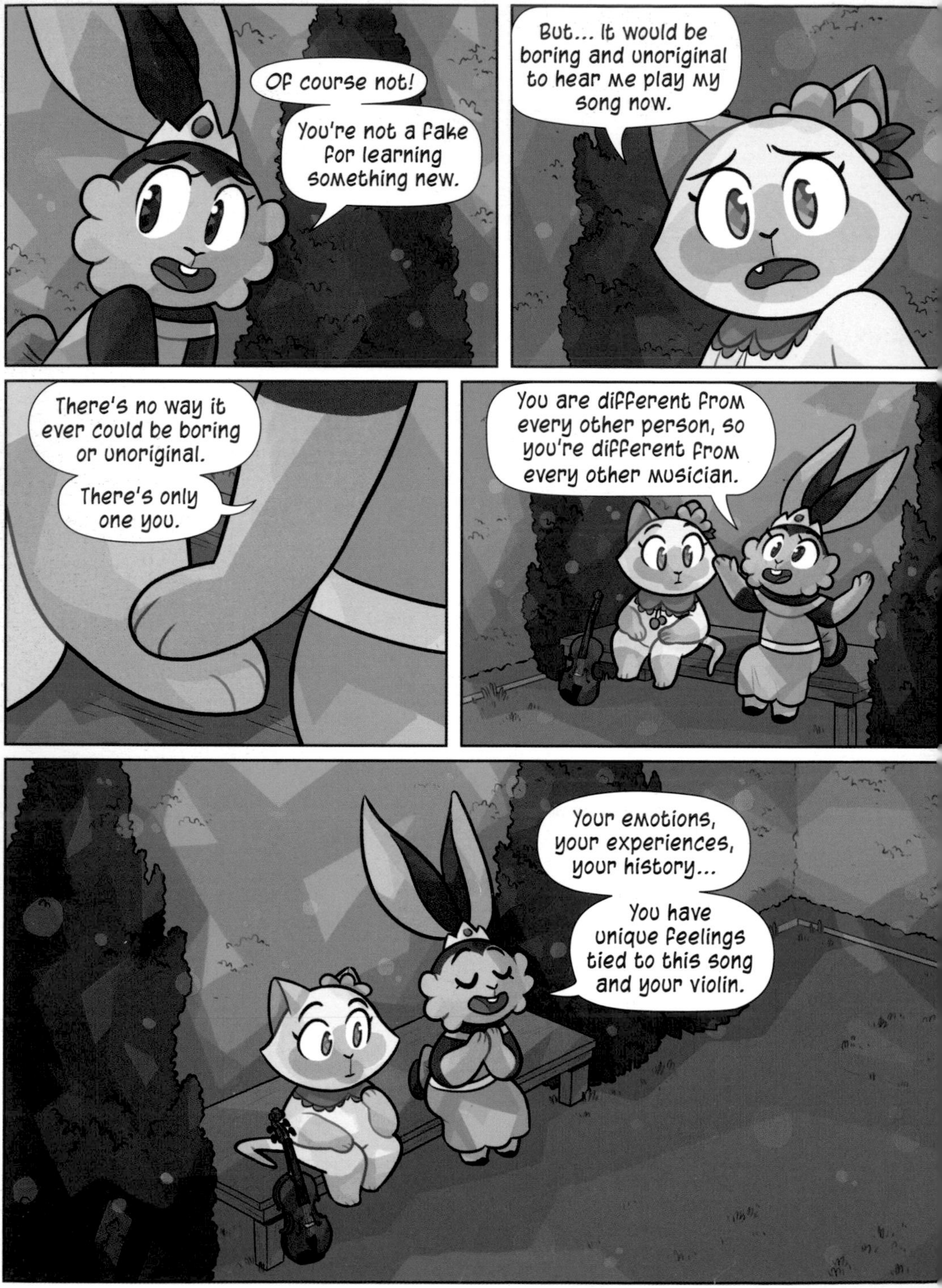
Of course not!
You're not a fake for learning something new.
But... It would be boring and unoriginal to hear me play my song now.
There's no way it ever could be boring or unoriginal.
There's only one you.
You are different from every other person, so you're different from every other musician.
Your emotions, your experiences, your history...
You have unique feelings tied to this song and your violin.

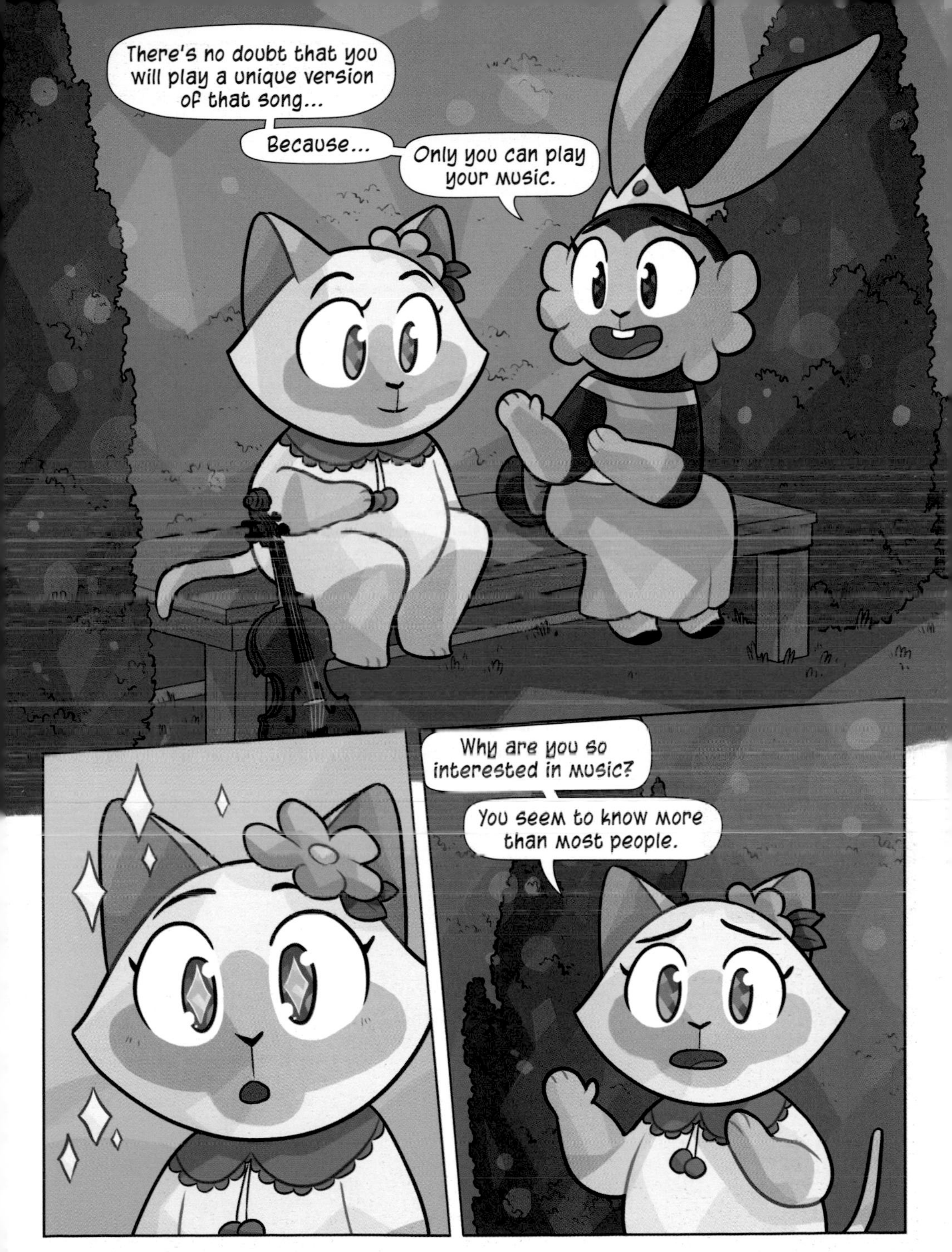
There's no doubt that you will play a unique version of that song...
Because...
Only you can play your music.
Why are you so interested in music?
You seem to know more than most people.

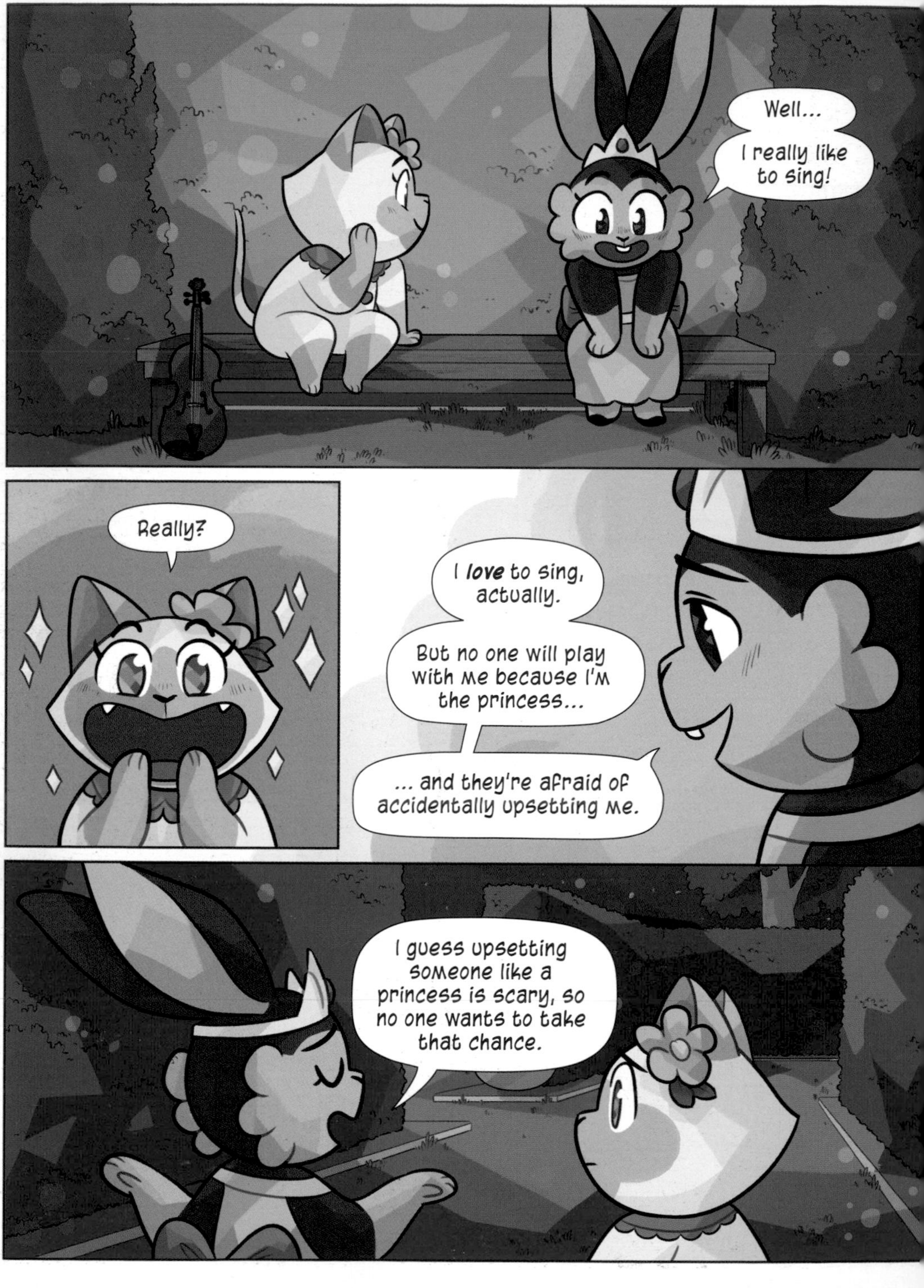
Well...
I really like to sing!
Really?
I love to sing, actually.
But no one will play with me because I'm the princess...
... and they're afraid of accidentally upsetting me.
I guess upsetting someone like a princess is scary, so no one wants to take that chance.

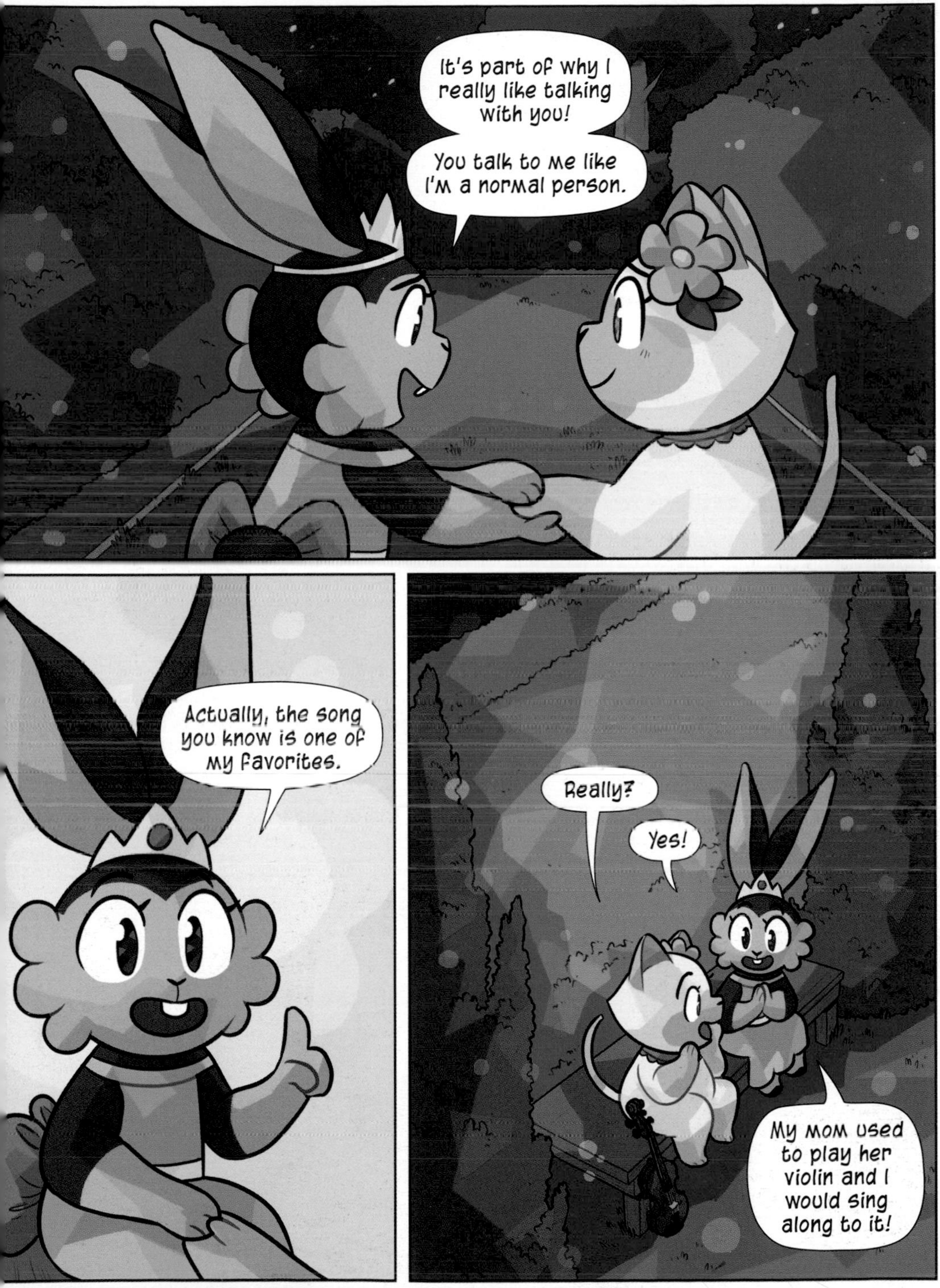
It's part of why I really like talking with you!
You talk to me like I'm a normal person.
Actually, the song you know is one of my favorites.
Really?
Yes!
My mom used to play her violin and I would sing along to it!

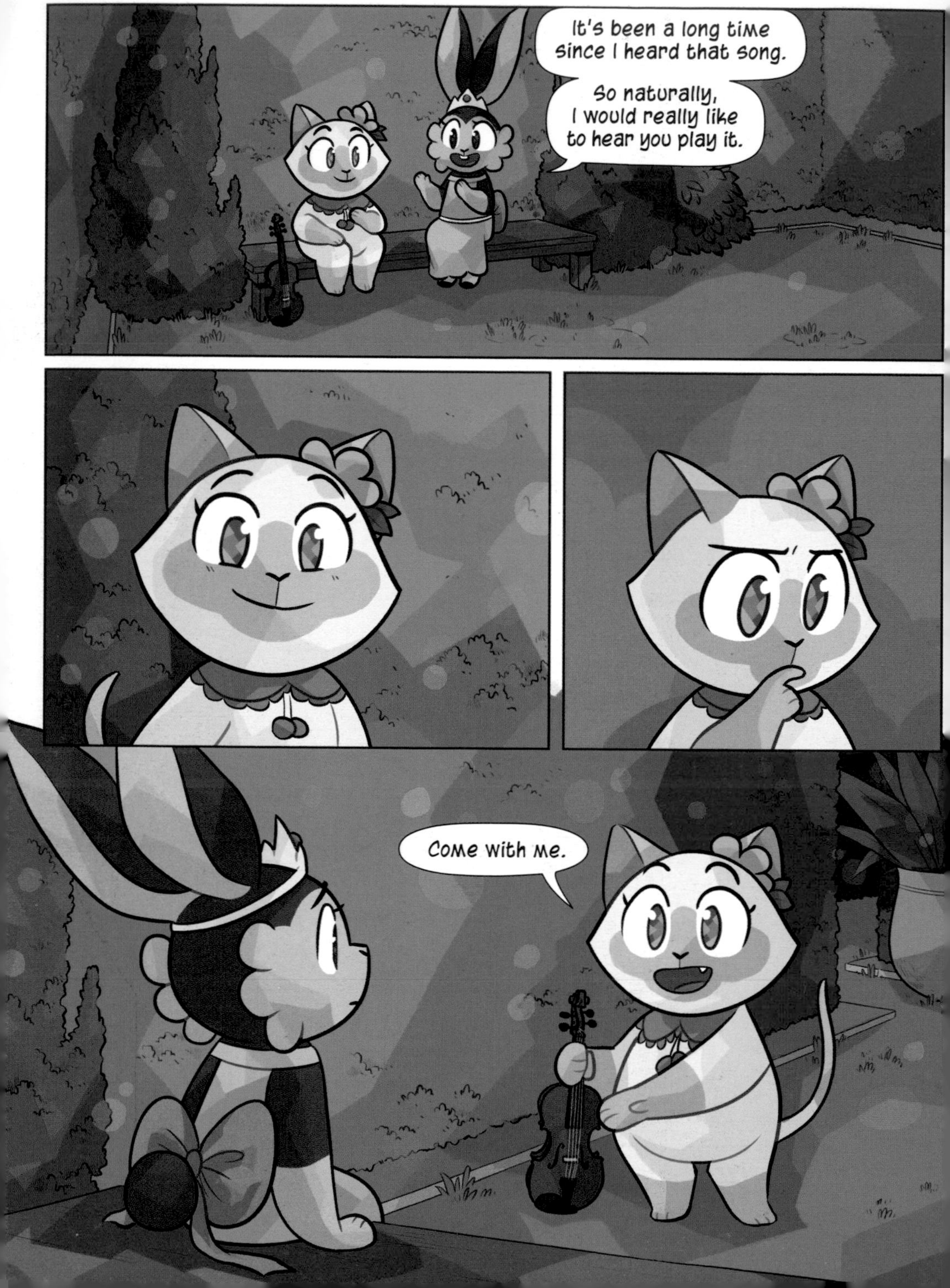
It's been a long time since I heard that song.
So naturally, I would really like to hear you play it.
Come with me.

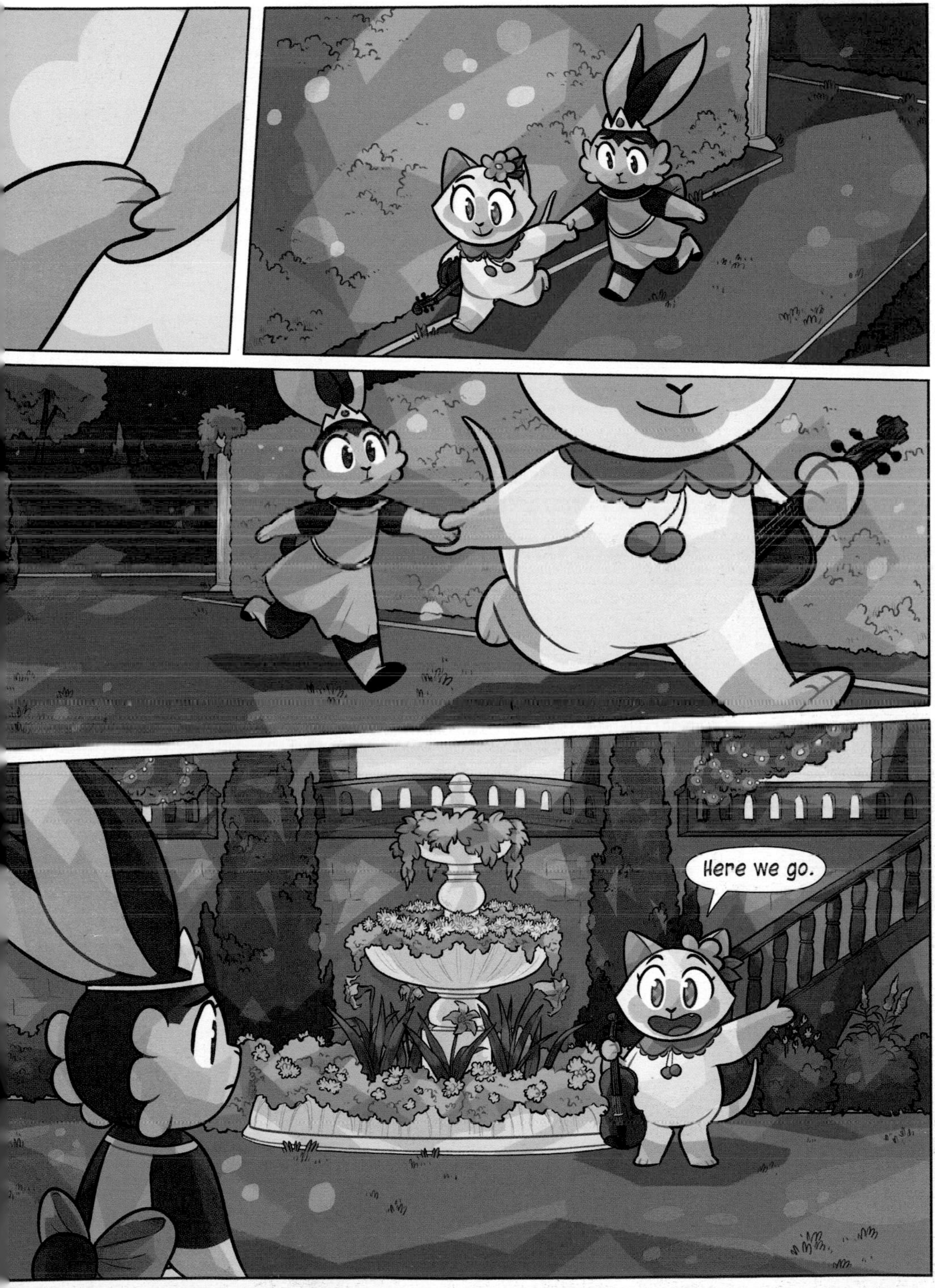
Here we go.

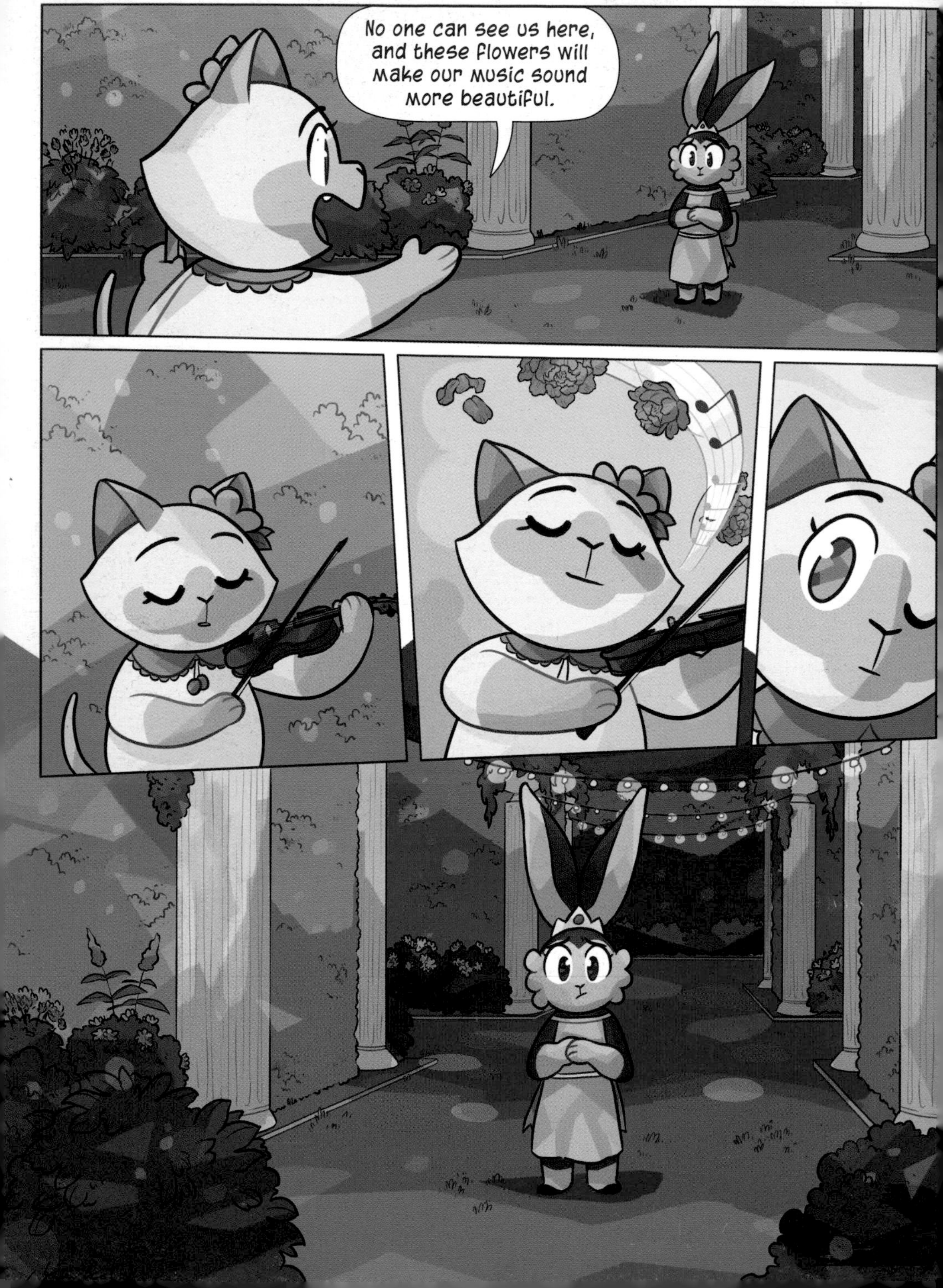
No one can see us here, and these flowers will make our music sound more beautiful.

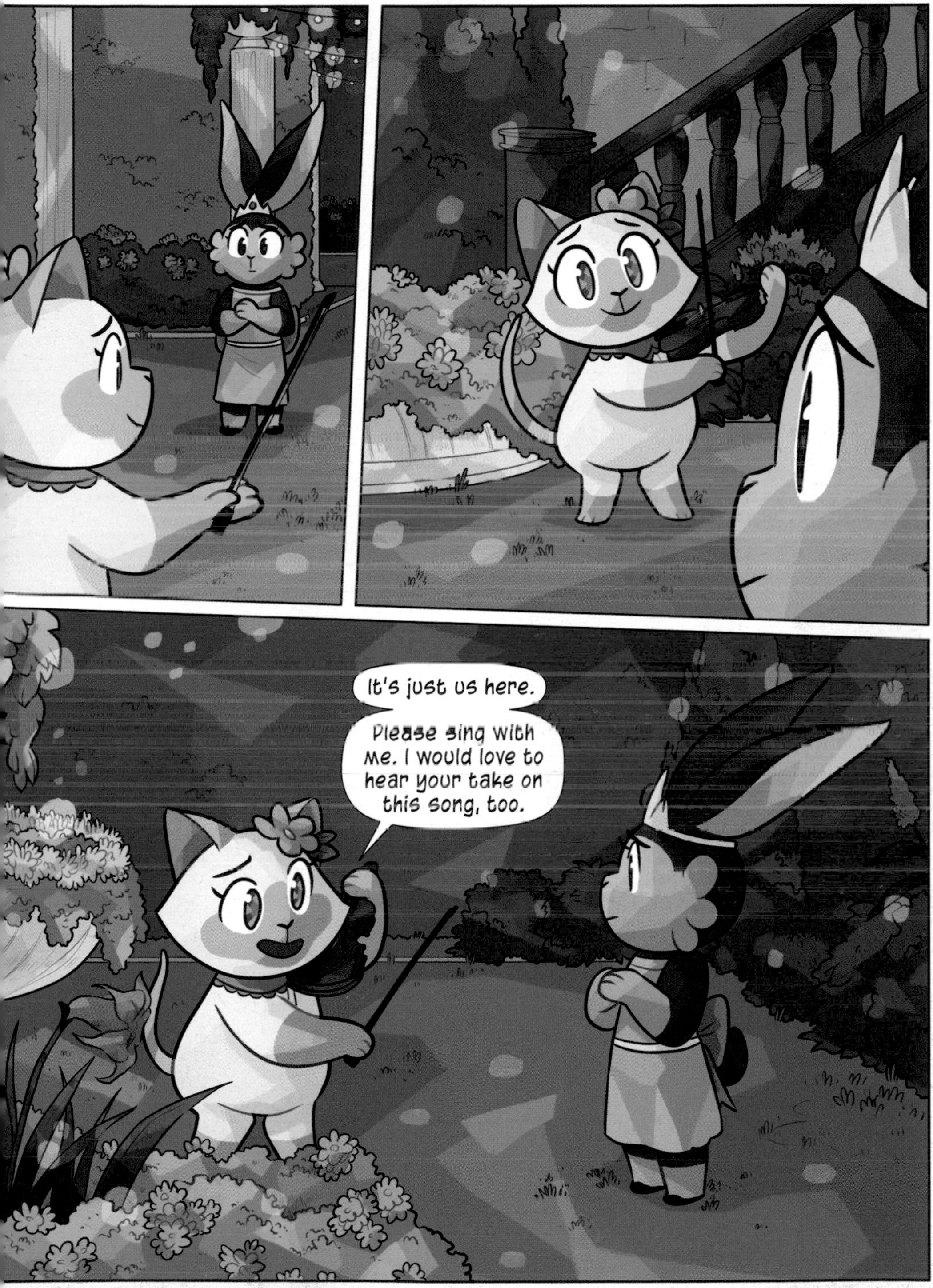
It's just us here.
Please sing with me. I would love to hear your take on this song, too.

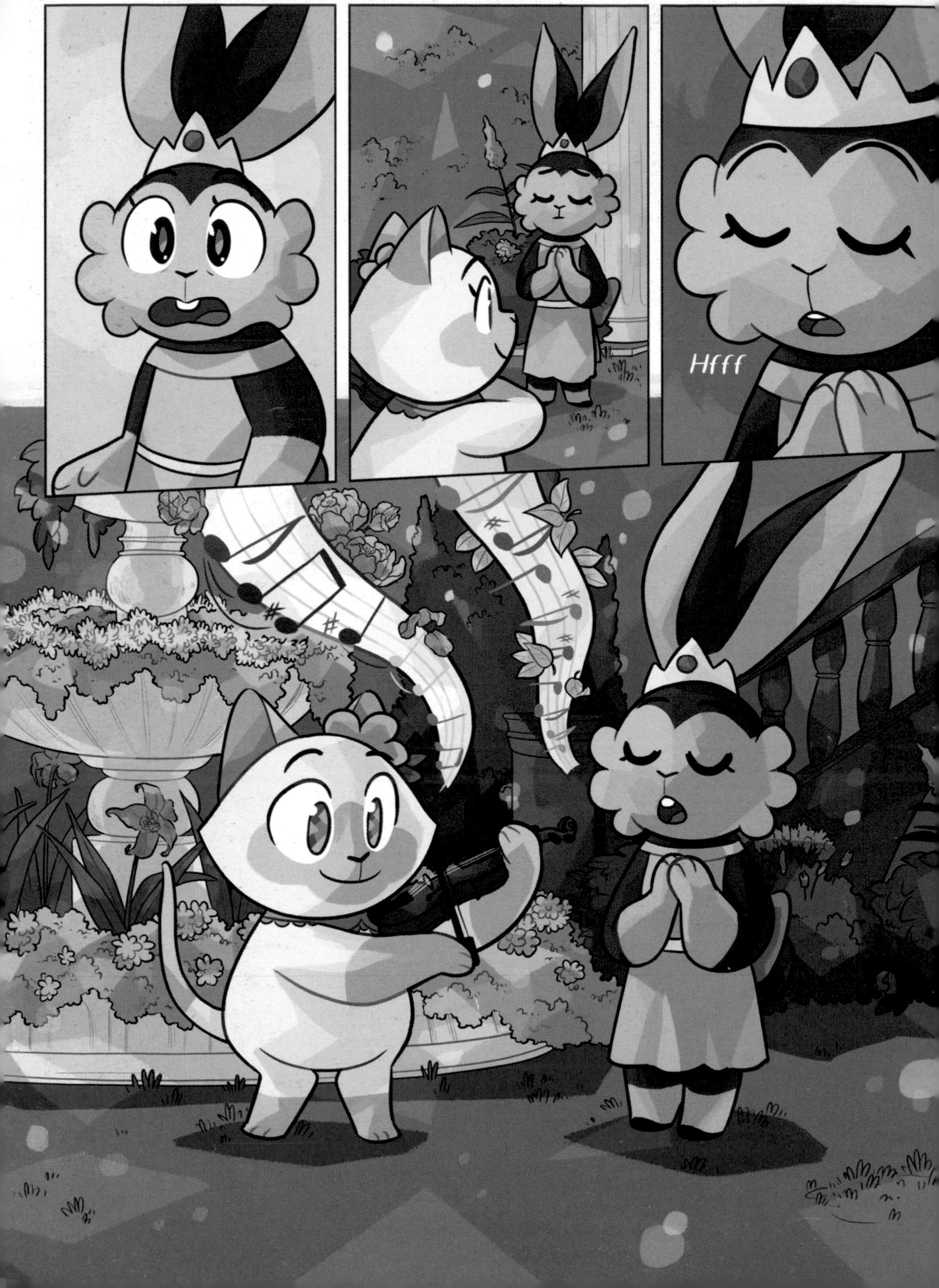
Hfff

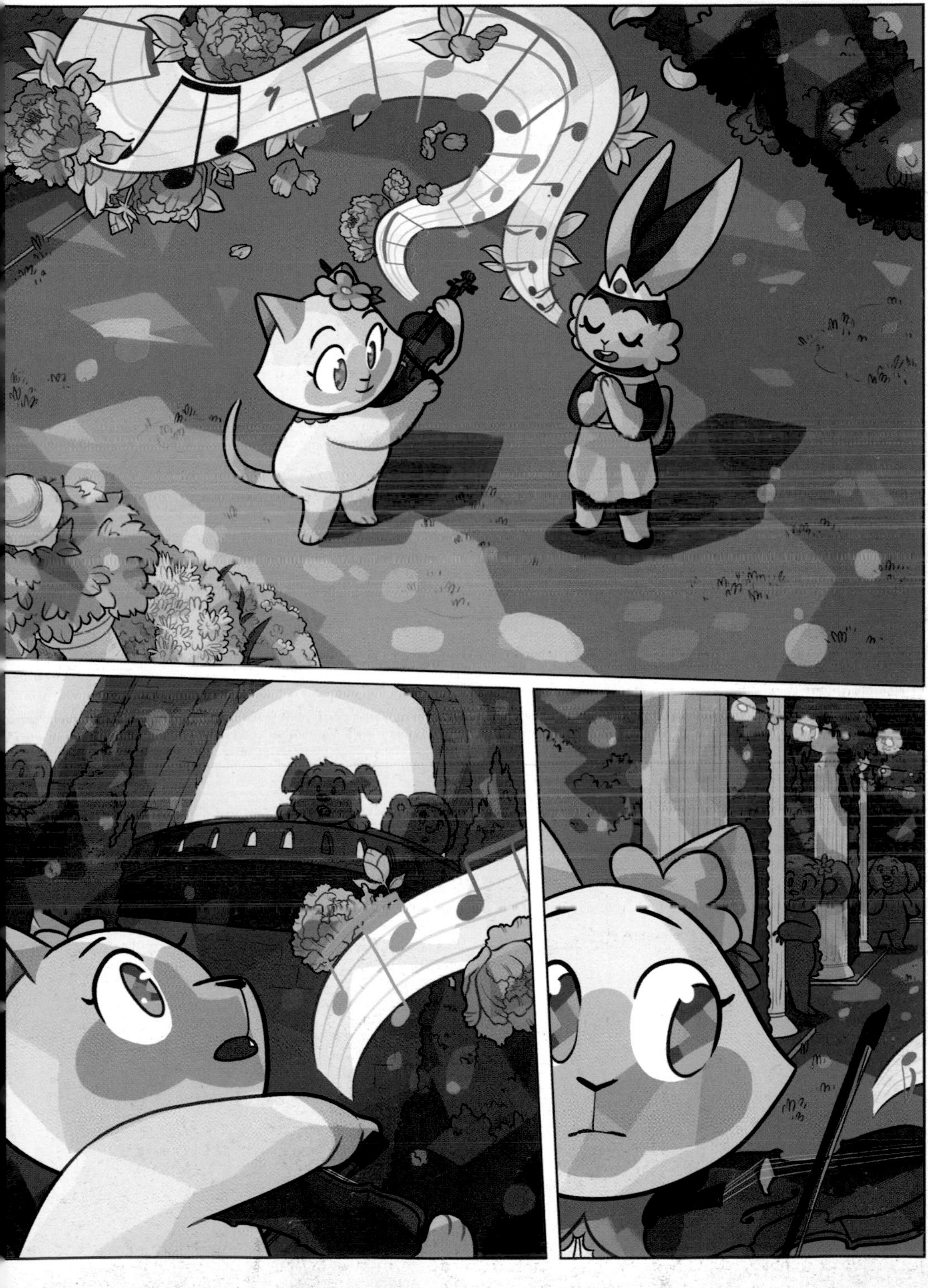

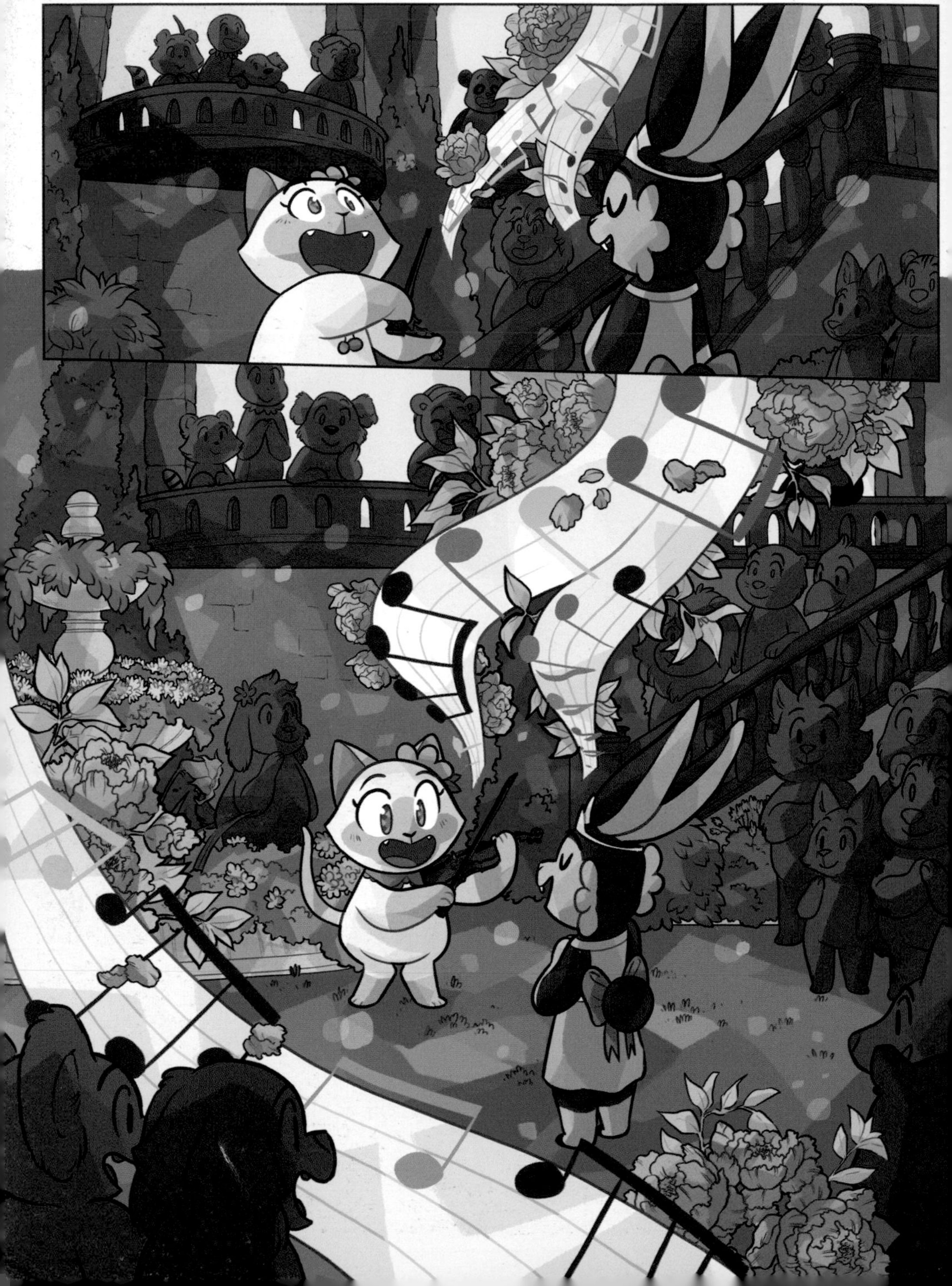

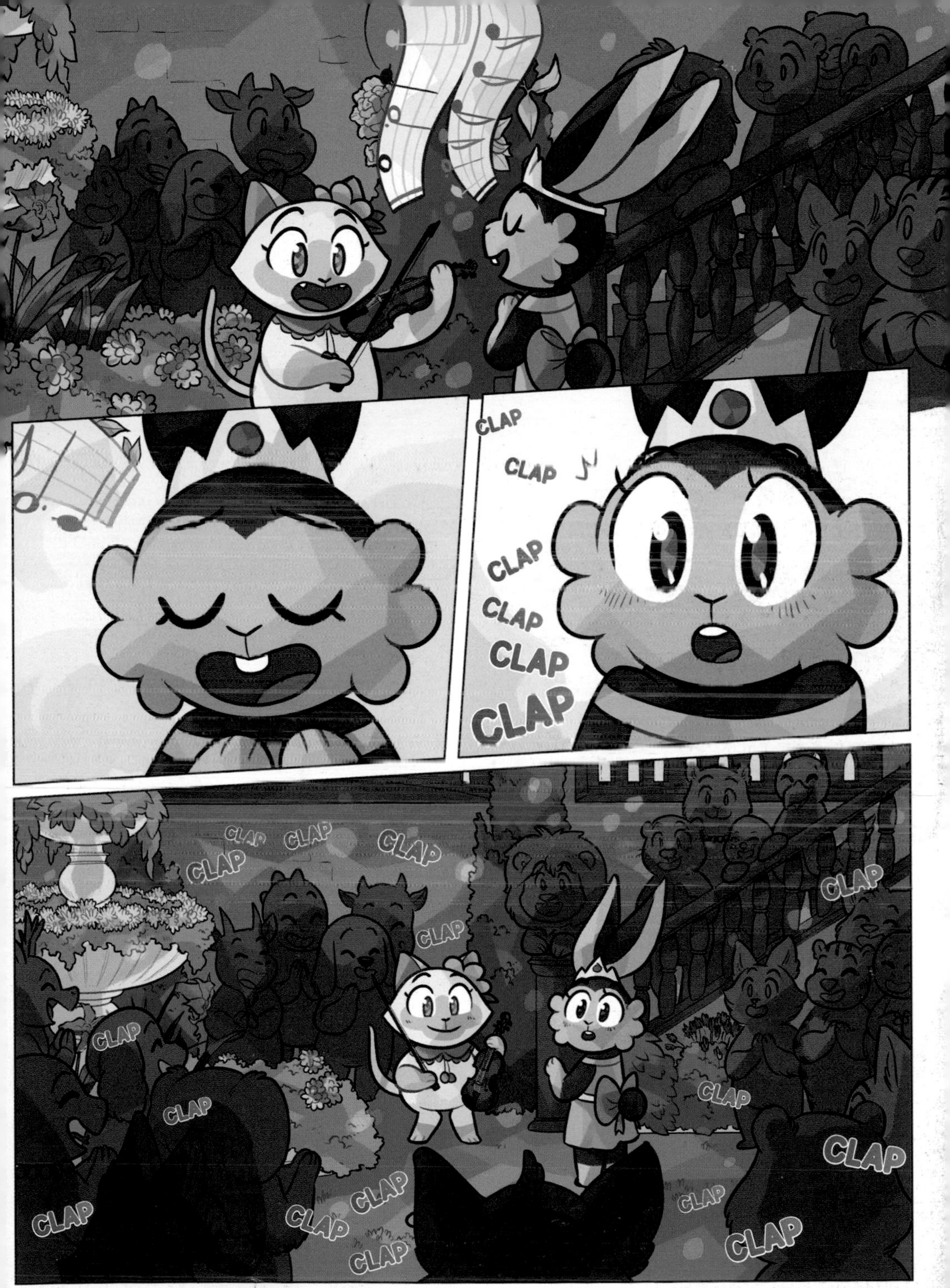
CLAP
CLAP
CLAP
CLAP
CLAP
CLAP
CLAP
CLAP
CLAP
CLAP
CLAP
CLAP
CLAP
CLAP
CLAP
CLAP
CLAP
CLAP
CLAP
CLAP
CLAP

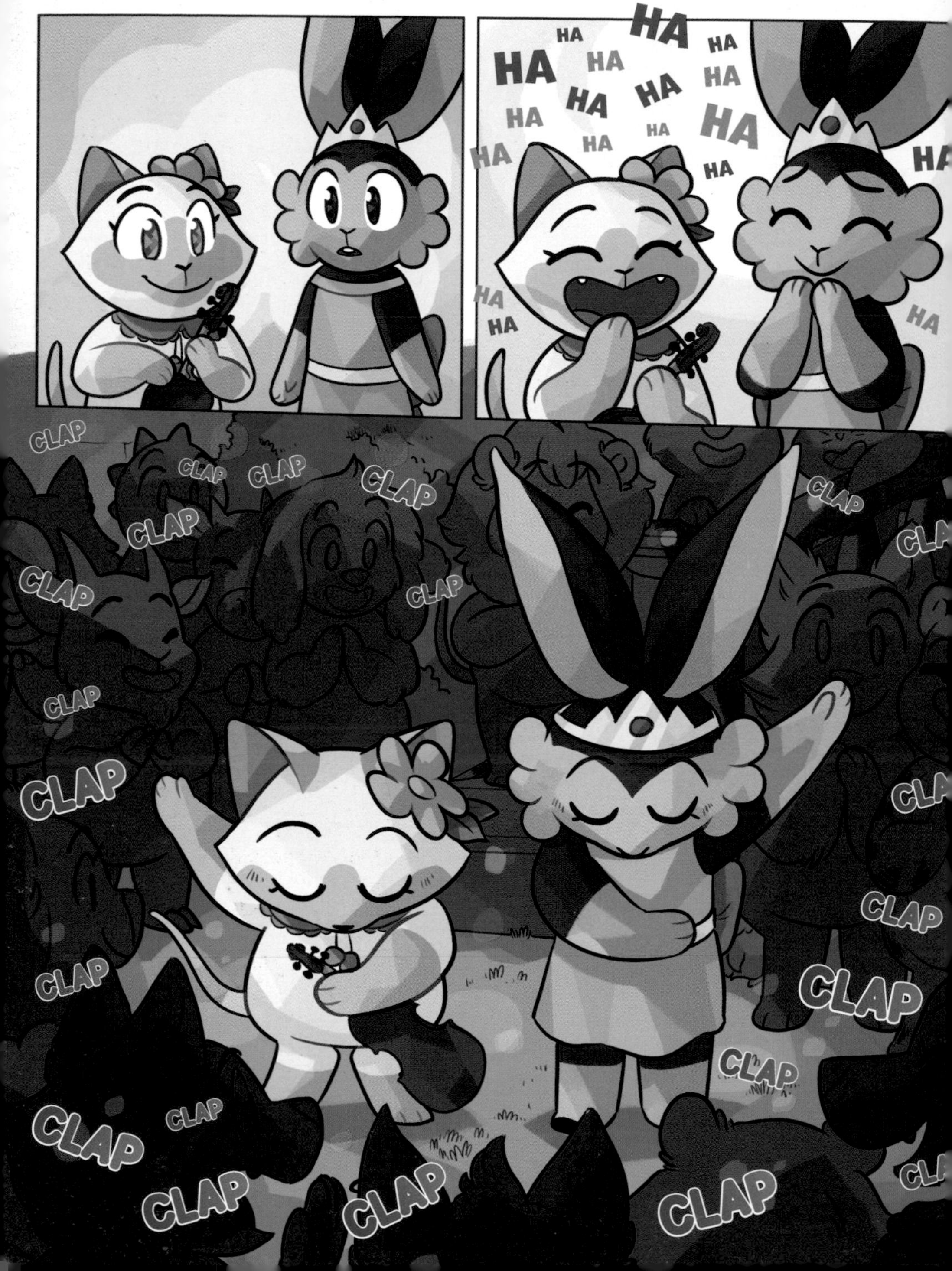
HA HA HA HA HA HA HA HA HA HA HA HA HA HA HA HA
HA HA HA
CLAP CLAP CLAP CLAP CLAP CLAP CLAP CLAP CLAP CLAP CLAP CLAP CLAP CLAP CLAP CLAP CLAP CLAP

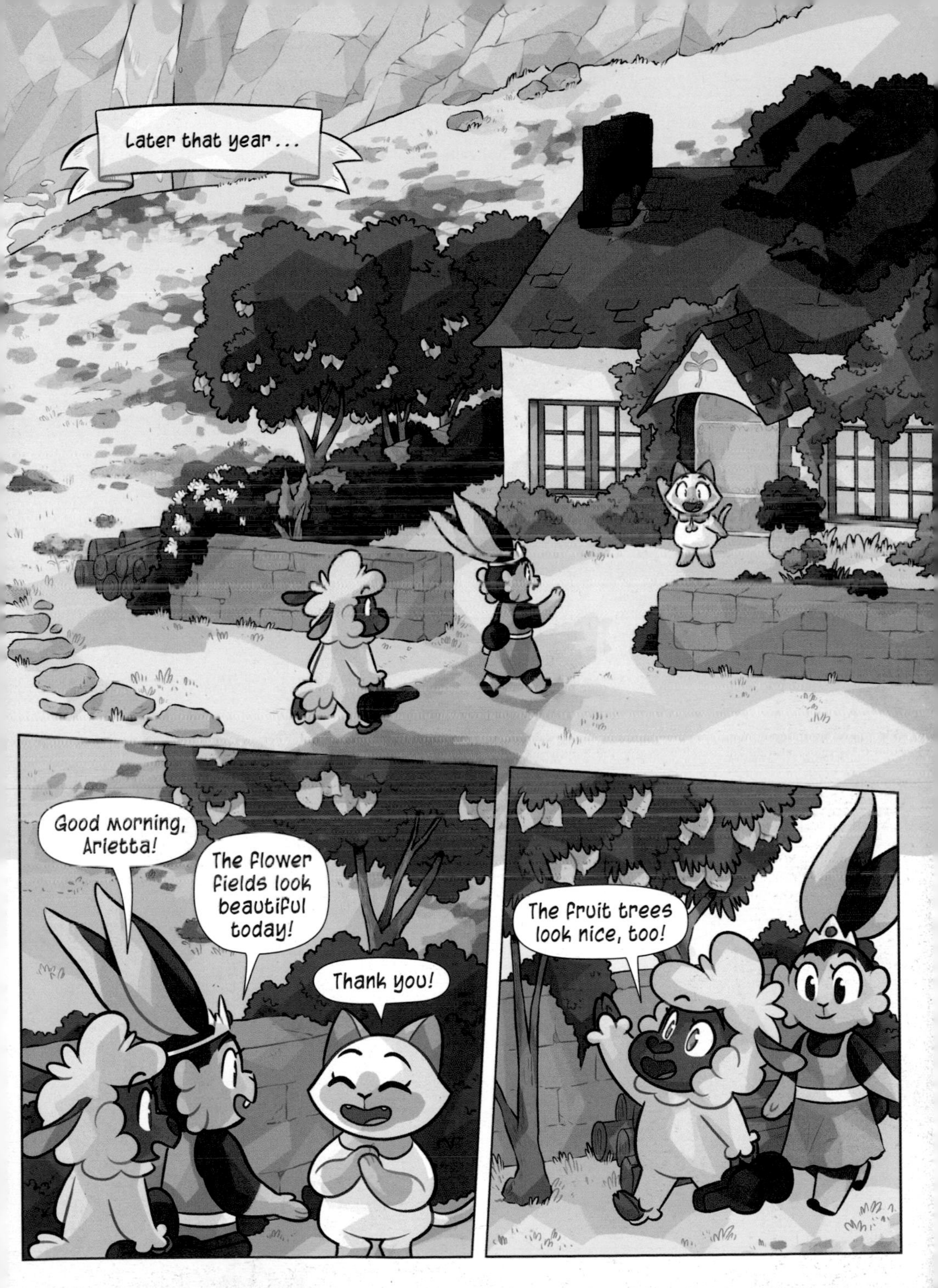
Later that year . . .
Good morning, Arietta!
The flower fields look beautiful today!
Thank you!
The fruit trees look nice, too!

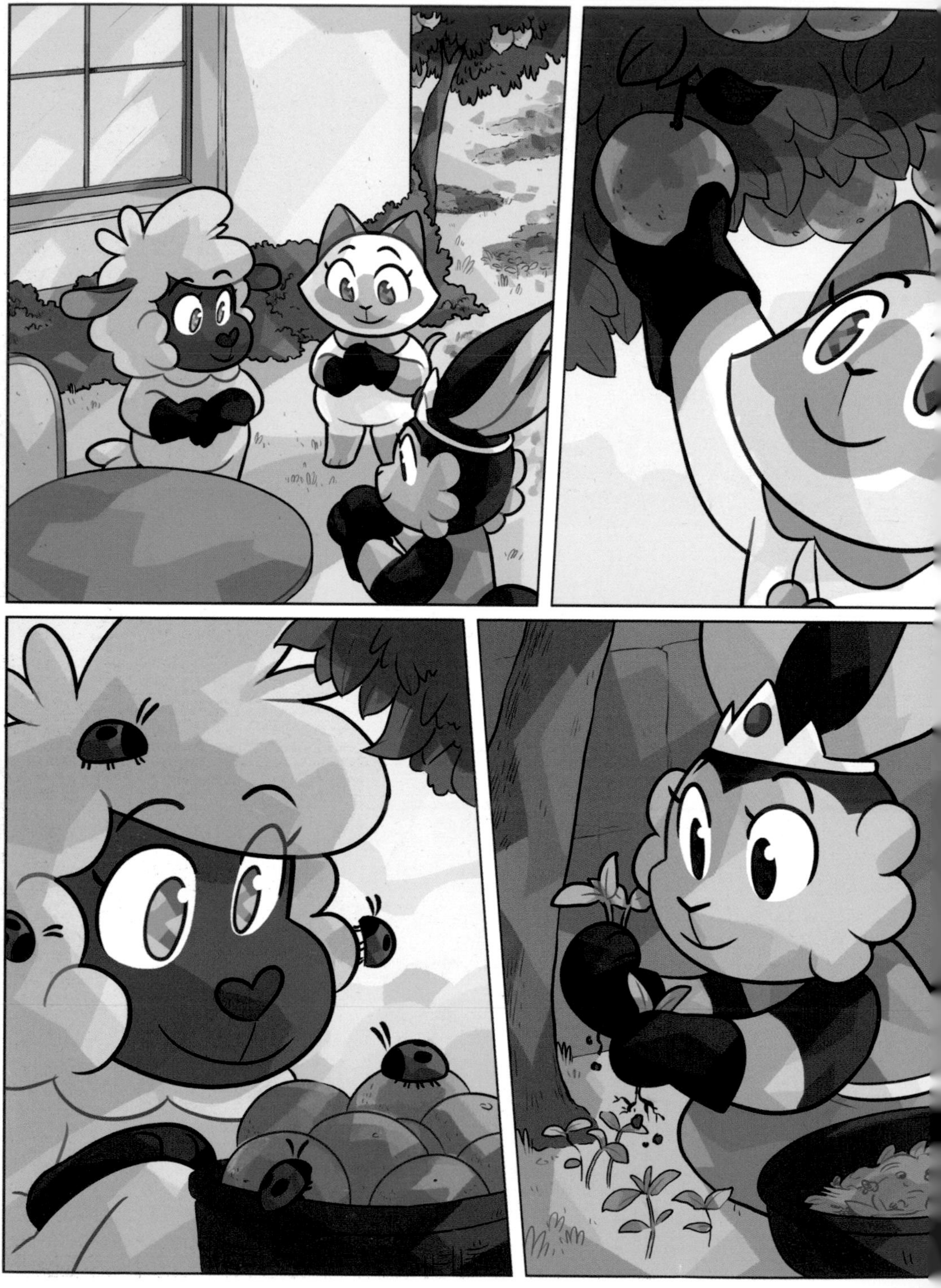

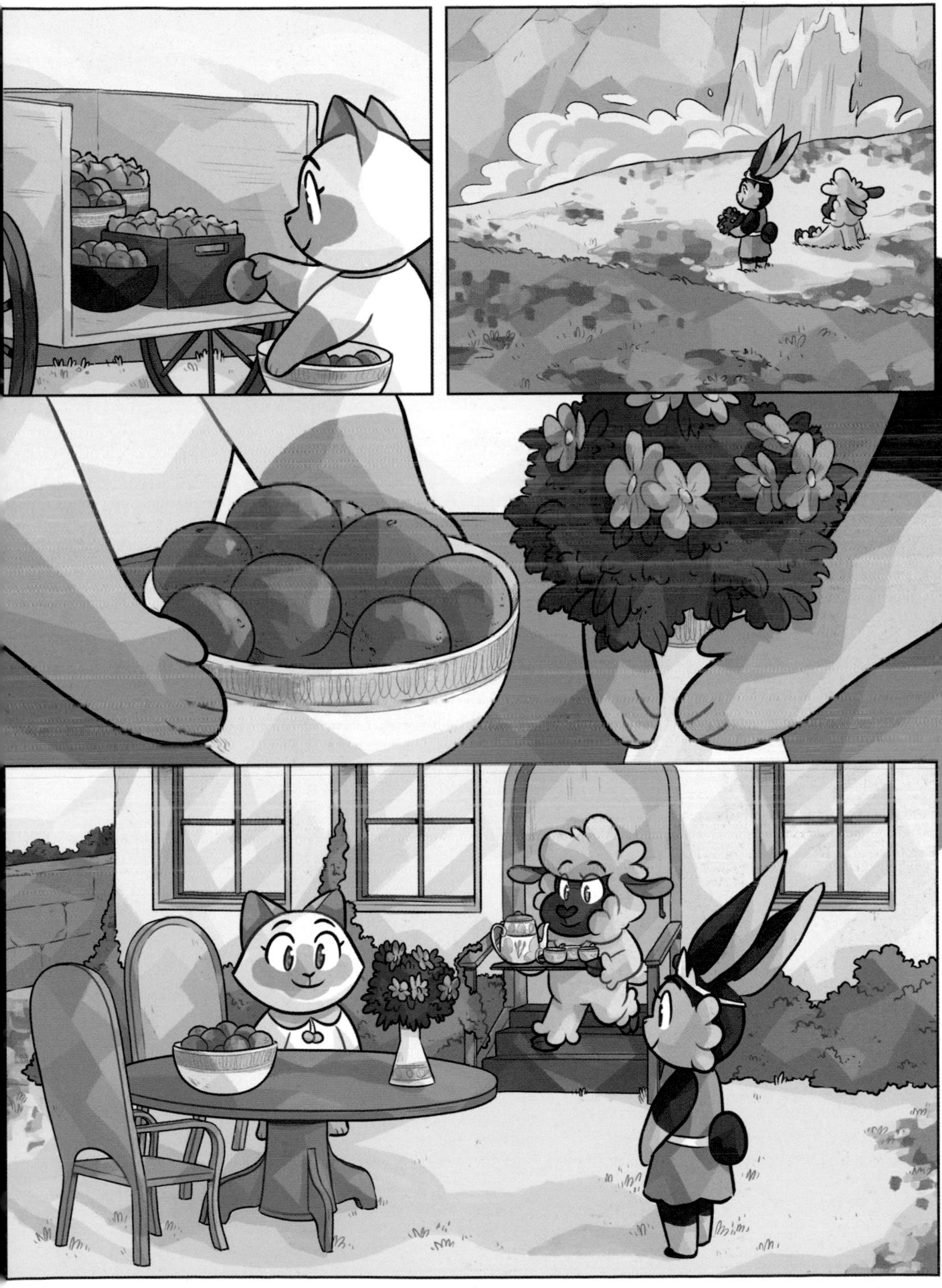

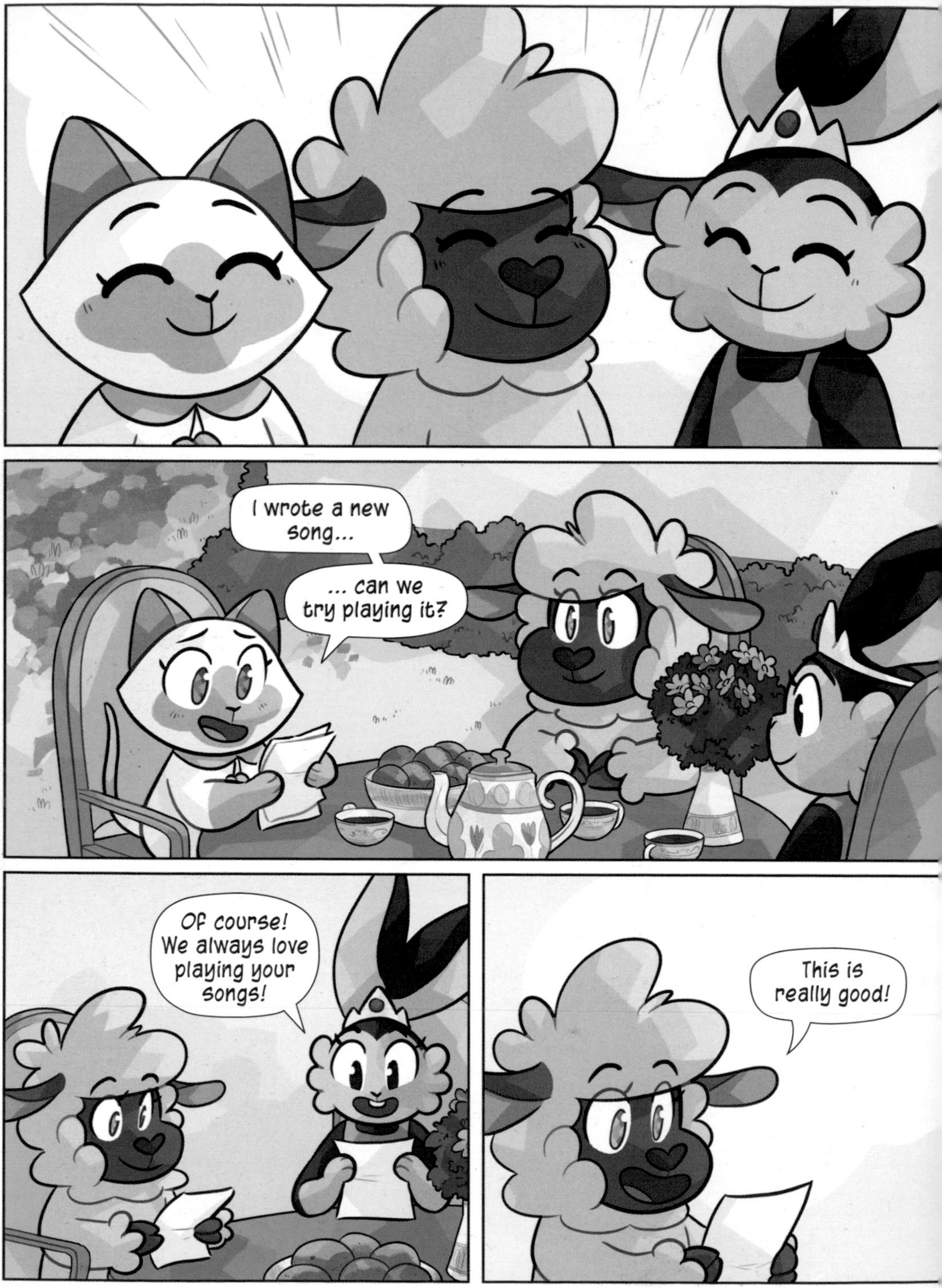
I wrote a new song...
... can we try playing it?
Of course! We always love playing your songs!
This is really good!

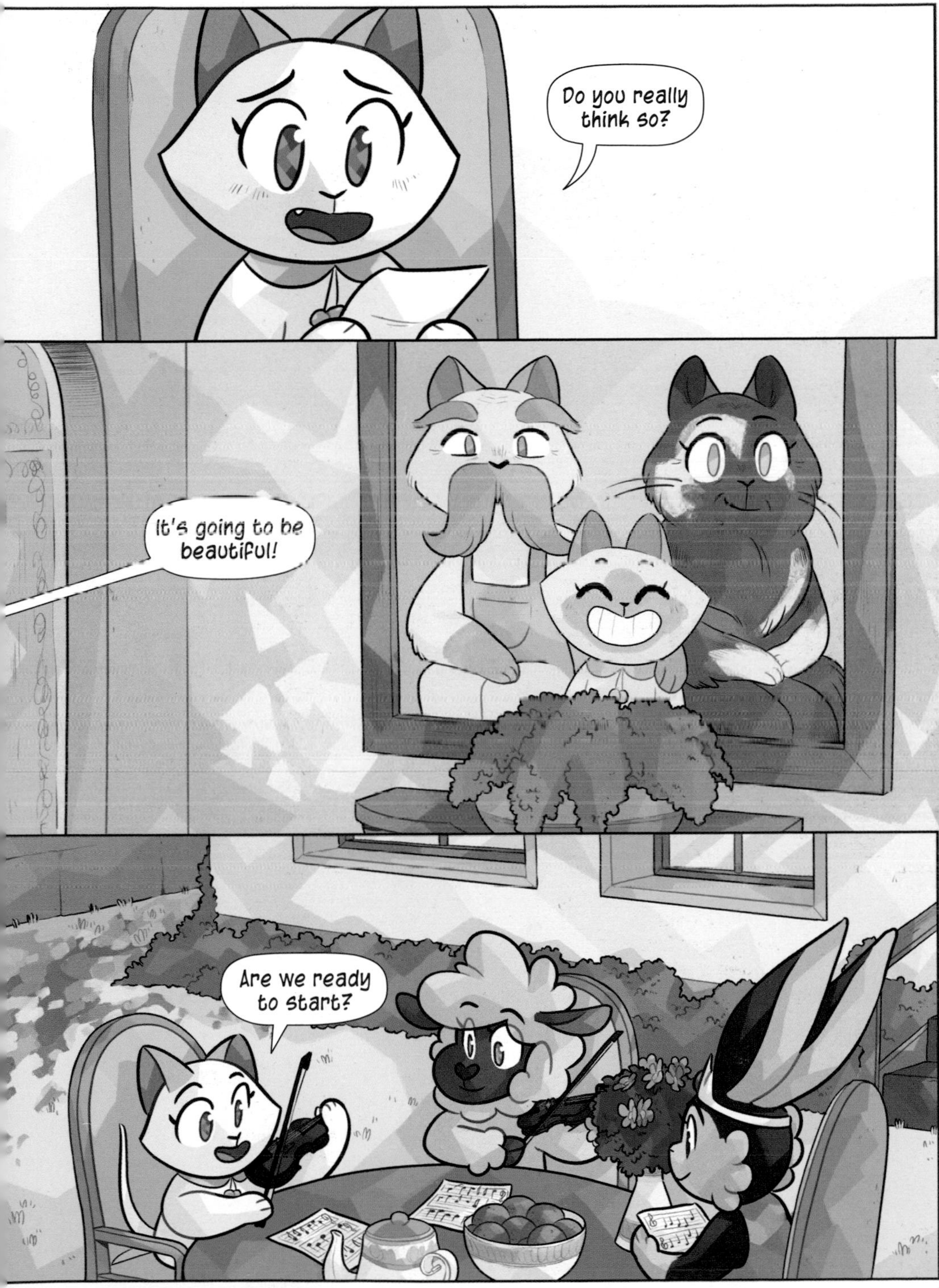

Do you really think so?
It's going to be beautiful!
Are we ready to start?

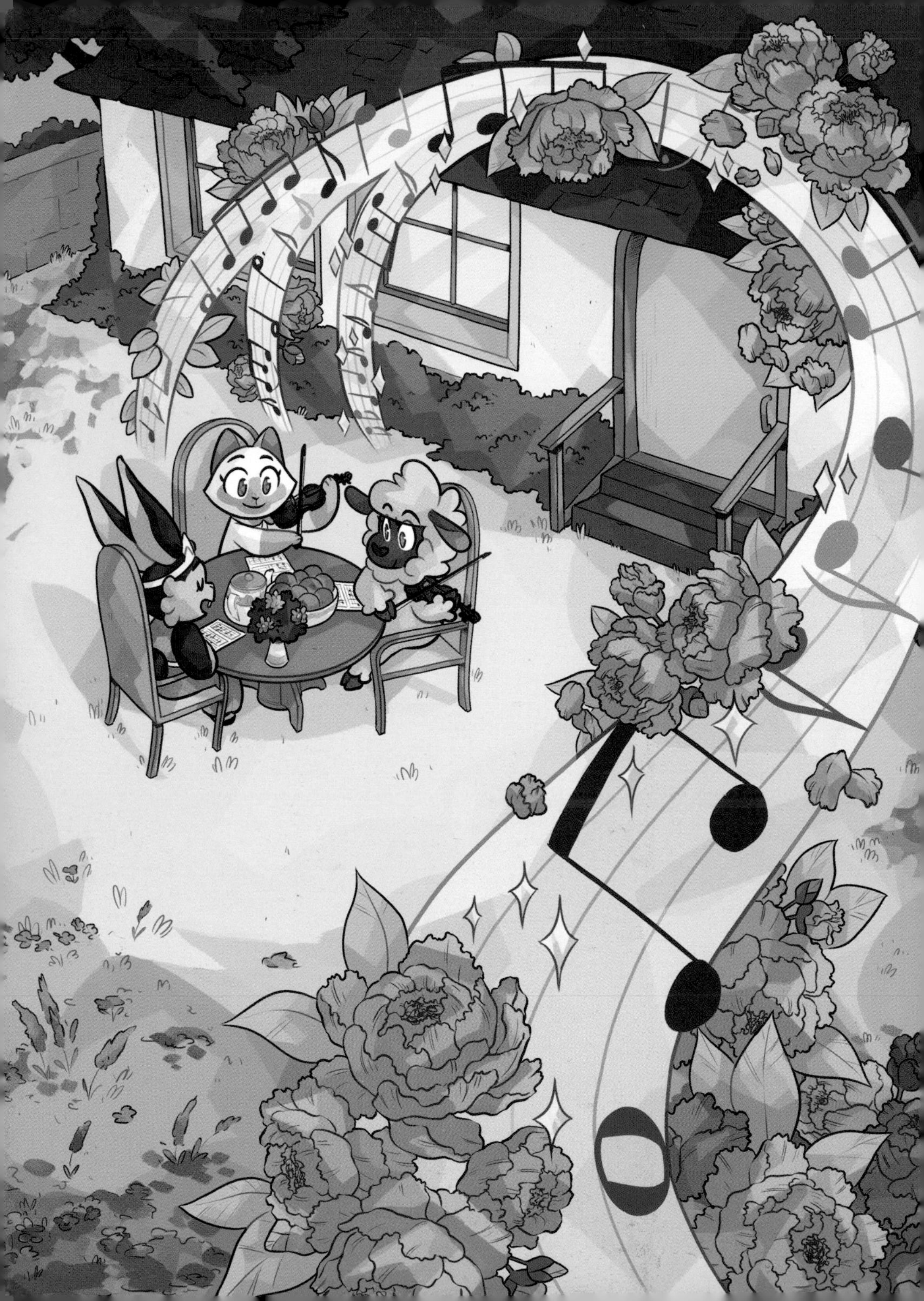

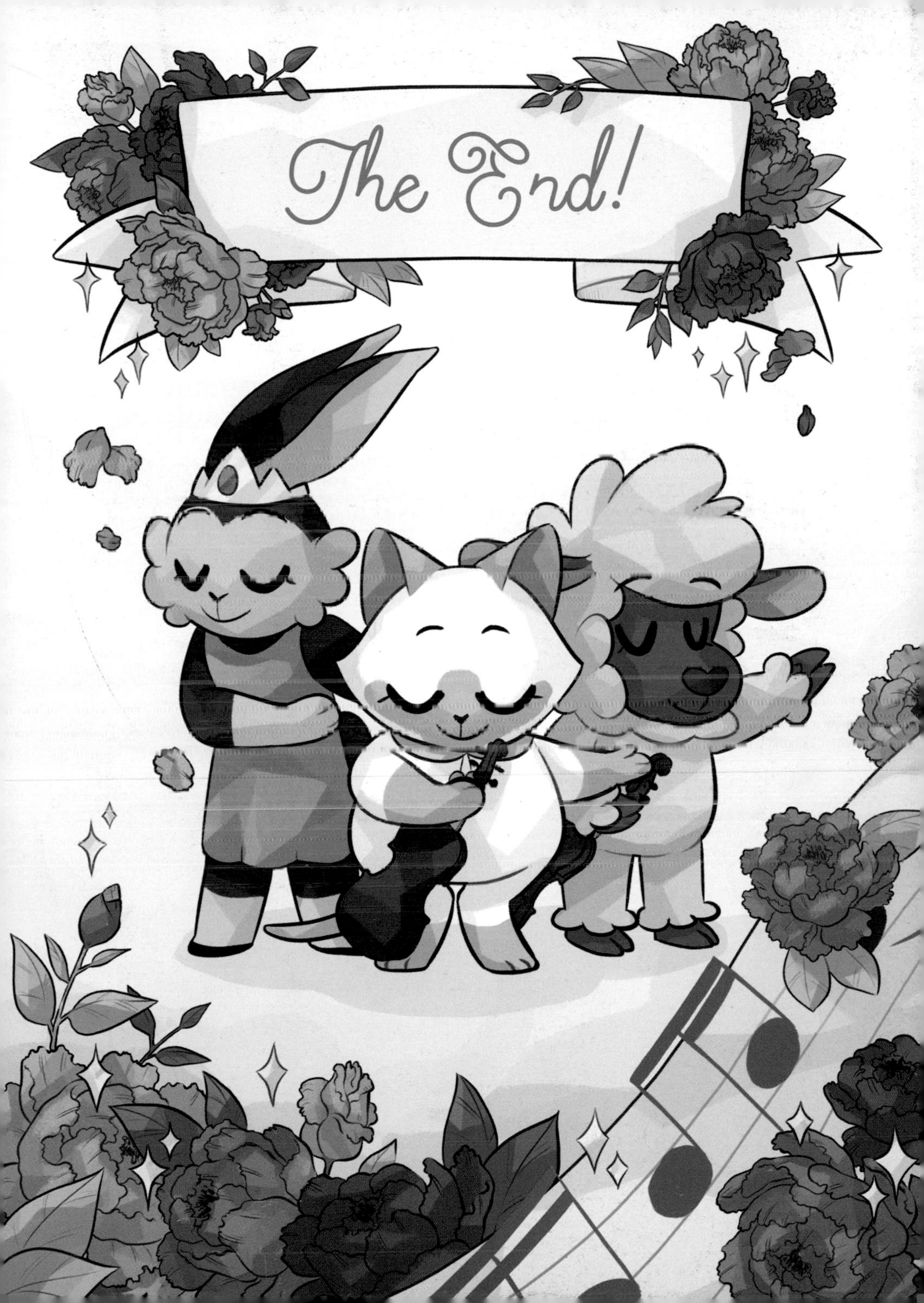
The End!

Acknowledgments

This book is for my husband, Rian, the sun in my sky. I love you always. Thank you from the bottom of my heart to the artists who helped Ashanti and me create this book: Binglin Hu, Sunmi, Mar Julia, Kaeti Vandorn, and Rel. To Eliza Berkowitz for seeing so much potential in this story, thank you for everything. Thanks to my editor, Ardi Alspach; art director, Heather Kelly; and the entire team at Sterling for all the love they have shown *Song of the Court* from day one. Thanks to Ari Yarwood for being a guiding light. I am eternally grateful to my agent, Steven Salpeter, for believing in this book and being my champion. Thank you to the foreign rights team, Sarah Perillo and Ginger Clark; the film department, Tim Knowlton, Holly Frederick, Maddie Tavis, James Farrell; and the rest of the team at Curtis Brown.

And thanks to you for reading.

You are worthy of love; may love always find you.